UNFAIR DISCRIMINATION

A
LEGAL
THRILLER

MARK
SHAIKEN

Published by 1609 Press LLC
Denver, Colorado

ISBN (print) 978-1-7345571-6-9
ISBN (ebook) 978-1-7345571-7-6
LCCN 2022916679

Cover Design and Interior Layout by *Damonza.com*
Editing by *Melanie Mulhall, Dragonheart, www.DragonheartWritingandEditing.com*

To Zac. I hope the world is a better place someday.

"Where justice is denied, where poverty is enforced, where ignorance prevails, and where any one class is made to feel that society is an organized conspiracy to oppress, rob and degrade them, neither persons nor property will be safe."

—FREDERICK DOUGLASS.

PROLOGUE

Saturday, April 6, 2024

THEY SAT IN the barn not far from the old farmhouse outside the town limits of Meadowfield, Kansas, population five thousand. The town was almost all White and mostly farmers, and those who weren't farmers made their living off the farming community. On the border between Kansas and Missouri, seventy-five minutes south of Kansas City, Meadowfield had two churches, a three block main street, a mayor, a city council, and mostly hardworking folks doing their best every day to make a living and put food on the table.

Eleven of them were in the barn after the sun had set that cool and crisp early spring evening, meeting to talk like they had done almost every Saturday night for years. The air smelled of hay in the barn and hogs in the pens. Nasty business, hogs in the pens.

The smell the hogs gave off bothered none of the eleven, even though the stench would bother everyone else in the world. It was a smell you got used to if you had to, and if you raised hogs for a living or lived in a town full of hog farmers, you had to, so you did. It didn't wash out of clothes. It didn't shower out of hair. The smell was something visitors to Meadowfield could taste in their mouths with each breath. It hung in the air like clouds float in the

1

sky, only not billowy, pretty, or moved along by the wind. Nothing moved the smell. Rain didn't wash it from the air. It just stayed.

Some of the eleven in the barn raised hogs. To them, hogs and their stench were money. Like their parents and grandparents, it was how they made a living. Raising hogs could be lucrative. Others grew wheat. It was less lucrative, but the world needed wheat. Hogs and wheat. Quite a contrast: the stink of pork versus the majesty of golden wheat waving in the wind. They wrote patriotic songs about wheat fields, but no one wrote songs about hogs.

They met in the barn to talk about things folks talked about when they believed they had lost their country to immigrants, and Blacks and other people of color, and Jews, and gays, and working women. And . . . and . . . and.

Sometimes they said it was time to take back their country, one way or another. Radicalized over years, influenced by social media and the inability to separate truth from lies, they became emboldened as the diseases of hate and intolerance egged them on, pushing them closer and closer to the edge of action.

The authorities knew about the eleven. The Anti-Defamation League and The Southern Poverty Law Center knew about them, tracked them, and labeled them domestic terrorists. The authorities knew them as a group of talkers, but no one knew if they would turn into doers. They didn't know either.

The Thirty-Six Thirties—that's what they called their little club. Formed by one of the eleven, it had been named after the 1820 Missouri Compromise, the law that permitted slavery in Missouri and south of latitude 36 degrees, 30 minutes.

Sometimes people called them The Thirties. They fancied themselves sovereign citizens over whom the state and federal government had no power. Domestic threats? That's what the authorities worried about. Right-wing subversives? That's what the ADL labeled them. The Thirties couldn't care less if some perceived them as a threat. If some perceived them as subversive. The Thirties were fine with the labels.

But this meeting was different. They weren't there to talk about the latest online posts. The ones with the usual vitriol spewed at everyone and no one in particular. They weren't there to talk about what was fake news and what was reality. At least, their reality. No, not that night.

That night they gathered to talk about Donnie Melanshin, a six-foot-four real estate businessman in town who, years earlier, had decided not to join the group. What did he and the wife believe in, the eleven wondered? Were he and his wife liberals living right there in Meadowfield?

Hell, the eleven thought, he wasn't even a farmer, just a real estate tycoon who now said he was in financial trouble. They knew he owed money to lots of folks, far and wide. He'd always paid, but no longer. The option of immediate and timely repayment of debt was not on the table, the businessman had said. He couldn't do that. So instead, rumor was that his wife and he had gone north to the big city—Kansas City—to talk to a fancy-dressing lawyer about options besides timely payment.

A true respectable farmer wouldn't do that, the eleven thought. But Donnie, the one who never joined, didn't farm the land. He didn't raise hogs. He didn't grow wheat. Land was his commodity. He and Lil bought and sold it. They owned it and leased it out to farmers. They brokered deals involving it.

They didn't live on a farm. They lived in town off Main Street in a big, historical house. They had fancy cars in the garage and maintained a significantly more lavish lifestyle than the eleven.

At one time or another, Donnie and Lil had purchased land from each of the eleven. Donnie liked to buy it over time and liked to use a form titled either Installment Land Sale Contract or Contract For Deed to do so. Each had the same terms. Under the contract terms, the seller retained ownership of the land while

Donnie and Lil paid them monthly. The contract said that Donnie and Lil didn't own the land until they made the last payment.

Up until then, one noted, Donnie and Lil had never missed a payment under any of the sale contracts. They had paid like clockwork.

As of the meeting in the barn, Donnie and the wife were in the midst of a large sale contract with Woody Clarke, the first of the eleven and group founder. It was his first sale contract with Donnie and Lil. Clarke had felt safe signing it because the contracts worked fine for others of The Thirties and, of course, the contract said he owned the land until Donnie and Lil made the last payment. So he thought the contract protected him. That's what he thought because he didn't understand how the sale contract worked under Kansas law.

That night, the eleven met as neighbors in a farming community with a common concern: the one who had never joined. They met to listen to Clarke talk as a creditor about the businessman who, for the last three months, hadn't paid Clarke the required monthly installment.

"Hadn't?" one asked.

"Or wouldn't?" one wondered.

"Wouldn't or couldn't?" one offered.

"No matter," Clarke said. "Figuring out whether he couldn't or wouldn't aren't important to me no more. All that matters is that them Melanshins didn't."

"Anybody know what went wrong in Donnie's world?" one of them asked of no one in particular. "Seems like he was doing just fine."

"I heard he financed the real estate operations with a big line of credit from a bank," another answered. "I heard the bank pulled the line and Donnie's world turned from greenbacks galore to no cash. I'm thinking that's what went wrong."

"Nah. That ain't what I heard," another said. "I heard he got overextended in some deals he made, though I don't know what those mighta been."

"I heard that the Kansas City lawyer he talked with was one of them immigrants," one of the eleven said.

The others agreed. They'd heard the same.

"Ain't about everyone in the big city one of them immigrant types?" one asked.

No one replied. Instead, someone else offered, "From somewhere in Russia, I heard."

"Russia? Sheee-it!" one exclaimed.

"His grandparents wasn't real Americans, so neither is he. His grandparents was commies, so this lawyer probably is too," one speculated.

"I don't care if he's from Mars," another said. "Woody gotta get his money each month or he's gonna need to talk to some legal suit in Kansas City himself."

Woody sat there on a hay bale, arms crossed on his chest, listening.

"I agree," one said. "I mean, the Melanshins are still getting big rent payments from their farm tenants each month, ain't they? What're they doing with that rent money, anyway? 'Cause they sure as hell ain't paying Woody with it no more."

"Maybe their tenants would pay Woody directly if we told them to," one suggested.

"Maybe so?" another replied, rubbing the gray and brown stubble on his chin as he considered the prospect of direct tenant payments.

There was silence as the reality of Woody not getting paid set in for the others. Woody already knew the reality.

Then another broke the silence and said, "Yep. I'm thinking Woody's gonna need him one of them big city lawyers as well."

They all agreed.

"So y'all think Lil and Donnie'll take bankruptcy?" one asked.

"How can they not?" another said.

"Anyone here know diddly about bankruptcy?"

"I'm thinkin' we all know something about it. How could we not, being in the farming biz?" one observed.

They sat in silence again, and then Clarke spoke. "I'm afraid I know quite a goodly bit about it." He looked around at his fellow Thirties. "This won't be my first time not getting my money from a former business buddy. Been through the bankruptcy wringer before. Gonna get a notice that he and Lil filed. Notice'll tell me that collection from them and their tenants are off-limits. It'll make me an offer to be on a committee to squeeze as much money out of him as I can."

Woody Clarke was the experienced one when it came to bankruptcy, and the others listened and learned.

"Committee?" one asked.

"Yeah, committee," Clarke, the experienced one, said.

"A committee of Thirties?" one asked.

"Nope. A committee of unsecured creditors," Clarke explained.

"You gonna get a lawyer?" one asked.

"Committee picks one and Donnie'll have to pay for it," Clarke said.

"I don't much like any of this, but I like that part," one said.

"And this lawyer'll get you paid back?" another asked.

"That's the aim," Clarke said.

One said, "Y'know, Donnie still owes me money for some equipment I sold him last year."

Another chimed in and said, "Me too. Guess that means we'll be on this committee as well."

There was silence again.

"Does this committee thing work?" one finally asked.

"Supposed to, but not every time," Clarke admitted. "Not every time," he repeated in a hoarse whisper, looking down at the ground and shaking his head.

"Then this committee's gonna need a damn good lawyer."

"For sure it will. And it'll have to hire one quick," Clarke said.

The experienced one looked at the others and nodded slowly as he chewed a stalk of hay. He was the one who had gone to college, at least for a while. He left college when he'd had enough and returned to Meadowfield, where he fit in and could find commonality with folks like the other Thirties. He was comfortable with them and he was comfortable with their views: *their* views, their *family's* views, and *his* family's views passed down since before the Civil War.

Now he would have to get comfortable with a big city lawyer who might not fit the mold of everything The Thirties stood for. Most big city lawyers didn't, he figured. Nothing he could do about that. At least not yet. Maybe someday.

1

AFTER OUR WEEKLY barn meeting adjourned at ten, I made my way to my Ford pickup truck and the five-mile drive back to my farmhouse. The moon was a sliver, and with no artificial light around, I couldn't even begin to imagine how many billions of stars twinkled in the sky. Rural America. Rural Kansas near the Missouri border. It's what I liked, and it's what I felt comfortable with.

Five miles on a two-lane dirt and gravel road with just me, my Ford pickup, and my thoughts. I lived alone, so I wasn't in any big hurry to get home.

Old Donnie and Lil owed some of us a goodly sum, and to me in particular, way too much. My folks left me thousands of acres of land. I sold Donnie and Lil four quarter sections—2,560 acres. We signed an installment land sale contract. The sale price was four-point-four million dollars. At the time, they still owed me four million. In my mind, they was paying me almost nineteen thousand a month, which worked out to four percent interest over twenty years. Not a bad deal for me at all. I could focus my farming on the land I needed and get paid a good sum for the land I didn't.

Didn't know Lil real well, but Donnie never struck me as the kinda guy who'd default. On the other hand, he also seemed like someone it wouldn't bother too much if he did. And if he did, I could see him trying to use the law to his advantage. The laws of this country were on the books to screw people like me. It wouldn't have surprised me if Donnie tried to use the bankruptcy laws for just that purpose. I was starting to realize that it'd be a slog to get what I could out of Donnie and Lil, and I knew I'd have to do it in front of a federal judge. And a bankruptcy judge at that—another illegitimate wielder of power I'd need to play nice in front of if I wanted to get my money back.

I'd been to bankruptcy court before. Watched the proceedings. Black-robed judge sitting up high with U.S. Marshals in the courtroom watching. Watching *me*. I could feel it when they stared at me. Yep. I knew this was gonna be a slog.

I thought of old Donnie pocketing the money him and Lil collected from the tenant working my land rather than paying me what was owed. I knew Donnie and Lil would have to learn that pocketing my money was off-limits. My land. Shit. My money, goddammit.

I'd been in Meadowfield my whole life. I grew up on my parents' farm, and they sent me across the state line to go to the University of Missouri in Columbia to become a Mizzou Tiger. Never finished. Got called back to the farm to help out my folks. I figured it was improbable that I went off to college in the first place. Didn't mind coming home. I never felt like I fit in with many of the folks I met at Mizzou. Not the ones from the big cities. Most of them Tigers I met weren't from the farm.

My parents passed long ago. Left me a large hog operation and all that land. They inherited it all from my grandparents. They worked hard to keep what they had. When they sent me off to college, I think they had mixed feelings about whether I should return to the farm when I graduated. They kept their feelings to themselves, but I'm sure they hoped I wouldn't. They never told me that, but I could see it in their eyes. A kid can tell things that way about his parents. But their dream that I would have a different life than them never happened. No. I came home and took over the farm's day-to-day operation. When they died, I owned it—and with it, my little piece of America. Just like them. But I could feel my little piece slipping further and further away each goddamn day. It wasn't what they'd hoped for, and it wasn't what I expected either.

It's every parent's hope to give their kids a better life than they had. Sometimes the parent fails and their kids lives ain't no better than theirs. I think my parents thought they'd failed.

As I drove, I thought that they—whoever *they* were—told you that anything's possible in this damn country. Dream and you can one day achieve it. But they didn't know. So many things weren't possible, at least not in this century. So many dreams wouldn't be coming true. At least not my dreams. Hell, maybe most dreams wouldn't. Leastwise, not anymore.

Oh, there's a rainbow all right. I'd seen it from time to time stretching across the Kansas sky from one end of the horizon to the other. Colorful, but truth is, there isn't no somewhere over it. Nah. Sometimes life is a series of nowheres. Nowhere over the rainbow for me, I guess. Not when I have to get up at four in the morning to run a farm in a country where we've lost our way, abandoned our history, mortgaged our present and future, and turned it over to those who'd sooner run it into the ground than abide by the wishes and intent of our founding fathers. Nowhere. That's the place where guys like Donnie can default.

Hence The Thirty-Six Thirties, a name I conjured up. More of a little social club than an organization, at least to that point. Like-minded folks who came together to exchange ideas, you might say. A club of twelve—well, really only eleven. I invited Donnie, but he never joined. Said it wasn't good for his business. Maybe, but I think he wasn't one of us 'cause he didn't think and believe like one of us.

We was a bit like the posse comitatus. The force of the county would be the literal translation. I'd heard it said before that we Thirties was a part of a far-right, populist, social movement. Conspiracy-minded. Anti-government. Anti-Semitic. Anti-colored people. Anti-immigrants. The true Israelites chosen by God to preserve civilization as it was meant to be, believing that the coloreds were nothing but Fourteenth Amendment citizens, not true Americans. Not like me and my kind.

All true.

The eleven of us had come together to start The Thirties, and I tried to pattern us after an original posse comitatus formed by Henry Lamont Beach, a retired Portland, Oregon, dry cleaner. A guy who pressed shirts for a living, if you can imagine that. I guess even dry cleaners have their limits on how much change in America they're willing to tolerate. Change ain't good. Not the kind of change we opposed. The Thirties were one of these posse groups.

I went online and kept up with the other posse groups. Feels like they made the internet for us posses.

This guy, Lamont, he had a simple belief: There was no legitimate government above the county and no authority higher than the county sheriff. We sorta thought the same from time to time. Some of the posse groups I kept track of refused to pay taxes. Some paid taxes with money they printed up. Sometimes the county clerk even took that fake money. No accounting for the competence of some county clerks—a power hungry bunch with no common sense. But on the other hand, that money was no more fake than the full faith and credit, no gold greenbacks printed by Uncle Sam in violation of the Constitution.

Some of the posse members had sued judges. Some had killed federal marshals. Most of the posses believed that the federal government had turned its back on folks like us. Abandoned us. Things in the farm belt were going badly. Always going badly. Hog prices were down and corn prices were up. Tax increases every year. All of that was bad for farming, and it was the government's fault. Politicians, Jewish bankers, corrupt feds, colored folks, working women, immigrants, south of the border folks flooding into this country, and the government—our government—all conspiring to oppress us God-fearing, White, Christians.

Us Thirties, we respected the posses. We believed what the posses believed. We read everything the posses posted on social media, but in the end, The Thirties was more of a talkers' club. At least up to that point. We was eleven folks with ideas and words, and yeah, we was angry and getting angrier by the day.

But we hadn't done nothing. Not yet. For example, I myself hadn't shot no one. I didn't know for sure, but I didn't think any of the others had either. So if I was a domestic terrorist back then, I guess I'd have to say I was more of a paper terrorist, willin' to use fraudulent legal documents and filings to intimidate public officials, law enforcement officers, and private citizens. I liked to think that I used the system against those who illegitimately perpetuated the system and tried to use it against me.

As I drove, I thought about old Donnie and Lil and bankruptcy. I realized that he'd most certainly try to use the system for his own purposes and file for bankruptcy protection. Protection from his creditors. Protection from me. And as a result, no payments to me and my Thirties colleagues. But I didn't think it would protect him from me.

Like I said at the meeting, people who owed me money had filed for bankruptcy before. The last time, I learned that these folks was supposed to treat creditors the same. No unfair discrimination in bankruptcy. Unlike in this great country of ours, where our government unfairly discriminates against us White, Christian folks every day. But them same feds and judges who daily ran our illegitimate government also run the system. So if Donnie and Lil filed, I was expecting nothing approaching fair treatment. Not in this system of ours and not in bankruptcy. No fairness without a fight.

Like I said, I was never much a system guy, and Donnie and Lil would try to use the system against me. But I'd turn the tables and use the system against them to get my money.

I figured Donnie'd file that next Monday morning. I figured no more time for talk. I figured time to take action.

I'm Woody Clarke, and this is my story.

2

Friday, April 12, 2024

THE DIFFUSED NORTHERN light streamed in through the floor-to-ceiling windows in Josephia Jillian Jones' high-rise condo on the southeastern edge of downtown Kansas City, Missouri. 3J to her friends. Golden morning light invited her to the new day. In the kitchen, Ronnie Steele brewed her a pot of Earl Grey tea and brewed a pot of French press coffee for himself.

"Hey, Jo," Steele called out. "If you don't drink coffee, why do you have this fancy French press and fresh coffee beans?"

3J leaned out of her bathroom, towel wrapped around her athletic frame, and called back, "It's for friends like you when they come over."

"Friends? Is that what I am? And 'come over.' Is that what I'm doing?"

"Yes, and yes. I mean, if you're not a friend, what are you? An enemy? And you're here, right? So I figure you must've come over to get here." 3J paused and then called out, "And you called me Jo. The only human in the world who ever called me that was my Papa."

"Didn't know that about your dad, but I guess that puts me in good company, eh?"

3J had made her way out of the bathroom and headed toward the kitchen, towel still wrapped around her. She frowned at Steele.

He couldn't tell if she was serious or not. "But I hear ya, so I'll stick with 3J for now," he said, retreating.

Several feet short of the kitchen island, she paused, smiled, and said, "Better." Then she whispered, "Come over here."

Steele did, drifting obediently toward her. And as he did, 3J's towel slipped off and fell to the floor. He smiled. How could he do anything else when looking at her in her Garden of Eden attire? He gently hugged her, and they kissed in the warm glow of the morning light.

"I gotta be in court in an hour, Mr. Steele," 3J said, pulling back. "No time for anything right now except clothing and tea."

"Hmm. I see. And the towel drop was a teaser?"

3J grinned. Steele was good for her, and the previous night's activities were long overdue. "Not a teaser at all. I don't want you to forget me as the day wears on."

He stepped back, looked from top to bottom to top again, and made eye contact. "Not a chance. How could I? Do you really have to be in court in an hour?"

"That's the fact."

Steele shrugged. "I suppose that's the life of a Greene Madison bankruptcy partner."

"The life of any bankruptcy attorney in any firm."

"Well, I too have obligations. Gotta get to the bar and get ready for the day. Can I come by tonight?"

"I'll text you."

"I'll be watching for it. G-rated only, please. No photos. I'm not likely to forget the live view here. Tea's ready for you in the pot. Thanks for last night. It was . . . nice."

3J stepped back, retrieved the towel, wrapped it back around her body, and feigned surprise. "Nice? That's the best you can come up with?"

Steele smiled. "More than nice. *Really* nice." He tried hard not to chuckle.

3J turned and headed to her bedroom, where she had laid out her lawyer's uniform—the day's business attire—on her bed. "We have to work on the breadth of your adjectives, my friend," she said over her shoulder. "I'm thinking you should work on words like 'epic,' 'memorable,' 'spectacular,' 'amazing.' You know, words that accurately and completely describe last night." She stopped short of the bedroom to turn, and before she turned, there was Steele, right behind her.

He grabbed her shoulders, gently guided her around to face him, looked her in the eyes, and said, "Magnificent. Last night was magnificent. Just like you."

3J looked up into his eyes and smiled. "Much better. For me too. Watch for a text." They kissed, and she moved into the bedroom with Ronnie following right behind her.

"So whatdaya got going today, 3J?"

"I'm in line to interview for several new cases Pascale and I will handle. Rural real estate Chapter 11s. If I get the gig, I'd represent the interests of the unsecured creditors. So I'm making a pitch for new business."

"How does that work in the bankruptcy world?"

"The debtors filed Monday. On Wednesday, the trustee's office appointed unsecured creditors to sit on an official committee. The committee is meeting at the courthouse to hire a lawyer today to help it assert its rights and represent the interests of all unsecured creditors."

"Rights and interests, eh? Do unsecured creditors have rights?"

"Sure they do," 3J said as she pulled on her gray pants, buttoned her white blouse, and reached for her navy blue blazer. "The Bankruptcy Code prohibits a debtor from unfairly discriminating against unsecured creditors, so normally that means they all get paid the same percentage over the same time period. My job, should I get hired, is to make sure that happens. Payments over as short a time period as possible."

"Unfair discrimination? That's a weird sounding one. Does that mean there's something in bankruptcy called 'fair discrimination,' and it's okay? I mean, maybe bankruptcy differs from the real world, but is there any kind of discrimination in the world that's not unfair?"

"That's the Bankruptcy Code for you. Not sure I'd compare it to the real world, though. I'll explain more later if you're interested, but now I gotta run."

"No worries. Good luck with your pitch thing. You'll knock them dead. You'll be . . . well, marvelous."

3J grinned again. "Watch for that text, Ronnie. Gotta finish getting ready. I'll see you at O'Brien's at the end of the day. I'm gonna meet Pascale there to talk about these new cases if I get hired."

"Well, I'll be there, as I always am, tending the bar and tending to the regulars. I'll grab my things and head out." Steele leaned in for a departure kiss and headed for the kitchen, grabbed a travel mug of coffee, and then made his way to 3J's door.

3J took her lucky shoes from the closet, a designer pair of deep red, sparkly shoes with scarpin heels. They were like Dorothy's ruby reds, but with high heels. As she put them on, she thought about how her life had recently turned on a dime with Ronnie Steele's sudden entry into it. Was it a passing fling or a relationship that had legs? It had been a long time since her last relationship, and she didn't want to screw this one up. The practice of law had gotten in the way of her last relationship. She resolved that it would not interfere this time and made a mental note to have a "talk" if necessary with the jealous paramour that constituted the practice of law's alter ego.

And then there was the impending retirement of her friend, law partner, and bankruptcy mentor, William Pascale. She worried how life at the firm would be without Pascale guiding her.

There was plenty to ponder. But she pushed those thoughts out of her head as she tried to focus on her presentation to a group of unsecured creditors in the bankruptcy cases of Donavan Isik Melanshin, his wife, Lillian, and their company, Melanshin Farms LLC. The Melanshins lived in Kansas, but they had formed their company in Missouri, so they were able to file the bankruptcy cases on the Missouri side of the bi-state Kansas City metropolitan area.

After the bankruptcy cases began, 3J had called the debtors' attorney, Jacob Steinert, for some background information. Steinert had told her he had delayed filing the cases for a few weeks while he waited for "Mr. Green"—the personification of money—to arrive. It was secret lawyer code for "awaiting payment of a retainer from the Melanshins." He reported that they went dark for a couple of weeks after he met them and delayed paying him a retainer. During that time, he wasn't sure they would follow through and hire him. But they wired him the money just in time because the Melanshins' creditors had begun to circle overhead like vultures waiting to pick meat off bones.

In Steinert's words, "From their story, I saw little meat on the bones left when we talked and heard no one making a motion to divide up the bones. Just angry creditors who wanted a piece of the Melanshins' hide."

3J had asked Steinert for information about the creditors, and he had forwarded to her the names and contact information for the twenty largest unsecured creditors. On that list were several corporate trade creditors, each owed about a million dollars, including the local farm cooperative and a neighboring one. Also on the list were individuals Steinert described as neighbors to whom the Melanshins and their company owed significant money. Steinert also reported that there were many creditors with collateral, including two with mortgages on the Melanshin house in Meadowfield and several others. Total debts were well over ten million dollars.

3J and Pascale had worked on cases with Steinert in the past.

He was a no-nonsense, experienced bankruptcy attorney who knew his way around the Bankruptcy Code and the courthouse. He was well respected by the judges and was a senior member in good standing of the small, informal group of Kansas City insolvency and restructuring lawyers.

When 3J asked Steinert what the Melanshins and their creditors were like, Steinert said, "3J, I don't know much about them yet. Donnie Melanshin told me there's a group in Meadowfield called The Thirty-Six Thirties, formed by one of his biggest creditors. He says it was a social club but at some point, it graduated to a fringe group with largely hater beliefs, and he never joined it. It's identified as a domestic terrorist group by some watchdogs. The Anti-Defamation League has a white paper posted about these types of groups. The Thirties have some out-there, right-wing views of the law and the world. Actually, in the world we currently live in, sadly, I'm not sure how out-there these kinds of views are. It seems there are way more of these fringe types than I ever imagined, and they're angrier and more strident than I ever understood. Many of them are hiding in plain sight.

"Melanshin says a guy named Woody Clarke formalized the group and named it four or five years ago. Melanshin told me he doesn't align with the members and their views. Maybe so. Not sure. Maybe he was telling me this because he thought it's what I would want to hear to take the cases."

Steinert had paused and then said, "The Melanshins seem to have run out of money. Even though they received rent from their tenants, they weren't able to pay creditors."

3J took notes.

"Y'know, 3J, I'm a little surprised they hired a Jewish guy like me as their bankruptcy counsel. But for whatever reason, they did. Even a little more surprising, I decided to take the cases . . . and their money. Am I crazy? Perhaps. What a freakin' world, right?"

3J had offered no response to Steinert's overview during the call. But as she made the short walk to the courthouse, she couldn't help but think about what kind of bankruptcy ride this would be if the unsecured creditors committee hired her. She found it hard to imagine a case in which the debtors lived in a town with a fringe group of haters and were represented by a Jewish lawyer while the creditors committee was comprised of "neighbors" who might be members of a fringe group and were represented by a Black, female bankruptcy attorney. It was the stuff of a morning news show exposé or an Apple TV+ series. Oh baby, how far we have come, she thought.

3J arrived at the courthouse, passed through the metal detector on the first floor, said hello to the U.S. Marshals stationed at the security checkpoint, and made her way to the United States Trustee's office on the second floor. Once there, she sat in a weathered, uncomfortable, creaky wooden chair outside a closed conference room door awaiting her turn to make her presentation. Within ten minutes, the door opened, a lawyer who had finished his pitch exited, and a loud voice from within said, "Next!"

3J rose and entered the conference room. There, around a large oval table, sat seven somber White men. Three were members of the The Thirties: Woody Clarke, Edward Daniels, and Sidney Perrin. The other four were representatives of creditor companies: a Meadowfield farm cooperative representative, an implement dealer, a credit card company, and a home repair contractor.

As 3J entered, The Thirties saw for the first time that she was Black. And a woman. A striking woman at that. Woody Clarke rose and pointed to a chair for her to sit in. Daniels and Perrin did not make eye contact. They had little contact with people of color in their lives and wanted to have even less. 3J made them feel uncomfortable.

The four creditor representatives had pads and pens in front of them and scribbled notes on the pads as each muttered, "Welcome," to 3J as she took her seat.

Tough crowd, 3J thought as she sat down. She was skilled pitching for bankruptcy business, and in short order, explained who she was and described her extensive bankruptcy experience. She also gave the creditors an overview of the Greene Madison law firm and its bankruptcy group.

She then explained the role of the committee and discussed how any bankruptcy repayment plan would normally treat unsecured creditors. She told them that committee members had a fiduciary duty to represent the interests of all unsecured creditors, not just their own interests. No one nodded in agreement. No one asked any questions. She saw no facial expressions of understanding or confusion, so she continued. "It's easy to discharge the fiduciary duty because, typically, unsecured creditors are all treated the same way by a debtor's repayment plan. So what's good for you is good for all unsecureds." She paused and looked at seven unemotional faces.

"If I could, gentlemen, I'd propose to use the remainder of my time to discuss what I see happening in these bankruptcy cases."

"Proceed," Clarke said simply without looking up from the table.

"First, I noticed that you, Mr. Clarke, signed an installment land sale contract to the Melanshins. In Kansas, the courts call those contracts for deed. Often, sellers mistakenly use this kind of contract thinking they'll retain ownership of the land until the buyer makes the last payment because that's exactly what the contract says.

"In fact, Kansas real estate law looks at the arrangement differently. The law says that the transaction is a sale of the land to the buyers on the day the parties sign the contract, and the law treats the contract as a mortgage on the land. For protection, the seller needs to file the contract in the county recorder of deeds office along with the mortgage records. If they don't, then in bankruptcy, the law characterizes the transaction as a financed sale, and the seller has none of the protections afforded by a recorded mortgage. Without that recorded mortgage, in bankruptcy, the seller is nothing more than an unsecured creditor. No land. No collateral.

"That's the reason, Mr. Clarke, that you're on an *unsecured* creditors committee," 3J said looking directly at Clarke, who offered no reaction. "The debtors owe you the balance of the purchase price, you have an unsecured claim for that amount, you don't own the land, and you have no legal way get the land back. Do you have questions on this point?"

Clarke stared at 3J as she spoke and blinked with his arms folded across his chest. He said nothing in response to her offer for a question and answer period.

"Second, the filed bankruptcy papers don't explain what led the debtors to need bankruptcy protection. Why did they stop paying creditors even as they continued to receive rent? The committee will want to get to the bottom of that. Also, the committee will want to lead the negotiations for a satisfactory repayment plan."

Again, there was nothing from Clarke, Daniels, or Perrin.

One of the other creditors asked, "How quickly can we begin those negotiations?"

"I'd expect the discussions to begin as soon as the committee has a good picture of the cause of the bankruptcy filings and the debtors present complete and satisfactory financial information, to include projections of cash flow into the future they'll use to repay each of you. So I would hope pretty quickly, assuming we get cooperation from the debtors in the committee's due diligence process. They have a good lawyer who knows how this is supposed to work. I'm sure he will encourage the Melanshins to cooperate. But you know the debtors. I don't. Will they cooperate?"

"Oh Donnie boy'll cooperate all right," Clarke replied gruffly. "He won't have no choice."

3J wasn't sure what Clarke meant but let the possibly veiled threat pass. She looked at her watch and said, "Gentlemen, it looks like my fifteen minutes are about up. If none of you have questions of me, I'll simply thank you for your time. And I'll look forward to hearing your decision." She stood, put her papers in her backpack, and strode out of the conference room. She was the last interviewee to pitch for the committee business.

Clarke rose and closed the conference room door so the committee members could have privacy to deliberate the selection of counsel.

Clarke studied his Thirties colleagues and the four trade creditor representatives. The committee members had completed interviews of six lawyers vying to be committee counsel. Clarke thought little of the first five candidates and wanted to summarily eliminate them and discuss only 3J.

Clarke believed that 3J was part of the reason the country was no longer great. After all, she was Black and a woman. But she had a law degree, and she was far more knowledgeable and far superior to the other five lawyers, based on the presentations he'd sat through. Moreover, it was the big city, and it would be hard to find a Kansas City bankruptcy lawyer who shared his views. He suspected there weren't many White Christian bankruptcy lawyers in Kansas City to choose from, though he admitted to himself that he had no way of knowing.

It sounded like she was a regular in front of the bankruptcy judge assigned to the Melanshin cases. He figured that was a good thing. Begrudgingly, he had no choice but to admit that she was the best he'd seen, and he knew he didn't have to like her to hire her. He didn't have to like that she was a reason the country was no longer great. Not at all. He needed the best option to get his money back from Donnie and Lil. Hiring a lawyer was just business. Black-and-white—no pun intended, he thought. He knew he'd have to navigate the situation carefully. He didn't want Daniels or Perrin to accuse him of compromising his make-America-great beliefs, but he was willing to stifle his beliefs in favor of repayment. Period. And they would too, but he'd have some convincing to do. Clarke called for a break before the group discussion began so he could have time alone with Daniels and Perrin. The other creditors were happy to adjourn to catch up on business and go outside for a smoke, leaving Clarke, Daniels, and Perrin alone at the trustee's conference room table.

"I didn't much like any of 'em," Perrin announced. "Of course, I don't much like lawyers at all, and I got no use for that Jones kind. What the hell kind of country lets colored women become lawyers? Nope, I cain't see her as my lawyer at all."

"Ditto," Daniels agreed.

"Look, fellas," Clarke said. "This here is just business. Donnie and Lil seem to be trying to screw us. Me in particular. They took my land. You heard Jones. I figured I may have a hard time getting it back. Jones says I ain't gonna get it back. Land or no land, they still owe me a ton of money. It don't look good for me getting all of that back neither.

"Far and away, this Jones lawyer made the best presentation. Sure, she's colored. Sure, she's a skirt. Sure, I want nothing to do with her kind. Sure, we gotta make sure that her kind don't take our country away from us. But I want my money, and I don't much have to like her, respect her, agree with her, or change my views about her and her kind to hire her if she's the most likely one to get me my money from Donnie and Lil. And she is, goddammit. I ain't gonna look past that she's colored and a woman. She's both. But she's got the right degree and I'm hoping the judge's ear as well. So I'm gonna ignore what she is for a few months while she does her thing and gets me and you paid back."

Clarke looked at his colleagues. They folded their arms and

frowned but said nothing. He continued. "Anyway, she ain't gonna be our lawyer. She'll be the committee's lawyer. Understood?"

The others frowned and continued to say nothing.

"So I need you guys to vote for her as the committee's lawyer when them other four creditors return. If you don't, then how're we gonna get paid?"

"Look, I hear ya', Woody," Daniels said. "But I gotta say, I don't like this one bit. Not a bit. The notion that some colored gal named Jones is gonna stand up in a courtroom on my behalf is almost too much for me to comprehend. Why cain't we find another lawyer? A White one?"

"These six were the only ones who wanted the business," Clarke replied. "We ain't got no time to start cold calling lawyers up here and see if they want the work."

Daniels' face contorted and then went blank. Perrin had a look of pain and deep contemplation.

"If we do this," Perrin said slowly, "I don't want this kinda thing discussed at our meetings back home. This'll just be between the three of us. Right? The others don't need to know that she's a colored lawyer and a woman to boot. And they don't need to know that we agreed to hire her. Right?"

Daniels eyed Perrin with a look of disbelief. "So just like that, Sid? You're gonna vote for this Jones lawyer?" He shook his head. "If that don't beat all. Well, here's my condition. If I vote for her like you want, then I don't want nothing to do with her. I mean, I'll go to some of these here committee meetings on the phone. But I want it clear. I don't want nothing to do with her. I don't want to come back to Kansas City and have to see her tell everyone she's *my* committee's lawyer. Woody, this is all your goddamn idea, so you'll have to be the one to deal with her, and you can report to us as needed."

Before Woody could respond, Perrin chimed in. "I agree. Anyway, you're the one with bankruptcy experience."

"All fine by me," Woody said, nodding his head in understanding. "Let's get them others back in here and finish this up."

The other creditor representatives returned to the conference room, and in short order, Woody explained the trio's thinking. The others agreed 3J was the best for the job. They weren't interested in talking about the different candidates. They all voted to hire 3J and put Clarke in charge of the interactions with counsel. Immediately after the vote, everyone except Woody Clarke retreated, leaving him alone to call 3J and convey the news.

When she answered the call, Clarke identified himself, told her she was hired, and explained that he would be her point of contact. "I wanna emphasize that I want my money from Donnie and Lil. ASAP," he said. "That's it. We all want our money. So I want an outline from you, step-by-step, saying what you're gonna do and how long you figure it'll take."

"I'll have that for you over the weekend, Mr. Clarke," she assured him. "Thank you, and please thank the other committee members for putting your trust in me."

"No trust involved at all. I don't trust lawyers. I don't trust Donnie and Lil. I don't trust the system. And I don't feel like I trust you. Hell's bells. I don't even know you and I don't need to. I just want my money, and you're gonna figure out a way to get it for me in the short run. That's my aim. You understand what I'm saying?"

"I understand," 3J replied, not knowing what else to say.

When the call ended, 3J replaced the office phone in its cradle and wondered if she should accept the representation after all. She put aside her concerns and decided it would be something new—a good learning experience.

3

Woody Clarke recalls Friday, April 12, 2024

AFTER THE COMMITTEE meeting, I got into my pickup for the seventy-five-minute drive back to the farm. I remember thinkin', goddamn lawyers. Goddamn Donnie and Lil. Goddamn system. Goddamn country of ours. It occurred to me that it wasn't so much our country anymore. They claimed it was theirs as well, and if they had their way, only theirs. Goddamn it all, I thought, and as I thought it, I sped up to eighty miles an hour. The old pickup truck's engine roared. I took my foot off the gas a little because there was no point in getting a ticket from a state trooper. Goddamn state troopers, I thought.

That Jones gal had mentioned one thing that made me think. It had been on my mind for a while. I wondered where Donnie's money went every month. He had a good tenant who, from outward appearances, paid all the rent on time each month. He had other tenants who paid as well. For several years, Donnie paid me like clockwork. Then he paid sporadically. Then, suddenly, Donnie's payments stopped, and the Melanshins and their company filed for bankruptcy. I wondered what in Christ's name was going on.

I thought about the situation the whole drive back to Meadowfield. No music. No talk shows. Just me and my thoughts. By the end of the drive, I decided I needed to have me a discussion with Donavan Isik Melanshin and his wife, Lillian. What a name old Donnie's folks gave him. Donnie once told me his folks misspelled his middle name, and instead of *Isaac* when they filled out the papers, they wrote *Isik*. He told me it meant "light" in Turkish, but he swore up and down that he didn't have a drop of Middle Eastern blood in his veins. He first told me he liked to go by DI, but when we formed The Thirties, we started calling him Donnie, and it stuck.

I knew I'd have to pay a little visit to old Donnie or DI or Donavan Isik or whatever the hell people called him and have a heart-to-heart. Something about his numbers made no sense to me. I figured I'd have to scour his spreadsheets. If Donnie was scamming, I knew I could figure it out. Then me and that Jones gal, we'd get him quickly back on the path to virtue, or in this case, payment.

Like I said, I hadn't never killed no one, but that didn't mean I hadn't threatened it, and it didn't mean no one never got killed on my behalf. Just sayin'. I decided it was time for Donnie and Lil to think they had more at stake than a repayment plan.

4

A FTER CLARKE'S CALL, 3J contacted Jacob Steinert to let
him know the committee had chosen her as its counsel
and asked to see the last five years of Melanshin financial
records. She told Steinert she was most interested in cash flows
showing where the Melanshins' money came from, how they used
it, and why their net cash flow appeared to have dried up.

"Of course," Steinert replied. Later in the afternoon, two boxes
of financials arrived at 3J's office.

3J prepared the papers required for her firm to represent the
committee for court approval and cleared other matters from her
docket so she could turn her attention to the Melanshin bankruptcy cases the next morning. Then she worked on the outline
for the committee, focusing on the information gathering phase.
She would share the outline with Pascale, get his input, and send
it off to the committee. After the committee digested the financial
information, she envisioned a meeting with the Melanshins and
thought an early start to the plan repayment dialogue was in order.

The busy day allowed her to ignore any thoughts about representing this particular committee and Steinert's comments about
the creditors. With Clarke and The Thirties on the committee, she

wondered why they decided to hire her and decided she was correct in her initial thought that it was a nutty, unpredictable world.

At quitting time, she stuffed her papers in her backpack, slung it over her shoulder, and made her way to the Greene Madison parking garage and her navy blue Prius. She was heading to O'Brien's to meet Pascale. They had met at O'Brien's most Fridays at quitting time for as long as she could remember to put a period and sometimes an exclamation point at the end of another busy week in the bankruptcy law business.

The familiar car ride took 3J past the National World War I Memorial just south of Union Station. It was a famous federal park site where she liked to walk early in the morning after a snowfall. Just her, the tall fluted shaft, and the surrounding national memorial grounds she shared with the ghosts of the World War I veterans who gave their lives before 1920 in the hopes of future peace. Private donations had funded its construction. Kansas City jazz band leader, Benny Moten, was one of the biggest donors, although it was unclear if he was ever permitted to visit the memorial—because he was Black.

The walks were her chance to take nothing but time and leave nothing but footprints in the fresh snow. They were her moments of solitude to slow the world down for a short while. Sometimes she took the walk at night so she could see the shaft's pinnacle flame, which was no more than rising steam illuminated by bright red and orange lights that gave the illusion of a burning pyre visible for some distance.

When she walked, she liked to think about the four sculptures crowning the tower. The Guardian Spirits represented protectors of peace, each holding a sword and named for a virtue: Honor, Courage, Patriotism, and Sacrifice. As 3J drove past the memorial, she thought about the four virtues. She recalled Steinert's comments about fringe groups hiding in plain sight and like the warrior ghosts, not always seen. She wondered if Americans had lost these virtues, and then she wondered if Americans ever really had them. She worried that they were nothing more than unachievable aspirations and not held by enough people to make them come true. The next winter's snow was months away, but 3J looked forward to walking the grounds when winter arrived. Her next walk in the snow might help her sort out her 2024 views of the four virtues.

She tuned her streaming service to a 1977 Chuck Mangione favorite, "Feels So Good," hoping she could forget the right-wing concerns swirling around the Melanshins' bankruptcy cases by listening to Mangione's upbeat approach to jazz composition. At least for a little while, Mangione's flugelhorn and Grant Geissman's soaring guitar solo took her to a happy Friday place.

The song ended as she arrived on Westport Road, parked the car, and entered O'Brien's, where the end-of-week crowd had already gathered. Pascale sat in a far corner booth. He had recently told the Greene Madison brass he would retire from the practice of law to pursue other passions, the list of which was still a work in process.

The staff at O'Brien's operated under the watchful eye of Ronnie Steele, who worked the bar. Earlier in the day, after 3J returned from her courthouse pitch, she had texted Steele to let him know he could come to her condo later in the evening when he got off his shift. She knew it would be late, but he wanted to see her again and she wanted him to be with her again. So it was an easy decision for her.

3J sat across from Pascale at the weathered oak table and sighed. Friday contentment. She grabbed the double-shot glass of Irish whiskey Pascale had ordered for her, held it up in silent thanks to Pascale, closed her eyes, and enjoyed the first sip. No water, no ice. Just caramel-colored, smooth, high-octane liquor.

"So you made a pitch today for business?" Pascale asked.

"I did," 3J replied.

"What type of case?"

"Rural real estate, as best as I can tell. I'm only at the beginning of understanding the case."

"Debtors' counsel?"

"Jacob Steinert."

Pascale nodded. "A good one."

"He's not sure why he took the case, Pascale, other than for the money. He says that some of the creditors belong to a fringe group of right-wing haters."

Pascale narrowed his eyes as he stared at 3J, asked no questions, and let the silence hang.

"I'm sure you're wondering why I pitched for this business," 3J said.

"Yes. Well . . . I was wondering that and a few other things, like why you would want this kind of added headache in life. And if they're haters, why do the unsecureds want you as their lawyer?"

"Steinert sounded a little disappointed in himself for agreeing to represent the Melanshins with all the right-winger stuff swarming around. I may be feeling the same way about the committee shortly." 3J sighed again as she studied the whiskey in her glass, but this time it was a sigh of conflict. She looked back to Pascale. "We humans can be a mysterious bunch if we're nothing else."

"Since you can be one of those mysterious humans like the rest of us, why *did* you want this case? Sounds like a whopper of a migraine in the making."

"I can't say that I *wanted* it. You do a lot of things you don't *want* to do when you're a lawyer, right? But I haven't had a committee engagement in quite a while. I'm not working on anything remarkably interesting at the moment, so I thought it would be a good change. I mean, the type of engagement would be good, not the part where I'll have to deal with the politics and beliefs of right-wingers." She paused and added, "Also, Robertson has the cases. I thought it would be an opportunity to appear before him in a role other than as debtors' counsel."

"Robertson" was short for Judge Daniel Robertson, one of the three bankruptcy judges in the Western District of Missouri. He was a rising star in the judiciary. 3J and Pascale had appeared in front of the judge many times and always looked forward to getting a case over which he presided. He dispensed bankruptcy justice with an even-keeled demeanor, and he made the correct rulings in a timely fashion. He was a favorite of the Kansas City bankruptcy lawyers.

"I get it. Maybe they hired you because you made the best presentation."

"Maybe. Who knows? I might get lucky and it'll turn out to be a fine experience."

"For you or for them?"

"Yes," 3J said, indicating for both. "I'm going to need some significant help on this one. I predict both court and couch time help."

"Happy to help in court. Happy to play social scientist and psychologist. My therapy rates are reasonable," Pascale joked. "Just let me know what you need."

"To start with, I'm going to need you to help review financials. The debtors ought to have money and net cash flow. But from what little I understand, they don't, and no one seems to understand why."

"Ready and able. Reporting for duty."

"I've got two boxes of information from Steinert already, so if you don't mind working on a Saturday during your wind down phase at the firm, can we dive in tomorrow morning?"

"Works fine for me. They're still sending me checks every two weeks, and in exchange, I write my time down. So far, the checks aren't bouncing."

Pascale looked into the golden-yellow Kansas wheat beer he was working on and then looked past the beer mug to 3J. "How's it going with Ronnie?"

Ronnie Steele and Pascale had both graduated from Kansas State University, Steele years after Pascale. Both played baseball there and had been close friends for years. Steele had been a criminal justice major in college and later worked on the vice squad for KCPD. When he retired from the force, he took the job running O'Brien's. Shortly after Pascale's wife and young daughter died in a car crash at the hands of a drunk driver, Pascale and Steele became even closer, taking in Kansas City Royals games at Kauffman Stadium and even the occasional Kansas City Chiefs game at Arrowhead when they could score tickets. Pascale needed the human companionship and the diversion that sports afforded, and Steele was there for him with an ample supply of professional spectator sports to put some sorely needed joy back into Pascale's life. Pascale felt indebted to Steele for giving him periods of respite from the persistent brooding over the sudden loss of his family.

"It's nice," 3J said as she smiled at Pascale's paternal question.

"Nice, huh? Seems like faint praise."

"Just kidding," 3J said without explaining her exchange with Steele that morning but trying Ronnie's descriptive words on for size. "It's actually marvelous."

Pascale nodded. "I'm happy for both of you kids. You deserve each other." Then Pascale added emphatically, "But please take it slow, Ms. Jones." 3J continued to smile, but he noted that in her silent response, she did not show any signs that she agreed.

"Uh, oh. Look at the time," Pascale said, looking at his watch. "I've gotta get home, grab the guitars, and head out for a practice session. I'll see you in the morning, say 9:30, if that works for you." He donned a fatherly smile and stood to leave. "Say hi to Ronnie."

"9:30 it is. Have fun playing whatever it is you're playing these days, Bill."

"Oh, just some new ideas I'm trying out about changing and stuff like that."

"You'll have to let me hear it sometime."

Pascale nodded and hustled to the door, waving his good-byes to 3J. After he left, 3J looked at her emails on her phone. Always connected, she thought.

Steele came to her booth. The bar was much too busy for him to sit and talk, but he asked if she wanted another one, on the house.

"Thanks, but I'll pass." She smiled. "I want to be awake and on top of my game when you close up here and come over."

"Come over? There it is again. Is that what I'm doing?"

"Okay. I want to be vibrant, witty, and desirable when you arrive later this evening at the condo."

"Better. You need to work on your vocabulary, 3J." Smiling broadly, he added, "But better. See you in a while."

3J's eyes lingered on Steele's fit frame as he retreated from the booth and returned to the bar. She wondered if he could feel her looking. She hoped so. She paid the check and made her way to the front door and the evening beyond. An evening to which she was looking forward.

Clarke had arrived back in Meadowfield and called Donnie after dinner. "What say I swing by your place first thing in the morning?" he suggested. "I got a few things you and me need to talk about and get straight."

"Okay, Woody," Donnie replied slowly. "Any hints about what things those are?"

"We can discuss it in person in the morning. Have Lil put on a pot of coffee. Could be a long discussion."

"All right, Woody. We'll be here." As he ended the call with Clarke, Donnie muttered sarcastically to himself, "Well, great." Clarke's demand for an in-person talk did not surprise Donnie. He expected Clarke to demand that payments on the sale contract be resumed immediately. Donnie figured that when he said no,

Clarke would get loud and pushy, and Donnie would have to tell him not to come around anymore.

Donnie wasn't looking forward to the confrontation. But he also knew that since he and Lil put their plan into action several years ago, the day would come. He felt he might as well get it over with, and Saturday at his house was as good a time and place as any. He'd let Steinert know about the meeting when it was over. He figured his lawyer would have some bankruptcy way of dealing with Clarke. Donnie thought the system would protect Lil and him and allow them to bring the last step of their plan to fruition.

How fitting, he thought. They'd use the system to their advantage. After all, Steinert told them that was what the Bankruptcy Code was designed to do: protect people like Lil and him from creditors like Woody.

Donnie smiled to himself as he considered how Clarke would react. He figured Clarke wouldn't be able to handle the realization that folks like Donnie and Lil would dare screw him using the very system he so vehemently resented. Donnie told Lil that Clarke would have a tantrum.

Lil had seen Clarke's tantrums a time or two. "Well, Donnie. He don't handle bad news well. No payments is pretty bad news. Old Woody is prone to tantrums, but this one ought to be a doozy. Maybe we should film it for YouTube?"

5

ATURDAY MORNING, BRIGHT and early, 3J quietly rose from her bed, leaving behind a sleeping Ronnie Steele, who had promptly arrived at the condo soon after midnight. They made love shortly after he arrived and then cuddled. No law talk. No bar talk. Like two teenagers. That was followed by more adult activities. They talked in the afterglow and then fell asleep in each other's arms. 3J wondered where he'd been all these years, and she suspected he wondered the same thing. She had a smile on her face as she drifted off to sleep and she had one when she awoke.

She shuffled to the kitchen and brewed her Earl Grey tea. It was Steele's day off from O'Brien's, so she didn't want to wake him. She got dressed, peeked in the bedroom at him, and made her way out of the condo and down to the street for the short walk north on Walnut to her law firm's offices. Steele had silenced his phone when he arrived the night before, so she knew an early morning text would not wake him. As she walked, she typed a message offering dinner that night at her favorite nearby restaurant, The Belfrey. The previous night had been perfect, she thought. Not moving slowly at all.

She entered the tower, made her way past the weekend security guard, and stepped into the elevator for the ride up twenty-seven floors. She planned to get started on the boxes an hour and a half before she expected Pascale to arrive. One of the boxes contained the debtors' historical cash flows, both personal and company, which she spread out on her desk.

At first glance, the cash flows appeared in order with nothing unusual jumping out. In the "cash in" section, she saw significant payments from tenants of various properties, including the Clarke land. In the "outflow" section, the Melanshins reported equally significant payments to cover rental-related expenses, real estate taxes, trade debt, mortgages, and considerable living expenses.

The Melanshins owned two luxury vehicles and an expensive car they'd bought for their kid. They had financed all three cars, and their monthly car payments exceeded three thousand dollars. They had done extensive repairs and improvements to their house and financed the house expenses with a home equity line of credit, HELOC. Now, besides a monthly first mortgage payment, they also had to make hefty monthly payments on the HELOC to the tune of twenty-four hundred dollars. Private college for their kid cost six thousand a month, and living expenses ran upwards of twelve thousand a month. 3J was looking at a burn rate closing in on twenty-eight thousand dollars per month, not including income taxes and payments of over eighteen thousand dollars per month to Clarke on the contract for deed. It surprised her that after taxes, the Melanshins could ever have made payments on the Clarke contract for deed.

Pascale quietly arrived at her office door and interrupted her concentration. "Morning. A penny for your thoughts?"

3J looked up, her striking hazel eyes gleaming, and smiled. "Welcome to our weekend. Thanks for doing this with me, Bill. I have a ton of information from Steinert. Let's grab the boxes, spread out on a conference room table, and try to figure this out."

They each grabbed a box, stopped by the coffee and tea station, and made their way to the small conference room they sometimes called the war room. It was their home away from home. Once there, they focused on the past five calendar years of cash flows Steinert had given them.

After forty-five minutes, Pascale broke the silence. "Looks to me like the problem isn't the cash receipts. Those seem pretty steady. Looks to me like they got overextended. They bought fancy cars, they spent a ton fixing up their house, and they have a kid in a pricey private college. They started to live large three or four years ago and have continued to do so."

3J nodded. "That's my take. They'll save some money for a while by not paying Clarke. That was a pretty significant self-inflicted wound Clarke suffered when he foolishly agreed to sell his land under an unrecorded contract for deed without advice of counsel."

"Yeah, that's wacky. Any self-respecting lawyer would have flagged the unrecorded contract as a real problem and advised against it. But I'm guessing Clarke found faulty solace in the contract's provision that he retains ownership until he receives the last payment."

"Steinert told me that the Melanshins had purchased land from other sellers under contracts for deed in the past. Sounds like performance under those other contracts went without a hitch. Clarke must have felt he was safe. Now he's run into a big hitch."

"Do you think the Melanshins knew the ins and outs of contracts for deed and then decided to take Clarke for a ride?" Pascale asked.

"It's a good question. I also wonder why the Melanshins started living large around the time they signed the Clarke contract for deed."

"Well, on their face, the financials don't seem to suggest anything out of the ordinary," Pascale replied. "People buy today and pay tomorrow, so the decision to live large isn't all that uncommon.

We'll have to keep an eye peeled for anything suggesting that something different is going on."

"Sort of the trust-for-the-moment-but-verify-in-due-course bankruptcy rule of thumb?"

"Exactly. And for the normal committee—and I'm not saying this one is going to be normal—the members would want to know that committee counsel considered and disclosed all possibilities."

"Understood."

"One other thing, 3J. I didn't see any tax returns in my box. Did you find any in yours?"

"Good catch. None. Neither Kansas state nor federal returns. I'll circle back with Steinert and see if he can email them over to us."

Promptly at 8:00 a.m., Woody Clarke arrived at Donnie and Lil Melanshin's home two blocks off Main Street in historic downtown Meadowfield. Clarke was chubby and short, not quite five foot eight. He stood on the Melanshins' wraparound front porch, ignored the sleek video doorbell, and rapped loudly on the door. Donnie opened it and looked down at Woody from the height of six foot four. Without an invitation to enter, Woody strode briskly by Donnie, past the wireless security panel, through the entryway, and into the living room with the newly renovated, large kitchen beyond.

It had been several years since Woody Clarke had been in the Melanshins' pre-Civil War home. He was dumbstruck by the lavish restoration and renovations they had performed on the main floor. He saw a marble floor entryway and highly polished wide plank wood floors. The kitchen had quartzite counters and gleaming smart appliances. There were all-new crown moulding throughout, high-end built-ins, and designer light fixtures. The furniture and electronics were clearly expensive. He was so surprised by what he saw that he said nothing for several minutes as he surveyed the interior, much as a child might gape at the spectacle of Disney World when seeing it for the first time.

Lil Melanshin said, "Brew coffee," to the coffee maker, and almost instantly, the machine began to brew a pot of drip coffee. She retrieved an antique sterling silver tray and placed an antique sterling silver urn and china coffee cups on it.

As the coffee brewed, Clarke slowly turned to the Melanshins. With a tone of disapproval that turned into a slow growl, he said, "So this is why you cain't pay me? Are you shittin' me?"

"Watch your language there, Woody. I don't want you swearing in front of Lil. It's not necessary."

"Like she ain't never heard it before? Bullshit! Ya hear me? This is all bullshit!"

Donnie didn't respond.

Clarke looked up at the much taller Melanshin and said sternly, "Donavan Melanshin, I came over here to set you straight on making payments to me you owe under the sale contract."

"I figured. And I hear you. You said that before. Here's the thing, Woody. We're stretched a little thin right now. We need to use our money to keep up payments to the banks on the house mortgage and the HELOC. We need to keep paying for our cars. We need to eat and pay the bills. And we got a kid in college. We had to pay our lawyer a big retainer. When we do all that, we don't have money left over for you right now. We just don't."

"Well, you damn well would if you didn't live so high and extravagant. A Hollywood flamboyant lifestyle right here in Meadowfield. Sheeit! You need to sharpen your pencil and find me the money. Y'hear me? You could sell this place and find some other place to live that costs a whole lot less. Then you'd have the money to pay me."

"We're not moving, Woody. We're not selling. We had our eyes on this old house for years, and now that we own it and have fixed it up to our liking, we're not going anywhere. We're not taking orders from you neither. We'll figure this out. But we're gonna do it with our lawyer in the bankruptcy cases. Not in our living room on a Saturday morning with you storming in here like you're in charge."

Woody was seething. Maintaining his cool was not one of his strong points. The lack of payments coupled with the Melanshins' unexpected lavish appointments was more than he could take, so he did what he usually did when he lost control: He bellowed. "You think your fuckin' Jew-boy lawyer is gonna get you out of paying me? Lilian Melanshin, you keep your damn coffee in your fancy urn! And you tell your coffee machine to shut the fuck off. And hear me good and clear when I say that you best both work on those eyes in the back of your heads, 'cause if you ain't paying me, then when you're walking forward, you'll need to be lookin' behind you as well."

"That a threat, Woody?" Donnie asked in a taunting tone, gazing down at Clarke and raising his eyebrows as he spoke. Clarke didn't scare Donnie. To Donnie's way of thinking, Clarke had proven himself repeatedly to be all bark.

Clarke jabbed his index finger up into the air toward Donnie. "It's a piece of real good free advice, Donnie. 'Cause if you ain't gonna pay me, your problems are just beginning. Y'hear me, goddammit?"

Woody turned, quickly made his way to the front door, and slammed the door hard behind him as he left.

Donnie looked at his wife, and the two smiled knowingly at each other as they each nodded. Lil spoke first. "Well, he ain't too happy, now is he, Donnie? Looked like he might bust a gasket there. D'ya think he's figured the plan out yet?"

"Not yet, Lil. Not just yet." Donnie smiled. "But I figure he will." Donnie looked down to the ground and said softly, as if he were still talking to Clarke, "Didn't say I wouldn't pay you back,

Woody, m'friend. Just not now, and when the time comes, just not all of it."

The couple were quiet for a moment before Donnie broke the silence. "I need to call Steinert and let him know that Woody's on the warpath."

6

Woody Clarke recalls Saturday, April 13, 2024

I LEFT THE Melanshin house as hot under my collar as I'd ever been. I remember thinking that no one screwed with me that way. Those two living the lives of luxury and paying everyone 'cept me would *not* fly.

As I drove, I had lots of thoughts swimming in my brain. I knew I needed to round up some of the boys and form my own little posse to take some steps that would set them Melanshins right. I could take care of this myself. I didn't need no lawyer.

Yep. What I needed was my own posse. Them feds passed the Posse Comitatus Act in 1878 so the military couldn't intervene when the Southern states set up Jim Crow. We still got that act on the books today, and it still lets the sheriff form a posse of citizens to suppress lawlessness in the county. Now, I wasn't no elected sheriff, but on this one, I was as close to a sheriff as one could be. And I felt in the right to form my own posse to enforce the pay-me-back-now law of the land.

I figured on starting small: a message to put a scare into them Melanshins. Donnie would know who sent the message even if he couldn't prove it. He'd then figure out a way to start up payments to me again. He'd realize I was serious, and them greenbacks would start coming my way again.

I figured on two or three of the boys to help me out. I knew I'd have to pay them something. It'd be worth it. I figured I'd start to round 'em up that night.

7

Donnie Melanshin recalls Sunday, April 14, 2024

THREE YEARS BEFORE me and Lil met with Jacob Steinert in Kansas City to talk about filing for bankruptcy protection, we wanted to get back at Woody Clarke in the worst way. We needed to get organized and come up with a plan.

The thing is, Lil is way better at organizing and figuring things out than me. My thing was buying and selling real estate in the farm belt. I was good at it. Sometimes I bought land with bank financing and sometimes I bought it over time, signing an installment payment sale contract with the landowner. I paid a fair price and I had a good reputation. I never missed a payment to a bank or landowner, at least not before Woody Clarke sold me his land. All them landowners wanted to know was that they'd get their money from me like clockwork. One of them even nicknamed me Clockwork Donnie. The name didn't stick, but I kinda liked the thought. It was good for business.

Now, Lil didn't get all too involved in the real estate business. We had kids to raise. Two back then . . . but now only one. One night we was up late talking and she tells me that an installment payment sale contract is called a different name by the Kansas courts. She tells me it's really called a "contract for deed." She asks me, "Donnie, do you know the legal effect of a contract for deed in this here state?"

I always knew Lil was as smart as any lawyer I'd ever met. She coulda gone to law school and been a great lawyer if she'd finished high school and gone to college. So I asked, "Like what legal effect?"

"Well, the contract says that the seller keeps ownership of the land until the buyer makes the last payment. But the law looks at it differently. The law in these parts says that when the buyer signs the contract, it becomes the landowner's right then. And the seller is like a bank. It has a mortgage. Now them banks, they record their mortgages so the world knows they have one, and so they can foreclose if you don't pay. The law treats the seller under the contract for deed like a bank with a mortgage. If the seller wants to protect himself, he has to record the contract like it was a mortgage."

I understood what she was saying, but I hadn't figured out the point. So I looked at Lil and raised my eyebrows for her to continue.

"So here's the thing I've figured out. If that seller don't record the contract and the buyer files bankruptcy, the seller can't record the contract at that point. The judge would treat the buyer as the owner of the land, free and clear, and would say that the seller has an unsecured claim against the buyer. No mortgage. No way to get protection. No way to get the land back from the buyer. That's it. The buyer wouldn't have to pay the seller under the contract until it did a bankruptcy plan. Even then, the buyer might get away with paying less than one hundred percent of what it owed."

I always listened real close to Lil when she was explaining things she'd figured out. On this topic, she had my complete attention. "Woody Clarke is trying to sell off significant acreage to raise cash. What if we bought acreage from him under one of these contracts for deed? He'd read over the contract and see that he'd keep ownership of his land until we made the last payment. And

I bet old Woody would sign right up. He wouldn't hire no lawyer. He hates 'em."

"If I'm understanding what you're telling me, we could screw old Woody if we filed bankruptcy later."

"Exactly what I'm saying."

But Lil had more in mind that she'd figured out, and this part involved our boy, Robert.

"Donnie, then I got to thinking. We ain't the only ones in these parts that have no use for Woody Clarke. There are others. So I got to scheming some more. Suppose we gave a quarter of the land to Robert after we signed the contract with Woody. Then we could lease the land to someone, and part of the rent could go to Robert and part to us. Then when we filed bankruptcy, we'd claim the rent for our part of the land but not the rent for Robert's part."

"How would that help us, Lil?"

"I figure we'd run out of money without all the rent in our pockets. We'd tell Woody we couldn't afford to pay him no more."

"I do believe we have the beginnings of a plan here, Lil," I said.

That Lil is amazing. She can figure stuff out. But you might ask, why would we go after Woody Clarke?

Bad things happen—sometimes unthinkably bad things. For me and Lil, that was the death of our youngest son four years before we filed bankruptcy. Lil had found Toby in his bedroom with a needle dangling from his arm next to a dark chunk of something on the night table. Stone cold dead from an overdose of what we learned was Mexican black tar heroin laced with synthetic fentanyl. Dead before he was eighteen.

We'd heard rumors that Woody Clarke's adult kid, Junior, was selling black tar heroin out of the back of his pickup truck near the regional high school. We felt certain that our kid purchased the deadly dose from the Clarke kid. And we was one hundred percent certain that Woody goddamn Clarke knew of the drug sales and looked the other way. We'd even heard that he found a way to benefit from the drug money. If that was true, we was pretty convinced Woody was in a little side business with his kid. Woody Clarke, the enabler of a goddamn drug pusher right here in rural, East-Central Kansas.

So it was pretty simple. Woody was the reason our kid was dead and Woody was gonna have to pay for that. It was time for him to go through some pain of his own. And with Woody Clarke, nothing would be more painful than getting screwed out of his land by us two Melanshins and the legal system.

So there you have it. Now, a while back, Woody started to exercise more influence on that social group of his. He came up with The Thirty-Six Thirties name. He followed other right-wing groups on the internet, some benign and some dangerous. He started to steer The Thirties toward his own views about America. Those weren't my views and I wouldn't join. Told him so right to his face. He didn't much like that, but he needed to know. And anyway, them meetings were Woody's chance to talk on and on. I didn't want to listen. Not to him. Not then and certainly not now.

Then Toby passed.

My oldest, Robert, was in a private college that cost me and Lil a pretty penny. But we was committed to getting him a top-notch education as his way out of Meadowfield if he chose that path. He certainly was getting that great education, and in the process, he questioned most of the beliefs The Thirties held. He shared his thoughts with us, especially after Toby died. Lil and me listened to him, and it got us to thinking and wondering.

Not that we was any kind of left-wing liberal types. That'd never happen. But we sure wasn't no Woody Clarke disciples neither. This was Kansas. Home of the Free-Staters. John Brown people. I didn't see no place for Woody Clarke in this state.

So I took Lil's plan and filled in some blanks. I knew my friend, Bill Pearson, was in the market to rent significant acreage to plant wheat. Pearson knew my views of Clarke and what he had done to

Toby. And Pearson had his own views of Clarke. "Bellicose, a bully, and an all-around bastard," was how Pearson described him to me. Pearson also didn't agree with all that Thirties hate.

So me and Lil, we approached Pearson with a business proposition. Sitting with us in front of our fireplace until late into the night, Pearson listened to us and readily agreed.

The proposition Lil had fine-tuned was straightforward. We'd buy four contiguous sections of land from Clarke under a contract for deed. Total of 2,560 acres. Clarke would read the contract but probably wouldn't talk to a lawyer 'cause he hated them. He'd see that under the contract, he'd retain ownership of the land. He wouldn't be smart enough to figure out what Lil had learned about how the law treats them contracts, and old Woody would sign on the bottom line.

We'd lease all that land to Pearson and then we'd deed a quarter of the land to Robert, but we wouldn't record that deed, so it wouldn't be part of the real estate records. Not yet. Now, by my calculations, the average rental rate for wheat land where Clarke's land sat was $120 an acre. Pearson would lease the land from us for $110 an acre. That was lower than the average wheat crop land rent but still within the local range. The lower price would make it worthwhile for Pearson to do the deal. Then Pearson would write two rent checks each month: one for $82.50 per acre made payable to us and another for $27.50 per acre made payable to Robert. So each month me and Lil would get $17,600 and Robert'd get $5,867. Robert would put the money in an account each month and hold those funds until we gave him further instructions. Robert's a good kid, and he and Toby had been as close as close could be. Robert hated Junior and wanted to get revenge on Woody Clarke, so he was happy to take part in Lil's plan.

The only wrinkle was that Pearson wanted the lease filed of record. He didn't trust Clarke. Wise man. Who would? Pearson wanted to make sure that no matter what Clarke might do, he'd be stuck with the terms of the lease. We were fine with that.

Pearson told us that he would go along with this scheming for three reasons. First, in the aggregate, he'd paid $110 per acre and thought that was about $10 dollars an acre per month less than the average and a lot less than some of the higher priced crop land in and around Meadowfield he thought was more comparable to the Clarke land.

Second, while we didn't share with Pearson the details of the bankruptcy part of the plan, he was pretty sure there was some unstated part of our scheme that would end up screwing Clarke. On that count, Pearson was all in.

Last, Pearson told us that he didn't see any downside. He'd pay a fair rental amount, whether he paid Lil and me all the rent or part of it. He figured he wasn't part of our plan. He was nothing more than a Midwest businessman in the farm belt growing wheat.

So I had the lease drawn up by a local attorney. It provided for the usual terms: legal description of the land, lease term, $110 per acre rent, dates and procedures for notification of lease renewal and cancellation, and a provision spelling out rights and responsibilities of each party. Then me, Lil, and Pearson signed it and recorded it. It covered everything. Well, everything except the details of Robert's share. Lil said that didn't legally need to be in the lease.

In the three plus years since signing the Pearson lease, Robert's gotten over $210,000, and I used our portion of Pearson's payments to help pay our bills, including pay to Clarke under the contract for deed. I knew Clarke was damn proud of the deal he'd struck and touted it to the other Thirties. But with Robert's private college education, the cars Lil and me drove, the car we got Robert, and the work on our house, our living expenses ballooned. I had other real estate deals, of course, and they were good for money too. Between Pearson and my other deals, we could keep going for a while. But after I paid taxes and Clarke, and after a few years of being more cash strapped than we had ever been before, we didn't have enough money to cover everything we had to cover and continue to pay Clarke.

So with less cash flow, we stopped paying Clarke, and it was time for me and Lil to drive up to Kansas City to see Jacob Steinert, a bankruptcy lawyer she found. We'd tell him a lot of stuff, but not about our plan and not about Robert's portion of the rent. That was Robert's. It wouldn't be part of the bankruptcy. To Steinert, we looked like two rural folks who lived beyond their means until it finally caught up to them.

We told Steinert about the contract for deed. He asked us if Clarke recorded the contract. We played dumb and said, "No. Is that a problem?"

"Not a problem for you folks. Big problem for this Woody Clarke fellow, I'm afraid," he replied as he wiggled his eyebrows and then smiled.

We didn't smile along with Steinert, but we sure wanted to.

Now, Lil had done some more snooping around on the internet about bankruptcy before we went up to see Steinert. "Always a good idea to learn a little something about what you're about to get into," she said to me.

Absolutely correct, as she always is. We wanted to use bankruptcy to pay less—much less—to Woody than we owed him. But we also had other creditors who had been good to us over the years, and we had no reason to screw them.

Lil figured it out. She's a bloodhound on the internet. She spent I don't know how many sleepless nights for weeks educating herself on payment plans in bankruptcy, and she learned that under a bankruptcy plan, we'd have to group creditors together in what the Bankruptcy Code called "classes." Creditors in each class got paid the same. We'd pay the creditors in each class over time. She figured out that usually, debtors had to group all unsecured creditors together in a single class. And if we wanted to have two classes of unsecured creditors and treat the classes differently, we'd have to convince the judge that we weren't unfairly discriminating against the class that'd receive less money. Unfair discrimination.

Fancy words. She thought that meant we could treat Clarke differently and pay him less if we came up with a good reason to do so.

"Y'mean like because he killed Toby?" I asked.

"That would be a real good reason, Donnie," she said. "The best. But we'll need more of a business reason. More like a good business story."

We both figured that we and this fella Steinert would have to put our heads together and come up with something that would fly.

I thought the whole thing was more than a little ironic. No unfair discrimination against a Thirties discriminator like Clarke. Just a healthy dose of business and the Bankruptcy Code.

8

Monday, April 15 through Wednesday, April 17, 2024

"HOW DID THE call with that Steinert fella go, Donnie?" Lil asked as Donnie came down from the upstairs bedroom he used as his office.

"Just fine. He knows what we want him to know. He's on alert about Woody and said he'd call the committee's lawyer to ask her to try and rein him in."

"Rein him in? Ha. Nobody's ever reined in Mr. Woody Clarke. At least not yet."

Donnie said nothing for a moment and then smiled. "Oh, old Woody's gonna find out what it's like to have a horse's bit in his mouth when the rider pulls up hard on the reins. Ain't too pleasant, I'd imagine."

"I do love you, dear," she said softly.

"As I do you."

Jacob Steinert answered his phone on the third ring.

"Jacob, 3J here. Thanks for the boxes of financial goodies. Pascale and I looked over the information on Saturday. It was a good start for us, but we didn't find any tax returns. Could you please send copies of the returns over as well?"

"3J, that's the thing. I don't have the Melanshins' returns," Steinert explained.

"Oh? I see. Did they file any in the recent past?"

"They say they did, but despite prodding, I have nothing."

"I'm sure I can get permission from Judge Robertson to subpoena them from your clients. Do you think a court order will help?"

"On this one, I don't know what will work. They readily filed the bankruptcy cases to get some protection, and yet when I talk with them, they're pretty cautious. They choose their words carefully."

He paused for a moment and then added, "Let's do this, 3J. I'll email them when we finish this call. I'll let them know I talked with you, and if they want the Bankruptcy Code's protections, they'll have to send over the returns pronto. In the absence of that, I'll let them know you'll get a court order and that if you have to do that, Judge Robertson won't be happy. They won't want to piss off the one person whose help and protection they'll need to get through their cases and reorganize."

"Works for me. Let's hope they see the light. If we're going to have these kinds of problems on the easy stuff like tax returns, Lord knows what'll happen when we get to the hard stuff. In the meantime, I'll try to suppress my own suspicious nature that they're trying to hide something they don't want me—and you—to see."

"One other thing, 3J. I heard from Donnie Melanshin over the weekend. He got a visit from one of your committee members, Woody Clarke. According to Donnie, Woody threatened him and his wife."

"What kind of threat?"

"Apparently, Woody told them that if he didn't start getting his payments, they'd need eyes in the back of their heads to protect themselves."

"So it's going to be one of those kinds of cases, eh?"

"I sure hope not. What's Clarke like?"

"I can see him as the threatening kind for sure," 3J admitted. "A little light on social skills. More than a little rough around the edges. But he tells you what's on his mind, and I imagine that's what he told the Melanshins. When he hired me, he let me know he didn't trust the system, didn't trust lawyers, and didn't trust me. Quite the vote of confidence. I can certainly see him as a guy who would take matters into his own hands. Luckily, he's not my client. But unluckily, he says he's my main committee contact. Let me try to talk to him and see if I can calm him down."

When 3J hung up, she emailed Woody Clarke and asked if there was a convenient time they could talk, saying she'd begun to review the financial information and wanted to report what she'd found thus far.

Minutes later, Clarke wrote that he could talk right then, and 3J called him.

"So far, I don't see anything out of the ordinary in the financial information. They bring money in and they spend it. They seem to have nothing left over to pay on the contract for deed."

"I've seen their house. And their cars. I've watched them conduct their affairs. They have a cable television rich-and-famous lifestyle," Clarke said emphatically. "That's where the money's going."

"Agreed. But it's not necessarily out of line in a bankruptcy case to maintain a lavish lifestyle. In bankruptcy, they're allowed to maintain the standard of living to which they've become accustomed. Look, I'm not done reviewing records, and there may be more to the story than simply an excessive lifestyle. I don't have tax returns, and I've asked for them. If I don't get them, I'll subpoena them."

"Don't wait too damn long on Donnie and Lil. A subpoena would be real good. It'll show them we mean business," Clarke replied.

"Mr. Clarke, debtors' counsel says that you may have threatened the Melanshins when you visited their house earlier."

Clarke chuckled. "Not me. Me and Donnie, we had us a chat in their kitchen. Friendly like. A heart-to-heart you might say. I told Donnie I wanted my money, and I do."

"Mr. Clarke, please know that you can't demand payments from Donnie and you can't threaten the debtors, directly or indirectly. If you do, you'll quickly get in trouble with Judge Robertson. That's not a place you or anyone else wants to be."

Clarke was silent for a long moment before replying. "I ain't scared of no Kansas City federal judge. And I've got matters under control. Don't need your help or advice on this issue. Didn't ask for it neither."

"Well, you *should* be worried about a federal judge's reaction to your conduct. I'm not giving you legal advice, but you really should hire a lawyer and get some advice about your personal situation."

Clarke said nothing, but 3J could hear him breathing heavily into the phone. Then Clarke asked brusquely, "Committee counsel, anything else you got for me as committee rep?"

"Nothing else."

"Good enough." Clarke hung up with a click and without a good-bye.

It was clear to 3J that Clarke had threatened Donnie, and whatever he had next in mind was coming, and coming quickly.

She switched gears and listened to the voice mail that had come in while she was on the phone with Clarke.

"3J? Steinert here. Talked with Melanshin. Won't bore you with the details, but he says he's emailing tax returns to me in the morning. As soon as I have them, I'll forward them to you. Call if you have questions."

3J was glad she wouldn't have to go to court to get the returns. Her goal was to try to identify discrepancies between the financial information she had and the information in the returns. As she reflected on next steps, she realized she likely was going to need help.

She wondered if Moses Aaronson and his investigative team could supply assistance. When she last engaged Aaronson, she learned he had extensive training in financial sleuthing and forensic accounting. She also figured Aaronson's team could get her some much needed background information about The Thirties, Clarke, and the Melanshins. She needed hard data, not rumor, conjecture, and innuendo.

3J decided to talk with Pascale about the idea of reaching out to Aaronson and to bring Pascale up to speed, but while she intended to sit down in his office for that conversation, once just inside his doorway, she stopped. Further entry into the room would be challenging. Pascale was in the midst of a months-long preretirement project to organize his office and sort his papers into three groups: What he needed to return to the firm, what he would keep and eventually move to his house, and what he should discard. 3J looked around in disbelief, observing even more papers and piles than she had become accustomed to seeing on his desk and furniture. It was as if the closer he got to retirement, the more mess there was, if that was even possible. She whistled and shook her head. "My Lord, Bill."

Pascale grinned. "Storm before the calm, 3J. Nothing to be alarmed about. It's all under control."

3J raised one eyebrow in response and then explained the tax return issue and the need to have someone with a finance background take a look at the Melanshin records. She reminded Pascale that Aaronson had that skill set and explained her conclusion that background checks were in order, at least at some level.

"He and his team did good work for us on the last go-round," Pascale said. "I think it's a good idea to reach out to Aaronson on both fronts. He can look over the info we have and see if anything jumps out. Maybe his crack techie, Rome, can simultaneously gather some information for us. What kind of information would you be interested in seeing?"

"Honestly, I would give Rome lots of room to wander around the internet and see what she can find. I could use a primer on right-wingers, their beliefs, their organizations. Some history and background for us. And anything specific she can find on The Thirties, Clarke, and the Melanshins."

★ ★ ★

The next morning, 3J and Pascale called Moses Aaronson. They had last engaged the New York City investigator on the Chapter 11 cases of six Kansas City jazz clubs owned by Kansas City music icons, Bey and Adam Rapinoe. Aaronson and his team were able to generate sufficient information to stop a disinformation campaign against the clubs and save them from an untimely demise. It was the first time 3J and Pascale had used Aaronson and his operatives, which he called the Moses Team. The speed and accuracy of the Moses Team's work and the skills of his tech wizard in London, nicknamed Rome, had duly impressed the lawyers.

"We have a new bankruptcy matter," 3J said as they got down to business. "I seem to recall you mentioned that you have a background in forensics accounting."

"That I do. In many of my engagements, I have had to shed light on the darkness where certain people attempt to tuck away their money for a rainy day. I find it all fascinating: the money, the people, the trail, the quest for financial truth. What do we have here?"

3J smiled. She had formed the opinion that Aaronson was quite a character but very good at what he did. He was a private eye's private eye who didn't like the label "investigator"—a throwback and old school in many ways. She had never met him and knew nothing of what he looked like. All she knew was that he sounded refined and educated with a distinct New York accent, much the way Michael Douglas sounded when interviewed.

"We represent an official committee of unsecured creditors. The bankruptcy arm of the Justice Department appoints the committee members to protect the interests of unsecured creditors. The debtors are Donald and Lillian Melanshin and their company, Melanshin Farms LLC. They live in rural Kansas, in Meadowfield, a farm community on the Kansas eastern border. They're more land barons and traders than folks who actually work the land. When they filed, the Melanshins owned a large tract of land totalling over twenty-five hundred acres, which they bought from one Woody Clarke. The Melanshins lease it to a tenant who grows wheat on the land. It's big business here in the breadbasket of the heartland."

"Fascinating," Aaronson replied. "I have worked on a number of agricultural cases in my career. And what is it that causes you to reach out to me?"

"We're looking into the Melanshins' finances. Standard stuff at the beginning of a Chapter 11. We have lots of financial statements, cash flows, income statements, and the like. Should have their tax returns by the morning. They owe significant money to this Clarke fellow. He sold the Melanshins the acreage under a contract for deed. Are you familiar with such a contract?"

Moses was not, so 3J explained how it worked and how the law deemed the Melanshins the owners of the land. "The thing is this. The Melanshins were able to pay Clarke for a number of years, but in the last year, they couldn't continue making regular payments, and then they stopped paying altogether. You'll see that their standard of living is eye-popping, especially for rural Kansas. But that still doesn't explain why they have no money to pay when they once did. We're looking for a deep dive to see if you can locate and explain any discrepancies. Might be nothing there, but better to know for sure."

"I understand. I am between matters, so I can begin as soon as you transmit the papers to me."

"Super. One other thing. Clarke belongs to a local right-wing group called The Thirty-Six Thirties. The group appears to be like other right-wing groups one hears about in the Heartland from time to time. Sometimes these groups are bad actors. Occasionally, they're violent. The group, and Clarke in particular, seem to harbor some anti-government beliefs. Some members, maybe many, are haters. We can get you the names of the group members we know of, and we're hoping Rome and you can dig up some things and help develop a profile for us. The devil is in the details, as they say."

"Haters, eh? I see. Certainly, we can help on this second part as well. This part should prove to be educational and potentially sobering, given the divided times in which we all continue to live."

"Great. Anything to add, Pascale?"

Pascale shook his head no.

"We'll send you a package and await your updates. Thank you, Moses."

Moses emailed his colleague Belita Davies—code name Rome—in London and explained the new engagement. He asked to speak with her the next day.

The next morning, Moses assigned Rome the task of developing a portfolio of background information on The Thirties, Clarke, and the Melanshins. After the call, Moses put on his cardigan sweater and his favorite navy blue beret and put the harness on Emily, his white, silky-furred rat terrier mix dog. The two went downstairs to the streets near the Flatiron Building in Manhattan and made their way south on Fifth Avenue to Madison Square Park for their early spring morning walk. Moses liked to go to the park to sort out a new assignment and come up with a strategy for the case.

It was Stop 'N' Swap day in the park. Locals dropped off possessions they no longer needed while others perused the boxes of goods in hopes of finding something they could use. The north end of the park was bustling, so Moses made his way to a bench far from the droppers and shoppers area to sit and think. Emily was happy to lie on the sun-warmed pavement at Moses' feet and snooze. Some of the park regulars knew Moses and Emily and waved to him on their way south to Union Square and Washington Park in Greenwich Village.

Before leaving for the park, Moses had taken a quick look at the financials and tax returns. He saw that a significant portion of the cash the Melanshins received over the last several years was from the lease of the land Clarke sold to them. Moses made some mental calculations and determined that at 110 dollars per acre, they should be showing rental receipts of about 23,460 dollars per month. But while the Melanshin income statement accrued income in that amount each month, the tax returns told a different story.

On Line 3 of their Schedule E, Supplemental Income and Loss form, the Melanshins reported that they actually received only 17,600 dollars per month, not over twenty-three thousand. Moses couldn't determine if they underreported receiving almost six thousand dollars a month or if the tenant underpaid. Either way, it was a discrepancy between the cash receipts in the tax returns and the income accrued in the income statements of over seventy thousand dollars annually and over two hundred thousand dollars in the last three-plus years. A significant amount.

If the Melanshins received two hundred thousand dollars less than the tenants owed them, that alone could explain a sudden inability to make payments to Clarke, Moses thought. But he wondered why they received less? He needed more information from 3J.

9

Thursday, April 18 through Saturday, April 20, 2024

THURSDAY EVENING, WOODY Clarke awaited the arrival of two handpicked helpers to carry out his Donnie Melanshin project. Promptly at 8:00 p.m., the two knocked on Clarke's front door. They entered, and Clarke explained the situation. He peppered his discussion with comments about how Donnie Melanshin was anti-Thirties, had used bankruptcy to get out of legitimate debts, was running up big bills, and was paying everyone except him. He told them that Donnie Melanshin and his wife needed to be taught a lesson.

The blond-haired one nodded. "What do you have in mind, Woody?"

"I figure a brick or two through the front picture window on his house. On the brick you can write, 'Pay up or pay the price,' and that'll get his attention for sure."

"What day and time do you have in mind, Woody?" the dark brown-haired one asked.

"Tomorrow around midnight. Will that be a problem?"

"Nah. That works," the first said as the second nodded.

They shook hands and the pair departed.

Clarke felt good about his plan. The bricks should shake up

the Melanshins, and the boys would damage their beloved home. He knew in his gut that they were using the home renovations to avoid paying him back.

He thought to himself that nothing could go wrong.

Friday morning, Moses got a call from Rome.

"I've been looking into The Thirty-Six Thirties group, but I realized I needed to step back and start with a broader view of the whole White Nationalists Movement in your country—if you can call groups like that a movement. They're simultaneously fascinating and horrifying, I must admit. But it's mostly horrifying and instantly repulsive."

"What have you learned?"

"These groups believe that they must reverse what they see as the loss of a White majority. The want to return America to a pre-Civil Rights Act era. That is pre-1964 in your country. They hate Blacks. They hate all other people of color. They hate Jews and argue that Jews are behind the plot to replace a White majority with a majority of people of color. And of course, they want to limit government and eliminate social welfare programs. Many advocate violence to further their ends. They seem to use the internet these days to organize. And they get many of their ideas from podcasts and fringe media that spew this stuff out 24/7."

Rome paused and then asked, "Have you heard of *Cablegram*, Moses?"

"I suspect you are not referring to the old-school way of transmitting messages across wired lines."

"I am not. I'm referring to a freeware app for instant messaging, video calls, channels, and encrypted chatting. It had over five hundred million active users as of a few years ago. It is dubbed a White supremacist safe haven by the Anti-Defamation League. It is also used to distribute child porn. Three Slavic cousins—supposed champions of unmoderated tools—founded it."

"And this is how groups like The Thirty-Six Thirties communicate?"

"Sometimes. The Thirties seem to be observers of the *Cablegram* goings on. Maybe they get their inspiration from *Cablegram* posts. Maybe the posts are their insight into the latest in the White Supremacist playbooks."

"Hmm. So they are using *Cablegram* to learn the latest?"

"Quite possibly. I will know more as I dive in. My guess is that they learn and then meet and talk about what they have read on *Cablegram*. They feed off each other's hate. I can reach that conclusion because they seem to post on Twitter and Instagram, so I have some electronic bread crumbs I have been able to follow so far."

"What else have you learned, Rome?"

"They seem to interact with similarly situated groups throughout Kansas and Missouri."

"How are you able to deduce that?"

"The other groups are more active on *Cablegram* and report discussions they have had with aligned organizations. The other groups mention The Thirties by name in their vitriol."

"Hmm. Very interesting."

"Yes. I would have guessed these groups would make efforts to avoid sharing beliefs so openly. But they have podcasts, and they are happy to share their views. They appear to be on government watch lists and are on the radar of the Anti-Defamation League and the Southern Poverty Law Center. I expected to report to you that they were hiding in plain sight, but they are not *hiding* at all. They seem to be surprisingly comfortable *appearing* in plain sight for all to see. Perhaps that is the point. They want others to feel threatened by them."

"Indeed. Rome, what have you been able to find out about Woody Clarke?"

"He is an interesting one. He attended the University of Missouri, but he dropped out, so he never got a degree. He fancies himself the founder of The Thirty-Six Thirties. Of all things, he's a descendent of one William Clarke Quantrill."

"I am not familiar with Mr. Quantrill."

"Mr. Quantrill was an infamous pro-Confederate guerrilla war leader during the American Civil War. Before the war, he was a schoolteacher and then a farmer. Around the time of the Civil War, he turned to a life of crime, stealing horses and slaves in Missouri and reselling them.

"The years before the Civil War saw the territory of Kansas mired in a violent struggle over whether it would be a slave state or a free state. Pundits named it Bloody Kansas at the time. The issue was supposed to be decided by a popular vote, but violent disputes over who could vote marred all election attempts. The Union admitted the eastern part of the territory as a free state only after the southern states seceded as the Civil War broke out.

"When the war broke out, Quantrill led a group of bandits nicknamed Quantrill's Raiders. The raiders included Frank James, brother of Jesse James. They liked to call themselves 'Terrors of the Border.' They roamed the Missouri and Kansas countryside near the border dividing the states with a goal to apprehend escaped slaves. Some think Quantrill's Raiders had taken up the Confederate states' cause in the war. But history has shown that they were not principled heroic warriors in the least. They were just a band of criminals plundering for profit and revenge. Pirates of the Midwest if you will."

Moses listened quietly as Rome continued to talk about Clarke's ancestor.

"Quantrill famously raided Lawrence, Kansas, a noted anti-slavery stronghold. He and his group massacred hundreds and destroyed hundreds of businesses and homes. He also raided Baxter Springs, not far from Meadowfield, where he attacked a Union post and killed over a hundred of the Union soldiers manning the post, mostly African Americans.

"Quantrill lived a life of infamy. Union soldiers finally killed him in an ambush of the raiders in 1865, one month after General Lee surrendered, ending the Civil War."

"Fascinating," Moses finally said. "Am I to assume that Mr. Woody Clarke is proud of this heritage?"

"Quite so. Posts about Clarke tout the lineage, and the source seems to be Clarke's on-the-record interviews during which he proudly recalls the days when Quantrill's Raiders terrorized Black Kansans along the border."

"Do we think that Clarke has the same tendencies as Mr. Quantrill?"

"You mean, is he violent and will he kill?"

"Correct."

"I would put answers to those questions squarely in the 'unclear' column for the moment. A search of police records in Kansas and Missouri shows run-ins with the authorities. One such run-in was at a White Nationalist protest of some sort in Columbia, Missouri, while Clarke was a college student there. The authorities arrested him, and while information is a bit sketchy, it does not appear Clarke attended the protest for a research project, nor did he land in jail for peacefully protesting."

"Ah. I see. And what have you learned about Donnie and Lillian Melanshin?"

"Not much on Lillian. Seems to be a housewife. Donnie Melanshin is mostly in the real estate business. He seems to have decided not to be a card-carrying member of The Thirties. His disdain for Clarke heightened when Clarke started to assert his influence on The Thirties. That was also about the time his son Toby died, based on a death record I found. The coroner listed the cause of death as 'drug overdose.'"

"Death of a son by drug overdose. That sounds tragic."

"Yes. The local county paper reported that Lillian Melanshin discovered her son in his bedroom, dead from an injection overdose. While there is no reporting I could find about what drug caused the overdose, that rural part of Kansas has been suffering through a black tar heroin epidemic for several years now. It is an inexpensive high, prone to fentanyl lacing, and it is the cause of many overdose deaths of youths in that region. Pushing the heroin also appears to be quite a lucrative business."

"I see. Is there any connection between any of the relevant hate groups and heroin?"

"Indeed. I found one surprising connection. Local authorities have arrested one Wallace Clarke several times for allegedly distributing black tar heroin. His nickname appears to be Junior. The prosecutor dropped the charges each time without explanation, so there are no convictions I could find. I did find some chatter, however, that the local prosecutor is a Thirties sympathizer."

"I take it that Wallace Clarke is Woody Clarke's offspring."

"Correct. A bad apple, it would appear. Records show that Woody Clarke's wife divorced him some years ago, left Meadowfield, and left Clarke to raise Junior by himself."

"Perhaps Junior is a bad apple that was spawned from a rotting apple tree."

"Indeed. So far, that is what I have found. How would you like me to proceed, Moses?"

"There are a couple of avenues to pursue, my dear Rome. First, see if there are any connections between Wallace Clarke, Jr. and Toby Melanshin. Second, I have reviewed the financial information provided by Ms. Jones. The Melanshins lease land they acquired from Mr. Clarke to a crop growing tenant. The financials suggest that they should receive significantly more lease income than they seem to. I want to know why that is. Perhaps a search of local records to locate the lease and identify the tenant?"

"I can do both, Moses. I will report back."

"I know you can and will, Rome. Thank you as always for your able assistance."

Moses then called 3J to report what he and Rome had discovered.

"This is turning out to be more sinister than I expected," 3J said. "We have the possibility that Woody Clarke's kid had something to do with the death of the Melanshins' kid. Then we have Donnie Melanshin declining to join The Thirties. And then the Melanshins purchased a significant tract of land from Clarke under a contract for deed that Clarke didn't realize could be the vehicle for him to get screwed in bankruptcy court. Way too many coincidences for my taste. And my mentor taught me that I shouldn't believe in coincidences, Moses. They're nothing more than connections and facts waiting to be revealed."

"Exactly, Ms. Jones. Connections and facts lurking in the darkness, awaiting the light to shine on them."

"What else have you discovered, Moses?"

"On the financial front, I have identified a significant discrepancy between the amount of money the Melanshins should receive each month and the amount they report receiving. On this point, I have more investigation to conduct. But I am wondering if you could gather information from Mr. Steinert on the lease."

"What types of information are you hoping to review?"

"The lease itself would be quite helpful. Rome is looking for it online, but if you can find a copy of it, that would be a great help. Information about the tenant could also be enlightening."

"Okay. Got it. Let me see what I can do."

Friday evening, the blond-haired one and the dark-haired one parked on the unlit street around the corner from the Melanshin residence in a gray, late model pickup truck. They carried two bricks, both with the inscription "Pay up or pay the price" written in indelible ink. They each wore a black balaclava pulled over their face to mask any identifying features.

At exactly midnight, they left the vehicle, made their way around the block, and walked halfway across the Melanshin front lawn. In one swift motion, each tossed a brick into and through the front picture window. A house alarm immediately blared and a dog began to bark. The two sprinted away, jumped into the pickup truck, and sped away.

As part of their home renovation, the Melanshins had installed a security system, including a front porch camera. The camera recorded the vandalism in real time, but the balaclavas masked the identities of the trespassers. The local sheriff's deputy met Donnie Melanshin at his front door at 12:30 a.m.

Donnie reported the incident, shared the camera video, and answered questions about who might have tossed the bricks into the house. Lil joined Donnie, and they were adamant that Woody Clarke or his crew had tossed the bricks, based on the inscription. The deputy sheriff looked at the damage, read the inscription, and confiscated the bricks as evidence.

"Well, folks, you owe lots of people lots of money," the deputy said. "Could be any one of them. Could be a local kid pranking you. Could be someone Donnie did business with in the past. And yes, it could be Woody. I'll find Clarke tomorrow and have a chat with him, but without something more than the bricks, all I'm seeing here is an insurance claim. I'll keep you apprised."

When the deputy left in his cruiser, Lil said to Donnie, "Local kid my ass. This is Woody Clarke all the way. What are we gonna do now?"

"We can replace the window, Lil. I say that we stay the course in bankruptcy and continue to hit him where it hurts: his wallet. He's all bark and no bite, and this window stunt ain't even much of a bite. I'll let Steinert know."

10

3J WAS AT her desk early Monday morning catching up on paperwork and trying to get ahead of the inevitable weekly tidal wave that accompanied the practice of law when Jacob Steinert called.

"The Melanshins took two bricks through their picture window a little after midnight on Saturday morning," he reported.

"Jesus."

"Exactly. Each brick had the same inscription: Pay up or pay the price."

"Bloody hell." She paused and then added, "Well, that has to be Clarke, don't you think?"

"He's certainly the leading candidate in my mind. But the local authorities threw out several other possibilities."

"Like what other possibilities?"

"Other angry creditors, business adversaries, and teenage pranksters. Although from the Melanshins' report, it sounded like pranksters was the cops' leading theory."

"That's ridiculous. They'd have to ignore the messages on the bricks to think it was kids."

"Agreed, 3J. But there's no hard evidence, and the Melanshins certainly owe lots of money to lots of folks."

3J silently contemplated the unlikelihood that anyone other than Woody Clarke was behind the vandalism.

"Oh, and the Melanshins' security camera caught the culprits on tape," Steinert added. "But it was dark, and they appear to have been wearing face coverings. So the camera captured no identifying details that were of any use."

"Any police cam footage?" 3J asked.

"It's Meadowfield, 3J. I'm not sure they even have police cams set up around town."

"What comes next then?"

"I've thought about this a bit, and I'd like to conduct an examination of Woody Clarke."

"As you know, he's not my client. The committee is. So fine by me."

"Good. None of my business, but I get the sense that it's likely he isn't going to acknowledge the difference between your representation of the committee and a personal lawyer representing him."

"Maybe not, but that would only be because he's not listening. I've certainly made the distinction clear. He gets it, albeit sometimes selectively."

"I'll get an order from Judge Robertson to permit the examination, and we'll see what comes of it."

"Okay. Good luck."

The call ended and 3J went to see if Pascale had arrived. Once again, he was sitting on his floor, sifting through papers. "How goes the battle, Bill?"

"Look at me. Sitting here on the floor in my suit sorting through papers. I'm disrupting my award-winning organization protocols that took me decades to perfect."

3J smiled. She wasn't sure she would call his method of saving documents "organization protocols." It was more like Pascale's legendary organized chaos document retention system. Either way, she didn't envy Pascale's need to go through everything.

"Geez, 3J. I'd like to set this aside for a while and get back to more of the law practice."

3J smiled. Years of mess had finally caught up to Pascale.

"I'd like to think that when I have a problem, I start at the beginning and work my way through it," he added. "The linear approach. But I feel like I'm caught in the middle, and I'm trying to dig my way out in multiple directions at the same time. Honestly, 3J, this sucks. I need a break."

"Then my arrival at your office is timely. We've got quite a situation brewing in the Melanshin cases."

3J explained her call with Moses, the information his team had discovered, and the possible connection between the Clarke family and the death of the Melanshins' son. She also told Pascale about the vandalism and Moses' preliminary review of the financials.

"Wow," Pascale exclaimed. "Lots to unpack. What a mess."

"Indeed. Here's what I'm thinking. Steinert will get an order from Robertson permitting him to examine Clarke under oath. At that exam, we should come ready to examine Clarke as well."

"That'll be potentially explosive, don't you think? I mean, you know Clarke will say his own lawyer has turned against him."

"I'm not sure I care what he thinks at this point. We're representing the committee, which has a fiduciary duty to all unsecured creditors. If Clarke is impeding the debtors' ability to stabilize and restructure, then it's my job to get to the bottom of the problem and if need be, report him to the court and to the trustee's office. And then have him removed from the committee."

"I hear you," Pascale said slowly with a raised eyebrow.

"We'll also need to get an order from Robertson to examine Donnie Melanshin under oath to get to the bottom of why the debtors have insufficient cash flow. I haven't talked to Steinert about that part yet."

"Well, Clarke will like that part of the plan for sure," Pascale said, nodding from his seat on the office floor.

"Interested in dividing and conquering?" 3J asked.

"If that gets me a respite from what I'm doing right now, absolutely."

"All right. Who do you want, Clarke or Melanshin?"

"I'll take Melanshin, given the choice."

"Okay then. We have our plan."

Judge Daniel Robertson pored over bankruptcy pleadings with his back to his office window, which overlooked the Missouri River from six stories up. Parties seeking or opposing relief. The life of a bankruptcy judge. It was Wednesday, the midweek day he usually set aside to try to reduce the pile that had collected on his desk.

Some might find it tedious and repetitive, but the judge enjoyed that he was there to provide answers to questions raised by the parties. While a far cry from his day-to-day life for years as a practicing bankruptcy attorney, he cherished his time on the bench and tried never to forget how lucky he was that the circuit court selected him to sit as a bankruptcy judge.

In his pile were requests in the Melanshin bankruptcy cases for permission to examine Woody Clarke and Donnie Melanshin, filed by Jacob Steinert and Josephina Jillian Jones. Something about the name of one of the proposed witnesses gnawed at him, although he couldn't put a finger on what it was.

He rose from his desk and headed down the hallway for the short walk to the small, no-window office of his law clerk, Jennifer Cuello. Jennifer had joined the judge the year before, and she jumped right into the fire when she discovered the anonymous campaign to put the Rapinoes' jazz clubs out of business. It was her discovery that ultimately led to the creditor's demise, with the help of an intense investigation by the Greene Madison legal team.

The judge found her hunched over her desk squinting with a look of concentration on her face as she read a printout of a case she had found on Westlaw in a research project the judge had assigned to her. The judge smiled and softly cleared his throat. Cuello looked up, smiled back at the judge, and said, "Uh, oh. Sorry. I hope you weren't standing there very long, Judge."

"Not at all. Good to see that you're so into whatever case you've turned up. Do you have a second to break from Westlaw and talk?"

"Of course. In your office?"

"Here will do just fine. My phone won't ring in your office," the judge said, smiling as he took his place in the spartan, padded wooden chair that faced Cuello's desk.

"Okay. What's up?" Jennifer asked.

"I'm reviewing pleadings and proposed orders today and came upon two in new Chapter 11 cases filed by Jacob Steinert, debtors' counsel. Josephina Jones and William Pascale are the creditors committee counsel in the case. Each side wants to examine the other's principal. So no real issue there. Pretty standard. But the name of one of the principals is vaguely familiar to me, and for the life of me, I can't place why. So could you do some Westlaw and Lexis-Nexis snooping around for the name Woody Clarke? He's from Meadowfield, Kansas."

"For certain, Judge. No other search parameters?"

"I'm afraid not. Not at the moment. Maybe something else will come to me on the drive home tonight. If so, I'll text you. I know this is different from your usual assignment because I'm asking you to research a person, not a matter of law. It's a pretty broad request, but see what you can find."

"Will do, Judge."

The judge headed back to his office. When he left, Jennifer wondered what she would learn from online Clarke searches. She knew the judge put great trust in her research skills, but this search would be different from her usual assignment. She wasn't looking

for a case that would answer a legal question. Rather, she was looking for information about a person. She was going to have to come
up with a strategy for a private eye, nonlegal search.

Rome decided to use a specialized online search engine called
CheckIt that she had helped develop five years ago. CheckIt aggre-
gated public records. With a name search, the engine searched
billions of records to develop a person's background, history, life,
and associates. In addition, Rome would need to search police
records. For that, she turned to an app called *SearchMine* that
maintained an extensive database of police reports and records.
Rome had developed her own search bot to assist in these kinds of
background check projects. She input the data Moses had given
her, set her search bot loose, stretched, and decided to go downstairs for a walk.

Rome was a London, England, native who had come to the
United States and Bryn Mawr College for her education and graduated with a degree in anthropology. Even though Bryn Mawr offered
no computer science classes at the time, with her exceptional technology skills, she returned to London hoping she could somehow
forge a career using her technological and investigatory skills. By
happenstance, she met Moses after she graduated, and he offered
her the chance to be his tech colleague. They had worked together
for almost seven years, and she relished the work he involved her
in. All were fascinating projects and all needed her skills

She lived in a tiny flat near London's Chelsea Farmer's Market,
but she didn't measure her universe by the size of her flat. Her
mansion was in cyberspace. She was a resident of the infinite size
of her digital world.

When she worked on a project, she spent long hours hunched
over her laptop at her small kitchen table or sitting cross-legged on
her bed. She wasn't a social creature by nature. Her need for human

connection was satisfied by her time on the internet helping Moses "shine light on the darkness," as he liked to say.

Stretching and walking were critical in reviving her, but she had learned that twenty minutes was all she could survive away from her computer. So she limited the duration of her walks to just enough time to get to the Chelsea Market and grab a cup of Ethiopian coffee brewed from beans roasted in a copper pan over an open flame before her eyes. The smell alone seemed to revive her.

After a caffeine break at the market, she returned to her flat and settled in for a long day of research to develop the requested backgrounds on what she hoped would be a stimulating engagement.

Against his better judgment, Donnie Melanshin took the call, even though the caller ID on his mobile phone showed it was Woody Clarke. He exhaled audibly as he asked in an exasperated tone, "Whatdaya want, Woody?"

"Damn shame about the bricks and your front window, Donnie. Damn shame," Clarke said. Then he added in a sarcastic tone, "Whoever would do such a thing, eh?"

"Is that why you called? To offer your condolences for the window?"

"Just being neighborly, Donnie. That's what us folks do for each other in Meadowfield, right? What's with the attitude?"

"I want to let you know, Woody, that when this call is over, I'm blocking your number on my phone and on Lil's."

Woody began to say something in response, but Donnie cut him off before he could get anything out. "And this call is now over." He terminated the call feeling a bit pleased with himself about the click Woody had to have heard on the other end, even though he also knew that Woody had gone from paper tiger to tiger with at least a few teeth with the brick-through-the-window incident.

After the abbreviated call with Donnie Melanshin, Woody Clarke concluded that the bricks through the Melanshin picture window were not enough. Donnie Melanshin was digging in. Clarke decided he needed to up the ante, and he still needed to know if the Melanshins had planned to screw him. He would have to figure a way to find out.

11

Friday, April 26, 2024

J ENNIFER HAD BEEN unsuccessful in her efforts to gather information about Woody Clarke. She found little of use in the Lexis-Nexis and Westlaw databases. There were many online background search sites, mostly fee-based, and some were less reputable and reliable than others. But she had no subscription to any of the search sites and didn't know the reputable services from the rest, so other than noting their existence, she had done nothing to access their databases. She was also concerned that searching a name that was as potentially common as Woody Clarke would yield too much information to sort through.

She sat at her desk staring at her computer screen, a distinct frown on her face, hoping that some new research tool or a new strategy would suddenly make itself apparent. She had found nothing about Clarke, and frustration was setting in. She thought she would need something akin to divine research intervention.

At that moment, Judge Robertson appeared at her office door with a huge ear to ear grin on his face. She looked up as a smile replaced her frown, and he said to her enthusiastically, "I remembered!"

She raised her eyebrows in anticipation but said nothing, silently inviting him to elaborate.

"I remembered. I took the dog out for a long walk along Ward Parkway when I got home last night. As I got to the Meyer Fountain Circle, I was trying to let my mind run free and focus on the dog and the walk. A Jackson County sheriff's car sped by with its siren blaring. I looked up, and I thought, *Sheriff!* That made me think of law enforcement, and that led me to think of the federal marshals. And then it came to me."

By now, Judge Robertson had taken a seat in the chair opposite Jennifer as she listened, still unsure where the story was heading.

"Judge, are you saying that Woody Clarke was a law enforcement officer?"

He smiled even more broadly, crossed his legs, and chuckled as he replied, "Nope. Far from it. Somehow, my cluttered brain played word association on the dog walk. Jackson County Sheriff led to U.S. Marshal, and that led me to remember a bizarre courtroom incident I observed some years ago in bankruptcy court."

Jennifer was still confused and furrowed her brow as she tried to follow the story.

"Before they built this building, I was over at the old courthouse in the post office building on Grand appearing for a bank in a newly filed Chapter 11 farm bankruptcy case. The debtor was a guy named Fred McKinley. Fred owned a farm west of Warrensburg, Missouri. A big farm. He filed the bankruptcy case pro se. No lawyer. Huge mistake, but he did it anyway. Filled out the papers as best he could in longhand and signed his name in red ink.

"That day, other farmers filled the courtroom. I imagine they were Fred's friends, family, and acquaintances. They were all in the courtroom, most with their arms folded across their chest, waiting for the judge to come in. Fred stood up front at one counsel's table looking pretty uncomfortable.

"I took a seat at the other counsel's table. The judge's law clerk peered into the courtroom for a moment to see if everyone was ready for the judge to come in. Then there was a big commotion at the back of the courtroom. The marshals had one of the spectators, a short roly-poly looking guy, pinned on the floor, facedown, hands behind his back. There were three marshals on his legs and lower back while a fourth secured handcuffs on the guy. They then stood the guy up and led him out of the courtroom.

"Today, the metal detector is on the main floor of the courthouse, far away from the courtrooms. In those days, the metal detector was on the same floor as the courtrooms. Turns out, this guy went through the metal detector and didn't set it off. But when he got to the courtroom, as he took a seat in the pews, he loudly boasted that the metal detector missed the forty-five caliber sidearm he had with him. And of course he laughed and made some comment about how bad the marshals were at their job.

"Someone in the courtroom heard him, was uncomfortable with the comments, went back out to the marshal manning the metal detector, and told the marshal what she heard. The marshal pushed the silent alarm button, and in seconds, four marshals came running into the courtroom and apprehended this guy.

"I later learned the guy's name was Woody Clarke, and he wasn't from the Warrensburg, Missouri, area. He was from Meadowfield, Kansas. He told the marshals he was at the hearing as a member of something he called The Thirty-Six Thirties. Said he was there to provide moral support for a Chapter 11 farmer's fight against my client, the big, bad bank. I learned later that he had no gun. He was just a big boaster who was talking at the wrong time in the wrong place and saying the wrong things around the wrong people."

The judge paused to let the story sink in.

"So you're saying that the committee chairman in the Melanshin bankruptcy cases has a federal criminal record as a result of the bankruptcy incident you've described?" Jennifer asked.

"Don't know if he has a record or what happened to him that day after the marshals intervened. But that's why I remembered his name. And now that I have, I would like to know more of what happened back then. So your assignment has changed. Can you please go down to the U.S. Marshals office and find Sal Viglione? Have you met him before?"

"I have not, Judge."

"Well, he's a marshal friend, and he was around in the nineties when this all happened. Tell Sal you work with me and ask him to see if there are any reports about the incident and about Woody Clarke that he can share with us."

"I'm on it, Judge," Jennifer said as she simultaneously stood and hustled out of her office even before the judge had a chance to stand and exit.

Jennifer took the elevator down to the U.S. Marshals office on the second floor of the courthouse and asked for Sal Viglione. Viglione came to the front reception area, and when he shook Jennifer's hand, she couldn't help but notice how large his hand was.

After inquiring how the judge was doing, he asked, "What can I do for the good judge and his trusted colleague?"

Jennifer gave Viglione a condensed version of the judge's story.

"Oh, yeah. I remember that crackpot, Clarke," Viglione replied. "I put the cuffs on him that day after my colleagues face-planted him into the courtroom carpeting and sat on him. It was a truly stupid stunt to pull in a federal courthouse. What an idiot. What did he expect would happen?"

"Do you have a report that you could share with the judge, Mr. Viglione?"

Viglione rubbed his chin. "Now, that's an old enough incident that we may not have digitized the reports from that time period yet. Give me a little time to figure out if they're digitized and get you copies of whatever we have."

Jennifer thanked him and returned to the judge's chambers to await the results of Viglione's search. In an hour, Viglione appeared in the judge's chambers with a manila folder containing thirty pages of information. He and the judge exchanged pleasantries and Viglione left the folder. Jill Walton, the judge's administrative assistant, copied the file and the judge brought it over to Jennifer.

"Jennifer, let's both look these papers over at the same time and see what we find."

An hour later, Jennifer was in the judge's office sitting in the large club chair facing his desk to talk about the Clarke papers.

"Looks like the marshals didn't recommend prosecuting Clarke, but they did their usual thorough background check on him," the judge said. "Yes, he was quite the character back then. Thirty-Six Thirties? They're on the domestic terrorist watch list. My Lord. After I read this, I figured it likely was an incredible stroke of luck that Clarke didn't actually have a gun that day."

"My reaction as well," Jennifer said. "The guy seems to subscribe to every right-wing theory out there. Immigrants are here at the behest of Jewish people to replace the true Americans, the White Christians. As if they weren't immigrants themselves." Jennifer paused for a moment and then continued. "Judge, I'm pretty sure I wouldn't make Clarke's Christmas card list in light of my Central American, Latino heritage."

"You wouldn't *want* to be on this guy's Christmas list, Jennifer."

"Judge, from my read, it doesn't look like the marshals thought Clarke was much of a doer. He was just a talker, at least at the time the incident happened."

"Agreed. Some talkers remain that way, but some graduate to action. Their beliefs leave them so frustrated and angry that eventually, some of them act out. Of those, some act out violently. We'll make sure we have a U.S. Marshal or two in the courtroom for any Melanshin hearings. Back in McKinley's case, Clarke was an observer. Here, he's a creditor and apparently, a big one. That might flip him from talker to doer, and I want to make sure the courtroom is a safe place for all the parties . . . and us."

"Will do, Judge."

"I've got to run out right now, Jennifer, but I'll sign both orders next week and allow an examination of Clarke and Melanshin. Then, let's keep an ear to the grindstone on these Chapter 11 cases. They've now risen to the top of our pile, I'm afraid."

Rome returned from her walk, poured a glass of water, sat on her bed, and began to review what her bot had discovered.

The searches revealed information about the lease between the Melanshins and Bill Pearson. The local real estate records contained the recorded lease, so securing a copy was simple. She emailed the lease to Moses.

She didn't find out much about the Melanshins. Her search into Woody Clarke's past, however, revealed much more, and the results were disturbing. He had been investigated numerous times by local and federal authorities for computer crimes he allegedly commissioned and the suspicious deaths of Black men along the border between Kansas and Missouri. Her search found a brief mention of the bankruptcy court incident. None of the brushes with the law led authorities to bring charges against him. But she knew that where there was smoke, there was usually fire.

She confirmed what she had previously discovered: that Clarke claimed to be a descendent of William Clarke Quantrill. And there were posts, not by Clarke but by others, reporting that at one meeting or another, Clarke boasted that the world would be a better place today if Quantrill and his raiders had succeeded in killing more Blacks and John Brown sympathizers.

Rome wondered why Clarke hired 3J as committee counsel, given his views of Blacks. While she didn't find posts under Clarke's name, she found posts by other Thirties discussing Clarke. As she read them, she concluded that Clarke was a real piece of work.

Rome also located evidence that Clarke's son had numerous run-ins with local authorities, including allegations of the sale of drugs near the regional high school. In the early stages of her investigatory training, Moses had drilled into her that there were no coincidences, and she wondered if there was a connection between the death of the Melanshins' son and the drug allegations against Clarke's offspring.

Rome drafted a detailed report of her findings for Moses and emailed it off to him with the promise that she would try to get more details. Rome closed her laptop lid, leaned against her wall, and quickly fell into a light, restless sleep. She excelled at many things in life, but sleep was not one of them. She often wondered if her constant connectivity led her to need, and get, less sleep than others. As she drifted off, she pondered what it would feel like to get ten hours in a row of a deep, restorative sleep.

After her brief nap, Rome decided to turn to a review of dark web information. She wasn't on the dark web to buy illegal firearms or drugs or to traffic in child porn. She was on the dark web like the many other users who availed themselves of the significant encryption advantages presented by the websites that operated there.

To search the dark web, she used the browser, Tor, and what she discovered was disturbing. In several right-wing chatrooms, she read accounts of a new Quantrill-like raider who, according to accounts, had slayed two Black farmers. The chatter spoke with reverence of this new raider finally taking action to rid the country of those Fourteenth Amendment citizens who sought to replace White Christians. The posts sent shivers up and down Rome's spine.

The posts did not mention Clarke by name. They referenced a group of like-minded Kansas farmers who gathered to plan ways to make America great again. With that information in hand, Rome did clearnet searches of the Anti-Defamation League's archives, as well as the Southern Poverty Law Center's archives to see if she could locate any ties. After thirty minutes, she thought she might have found that connection: an entry in the ADL's database of right-wing fringe organizations, one in Kansas calling itself The Thirty-Six Thirties and labeled, "potentially dangerous."

The ADL reported that Wallace "Woody" Clarke likely founded The Thirty-Six Thirties, and while there had been no arrests of group members for terrorist-related activities to date, the ADL reported that The Thirty-Six Thirties were capable of such activities and therefore were capable of violence.

Rome concluded that she had enough information for a report in which she could credibly suggest that Clarke might be capable of violence. She forwarded the supplemental report to Moses, who wrote back quickly that Rome should be available for a call with the lawyers in twelve hours to discuss these matters.

Rome wrote back, "No problem, Moses. Just let me know when."

As she closed the lid of her laptop, Rome wondered if the bankruptcy process could deal with a fringe group and a potentially violent person like Clarke.

12

Monday, April 29 through Wednesday, May 1, 2024

MOSES FORWARDED ROME'S preliminary and supplemental reports to 3J, and first thing Monday morning, Moses and Rome were on a conference call with 3J and Pascale, who were on a speakerphone in 3J's office.

"We've read the reports and the information about Clarke and his Thirties," 3J said. "It's chilling. So where should we begin, folks?"

"Let's first discuss the financials," Moses replied. "There is a discrepancy between the Melanshin income statements reporting over twenty-three thousand dollars in accrued income each month from real estate leases and the Melanshin cash flow statements reporting actual receipt of cash from those leases of less than twenty thousand dollars a month. In the public records, Rome was able to locate the Melanshins' lease of the land they purchased from Clarke. It calls for payments of over twenty-three thousand, so on an accrual basis, the income statement appears to be true to the terms in the lease.

"We have two possibilities. Either the tenant paid more like seventeen thousand six hundred dollars per month and the Melanshins took no steps to enforce payment of the higher amount or the tenant paid the full amount under the lease, but not all of it to the Melanshins. Since I cannot determine which possibility is correct from the public domain, you will need to delve into that in your examination of Mr. Melanshin. Questions?"

"Is there any evidence that the Melanshins increased their spending over the last several years?" Pascale asked.

"Most definitely. They significantly increased their spending. Luxury items, home improvements, cars, private college for their son, lavish trips abroad."

"Is there any evidence that the Melanshins intentionally increased their spending to reduce their net cash flow and thereby engineered insufficient cash to pay Clarke under the contract for deed?" Pascale asked.

3J looked up from her notepad when Pascale posed the question and wondered what led him to suspect an intentional reduction of net cash flow. She made a mental note to ask Pascale about his inquiry.

"It is certainly possible, Mr. Pascale. Lifestyles can certainly change when people have increased cash at their disposal. Here, however, there is no evidence that the Melanshins came into more cash. Rather, they seemed to have made a decision to live the good life. Based on the information gleaned by Rome, it appears that decision to live it up coincided with the death of their son Toby."

"Okay. Thank you, Moses," 3J said. "Rome, what do you have for us?"

Rome went over the right-wing fringe information she discovered about Clarke, the group named The Thirty-Six Thirties, and the possibility that Clarke had something to do with the unsolved murders of Black border farmers. 3J had read about the Clarke revelations in Rome's report and listened quietly as Rome highlighted parts of the report. Rome added to her written report that she had discovered Clarke had a run-in with the U.S. Marshals in the 1990s at a bankruptcy court hearing. She reminded the lawyers that others reported Clarke had claimed to be a direct descendant of William Clarke Quantrill, of Quantrill's Raiders infamy, and who also slaughtered numerous Black Kansans along the Missouri border before and during the Civil War.

"Yes, we saw that in your materials," 3J said. "Jesus. What a world."

Rome ended her presentation with her conclusion that Clarke was likely capable of violence, whether to further the cause of right-wing fringe groups or to rid the world of people Clarke believed were trying to replace him and his White Christian cohorts.

"Good people, if I may go out on a limb," Moses said, "I sense that Clarke is as capable of bad acts against the Melanshins as it appears he is in reviving his Civil War relative's infamous attempts to purge his part of the countryside of people of color. Since Clarke is your client, I wonder how you will be able to handle this type of situation."

"Moses, Clarke is not our client. He's a creditor on the committee. None of the committee members are clients. The committee itself is our client. So if we need to, we'll ask Clarke the hard questions, and if he doesn't like it, setting aside for the moment the developing story that he might be violent, my response to any objection he might raise to my questions would be, 'Tough.'"

"Ahh. I understand, Ms. Jones. We will continue to delve into these matters for you and share any updates. And please do not take Mr. Clarke lightly. There are too many red flags to brush aside the possibility that he may react in an unpredictable and dangerous manner."

"Understood. Thanks to both of you for the quick work," 3J said.

When the call ended, 3J and Pascale looked at each other but said nothing. Time seemed to slow for both of them. After a few moments 3J asked, "Bill, what led you to ask if the Melanshins engineered a reduction in cash flow?"

"Just a gut reaction. Seems to me that there is a bit of a Hatfield and McCoy dispute brewing here. If the Melanshins have it in for Clarke, and if they're planners, it might make some sense for them to spend money so they won't be able to pay Clarke."

"Hmm. I see."

"Let's play the Clarke examination out, 3J. You could examine Clarke after Steinert takes his shot and hit him with questions about Quantrill's Raiders, dirty tricks, violence, and all of his political bullshit. Or you could share with Steinert what we've learned from Aaronson and Rome and let him take the shots."

"I'm not inclined to shy away from directly asking Clarke whatever needs to be asked when it's my turn to question him," 3J said firmly but in a measured tone. "I have a job to do. If Clarke's a bad actor and he's impairing the other unsecured creditors from getting paid, it's the committee's duty and ours as committee counsel to investigate it and take steps so the unsecured creditors get paid."

"My first and foremost concern here is your well-being."

"I get it. But I don't like options that involve me doing less than my full duty," she said, frowning. 3J paused, then smiled and said, "No corner cutting. That's what my firm supervisor taught me. Right?"

Pascale nodded but continued to look worried. "Understood, but we still shouldn't take Clarke lightly. So instead of conducting his examination at a lawyer's office, suppose we do it at the Western District courthouse."

3J said nothing, waiting for Pascale to elaborate.

"The courthouse comes equipped with security—the best in the land, the U.S. Marshals. Clarke will have to walk through a metal detector to enter. If he gets out of control at any point in the examination, we'll find a marshal to either calm him down or walk him out of the examination room—maybe right into an orange jumpsuit and a holding cell."

Pascale paused and then completed his thought. "And Rome reported that Clarke had that run-in with the marshals in the old courthouse. In the new courthouse, he might temper his conduct, knowing they're nearby. The marshals might enjoy helping him adjust his conduct like they did in the old days."

3J said nothing for a few moments while she considered the proposal. "Well, I have to admit that I don't hate the idea. But I need to talk to Steinert and get his buy-in. We'll also have to reach out to Judge Robertson and see if he's willing to sign the examination order and direct a courthouse examination venue. I guess that means we'll have to examine Donnie Melanshin at the courthouse as well."

"Agreed," Pascale said. "Should I call the judge's chambers after you talk with Steinert?"

"That works. Thanks, Pascale."

3J called Jacob Steinert to suggest the date and venue for the examinations. To her surprise, he thought the courthouse venue was a good idea and a way to have the marshals at the ready. He said he would take care of explaining this to Donnie and Lil Melanshin and would let 3J know if he ran into resistance from them. The two agreed to take the examinations in two weeks. In short order, he called 3J back and said the courthouse venue would work.

3J reported to Pascale that Steinert had agreed. With 3J in his office, Pascale then called Judge Robertson's chambers and spoke to Jennifer Cuello, explaining that he was calling on the Melanshin bankruptcy cases. "The judge should have our request to examine Donnie Melanshin, as well as the debtors' request to examine one of the committee members, Woody Clarke. We've talked with Mr. Steinert, debtors' counsel, and the lawyers agree that it would be best if the judge's orders approving the examinations direct us to take them in the Western District Courthouse. With this background, I am hoping you might be able to talk with Judge Robertson about that possibility, and if he is so inclined, let me know if he needs any further information from us before issuing an order."

Jennifer listened carefully as Pascale explained the unusual request. She made a mental note that Pascale had not explained why the lawyers thought it best to use the courthouse to examine the parties. But she asked no questions and simply said, "I understand, Mr. Pascale. Let me talk to Judge Robertson, and I'll get back to you."

After the call, Jennifer went to the judge's office, and when he looked up, she asked if he had a moment to talk about the Melanshin cases.

"Certainly. What's up?"

Jennifer explained the call from Pascale and the request. As she finished, the judge smiled. "I'm not sure I remember Bill Pascale in the courtroom the day Mr. Clarke got carpet burns on his face, but it sure sounds like Mr. Pascale might be aware of the history. Or perhaps there's some new history Mr. Clarke has made. That would not surprise me. But I don't have to think about this too long. Whether Mr. Pascale knows of the incident or not, it's a good idea to have Mr. Clarke walk through a metal detector and have the marshals nearby. Let Bill know I will grant his request. I'll also order that Clarke and Melanshin must cooperate with the lawyers in the examinations and conduct themselves appropriately in the courthouse at all times."

"That sounds like a good idea, Judge," Jennifer said.

"Then please let Viglione know the date and time of the examinations. He should be on standby on the examination day. And he might want to greet Mr. Clarke in the courthouse lobby and renew an old friendship."

"Sure thing, Judge."

As Jennifer rose to return to her office the judge added, "These Melanshin cases are shaping up to be quite unusual."

Late Monday afternoon, Judge Robertson issued the two orders directing the examination of both Clarke and Melanshin at the courthouse at a time and date mutually agreeable to the committee and the debtors. 3J, Pascale, and Steinert talked and agreed that a process server should serve Clarke with the order directing him to appear and that Steinert could deliver the Melanshin order to his client. 3J and Pascale suggested their process server, Anthony Rosini, would be a good choice to serve Clarke. Steinert knew Rosini and agreed.

Tuesday morning, Pascale called Rosini and put him on the speakerphone. "Anthony, my man. Bill Pascale and 3J here. How are ya?"

"No complaints at all. I'm putting the nose to the grindstone every day. Say, I heard a rumor you were hanging up the bankruptcy cleats. True?"

"That's the plan, at least so far."

"Well, best of luck, and I hope you'll invite me to the send-off party."

"You'll be on the guest list for sure. We have a new project for you. Service of an examination order on a member of a right-wing fringe group. The group is on the Anti-Defamation League's list of domestic terrorist organizations."

"No shit?" Rosini whistled before adding, "Right here in Kansas City? Not that I doubt their presence here. They're everywhere."

"No, not exactly here," Pascal explained. "He's in Meadowfield, Kansas, a border town off Highway 69 and K-7, south of here."

"Well, you guys certainly come up with interesting projects for me. Guess I won't be telling this fella that I'm one of those Italian immigrant types. Might pull a shotgun out and hustle me away."

3J listened to the banter and was concerned. "No kidding around here, Anthony. This guy is a potentially dangerous one."

"Apologies if I gave you the impression I was joking around." Rosini, a former Jackson County Sheriff, was a large man—over six feet tall and a hair under two hundred pounds, most of it still rock-solid muscle. But that didn't mean he was cavalier about serving dangerous people. "Not to worry, 3J. I hear you loud and clear." He paused before adding, "Folks, to serve this guy in the safest manner possible, I'm thinking I should pretend I'm a county official who made a tax mistake and wanted to personally bring him a refund check and apologize for the mistake."

"You think that would work?" Pascale asked.

"It should. Regardless of whether you're right-wing or left-wing, everyone wants money back from the gov, and a taxation department apology would be icing on the cake, right?"

"Sounds like you've done this before," 3J said.

"Yep. Get me the papers and the location and I'll get it done."

When they ended the call, 3J expressed some concerns to Pascale. "Bill, everything about this guy Clarke gives me the chills. Even with something as simple as service of process, my thoughts immediately go to a dark place. Rosini knows what he's doing, but he needs to be careful."

"Anthony will be careful. In and out quickly. That's his style. He's been at this a long time. He's a pro, and he'll be fine," Pascale said to allay her fears. But privately, he shared 3J's concerns. He could tell the cases were turning out to be messy.

The next day, 3J delivered the Clarke examination order to Rosini.

Rosini had dressed as he thought a county official might dress in a button-down shirt opened at the collar, a dark knit tie, khaki pants, and loafers. No sports coat. He headed for his car and a rendezvous with Woody Clarke. Rosini had learned that Meadowfield was forty miles from the county seat, and he hoped Clarke was far enough away from the county offices that he didn't know all the county employees, let alone someone lower down on the totem pole in the taxation department.

Rosini arrived at Clarke's hog farm in about seventy-five minutes and found Clarke in a work shed behind the farmhouse. He knocked on the shed door, and Clarke came out. Rosini performed his roll as county official, explaining who he was and why he was there. A mixture of soot, dried hog pen mud, and engine grease covered Clarke from head to toe. As he listened, he held a greasy rag he used to try to wipe some of the grease from his hands. Rosini decided to dispense with a handshake.

As Rosini finished his story, he handed Clarke the envelope containing the examination order. Clarke was in no condition to handle a valuable check, so he took the envelope without opening it and grumbled a thank you before turning back into the shed. Rosini quickly returned to his car for the trip back to Kansas City.

Later in the afternoon, Clarke cleaned up and sat down on his porch to open the envelope. Instead of a county issued check, he found the examination order and immediately went inside to call 3J.

"What in the hell is this, lawyer of mine?" Clarke growled when 3J answered the call.

"Mr. Clarke, the debtors want to take your examination under oath. The law entitles them to do so. There's nothing anyone could do to prevent it. I have a similar order to examine Donnie Melanshin. And I'm just not your personal lawyer in this case. I'm repeating myself, but at this point, you need to consider hiring a lawyer to represent you, especially at the examination."

"Not gonna happen, counselor. Don't need one. Don't need you to tell me what to do. Why at the courthouse?"

3J decided to fudge the truth and replied, "Not terribly out of the ordinary. Sometimes the lawyers take the exams in their offices and sometimes at the courthouse. These will both be at the courthouse."

"Where are we on gettin' me paid?" Clarke grumbled.

"The process of getting all unsecured creditors paid will commence in earnest after we get some information from Melanshin in the examination. So the sooner that happens the better. The sooner we can examine Melanshin the sooner we'll get this process under way."

"Lots of words, counselor, but they don't mean nothin'. Sounds like the short answer is that we're nowhere yet on gettin' me my money."

"Not nowhere, Mr. Clarke, but it's a process."

"Process means no money and nowhere in my book. Christ almighty! What a goddamn system. No wonder this country is going down the shitter. Don't I have rights? Ain't the law supposed to protect me? How does anyone get paid back anymore? Goddammit!" Clarke yelled into his phone.

Before 3J could say anything in response, Clarke hung up on her.

After the call, Clarke tried to return to the shed and concentrate on his repair work. But all he could think about was his suspicion that the Melanshins had a premeditated plan to set him up for selling his acreage without being paid for it. He knew he had to prove it. The more he thought about their premeditation, the less he could concentrate on repairing his equipment and the angrier he got.

13

*Woody Clarke recalls Wednesday, May 1
through Sunday, May 5, 2024*

WHEN MY CALL with that colored lawyer ended, I was fuming again. Between Donnie and that Jones gal, it had quickly turned out to be one big shitty day in the heartland. I needed to know what Donnie was up to. I was coming to the realization that I'd have to spy on him to figure it out, but I wasn't sure how.

Then I thought that perhaps there was a tech way to do it. Y'know, like you see in the movies. While I hadn't kept up with tech all that much since college, I felt like I was a reasonably quick learner about internet things and certainly better with the tech stuff than most of The Thirties boys. Even so, I sure didn't know enough about technology to know how I'd find out what I needed to know about Donnie.

But I knew a teenager I thought might know. You know them teenagers these days. They got that extra strand of DNA that allows them to understand almost everything online and tech. Now this kid, he was helping my son grow that little business of ours at the high school. This kid wasn't in The Thirties. Not yet. Still too young. But I knew his old man was a Thirties sympathizer, so I figured the kid would help me out, and I thought I could trust him. I'd invite him over and have a heart-to-heart about how.

So I call the kid, and he's able to come over to the farmhouse later in the day. I sit him down and tell him what I need, and he tells me he's reluctant. The cure for reluctance is good old money, which every teenager I ever met wants and needs more of. So I offer him money, and he tells me that he can teach me how to eavesdrop on the Melanshins but he wouldn't do it himself.

To my surprise, he asks me what their kitchen is like. I tell him it's all brand new. He asks me what kind of appliances they have, and I tell him about the stove, the fridge, the coffee maker, and whatever else I could remember from my visit. He says I'm in luck because he figures that some or all of those electronics are smart appliances. I ask why that matters.

He says, "They're all computers that happen to be something else like a coffee maker or a fridge." He tells me that some of the appliances probably have a microphone, and with a little luck and his instructions, I can log in to the appliance and use its microphone to listen.

I tell him I figure the coffee maker has a mic because Lil told it to brew a pot of coffee and it turned itself on.

And he says, "That's good. That's real good." He says I could use the coffee maker to listen in on what they're talking about.

I'm amazed and whistle. "No shit?"

He says in response, "No shit, Mr. Clarke. Welcome to the twenty-first century. Is that what you're angling for?"

"Absolutely."

Then I ask him if it'd be hard for me to learn. He says, "Nah. You know how to work the internet. I can teach you how to do this. You'll need a little luck. Hopefully, the Melanshins haven't added their own passwords to any of the smart appliances."

He teaches me what I need to do. He shows me this website called Reveal where I could open an account and run a search to find the smart appliances in the area. He then shows me that Reveal has a geolocator to show me the smart appliances in the Melanshin house.

Once I found them, he taught me how to log in to the appliance. I had some questions after I practiced what he told me. After a few days, I figured it out, and it worked, and to get right to the bottom line, here's what I heard through the microphone in their damn coffee maker on that Sunday morning:

"Lil, I talked with Steinert about Clarke, and Steinert says he'll continue to monitor the situation. He also talked to me about my upcoming examination by that Jones lawyer at the courthouse and said he would examine Clarke at the same time."

"Honey, when they examine you, are you gonna tell the lawyer about the plan I sketched out?"

"I don't see anyone asking if we planned to take his land without paying. Look, I didn't make Clarke sign the contract. I didn't prevent him from taking the steps he mighta shoulda to understand the contract. Didn't tell him not to go to a lawyer. I didn't stop him from recording it. All Clarke, not me. Nothing to tell."

"I agree. All Clarke. What about our expenses?"

"What about 'em, Lil? They are what they are. They're real. They ain't fake. No one's gonna ask me about our plan to reduce our cash flow on purpose, right? And why would they ask? We ran out of money. We filed. Just another married couple in bankruptcy."

"Yeah, probably not."

"Don't want to lie, Lil, and don't think we did anything wrong here, but I'm not gonna explain it unless someone asks me the right question."

"Sounds right, Donnie. But it's always good to prepare."

There was silence as I heard some shuffling, and then Lil continued. She mentioned Robert, and I knew he was their kid in college.

"What about the payments to Robert?"

"Robert owns part of the land we bought from Clarke. The bankruptcy papers asked what transfers we made in the last two years. We gave Robert his interest in the land at least three years ago. We done nothing wrong. The rent payment ain't made by us, so it ain't a transfer we made. As a part owner, Robert is entitled to a part of the rent. Right? Again, we done nothing wrong in filling out the bankruptcy papers."

"I know, Donnie. I'm thinking all of this through."

"One reason I love you, Lil."

"Do you think Clarke has figured this out yet, Donnie?"

"Him? Nah. He ain't there yet. And remember, he's Woody Clarke. He'll take some time to get there. And then again, he may never get there, Lil."

I made a thumb drive of the conversation I recorded on my computer. And there I had it. Premeditated. Donnie and Lil planned a way to screw me. I suspected it, but now I knew it for certain. Dammit. They stole my land. They'd been skimming money to their son, Robert. I wondered if Pearson was in on this as well. Never had much use for him either.

I decided I'd have to get that thumb drive to that colored gal before the examinations. She could use it to make Donnie and Lil start to squirm. I figured repayment would follow that squirming.

14

Tuesday, May 7 through Thursday, May 9, 2024

3 J was at her desk at 8:30 a.m. when one of the Greene Madison office couriers brought a small padded envelope to her. It was postmarked Meadowfield, Kansas, and there was no return address. Inside was a small thumb drive and a business card from Woody Clarke.

3J was familiar with the firm's policy barring insertion of an unknown thumb drive into her laptop's USB port to guard against releasing a virus into the firm's network. Following the required protocol, she took the thumb drive down two floors to the director of litigation support, René Alvarez-Thompson. Alvarez-Thompson and 3J had worked together on matters too numerous to count, and 3J both liked and trusted her with most of the day-to-day tech issues that arose in 3J's practice.

Alvarez-Thompson took the thumb drive and told 3J she would be back to her in an hour or two. Ninety minutes later, Alvarez-Thompson called 3J and reported that the drive was clean and contained one large audio WAV file, which she had loaded onto the network so 3J could open and listen to it. As Alvarez-Thompson spoke with 3J, an email arrived on 3J's desktop with a network link to the audio file.

Pascale showed up at 3J's office with his morning coffee. "What's on tap this morning, 3J?"

"It's starting off as one of those best-laid-plans kind of day. I was going to start outlining my questions to ask Clarke at the examination when a padded envelope arrived at my desk postmarked from Meadowfield but with no return address and no explanation. Inside was a business card from Clarke and a thumb drive that I had Réne clear for viruses. It was clean. The drive has one audio file on it. I was about to listen to it. Pull up a chair and make yourself comfortable."

The two listened as Donnie and Lil Melanshin discussed the status of their plan and how Donnie might handle questions in the upcoming examination. The conversation was more than enlightening. As the audio file ended, 3J looked at Pascale, and in a hoarse whisper said, "Shit, Pascale."

"Exactly. Clarke must've somehow bugged the Melanshin kitchen and listened in as the two talked about stuff I'm sure they thought no one would hear." Pascale paused and after a few seconds, he mimicked 3J's whisper. "Jesus."

3J slowly shook her head. "I guess that just about covers all the commentary two bankruptcy lawyers could possibly offer. Not sure what we should do with this. Are we obligated to turn it over to Jacob Steinert? Is it a privileged communication between husband and wife? And most importantly to me, how in God's name could Clarke have recorded them?"

Pascale nodded. "This is the kind of stuff you see in the movies. How could he have bugged them?"

"Not sure. How would he have gotten into the kitchen alone to do that?" 3J mused.

"This stuff is way over my pay grade," Pascale said. "I have no idea, but I agree with you. We ought to know how it might have happened."

"Why do you think Clarke shared it with me?"

"Plain sight, like Rome said. But they're not hiding at all anymore. I bet he's proud he bugged the debtors and wants you to know about it."

They were both silent for a while. Then 3J said, "Y'know, Bill, we should get some insight from Rome about how this recording could be possible or at least find out if she has any specialized knowledge about this area of sleuthing. I'll send her and Moses the audio file, explain the situation, and set up a call."

Later in the day, 3J, Pascale, Rome, and Moses met on a conference call.

"Fascinating development, to say the least," Moses said. "Rome can provide some intriguing insights into how Clarke might have recorded the conversation."

Rome took it from there. "There are some traditional ways and some more modern ways a person might record an audio file like the one you sent us. The more traditional way is how Hollywood has typically portrayed the issue. Someone infiltrates the subject's home and plants a bug in the form of a tiny little transmitter they stick to a lampshade or the underside of a counter or desk. The transmitter then wirelessly sends conversations or other sounds it picks up in the room to a remote receiver. The person listening on the receiver end then simply records the conversations.

"Two downsides of using a bug are that someone has to plant it and the homeowner might discover it. Someone would have to be physically in the room to plant it—for instance, a guest left alone in the room or someone there surreptitiously. This person would have to affix the transmitter without the homeowner knowing about the bug. In Hollywood, if it is an infiltrator, that person might pick the front door lock when the homeowners are away. But many homes have pretty effective security systems these days, so an infiltrator would have to disable the system before picking the lock. No small task. And if there is a dog in the house, the infiltrator would have to deal with the dog once inside. Layers of complications.

"I cannot say if that happened to the Melanshins, but it is certainly one possibility. Any questions so far?"

3J looked at Pascale, who shook his head. "No questions so far," 3J replied.

"Excellent," Rome said. "Then let's transport squarely into the twenty-first century. Have you heard of something called an IoT?"

"An IoT? I don't believe I have," Pascale said.

"Me neither," 3J added.

"IoT stands for 'Internet of Things.' It is a phrase coined in 1999 by Kevin Ashton, a British technology researcher. IoTs are all the different kinds of internet-connected devices that are not traditional computers. Things like fitness trackers, headphones, wireless music systems like Sonos, and cameras. Also smart devices like smart watches, smart kitchen appliances, smart lighting, and smart thermostats. Washers and dryers are in there, as well as cars, traffic lights, airplane engines, home security systems, and televisions. And speakers like Google Home, Apple Homepods, and Amazon Echo devices. To name but a few. There are even voice-controlled devices now that can connect to and take control of numerous IoTs so the consumer can communicate to all of the devices through a single product. There are literally billions of IoTs in existence."

Pascale leaned back in the chair and closed his eyes and 3J leaned her elbows on her desk and rested her chin on her clasped hands to get closer to the speakerphone.

Rome continued. "It is common knowledge that, at least to date, IoTs are not secure, especially the older ones that people have in their homes. The IoTs have IP addresses, and there are search engines to find them. For example, one search engine is Reveal. With an account, you can search for IoTs in a region, and then employing Reveal's geolocator function, you can generate a map showing where those devices are located. Using the geolocator, Clarke could identify the IoTs in the Melanshins' house.

"Most IoT device firmware does not offer the same level of protection as computer and smartphone operating systems have. For example, in a Reveal search, one can see images generated from any IoT device that uses a camera, like a security camera."

"Rome, what about passwords?" Pascale asked.

"Excellent question, Mr. Pascale. Many people never bother to change the login credentials on their IoT devices. They may not know they can change the credentials or they don't know how to do it. Or they ignore the risks of not changing the credentials. Many IoT devices do not permit the owner to change the credentials."

"I see," Pascale said slowly.

"Think about it," Rome said. "We talk to our Echoes and Homepods and ask for the weather report, and Alexa or Siri answers from remote servers. We talk to our coffee machine and tell it to brew for us and it does. We talk to our smart television and ask it to search for one movie genre or another and it does. We tell our music system to play a playlist and it does. Everyday IoTs help us perform everyday tasks. Many of these devices have a microphone. Clarke could get a Reveal account, perform a Reveal search, find the Melanshins' IoT devices, identify one in their kitchen without password protection that has a microphone, and then eavesdrop."

Rome paused.

After a moment, 3J said quietly, "I feel like I need to disconnect my appliances and technology in my condo when I get home tonight."

"Indeed. A common sentiment when one first learns about IoTs, Ms. Jones. It is a very connected world we live in. The convenience of the connectivity carries with it risks that most consumers are unaware of or simply choose to ignore. Some people love all the connectivity. But others seek to remove themselves from the grid, so to speak, when they learn of the dark side to the technology."

Pascale, normally technologically challenged, simply said, "My Lord."

"Do you know how high-tech the Melanshins are and if Clarke or any other person has intimate knowledge of their technology?" Moses asked.

"We don't, Moses," 3J replied. "At least, not at this point."

"Hmm, I see."

"That is my overview for you," Rome said, concluding her explanation of IoTs. "You now have lots of information to consider."

"This presentation was eye-opening and thought-provoking," 3J admitted. "Bill and I need to figure out how to deal with this and the audio file. I'm not sure if the audio file is even fair game. It's becoming apparent to me that making the recording undoubtedly violated one law or another."

"We certainly understand, Ms. Jones. The modern era presents issues that older laws may not have contemplated. And high-tech tends to look the other way when these issues raise their heads. While we shed light on matters that lurk in the dark, there are things we should perhaps very well leave in the dark, like a private conversation between husband and wife. In any case, please let us know how we can help in this matter. And good luck."

When the call ended, 3J and Pascale looked at each other and said nothing for several minutes.

"Rome can certainly take a sunny day and quickly blow in the storm clouds," Pascale observed, breaking the silence.

3J nodded in agreement as she bit her upper lip absentmindedly.

"So where do we go from here, 3J?"

She switched from a nod to shaking her head from side to side. "We should talk about this issue by issue and see if we can come up with a plan for each one. Otherwise, I'm more than a little over-whelmed by the totality of what we heard from Rome and what we heard on the audio file. And the examinations are only days away."

"Makes sense. Which conundrum do you want to tackle first?"

"Let's start with the bankruptcy stuff. At least there, I feel we have half a chance to get the strategy correct."

"Agreed. The tenant pays a portion of the rent to Robert. I think I read that Robert is their son. Is that kosher?"

"Sounds like there may be an unrecorded deed transferring part of the Melanshins' interest in the land to Robert," 3J said.

"And that transfer may've happened more than two years ago. So it wouldn't be a transfer the Melanshins had to report on their Chapter 11 bankruptcy papers."

"Agreed. No failure to report, so no improperly hidden asset there. And it looks like some of the rent goes to the Melanshins and some to Robert each month."

"Correct. But is that improper?" Pascale asked. "I mean, if Robert owns part of the land, isn't he entitled to part of the rent?"

"Perhaps. Honestly, I'm not entirely certain." You know, Bill, the deed to a relative might be a fraudulent transfer, and if it was, then Robert's rent payments could be fraudulent as well."

"Yes, I'm with you. It might be fraudulent if it was a transfer for less than reasonably equivalent value at a time when the transferor was insolvent or rendered insolvent by the transfer."

"Right. If this transfer occurred more than three years ago, before the Melanshins started to incur their heightened lifestyle debts, they probably weren't insolvent and the transfer probably didn't render them insolvent," 3J said, analyzing the insolvency issue further. "You know, if they transferred the land to a relative with the intent to hinder, delay, or defraud creditors, it could also be a fraudulent transfer."

"True, but would a transfer of part of the land they didn't ever pay for to their only son when they weren't financially stressed qualify as an intent to hinder, delay, or defraud?" Pascale rubbed his chin. "I mean, because Clarke didn't record the contract for deed, in effect, the Melanshins got this land mostly for free."

"Well, I have my doubts about whether these facts add up to an intent to defraud creditors," 3J replied. "So for purposes of trying to work through this, let's assume for the moment that the transfer was a good one, and therefore, the rent payments each month to Robert were also fine."

"They won't be fine in Woody Clarke's mind for sure, but Clarke aside, agreed. Next up, the apparent scheme to dupe Woody Clarke out of his land."

"Yeah. I kind of agree with what I heard Donnie Melanshin saying on the audio. No one made Clarke sign the deal. No one prevented him from seeking legal advice. He kind of brought the problem on himself."

"I agree," Pascale replied. "Based on what Rome dug up, if the Clarke family had something to do with the death of Toby Melanshin, I can certainly understand the Melanshins' motivation to get back at Clarke. It's human nature. But can we say that a Melanshin plan to screw Clarke was legally improper."

"Not seeing it was improper, Pascale. I see a savvy real estate businessman, maybe with some pointy elbows, who took advantage of Clarke. But savvy businesspeople negotiate advantageous deals every day without legal exposure."

"Agreed. We all learned in law school contracts class the famous Latin phrase 'caveat emptor.' Buyer beware. Well, we're looking at the seller version of that. What would that be? *Caveat venditor?*"

3J nodded. "And isn't this Clarke's problem, not the committee's?"

"Absolutely. Not a committee's issue," Pascale agreed. "Next up, the recording. Who made it?"

They agreed that Clarke either made the recording or had someone do it for him. He'd even been brazen enough to include his business card when he sent it to 3J. Whether it was an illegal wire tap was something they were less sure about; 3J wondered aloud if they could trace the recording back to Clarke in some way and realized that was something they should have asked Rome. She made a note to do so. Questions of what was best for the committee also came into play, as well as whether marital privilege was involved and if the recording could be used in court. The issues kept coming.

"Let's pause here," 3J finally said. "My head's swimming. I'll need to do some research. Then we can circle up and finalize how to deal with Steinert."

The next day, 3J stepped away from her desk after hours of research and walked over to Pascale's office to find him sitting with his back to his desk, chair turned to the window, hands clasped behind his head, looking out over downtown Kansas City. He heard her enter and slowly spun his chair around.

"What did you find out, 3J?"

"This marital privilege stuff is as clear as mud in federal court. Some courts say that even if there is a privilege, it doesn't apply to business matters a married couple discusses. Others reject that and apply the privilege no matter what topic the couple discusses. Still others say there is no such privilege. More often, a particular court has had nothing to say about it either way, so a litigant in that court has no idea what the rule is."

"Hmm. I see. And what of our particular court and our particular judge?"

"Judge Robertson and the other judges in the Western District have had nothing to say about it. No stated rule they follow."

Pascale listened attentively as he absentmindedly rubbed his forehead, finally asking if her research had helped her come up with a strategy on dealing with Steinert.

"Well, if we tell Steinert in advance, it's likely he'll say he won't permit us to use the recording. And in the examination, he'll go after Clarke about making it. If we don't tell him in advance, he'll be pissed, but he'll still take the position that we can't use the recording, and he'll still go after Clarke. Same result each time."

Pascale nodded. "Agreed. Setting aside when Steinert finds out about the recording and how he reacts, I suppose Clarke sent us the recording because he thinks it shows the Melanshins have done something wrong, and he wants the committee and its counsel on his side."

"Undoubtedly."

"Do we agree that on this issue, the committee is on Clarke's side?"

3J took a deep breath and sighed. "Yeah . . . not so sure. I've been pondering that question. My gut reaction is that the committee is going to be on the Melanshins' side on this one. They did nothing legally wrong. The unsecured creditors benefit from Clarke's loss of the land. Maybe the Melanshins even find a way to treat Clarke differently than other unsecured creditors without unfairly discriminating against him."

"I agree. On that last point, it even seems to me that the committee and the Melanshins can work together to find a way to treat Clarke differently."

3J's eyes widened. "Jesus, Pascale. He'll have a tantrum and then a stroke if he thinks the committee will challenge him head-on."

"Yes, I imagine so. And maybe a stroke will be the least of his reactions. Getting paid less could push him over the edge. Remember Rome's conclusion about Clarke's tendency toward violence."

"Oh, I remember," 3J said with a deadly serious look on her face. "Seems to me that this discussion has led us to a strategy: Tell Steinert. No downside and no different results. Then tell Clarke. Then tell the entire committee."

"I agree. And if the rest of the committee is going to be adverse to Clarke, he'll need to drop off the committee."

"Yep. So when he appears for his examination, it'll be Woody Clarke, creditor, not Woody Clarke, committee spokesperson."

"Afraid so, 3J. That will make an already difficult examination exponentially more so."

"Perhaps. I was thinking it might make it easier for me to be forthright with him in the examination if he's no longer on the committee."

Pascale nodded. "What next?"

"Let's start with Steinert in the morning. Then I'll have to call both Clarke and the committee members."

"Sounds like a plan."

When 3J and Pascale had their phone call with Jacob Steinert later that morning, Steinert said nothing as they revealed the content of the recording and promised to deliver to him a copy of the thumb drive. When they finished, Steinert remained silent for an uncomfortable period and finally said, "Strange bankruptcy cases. I'm going to need to think about this and do some research before I figure out how to respond."

"Jacob, I can tell you that I researched the issue of marital privilege and learned that Judge Robertson hasn't written anything stating his view," 3J replied. "Neither have the other judges in the Western District."

"Ahh. I see. So we may not know if the recording is admissible or not."

"Correct."

"Well, I need to get with the Melanshins and talk this out. There's a bit of law here. Should the recording see the light of day in court or the examinations? But first I need to get to the bottom of my clients' failure to share this little scheme with me. Not saying that I expect all debtors to share everything with me. We all know that when it comes to 'the truth, the whole truth, and nothing but the truth,' debtors often struggle with that middle element. But on this one, I can't help them if they don't let me. Let's do this. I'm scheduled to talk with them this afternoon anyway. Let me have that conversation with the Melanshins, and then the three of us can resume this discussion. Okay?"

"That works for us, Jacob," 3J said. "We'll hold off on any further discussion on this matter with Clarke and the committee until we hear back from you. I'm not looking forward to the Clarke discussion and would prefer to have only one discussion on this topic. It would be best when I talk with him if I know the debtors' position on the recording."

When the call finished, it was lunchtime, and Pascale suggested he and 3J continue the discussion over lunch. They settled on Danny Edwards Blvd BBQ, one of 3J's favorites.

Danny, a local fixture, had been in the barbecue business since he was a kid, starting out working for his father, who opened his barbecue restaurant business in 1938. Originally downtown near the county courthouse, Danny's first joint was a tiny thumbprint of a restaurant on Grand Boulevard known as Lil' Jake's Eat It & Beat It, just behind the Greene Madison offices. A large pink pig statue stood outside the front door greeting diners. The patron line snaked outside, and once they made their way inside and ordered, they sat together and ate family style. Many were lawyers and judges on a lunch break from a trial. Each day, the crowd sat shoulder to shoulder and discussed the courtroom goings on without apparent concern that their table neighbors could hear most of what they were discussing. It was a favorite destination for the Greene Madison crowd.

When the city seized his Eat it & Beat It location under eminent domain powers to clear the way for the Sprint Center construction, Danny moved the restaurant to a much larger building in front of the freight train tracks on Southwest Boulevard south of the Crossroads District. Taking his pink pig, reputation, smoke, and secret rubs and recipes with him, his new locale offered much more dining space and privacy. And like he had done at Eat It & Beat It,

Danny greeted almost every diner who entered from behind the counter, offering his infectious smile and smoky aromas.

3J and Pascale arrived, greeted Danny, and ordered. Then they found a table and waited for the staff to call their number. 3J had ordered pulled pork topped with coleslaw and sauce, served on a toasted kaiser roll, while Pascale had ordered Danny's burnt ends sandwich, a Kansas City delicacy called an Old Smokey.

When the food arrived, they talked as they ate.

"Look, 3J. I've been thinking about what Rome reported to us. I'm concerned. When you examine Clarke, we should expect him to be belligerent. When you tell Clarke the committee isn't backing him, surely he'll be unhappy with the system he hates. But he'll also be unhappy with you, a Black female attorney, and with Jacob, a White Jewish attorney. Let's be truthful here. He already hates you and Steinert. Blacks and Jews—the root of all things evil in the world according to folks like Clarke and the subject of hate for centuries. Your conversation with him will cause that hate to bubble to the surface."

"I know, and I appreciate what you're concerned about. But I don't see alternatives to doing my job. And I expect Jacob will do his as well."

"Well, there are ways to do your job and then there are ways to do your job."

"Meaning?"

"Meaning a couple of things. First, we should let the firm's management know we're concerned and let them implement some security protocols so no one can get into the firm's halls unless they're cleared." Pascale paused.

"Who would you define as firm management for this issue, Pascale?"

"I'm thinking a very limited group. Only Bob Swanson to start with."

Swanson was the firm's managing partner in whom both 3J and Pascale had a great deal of trust.

"I'm okay with that, Bill. What else?"

"We should consider turning Rome loose on more dark web and clearnet forums. She can follow the chatter out there once you inform Clarke of his plight in these bankruptcy cases."

"Hmm. When you say 'turn her loose,' are you suggesting that we tell her she can do things she shouldn't be doing under the law?"

"Not exactly. I'm suggesting that we tell her to be more aggressive but warn her not to hack into anyone's computer in doing so."

"Yeah, we'd have to be pretty careful in that communication," 3J said skeptically.

"I'm going to suggest that I take care of Rome, 3J."

3J's eyes got wide and her eyebrows shot up on her forehead. "You mean to insulate me from whatever Rome ends up doing?"

"No, but you have enough on your plate without having to monitor Rome's activities. I'm suggesting that you can entrust Rome to me."

"I understand the sentiment and I appreciate the insulation, whether it's because my plate is already full or because you're implementing some plausible deniability scenario to protect me if things go south. Let me think on this and let you know in the morning. What else?"

"For the moment, that's it."

3J's attention lingered on Pascale's phrase, "for the moment." She wondered if he had other things to suggest they implement. As great as Kansas City's barbecue was, she knew that sometimes, real life took the pleasure right out of the hickory smoke.

That night, when she met Ronnie Steele for a late bite at The Belfry, 3J shared the whole story with Steele, explaining the case, Clarke, Quantrill, the raiders, The Thirty-Six Thirties, the recording, and Pascale's lunchtime suggestions.

In the background, Chef Tio's sound system played a Houston Person set of his signature saxophone soul jazz. Person's saxophone laid down a full-bodied, swinging style of jazz, marrying his rich tone with a rhythm and blues organ and beat. 3J always found his style passionate and soothing—and she needed soothing.

"Damn, 3J," Steele said when she finished. "And these are the cases you pitched for in your presentation a few Fridays ago?"

"Yep," she replied.

"And you wanted these cases? Why?"

She sighed, shook her head, and smiled. "Been asked that a lot lately. It's what us lawyers do. No different for us Black female lawyers. We need work so we pitch for business. It's the job. It's how I get paid."

."Well, I'm with Pascale on this one. His sentiment is a good one. This Clarke guy begs for a cautious approach to the 'job,' as you call it. You gotta be real careful with nutbags who have the capacity to act out."

3J nodded. "I'm worried for Jacob Steinert as well."

"I'd be worried too if I were him."

They both contemplated in silence. In the background, Person played "Detour Ahead" from his 1997 album, *Person-ified*. The music was perfect for thinking, and 3J wondered if the song was telling her something about the future of the Melanshin bankruptcy cases.

She and Steele finished dinner and headed out of Chef Tio's place for the walk north to downtown Kansas City and 3J's condo. They held hands as they walked but said nothing. That evening, the Melanshin developments seemed to interfere with any thoughts of romance.

Pascale had always told her the law life could give the love life a run for its money.

15

Friday, May 10, 2024

THE NEXT MORNING, 3J arrived before 8:00 and walked past Pascale's office expecting to see his door closed. Instead, his door was wide open. Once again, he sat with his back to his desk, hands clasped behind his head, looking out his north-facing windows to the Kansas City skyline beyond.

This time she stepped over his growing piles as she entered, removed papers from his club chair, and as he turned to face her, asked, "So what's up with this gazing-out-to-the-city-beyond thing you seem to have going on?"

Pascale smiled. "Oh, I don't know. Moments of quiet reflection are always a good thing if one doesn't abuse the opportunity to do so too often."

"And what are your moments telling you? Maybe a sabbatical rather than a retirement?"

"Oh . . . I don't think the moments are quite telling me that, 3J. No . . . not that."

"Then what, if you don't mind sharing?"

"Don't mind at all. Just some more reflections on the professional past. For me, a long career. I can reflect on that, and looking out the window is an easy way to enter the reflection zone." He paused and smiled wistfully. "But too much career reflection can be a bad thing. It can be all-consuming, and unless one is careful, it can completely occupy the present. I don't want that to happen. I need to leave room in the present so I can map out the future. Planning and dreaming. I seem to be in a delicate place right now. I'm making peace with my long career to make room in my life for what might come next."

"Ahh. I see. And your arrival here earlier than customary?"

"Gives me a chance to start to make room for the future without interruption from the inevitable present that is still the law firm life. Despite the changes in my life that may be coming, at least for the immediate future, I'm still under the law firm's spell."

"Good to know. I had a chance to think about the Melanshin case suggestions you've made so far, and I've talked with Ronnie about them as well. Hope that was okay?"

"Of course. I expect his input is invaluable."

"Where I've ended up is this: I'm okay with you talking to Bob Swanson so we have a little more security than usual. Let's keep the circle of management that knows about this as small as possible. I'm also okay with you talking with Rome and keeping me in that loop on a need-to-know basis. Let's make sure she knows the boundaries of what she can and can't do for us."

"Excellent. I'll take care of both today. I might also suggest that I call Jacob Steinert and have a discussion with him."

"I'm okay with that as well, Bill."

3J rose out of the chair and turned to head for her office. Midstride, she paused, looked back to Pascale, and said, "Look Bill. I'm worried that we may be trying to find a problem to fit the solutions you came up with."

Pascale nodded and said nothing.

3J sighed. "But I guess there's no good reason not to take some steps. Actual problem or not, better to be prudent."

Pascale nodded again. "Examinations are Monday, 3J. You ready and still up for it?"

"I'm ready, and it's my job to be up for it, so I am and I will be. You?"

"I'm ready. Should be another one for my memories file for sure."

Pascale set up a call with Rome and Moses, and later in the afternoon, they spoke. He explained the concerns he and 3J had about Woody Clarke's reactions to the events as they unfolded in the case and said they wanted Rome to monitor online chatter.

"Very well," Rome replied when he was done. "I suppose to be efficient, I could pretense my way into several chatting platforms where folks like Clarke exchange ideas, believing they are safe from the intrusion of people like me. I can create some profiles, use them to gain access to groups, and see what I can see."

"So no hacking?"

"I'm not proposing any hacking. If it becomes necessary, I'll come back to you for further authority."

"Rome, would this be on the dark web or the clearnet?"

"I anticipate it would be on both."

"Could someone trace the profile you create back to you and then, of course, to us?"

"There are certainly ways to try to match up an anonymous presence on the internet with the real human behind the curtain. You learned that in the recent jazz club bankruptcy cases. In those cases, the person posting left years of breadcrumbs that we could access with a team of sleuths. Those breadcrumbs were real, not the result of a recently created artificial person designed to mask an identity. Here, I would be careful to create several profiles that would leave no breadcrumbs. The profiles would contain enough details to support entry into different groups where like-minded right-wingers exchange ideas. Then we would hope for exchanges reporting what Clarke is doing."

Pascale listened silently as Rome spun out her suggested course of action. Her plan was legal and as sound as he could expect. It gave her the best chance to get in and get out of the chatrooms without anyone figuring out her true motive. He agreed to the plan, as did Moses.

When he hung up, Pascale spoke with the firm's managing partner, Bob Swanson, to fill him in and explain the need to take some precautionary measures to be on the safe side. The firm's security system already made it difficult for someone to walk or ride the elevator between floors. To change floors, one had to swipe a key card to enter the stairwells or elevator to walk or ride between floors. Only lawyers and staff had the key cards, so a visitor to the firm could access only the reception area on the twenty-ninth floor and could only move to other floors if escorted by someone with a key card.

The firm's security system went a long way to preventing a guest from traveling to floors where they didn't belong, but after hearing the overview of the Melanshin bankruptcy cases, Swanson shared Pascale's concerns and agreed that he should order more security. After considering options, he decided to place a plainclothes security guard in the reception area and another on the twenty-seventh floor where 3J and Pascale officed.

Satisfied with the beefed up security, Pascale thanked Swanson and returned to his desk to call Jacob Steinert. Pascale explained that he and 3J had concluded the committee would likely have to pick sides between Clarke and the Melanshins and revealed they would recommend to the committee that it was more advantageous to side with the Melanshins.

Steinert listened, and said only, "I see."

"When we make that recommendation to the committee, we foresee that several things are going to happen. First, the four members of the committee who are not members of The Thirty-Six Thirties will outvote Clarke and his two cohorts, accept the recommendation, and instruct us to proceed. Second, that will make the committee adverse to Clarke. We think he will then do everything in his power to thwart any of your reorganization efforts. And in doing so, he will adversely impact the prospect of payment to unsecured creditors. His likely conduct *may* disqualify him from serving any further on the committee."

Steinert continued to listen without interrupting and commenting.

"Last, we worry that Clarke may then act out. We've been gathering information on him, and he's bad news. We fear he's capable of doing bad things. If he does act out, it seems logical to assume his ire will turn to the Melanshins, 3J, and you. We worry that whatever he does will make the bricks through the window and the unauthorized recording of the Melanshins seem like minor infractions."

Pascale paused to give Steinert a chance to talk, but Steinert said nothing for several moments. "I appreciate you looping me in," he finally said. "Is this a heads-up call or is there something you want me to do, Bill?"

"Let me tell you what *we're* doing, and then we can figure out if there's something you might want to do."

"Certainly."

Pascale explained the new security measures Greene Madison was taking at the downtown offices and then presented an overview of Rome's plan.

"Bill, I'm just a solo practitioner," Steinert replied. "I don't have much in the way of security here. We have a key card we use to access the door to our office when we get off the elevator. But normally, that door is open during working hours. We use the same key card to access and ride the elevator after hours, but that's only activated after 6:00 p.m. I guess I could hire a security person to sit in my lobby, but I'll need to think a little bit on that idea. And for how many weeks or months would a security person have to sit there?"

Pascale said nothing, allowing Steinert to continue to contemplate the situation.

Steinert continued after a moment. "Your private investigator idea sounds interesting. Are you and 3J willing to share what the investigator learns?"

"Yes. We'll share."

"If the investigator turns up what I guess law enforcement calls 'credible threats,' I might consider hiring a security person."

"Understood. This is a very unusual situation. You don't see this kind of stuff too often in the bankruptcy world. 3J and I felt you should be aware of everything as we find out."

"I appreciate that, Bill. Y'know, some years ago I had a livestock rancher client for whom I filed a bankruptcy case. He was a little like Clarke in many respects. The client fired me after the judge signed an order granting the bank's request to repossess the collateral—cattle. It was my shortest engagement as debtor's counsel.

"The order required my client to cooperate in delivering the cattle to the bank. As he fired me, he decided that if he couldn't have the livestock, neither should the bank, and late one night, he opened up the gate to his fields and let the cattle escape. It sent the bank scurrying all over the county looking for the collateral. Some cattle had brands. Some didn't. Unbranded cattle were nearly impossible for the bank to identify. I guess that was the point of my former client's actions. The bank never recovered all the cattle and never got whole.

"The judge had the marshals pick up the former client and bring him into court for a contempt hearing for failing to cooperate with the bank as the judge had ordered. In the courtroom, the farmer had no lawyer because he had fired me and didn't want a replacement. I decided to come over to the courtroom to watch the hearing. What a shitshow. Representing himself, he screamed at the judge, and some of the stuff he yelled was crazy shit. Nonsensical stuff about the judge and bankruptcy and the law and the posse comitatus and county sheriffs and our country and yes, Jews. Presumably the judge and me.

"The judge found him in contempt. The marshals fitted him for an orange jumpsuit, took him away, and put him behind bars. He became known as the 'unafarmer' around the courthouse, a bad play on words. You know, Ted Kaczynski, the Unabomber. Kaczynski delivered his manifesto to the FBI in 1995, claiming to explain his motives.

"My former client screamed his own manifesto every time he appeared in court, so everyone knew who he was and what he thought. I remember one hearing where he appeared shackled and dressed in orange, flanked by U.S. Marshals. He pointed at the judge and yelled that he didn't acknowledge the judge's power or authority over him. Crazy stuff. Maybe he wrote it all down at some point and published it somewhere. Don't know. Don't want to know.

"Long story short, maybe the best thing that could happen here is that Clarke gets enough rope to go bonkers in court and Robertson has the marshals take him away."

Pascale smiled as Steinert recounted the story, legend around the Western District courthouse. He had heard it many times at one conference or another. But he never heard Steinert recount it. "I can see some similarities, Jacob. We need to be careful here. Let's see what the investigator turns up. Then we can decide if we have another unafarmer on our hands, this one, perhaps with a tendency towards violence."

After the call, Pascale went to 3J's office to explain his discussions with Swanson, Rome and Moses, and Steinert. They agreed that the situation was a mess, and Pascale agreed with 3J when she suggested she wait to give Clarke the bad news after the examinations.

"Let's see if Rome can turn up something," Pascale said. "She's good at turning over rocks, and this time, I have a feeling that all kinds of things will scurry out."

16

Saturday, May 11 through Sunday, May 12, 2024

SATURDAY MORNING, 3J sat at her desk finishing an outline of her examination of Clarke. Pascale was around the corner, cleaning. Both in on the weekend. Par for the course.

She thought that it might be difficult to focus and block out the distractions of Rome's investigation and Clarke's omnipresent personality, but she powered through. Then her desk phone rang. No caller ID. She knew she should let the call roll to voice mail, but she ignored that logic and raised the receiver to her ear against her better judgment. "Josephina Jones."

"I ain't heard nothing from you since I sent you the recording," Woody Clarke said without greeting.

"Well, Mr. Clarke, your envelope was a little short on explanation, don't you think?"

"Did you listen to the recording?"

"Yes. Indeed I did."

"And?"

"And what, Mr. Clarke?"

"Whata we gonna to do with the recording? Whata we gonna do about these goddamn Melanshins?"

3J sighed, regretting that she hadn't let the call roll to voice mail. "Mr. Clarke, I am not entirely sure anyone can use the recording in court or in the examination of Donnie Melanshin."

"Jesus! Why the hell not?" Clarke yelled.

"Something called the marital privilege. Often, communications between a husband and wife are off-limits in court like communications between lawyers and their clients."

"Goddamn it! If that don't beat all."

"In my view, the Melanshins will have to consent for me to be able to use the recording."

"Well, they ain't gonna consent. They ain't crazy. What a fuckin' system we got here. The bad guys get off on a technicality, and all because they're married and you're telling me you cain't use my recording."

3J noted that Clarke called the thumb drive "my recording." She decided it was time to give Clarke the honest truth. No point waiting until after the examination. As Pascale and she had discussed, she explained that the recording was obtained illegally, it was subject to a marital privilege, and that it was generally in the interest of the unsecured creditors for the Melanshins to own the land formally held by Clarke and try to pay Clarke differently than the other unsecured creditors. To that end, she explained, her recommendation to the committee would be to support the Melanshins' reorganization efforts, even if that meant the committee would end up adverse to Clarke. Clarke listened without comment.

When 3J finished, she could hear Clarke breathing, but he said nothing. Then Clarke hissed, "You colored bitch! You have no idea who you're fuckin' with here. This ain't no game. You got hired to get me paid. Now you think you and that damn committee are gonna fight me? And you're gonna fight me alongside Donavan Isik goddamn Melanshin? Well, you listen here. Gloves off, Jones. You're in the ring with me now, and you need to make sure you keep your hands up or you're likely to get hurt, if you know what I mean."

"Mr. Clarke, I don't take kindly to threats. You need to resign from the committee."

"I ain't firing you and I ain't done with you."

"Mr. Clarke, you can't fire me. Only the committee can. It would be best if you resign from the committee and find a lawyer to carry out your wishes . . . or at least some of them. If you don't resign, I'll have to seek authority from the committee to have you removed."

"Listen, sister," Clarke hissed, "don't tell me what I can and cain't do. No woman tells me what to do, 'specially no colored woman with an attitude!"

Trying to maintain her composure, 3J countered, "Mr. Clarke. This call is not productive. I'll see you at the courthouse first thing Monday morning."

As 3J began to say the word "Monday," Clarke slammed the receiver down and ended the call.

3J's hands were trembling, and as she placed her receiver in its cradle, she struggled to maintain her composure. The last thing she wanted was for anyone in the firm, Pascale included, to see her in an uncomposed state. While she momentarily thought she wouldn't report the call to Pascale, she quickly decided she had to. He needed to know the up-to-the-minute news, and the call was certainly the lead story.

He was concerned enough to direct her to not go to the garage alone. Her visceral response to the order must have been obvious because he immediately softened the order to a suggestion. She agreed to let him walk her to her car when she was ready to leave and beyond that, she wanted to take it one day at a time.

Later in the day, Pascale emailed Rome, asking if she could talk. In seconds, Pascale's mobile phone rang.

"Rome, can you give me an update please?"

"Certainly, Mr. Pascale. I am making progress. I have created several online profiles and taken steps to add credibility."

"What does that mean, Rome?"

"I would describe it as digital backfill. I have some associates in the digital world who have helped me create it. If someone background checks the personalities, they will find information I've created to support each personality's legitimacy. I don't have the capacity to create digital backfill to the degree of an MI-5 or FBI, but it will survive a modest investigation."

"I see," Pascale said slowly.

"With those personalities in place, I have joined a select number of groups, and I am monitoring the chatter."

"Anything so far?"

"Minimal chatter until this afternoon when all of a sudden, The Thirty-Six Thirties' chatter picked up dramatically."

"In what way?"

"Someone with the handle A Quantrill Raider began posting some serious vitriol about Black women, although you might imagine, AQR, as I'll call the person, did not refer to that segment of the human race as either Blacks or women. AQR's posts are prolific. Every half hour or so, there is a new post."

"Apart from ranting about Black women, are you able to glean any patterns so far?"

"Indeed. I can see a pattern forming. AQR has moved from general vitriol to a specific call to form a posse of raiders, as AQR calls them."

"A posse? Jesus. Like Marshal Dillon in Gunsmoke? For what purpose?"

"So far, AQR is circumspect. I have a bot researching the net for past AQR posts. Often, as we learned in the Rapinoe cases last year, some posters are lax in maintaining their own anonymity, and they repeatedly use the same handle. My sense from what I am seeing so far is that AQR is fond, even proud, of historical references. The posts contain some historical references to William Clarke Quantrill's Civil War cleansing campaign in which he and his raiders attempted to rid the Kansas border towns of Blacks and free state sympathizers."

The revelation shocked Pascale. "My god, Rome. This stuff is just chilling. Right here in this day and age."

"I am afraid that after one has read the posts in the far right chatrooms, the phrase 'this day and age' serves little purpose. For many of the posters, it means the day and age that existed prior to the Civil War. I suppose they would say that was their heyday, if you will."

Pascale said nothing for a few moments as he started to absorb what Rome said. Then he said slowly, "Rome, I need to have a discussion with only you. Not 3J. Not Moses. Not anyone but you and me. Can we agree to that?"

"I understand, Mr. Pascale. Proceed."

"It's more than obvious to me that AQR is Woody Clarke. The difficulty will be to learn what he's up to in time to stop him from doing whatever he intends to do. We aren't going to have a great deal of time. So in addition to your bot and your fictional personalities, what else might stop Clarke and his raiders."

"Mr. Pascale, are you asking me if there is a technological way, perhaps not entirely compliant with laws, to link Mr. Clarke with AQR and then find out what he plans?"

Pascale said nothing as he wondered if he would really go to the dark side. "Rome, I would like to understand if there is a way, and if so, what that might be. Then the two of us will decide if that's what I'm asking you to do."

"To start with, I would be looking for something that would get us access to Mr. Clarke's tech. His computer. It would be helpful to gather a bit of computer intelligence on Mr. Clarke. I wonder if you could reach out to Donnie and Lil Melanshin and gather some information for me."

"If I did reach out to the Melanshins, what would I ask them?"

"The question I have in mind is this: Does Woody Clarke game on the internet? If so, it could provide me a way to infiltrate his computer. Once in, I could review his texts and emails and perhaps, with some luck, we would learn what he is planning."

Pascale listened quietly. What Rome was saying was simultaneously what he hoped to hear and what he dreaded hearing. But the dread faded quickly. He was fast coming to the conclusion that he needed to do something to try to head off a huge problem for 3J he saw approaching on the horizon. In so many respects, she was the most important thing in his world. He'd lost his wife and daughter in a car wreck, and he couldn't bear the thought that something could happen to 3J if he could have done something to prevent it but didn't.

"Gaming? Really?"

"Yes. Gaming. There are more than two-and-a-half billion gamers worldwide. Sixty percent of Americans play games daily. Twenty-six percent of them are over thirty-five years old. During the pandemic, the numbers skyrocketed. We were all in lockdown. Gaming connected people online when they couldn't connect in person. It was and is very popular in rural America, and it is surprising to those who have never gamed to learn how prevalent it is. Clarke is divorced and lives alone, so it may be that he is one of the legions of people who game."

"Okay. I understand. I'm not sure if the Melanshins will know whether Clarke games, but it's a small town so maybe they will. Can't hurt to ask. But you talked about infiltrating his computer through gaming. How?"

"There are some options. One would be to goad Clarke into playing a new, unreleased war game against me. To do so, he would have to download a plug-in for his web browser. A plug-in I altered. That plug-in would release malware onto his computer hard drive without him knowing it. With the malware in place, I could read his communications, whether email, text, or online."

"Over my pay grade I'm afraid."

"Let's just say that if I can get him to add the plug-in, I can use it to access Mr. Clarke's computer . . . if you choose to go down this path."

Pascale took a deep breath and let the air out slowly. "Okay. I see. I need to think on this. I'll be back to you very shortly, Rome. Thank you."

That evening, Pascale sat cross-legged on the floor of his bedroom, his back against the foot of his bed with his Martin acoustic guitar resting on his legs. He absentmindedly played the guitar as he thought. His "girlfriend," the Martin, was such a good listener and always there for him. When he finished his call with Rome and left the office for the day, he'd wondered if he would agonize over the decision to allow Rome to cross the line. He surprised himself because there had been no internal debate and no agonizing over the decision. In this limited situation, he decided that whatever it took was not only the right thing to do but the only thing to do.

He finished his chord progression—Cmaj7, C7, Dm, D#dim7, Cmaj7, Dm, Fdim7, Cmaj7, G aug, Cmaj7, which were the beginnings of a song he'd been working on—and softly strummed the chords over and over. Sometimes the words came first. Sometimes the music. Sometimes they seemed to come at the same time. This time, it was the music first. That was good because the music helped him focus. Playing the chords would lead to the words. It always did.

As he played, he drifted and pondered. After fifteen minutes, he stood, gently laid the guitar on his bed, retrieved his mobile phone from his night table, and phoned Jacob Steinert. It was 10:00 p.m. on a Saturday. Normally, Pascale wouldn't consider phoning Steinert at such an hour on the weekend, but nothing about what lay ahead was going to fit into the normal category. Steinert answered on the third ring.

Fortunately, Jacob Steinert took the Saturday evening call in stride, so Pascale quickly got down to business, not wanting to interupt his peer's evening more than necessary but knowing the call really was necessary.

"I need to ask you to find out something from the Melanshins. It's going to sound a little wacky, but it's important. And I need you to be willing to ask them without also asking me why I need to know."

"Hmm. Not a typical lead-in to a request from counsel in one of my cases," Steinert replied. "Unusual, but I'm intrigued. I'm listening."

"I need to know from the Melanshins if Woody Clarke is a gamer."

"A what?"

"Y'know. Someone who plays games on the internet, on one website portal or another."

"I must admit, Bill, I didn't expect that, let alone at ten on a Saturday night. And this is the point where I'm not supposed to ask why in heaven's name you want to know that?"

Pascale remained silent to give Steinert an opportunity to consider the request.

"Sure. What the heck. I'll ask them and get back to you shortly."

"Thanks, Jacob."

The call ended and Pascale returned to the floor, his girlfriend's rosewood fretboard, and his chord progression. He wouldn't have long to wait for Steinert's response. An hour later, Steinert called him back.

"Bill, turns out, Donnie Melanshin called me shortly after you and I finished our call. He had a quick bankruptcy question. You know the drill. Connectivity 24/7 these days. And he's the client, so I took the call. We talked and I answered his question. Then, since I had him on the phone, I posed your question to him. Much to my surprise, he told me that Clarke fills his evenings with several gaming sites he likes to frequent. When I asked Melanshin how he could possibly know this, he replied that it was common knowledge in Meadowfield. Small town. Clarke boasts about his gaming prowess. Everyone knows almost everything about everybody, I guess.

"One site Clarke likes to visit runs some kind of role-playing war game where Clarke can select which war to fight in. He can choose from past historical wars and future science fiction wars. He can also fight with other players who visit the site. Multiplayer RPG. The online warriors can communicate in a chatroom. Clarke likes to talk about his gaming conquests, almost like a gambler likes to brag about his successes at the craps table. I can text you the name of the sites he frequents and the games he likes to play."

"Yes, please do. And thanks for this, Jacob. You don't know how grateful I am for the information and for your willingness not to ask why I wanted to know."

"No 'why' question at this point. But if this leads to something that's going to come up in the bankruptcy cases, I sure would appreciate a heads-up and a preview."

"Absolutely, Jacob. Thank you. See you at the courthouse Monday morning."

By then it was midnight in Kansas City. Pascale calculated that it was early morning in London and decided to phone Rome, hoping she was awake. Rome answered and took the gaming information from Pascale. She had no questions.

Pascale paused before saying anything else to Rome. He had finished pondering when he called Steinert. His Martin girlfriend had helped him make his decision. But now he paused to give himself one more clear chance to back away from what Rome might do if he turned her loose. He was ready. No backing away. He had to try to protect 3J.

"Rome, do it," he said.

Rome had an extensive network of techies worldwide. Within the network, her reputation, developed in college and extended working for Moses, was legendary. It was a close-knit group. Most had never met each other in person but described their interactions on the internet as "meeting in person" and their communications by chatroom, texts, and apps as "talking."

One man in her network was developing a new war game, a web-based game rather than one to be downloaded to a gamer's hard drive. To enhance the online browser experience, he developed a small proprietary extension for a gamer to download and install as a browser plug-in. His upcoming release had gained a great deal of positive press. Gamers filled the internet with information about the game and him. Only two weeks ago, he'd announced its long awaited name, *Ruckus*.

One element was a high resolution, virtual reality where the gamers could fight in different Civil War battles. One was the famous Kansas City Battle of Westport, often referred to as the Gettysburg of the West, the largest Civil War battle west of the Mississippi.

Rome well knew that plug-ins could be a privacy nightmare. And she understood that most computer owners used plug-ins without knowing they could turn out to be malware and without taking sufficient care to guard against that. With her friend's permission, Rome had taken the plug-in beta and added code to it. She assured her friend that she would push the altered plug-in only to Clarke. If she could get Clarke interested in testing the game, he would have to download the altered plug-in, and through it, she could drop malware into his computer without him knowing.

That malware would allow her to read his emails remotely as it logged and transmitted his activity. It would also expose his chatroom passwords to access his posts and reveal if he was AQR. When she finished her mission, she would push out an update to the plug-in, deleting the malware. If it worked, Clarke would never know what she had done. To whet Clarke's appetite, Rome crafted a teaser to get him to play *Ruckus*: "AQR, I hereby challenge you to a duel on the newest war gaming site, *Ruckus*. The website is in its final stages of development and testing. It's not open to the general public at this time. Test it with me. Let's see if you're as good as they say you are. Click here and let's get it on. Alexander Frank James."

Rome's research of Quantrill's Raiders revealed that one of the Civil War gang members was Alexander Frank James, infamous brother of the even more infamous Missouri bank robber and outlaw, Jesse James. She hoped the reference to Frank James would pique Clarke's interest, given his obsession with Quantrill's Raiders. She also hoped that the challenge to fight on a not-yet-public gaming site would appeal both to his expected desire to play on cutting-edge websites and to his braggadocio.

Rome had created an online profile for Alexander Frank James, or AFJ as she called him. With the help of her cohorts, they back-filled data about AFJ to provide cover if Clarke investigated, as she expected he would. She hoped Clarke *would* research *Ruckus* and conclude it was legitimate. After all, other than the Rome-altered plug-in, it was.

She had to move quickly. She hoped for an AQR versus AFJ matchup. And soon. She feared that any delay could mean physical harm to 3J and others, and she had no interest in facilitating harm to anyone by failing in her mission.

17

Monday, May 13, 2024

E XAMINATION DAY. 3J and Pascale made their way to the courthouse for a day of testimony from Donnie Melanshin and Woody Clarke.

At 8:00 a.m., they entered the large main floor of the Charles Evans Whittaker Courthouse, a six hundred thousand-square-foot, crescent-shaped federal building. Named for the only United States Supreme Court justice to hail from Kansas City, Missouri, it was an impressive structure. Pascale silently reflected as he entered that the building was a grand place to practice law.

The two lawyers greeted the three U.S. Marshals who worked for the Marshals Service Judicial Security Division at the security station. They emptied the contents of their pockets into a tray, showed their Missouri driver licenses for identification, and placed their briefcases and the trays on the conveyor belt that ran the items through an X-ray machine for the marshals to inspect the contents. As the trays made their way through the X-ray machine, they each stepped through the metal detector that constituted the entryway to the staircase and elevator banks. On the other side of the metal detector, they retrieved their belongings. All this was standard procedure at federal courthouses throughout the country.

They headed for the staircase and the walk up to a second-floor conference room provided to them by the marshals for the examinations. As they headed for the staircase, they noticed a fourth marshal standing near the security station watching them: Sal Viglione.

Before they got more than four steps up the staircase, Woody Clarke arrived and silently approached the security station. 3J and Pascale paused on the stairs and turned to watch and listen. The marshal told Clarke to empty his pockets into the tray and Clarke deposited a pack of cigarettes and his wallet. Clarke showed them his Kansas driver's license. As Clarke was about to step through the metal detector, a smileless Viglione approached the machine and blocked Clarke's passage.

In a deep, authoritative voice, he said, "Why, Mr. Woody Clarke. It *is* you. I heard you were coming here today, but I needed to see it with my own two eyes. Remember me? Long time no see. I hear you're at the courthouse today to be examined under oath. Are you going to be a good boy today and on your best behavior, or are we going to have to reprise the little courtroom interaction we had with you some years ago?"

"I remember you. I ain't gonna talk to you," Clarke replied harshly.

"Ahh, but you just did, Mr. Clarke. You just did and you will."

"Look. I got me an order says I gotta go upstairs and testify. You're in my way. You gonna get out of my way so I can comply with the order, or am I gonna have to tell the judge that you're the reason I had to violate it?"

"Remain calm, Mr. Clarke. Do us a favor now and step through the detector," Viglione said as he moved several steps back from the metal detector on its secure side.

As Clarke stepped through, the metal detector sounded an alarm, indicating that he had something on his person that he'd failed to place in the tray.

Viglione moved back toward Clarke, who smiled at the marshal. "This is not a game, Mr. Clarke. Step back through the machine, sir, and like the good man said to you in the first instance, empty *everything* out of your pockets. I'm only going to say that to you once."

Clarke retraced his steps, reached into his pockets and removed a metal cigarette lighter. He smiled broadly, held up the lighter with two fingers for all to see, and said, "Why, I must've overlooked this, boys. A cigarette lighter. Nothin' else. You can cancel your red alert." He placed the lighter in a new tray and walked through the metal detector without setting it off.

As Clarke passed through the metal detector the second time without incident, one of the marshals reached for his portable metal detector wand and said, "Please step over here, sir," pointing to an area next to the end of the conveyor belt.

"Why?"

"Sir, step over here," the marshal said, repeating himself and ignoring Clarke's question.

Viglione walked over to Clarke. "Additional screening, Woody. Random spot check. Step over there and let this good man wave that wand over your body. That is, if you want to go upstairs."

"Why me? You ain't singling me out now, are you? That would violate my rights, and you wouldn't wanna get caught doing that in a federal courthouse, now would ya?"

Viglione smiled and shook his head. "No one's violating anyone's rights. Anyone who walks into this place agrees to be scanned. Some we wand to make sure the machine got it right. Some we frisk. Some we don't. That's why it's called 'random.'" Continuing to smile, Viglione added, shaking his head, "Y'know, sometimes, it's just your time and your turn."

Clarke narrowed his eyes and his body tensed as he stared at Viglione. Then he relaxed his body, shrugged his shoulders, and walked toward the marshal waiting with the wand. Once there, he raised his arms straight out from each side of his body while the marshal moved the wand up and down and from side to side across Clarke.

"You're clean," the marshall said. "You can retrieve your belongings and go upstairs."

As Clarke made his way to the elevators, 3J and Pascale turned to continue up the steps. Pascale shook his head. "What the hell was that all about? It's going to be one of those days."

The lawyers arrived at the examination room and saw that the court reporter had completed setting up her dictation machine. An oval table filled the room. At one end sat the court reporter. By agreement with Steinert, first up would be Pascale's examination of Donnie Melanshin. Pascale and 3J sat at the reporter's end of the table facing the chairs where Melanshin and Steinert would sit.

Pascale looked at his notes as Melanshin and Steinert arrived and took seats opposite him. Clarke arrived last and sat at the end of the table opposite from the court reporter and as far from Melanshin and the lawyers as the room would allow. Since the lawyers were not taking the examination in conjunction with an ongoing lawsuit, they permitted Clarke to be present during Melanshin's testimony. Pascale figured it would be one less thing to argue about with him.

The court reporter administered the oath and Pascale started the questioning with the usual background inquiries to identify Melanshin for the written record. As of that moment, he and 3J were still uncertain if Melanshin would consent to the use of the recording. Their uncertainty would quickly end.

"Mr. Melanshin, I have here what I've marked as Exhibits A and B. 'A' is a thumb drive my colleague received in the mail from Woody Clarke with an audio file on it and 'B' is our firm's transcription of the audio file. Are you familiar with these exhibits?"

"I am."

"Are you prepared and willing to talk about the matters contained in the recording today?"

"I'll talk to you about them. Lil and me, we have nothing to hide."

Drama averted. No marital privilege to deal with.

"Lil is your wife?"

"Correct."

"Have you listened to the recording?"

"I have."

"Does the recording accurately reflect what the two of you discussed?"

"It does."

"Where were you and Ms. Melanshin when you talked?"

"At our kitchen table."

"Do you know who recorded you?"

"I don't for certain but I suspect that Woody Clarke made the recording without our permission. Rumor at the coffee shop in town is that he's bragged to some folks about making the recording, but I don't know how he did it. Woody doesn't do too many things that he doesn't brag about. Something about a website named Reveal."

"Do you know how Mr. Clarke made the recording?"

"I don't."

Pascale then took Melanshin through the entire recording and in doing so, made a record of the Melanshins' plan to buy the Clarke land under a contract for deed and the need to file for bankruptcy protection.

"Have you formulated a bankruptcy plan yet, Mr. Melanshin?"

"Thinking about selling the land we bought and using it to pay back creditors. No decisions yet, though. Rest assured, it's in process with our lawyer."

"Have you decided if you are going to pay Mr. Clarke back in full?"

"Not yet, but not likely. We want to pay back all of our other creditors, and I don't think we can afford to do both."

Clarke leaned forward in his chair as Donnie explained the treatment he would get under the plan.

"Have you and Ms. Melanshin thought about whether treating Mr. Clarke differently would amount to unfair discrimination under the Bankruptcy Code?"

Before Melanshin could answer the question, Jacob Steinert interceded. "Counsel, I do not believe Mr. Melanshin can answer that question without revealing communications that are subject to the attorney-client privilege. So I object to the question and I advise my client to assert the privilege and decline to answer that question."

While Steinert spoke, Melanshin calmly looked down to his folded hands, which rested on the table. And as Steinert spoke, Clarke became visibly agitated. From the look on his face, 3J thought he would have an outburst. But perhaps recalling what Viglione had said to him in the courthouse lobby, Clarke slowly leaned back in his chair and folded his arms across his chest. A passive look came over his face.

When Steinert finished making his objection, Melanshin looked up at Pascale and then over to Clarke. As he held eye contact with Clarke, he said calmly, "I assert the attorney-client privilege and decline to answer."

As he finished, he looked back to Pascale, who said, "Very well. I understand."

Pascale then took Melanshin through his various financial documents and questioned him about expenses and cash flow. Basing his question on Moses Aaronson's analysis, he said, "Mr. Melanshin, your tenant Bill Pearson, pays you one hundred ten dollars per acre, correct?"

"Yes."

Pascale showed Melanshin his most recent income statement. "On your income statement, you accrue rent amounting to one hundred ten dollars per acre. Do you see that line?"

"Yes."

"So on an accrual basis, you are reporting 23,467 dollars per month of rental income from Mr. Pearson?"

"Sounds about right."

Next, Pascale showed Melanshin his tax returns. "But on your tax returns, you report receipt of cash from Pearson amounting to only eighty-two dollars and fifty cents per acre, not one hundred ten dollars. Correct?"

"Correct."

"On a cash basis, you are reporting receipt of seventeen thousand six hundred dollars per month. Correct?"

"Again, sounds about right."

"That's a difference of 5,867 dollars per month and over seventy thousand dollars per year. Correct?"

"If that's your math, I'll trust it's correct."

"An aggregate discrepancy of well over two hundred thousand dollars, since you and Ms. Melanshin signed the contract for deed with Mr. Clarke?"

"Well over two hundred thousand dollars," Melanshin replied, agreeing with Pascale.

"Can you explain that discrepancy?"

"Like me and Lil talked about in the kitchen, some years ago, we transferred a quarter of the land we bought from Woody Clarke to our son, Robert. So a quarter of the rent is his. Pearson sends Robert a check for a quarter of the rent each month and a check for the rest of the rent to me and Lil."

"Is that set out in the lease?"

"No."

"Why not?"

"Didn't seem important to be in the document. Me, Lil, Robert, and Pearson know what the deal is."

"Did Robert pay you for his one-quarter interest?"

"No."

"Why did you transfer the land to Robert?"

Melanshin looked down at the tabletop, closed his eyes, paused, and took a deep breath. Slowly, he opened his eyes and looked up at Pascale. "This part ain't on that thumb drive recording, Mr. Pascale. Not too many years ago, we had two kids: Robert and our youngest, Toby. Toby was a good boy. But someone sold him black tar heroin, and Lil found him dead in his bedroom with a needle still in his arm and a chunk of the heroin still sitting on the night table. The coroner told us that someone laced the heroin with synthetic fentanyl. Not a day goes by that we don't remember Toby and grieve. When something like that happens to your kid, why, you take stock of what you had and what you have left. We had our oldest boy left. That was it. We decided that we shouldn't wait until we were near dead to start to share things with him. So we decided to give Robert part of the land we leased to Pearson."

The story and the way he delivered it to Pascale came across as sincere and highly credible. "How did your son, Toby, get the heroin?" Pascale asked.

Melanshin unfolded his hands and rested them, palms down and fingers spread on the table, before answering. "So that's the thing. Mr. Clarke over there has a son older than my boys and that son of his sells drugs at the high school. Mr. Clarke knows about it and facilitates his son's little business. Me and Lil think that Mr. Clarke takes half the drug money his son brings in. So we think Mr. Clarke over there killed our son, Toby."

Both times Melanshin said "Mr. Clarke over there," he tilted his head in Clarke's direction but didn't look over at the man. He maintained constant eye contact with Pascale, and the pain and anger in his eyes were obvious.

As Melanshin finished speaking, Clarke stood up, pounded both hands on the table and yelled, "That's a goddamn lie! Donavan Isik Melanshin, you ain't got no proof to back that up. None at all!"

Pascale stood and said forcefully to Clarke, "The witness is testifying. It's an examination, not a court hearing. He can tell me his thoughts and beliefs. The court's order directs you to cooperate and act appropriately. This outburst is neither. You, sir, will either sit down and remain quiet until it is your turn to testify or we will not hesitate to have the marshals remove you and perhaps take you into custody. Up to you, Mr. Clarke, but we can always take your examination through cell bars. Do you understand?"

Clarke said nothing, waved his hand at Pascale in disdainful disagreement, and sat down.

Pascale then returned to questioning Melanshin. "Do you have any evidence about the source of the heroin, Mr. Melanshin?"

"Don't need none. Everyone in Meadowfield knows that Junior—that's what they call Clarke's kid around town—sells drugs at the high school from the back of his pickup. Ain't nothing anyone can do about it. But they all know about it."

Pascale finished his questioning of Melanshin, who left to return to Meadowfield. Without taking a break, Clarke took the seat vacated by Melanshin, Pascale and 3J moved two seats over, and Steinert took Pascale's seat.

The court reporter asked Clarke if he swore to tell the truth, and with his raised right hand, he answered, "Of course," his voice dripping with sarcasm.

As soon as Clarke lowered his hand and directed his gaze across the table, Steinert asked, "Why don't you tell us how you managed to listen in on my clients' private kitchen table conversation."

Clarke smiled. "IoTs," Clarke said proudly.

"Say again, sir?"

"IoTs. Internet of things. Complete with microphones and operating systems. A search on Reveal and I was in and listening, I believe through their older smart coffee machine, if I recall correctly."

"You know that is a crime, right?"

"No more of a crime than what those two clients of yours did to me. All premeditated. Kind of fits the mold for how your people operate. Take things from others. Collect your wealth on the sweat of the rest of us. You're the expert in that. Maybe you put them up to the plan to screw me."

"My people, eh? What people would that be?"

"I heard you people call yourselves the chosen people. You run everything from behind the scenes. You're hard at work populating this country with coloreds and immigrants and running us White Christians out. That's the plan, ain't it?"

Ignoring Clarke's question, Steinert asked, "So is it your testimony that because I am Jewish, I came up with a plan to have you sell your land to Donnie and Lil Melanshin?"

"Exactly. Wouldn't surprise me."

"Do you also believe I told the Melanshins you would not do what any normal businessman would do and get advice from a lawyer before signing the contract for deed?"

"Is that a question, counselor?" Clarke asked, smiling.

"It was, but we can skip past the need to have you answer that one."

"How much did the Melanshins agree to pay you over time for your land?"

"Four point four million."

"Could they afford that?"

"They could and they did afford it for a few years. So yes, indeed. Then they decided to live large and screw me in the process. Still can afford it. That's my belief. They just choose not to pay me."

"Mr. Clarke, does Mr. Melanshin need to keep doing business with you in order for him to stay in the real estate business?"

"Apparently not. Pretty clear to me that he wants nothing to do with me no more. I don't need to have nothing to do with him neither as soon as he pays me back."

"You run a large hog operation. Is that correct?"

"Yep."

"Do you need to do business with Mr. Melanshin to continue to run your hog operation?"

"No, and like I said, I don't want to do no more business with Donnie. Lil neither. Just want my money for my land."

"So you envision no further business deals with Mr. Melanshin?"

"Damn straight."

"Did you look over the creditor list in the Melanshins' bankruptcy papers?"

"I sure did."

"Are you the only creditor he was buying land from before the bankruptcy filings?"

"I don't believe so. But I'm the only one he plotted to screw. The recording is how I know this was all a setup to get my land. I'm the only one getting screwed here." Clarke began to get angry, and as he did, his voice began to quaver.

"Mr. Clarke, someone in Meadowfield reported to me that you said if Donnie and Lil didn't pay you back and quickly, you couldn't be responsible for what might happen next. Do you remember saying that?"

"Maybe I did. What of it?"

"What did you mean?"

"Look. I ain't gonna keep cooperating with you if you keep asking me stuff that doesn't matter."

"You don't think a threat is something that matters?"

"Wasn't a threat. I'm stating a fact."

"What fact was that?"

"You ain't taken over this country yet. I still got my rights."

"To what rights are you referring?"

"Why, a right to enforce the law."

"What law would you be looking to enforce?"

"The law of the land. The pay me the fuck back what you owe me law."

As Clarke dueled with Steinert, 3J and Pascale stared at him.

Clarke sounded crazy and dangerous. A terrible combination. 3J wondered what Clarke was going to be like when she, a Black woman who had already tangled with Clarke on the phone, took her turn to question him.

Steinert announced that he had only a few more questions but wanted to take a short break before finishing up. The three lawyers stepped outside the room to stretch and compare notes.

"I was looking for ammunition that would support treating Clarke's claim differently than other unsecured creditors," Steinert said. "Something the judge could hang his hat on in ruling that we didn't unfairly discriminate against him. I think I've got all I'm going to get from him on that score. He's a different kind of creditor than the others. Neither Clarke nor the Melanshins need each other going forward. No business to conduct with each other. Do you think that's enough?"

"Not sure," 3J replied. "But couple that with the fact that Clarke is a bad actor and made an illicit recording of the debtors and maybe we have enough for your clients to pay him a lot less over a long period while paying the rest of the unsecureds quicker and in full. That could form the basis for an agreement with the committee."

Pascale jumped in. "This guy is completely bad news. We're going to have to hope Robertson will let the debtors treat him differently. Otherwise, he's owed a lot of money, and I'm not sure how the Melanshins can swing the repayment of such a large debt."

As they finished up the break, Sal Viglione walked past them and asked, "Everything okay in there, folks?"

"Well, it's different, that's for sure," 3J replied. "But other than some snarky comments and loud talking, so far, it's fine, Marshal."

"Good to hear. You know where we are if you need us."

Once back in the conference room, Steinert finished up quickly, ending by saying, "No further questions."

As he uttered the words, Clarke rose and began to leave. With his back to 3J, he said loudly, "You folks have a nice talk with that marshal fella, eh?"

As he neared the door, 3J replied, "Mr. Clarke. You cannot leave yet. I have questions I need to ask you as well."

Clarke wheeled around. "What the hell you talking about? You're *my* lawyer!" Clarke yelled.

"For the last time, Mr. Clarke, you well know I am not your lawyer. I am the committee's lawyer. Now, please sit down, and let's get to the questions. The sooner we get your answers on the record, the sooner this will be over for you and us."

"I'll give you fifteen minutes and then I'm out of here!" Clarke whispered hoarsely.

3J ignored his comment.

He retook his chair and 3J sat opposite him.

"I remind you, sir, that you are still under oath and sworn to tell the truth," 3J said.

Clarke said nothing.

"Mr. Clarke, why did you send me the thumb drive?"

"I want you to use it against Melanshin and get him to pay me back. Jesus, woman. You heard what he said. He ain't gonna pay me back in full and he's gonna sell *my* land to pay everyone else back in full. If that ain't the biggest screwing in the history of the planet, then I don't know what is."

"Mr. Clarke, wouldn't it be in the interest of the many other creditors in these bankruptcy cases for Mr. Melanshin to sell the Pearson land and pay them back in full?"

"It ain't the goddamn Pearson land. It's *my* land. The Clarke land!" Clarke barked as he slapped his left hand on the table. "I cain't believe you're gonna side with these folks here and sell *my* land to pay *his* creditors."

"Whatever name you wish to give to the land will be fine, but you need to answer the question, Mr. Clarke."

"I ain't gonna answer that question. I shoulda known a colored gal like you cain't understand what's going on here."

"Help me understand, Mr. Clarke. To use your words, what *is* going on here?"

"I'll tell you what's going on here. I got me a colored gal and a Jew conspiring to take away my land and use it to pay everyone else—a Fourteenth Amendment citizen and a commie Jew that don't belong here." He pointed to Steinert and shook his head in disgust. "That's the way of the world these days, at least if folks like you and him get their way."

"Your business mistake plays no part in where you find yourself today, Mr. Clarke?" she asked.

"My only mistake was not seeing these Melanshins for what they are: thieves, plain and simple."

"Mr. Clarke, did your son, Wallace, sell heroin to Toby Melanshin?"

"I ain't gonna answer that question. It's got nothing to do with these bankruptcy cases."

"So you are refusing to answer that question."

"I told you what I'm not gonna do. You heard me."

"Mr. Clarke, what is the mission of The Thirty-Six Thirties."

Clarke paused before answering the question. Then he smiled a thin, evil smile, and said, "Why, it's just a group of like-minded folks that meet and talk. Private conversations. None of your damn business and none of the business of that Jew lawyer over there neither. No mission."

"Did you form the group?"

"I did."

"Are you the head of the group?"

"I am."

"Did the group talk about ways to make the Melanshins pay you back?"

"I ain't gonna tell you what the boys and me discussed. Private.

Kinda like the attorney-client privilege, I reckon," Clarke said, smiling.

"Would the court reporter please mark the parts of the transcript in which Mr. Clarke has declined to answer a question so the Court can easily review it when we ask for an order directing Mr. Clarke to come back and answer."

"An order? What a bunch of shit!" Clarke said loudly. "You know that Pledge of Allegiance? In your world, it's liberty and justice for some, but not for all. Not for me. We're done here. Never shoulda had the committee hire a colored bitch like you!"

Clarke rose, turned, and left the room and the courthouse.

Examination day over.

3J shook her head in disbelief. For the record, she said, "It is 11:53 a.m., and Mr. Clarke has left the examination before I have finished questioning him. We will hold the completion of the examination open until the Court directs next steps."

As she gathered her papers, she said, "I knew this was going to be a tough day. I knew Woody Clarke was going to be like no other witness I've bumped into before. But he exceeded all expectations. And now he's gone."

As everyone left the conference room, Steinert added softly so only 3J could hear him, "Well, you and me certainly didn't win over any right-wing converts today, now did we?"

18

Woody Clarke recalls Monday, May 13, 2024

BACK HOME IN Meadowfield, I sat at my desk. Examinations over. Shitty drive back to Meadowfield. Shitty marshals. Shitty Viglione. Shitty lawyers. Shitty Melanshins. Shitty day.

No need for me to stay and answer those two shitty lawyers' questions. Screw 'em.

Good thing I lived alone. Not sure what I would have said or done to anyone I lived with at that moment. I was not in a good place at all.

That damn bitch colored lawyer. Serving me with a court order. Telling me I had to get off the committee. Telling me that the committee was on Donnie and Lil's side, not mine. Asking me questions like she was on Donnie and Lil's side. Telling me that she'd get another order against me to make me testify. That colored bitch had really pissed me off. So had Donnie and Lil. So had their damn Jew lawyer. Everything about the Melanshins' bankruptcy cases was pissing me off.

And that damn judge, ordering me to cooperate. Jesus. How did he ever get to wear a robe in the first place?

They were trying to sell my land to pay everyone else off after screwing me out of my land. I knew there came a time. There's only so much any man can take. My mind was racing. This fuckin' country. So much change. Left me angry. And threatened. And alone. Didn't like to feel threatened. Didn't like people takin' stuff away from me. Liked my freedoms. I liked being in control. Didn't like to feel cornered. Didn't like to feel there's nothin' I could do.

I sat trying to focus and gather my thoughts. I reached the conclusion that at least in the goddamn bankruptcy case, I could do something. I could be in control, and I wouldn't be alone.

I decided it was time for me to act. No more thinking and talking. I wasn't gonna wait for them Melanshins to sell my land. *My land*, damnit! Not *theirs*. *Mine!* I knew there would be no more waitin' for things to happen. It was time to *make* things happen.

I wanted me a posse. The new raiders. Maybe five of them I trusted. Plus me. With them, we could fan out and send some real direct messages. Message to Donnie and Lil, message to Ms. Josephina Jones, and a message to that Jacob Steinert. A message they'd remember. I wasn't talking about an electronic message like a text. No. I had in mind an old school physical message for each of them.

Didn't think we necessarily needed to kill the targets. Not this time and not yet. Roughed up, that's all we needed. Me and another raider would take Jones. I wanted that one. Smug, smart-ass, colored bitch. She was mine. I'd assign a pair to Donnie and Lil and a pair to Steinert. We'd send our messages at the same time. A coordinated, simultaneous strike.

I felt that we needed to make this happen soon, so I decided to call a meeting in my barn. My new raiders would come. They'd be all in. I'd send out an encrypted message on *Alert*, a private chatroom app I liked to use. A cipher like the Confederate generals used in the day. The boys could decode it. The other posses could as well. They all had the key from me. They'd all know. They all needed to know.

Having made my decision, I thought I needed to get online and play my games. Kill some opponents. It was the only thing that helped calm me down at times. I was always the Confederate. I always won. Just like them Graycoats shoulda.

The South will rise again, I thought. And as I started to play, I thought it was just like I told Jones. "I'm coming. You was warned."

19

Tuesday, May 14 through Sunday, May 19, 2024

WOODY CLARKE SAT at his desk reading and rereading the AFJ message. It intrigued him, but he was cautious. He wondered who was behind the handle Alexander Frank James. He wanted to be one of the first to beta test *Ruckus*, but first he needed to know more about AFJ. He discovered that Alexander Frank James was a handle for Alan Jackson, and from what he could tell, Jackson belonged to all the right forums. And as a bonus, he appeared to live near Pecan Grove, Arkansas, a posse stronghold.

Clarke next investigated the *Ruckus* beta website and liked what he learned. It was a sophisticated and robust role-playing game with character development. It offered his character the ability to get stronger, and as it did, he could inflict more damage on his opposition. It also gave his character a variety of killing tools and weapons. The graphics were top-notch and offered different high resolution battlefields. There was attention to detail and nonstop action. In his view, it might be a successful attempt to recreate in-the-trenches warfare, especially at famous Civil War battle locations. All that was to his liking.

Everything seemed legitimate to him. He wrote Jackson back

and said he would play. They agreed on a time, 10:00 p.m. on Saturday.

To practice in real time, he downloaded the game's plug-in, altered by Rome. Rome received a notice as soon as Clarke downloaded and activated the plug-in in his browser. As he began to practice on the site, the plug-in began to transmit his activity—emails, browsing history, and passwords. She was in.

As the information from Clarke's computer started to come in, Rome needed a way to parse through it. She had developed an app several years earlier that used a type of search engine technology to wade through documents and identify those with a key word or phrase. Her initial key word searches were straightforward: Josephina, Jones, Steinert, Jacob, Donnie, Lil, and Melanshin. She would have others, but she thought that by starting with simple, relevant names, she might get lucky and find her answer more quickly.

The shear volume of material for her app to analyze was daunting. But her only course of action was to allow the app to do its work while she waited and hoped. She took her walk, drank her coffee, and lay on her bed, but sleep evaded her. Since she was wide awake, her thoughts turned to the upcoming game with Clarke.

Rome had gamed during and after college. It was not good for her health. She learned that she had an addictive personality, and she got easily hooked. A doctor called it an impulse control disorder. Already a socially challenged wallflower in college, the gaming world was dangerous for her. She tried but was unable to set time limits. Her already challenged social life evaporated. When she did impose a moratorium, she lost her appetite, suffered sleeplessness, and became agitated. She finally sought help and now stayed completely away from gaming. She felt that her current sleeping difficulties were a fallout from her gaming days.

Now that Clarke had accepted her challenge, she thought

briefly about her return to the gaming world, even if it was a limited engagement. She knew she was not there to play Clarke. That did not matter. She was there to see what Clarke was up to and help prevent it. While any contact with an online game worried her, she would see the mission through to the end to help 3J.

Early the next morning, Rome began to look through the information her app had culled. Much to her surprise, there was little about either Jacob Steinert or 3J. There was a growing amount of information about Donnie and Lil Melanshin, but she expected that. After all, Donnie and Lil had owed money to Clarke for years before cutting off payments.

But she had expected more hits for 3J and Steinert. She wondered what she was missing. With one of Clarke's passwords, she was able to access a *Cablegram* account he used to post notices and information. Most of the posts seemed innocuous to her except one he had posted late on Thursday evening that read "DPTSVLCRZ-BAMYHB." The letters were gibberish. She thought it could be a cipher, and ciphers were not exactly her specialty. She generally knew about them from some of her college anthropology classes, but she didn't count herself an expert in the field, and she was going to need help.

She wanted to keep her promise to Pascale to not let Moses know about this project for Pascale, but she also needed Moses' help—and quickly—if she was going to have any chance of giving Pascale what he wanted. She saw no alternative but to involve Moses and read him into the project. She didn't look forward to telling Moses that she'd gone behind his back. She had never done anything like that, and she had no idea how he would react.

She phoned Moses, and like a child confessing to a parent that she had done something wrong, Rome explained her calls with Pascale, the overriding concern for 3J's safety, her suggestion of what she could do to help, and Pascale's decision to authorize her plan. Moses listened. When Rome finished her explanation, Moses remained on the line silently, and Rome resisted the urge to fill the void by saying something—anything.

After what appeared to Rome to be many minutes, Moses spoke. "What is the status of your work on the project."

Rome brought Moses up to speed on the information her plug-in had generated and how the information had been disappointing. She explained that she thought she had found a cipher, and while they talked, she texted it to him. She waited while Moses looked at his mobile phone to see the text.

"Hmm. Well, this *is* an interesting development. These letters definitely appear to be part of a cryptographic system that transposes or substitutes the letters according to a predetermined code, usually activated by a key."

"But what code and what key?" Rome asked.

"Indeed. The two most important questions. Our friend Mr. Clarke is turning out to be quite an enigma wrapped in a mystery. He is communicating by cipher. To whom? You do not see too many people doing that unless they have something significant to hide." Moses paused and then said, "Mr. Clarke, what exactly are you hiding and from whom?"

He paused again, as if giving the matter some serious thought. Then he said, "Rome, let's do this. Let's start by talking about what we know about Mr. Clarke. That may reveal exactly which cryptographic system he would likely use. That assumes, of course, that he has not invented his own unique system. If he has, I fear we will never be able to decrypt these letters in time for the message to be useful to Mr. Pascale."

Rome began. "We know he went to the University of Missouri, and before he dropped out, he took American history classes. We know he returned to his parents' farm, and today he owns significant acreage on which he raises hogs and grows wheat."

Moses continued. "He is the leader of a right-wing organization he named The Thirty-Six Thirties. In that name is more

American history. The group has made it onto various domestic terrorist lists, but the members do not appear to have done anything other than communicate their views."

"We know he games," Rome said, "and I now know that he regularly visits private, right-wing chatrooms where he talks about taking America back, bad-mouths every minority group imaginable, and seems to extol the pre-Civil War world."

Moses and Rome both had a moment of silence before Moses said, "Civil War. Gaming. Right-wing groups. My dear Rome, as I recall, there was a cryptographic system used by the Confederate Army during the Civil War to keep their leaders' strategy out of the Union Army's hands. I believe the Southern army was partial to a variation of a sixteenth-century Vigenère cipher that used a table consisting of twenty-six alphabetized letters across and twenty-seven letters down: A through Z across in the first row, B through A in the second row, C through B in the third row, and so on. The last row repeated A through Z. Have you any experience with the Vigenère cipher?"

"I have not, Moses."

"Google it while we are talking. You will surely find the table somewhere online."

Rome began searching, and Moses continued. "While you look, a little history. At some point, someone gave it the nickname '*le chiffre indéchiffrable,*' French for 'the undecipherable cipher.'"

Rome listened as she entered the phrase "Vigenère cipher" and immediately saw the table Moses described:

```
ABCDEFGHIJKLMNOPQRSTUVWXYZ
BCDEFGHIJKLMNOPQRSTUVWXYZA
CDEFGHIJKLMNOPQRSTUVWXYZAB
DEFGHIJKLMNOPQRSTUVWXYZABC
EFGHIJKLMNOPQRSTUVWXYZABCD
FGHIJKLMNOPQRSTUVWXYZABCDE
GHIJKLMNOPQRSTUVWXYZABCDEF
HIJKLMNOPQRSTUVWXYZABCDEFG
IJKLMNOPQRSTUVWXYZABCDEFGH
JKLMNOPQRSTUVWXYZABCDEFGHI
KLMNOPQRSTUVWXYZABCDEFGHIJ
LMNOPQRSTUVWXYZABCDEFGHIJK
MNOPQRSTUVWXYZABCDEFGHIJKL
NOPQRSTUVWXYZABCDEFGHIJKLM
OPQRSTUVWXYZABCDEFGHIJKLMN
PQRSTUVWXYZABCDEFGHIJKLMNO
QRSTUVWXYZABCDEFGHIJKLMNOP
RSTUVWXYZABCDEFGHIJKLMNOPQ
STUVWXYZABCDEFGHIJKLMNOPQR
TUVWXYZABCDEFGHIJKLMNOPQRS
UVWXYZABCDEFGHIJKLMNOPQRST
VWXYZABCDEFGHIJKLMNOPQRSTU
WXYZABCDEFGHIJKLMNOPQRSTUV
XYZABCDEFGHIJKLMNOPQRSTUVW
YZABCDEFGHIJKLMNOPQRSTUVWX
ZABCDEFGHIJKLMNOPQRSTUVWXY
ABCDEFGHIJKLMNOPQRSTUVWXYZ
```

As she gazed at the table, mesmerized by its symmetry, Moses talked.

"Quite ingenious in its effectiveness and simplicity. To encrypt, the message writer and the recipient must have a shared phrase. With that phrase, called the 'key,' the writer can encrypt the words of a message and send them to the recipient. With the key, the recipient can decrypt and read the message. Without the key, it would be virtually impossible to decrypt the message. So no pun intended, but the key is the key.

"For example, if the key was 'NewYorkCity' and the message was 'saveme' using the table, the writer would find the first letter of NewYorkCity—the N—in the first row. Then they would find the row that begins with the first letter of the message, the S, and where the N column intersects with the S row, we have our first letter of the cipher: F. The sender would do the same for the second letter of the key and the second letter of the message, and the second letter of the cipher would then be E. Then the sender would move on to the third letter of the key and the message and so on until they had cloaked all the letters of the message. The full cipher would be 'fercav.' The recipient would then reverse the process to decode the cipher and reveal 'saveme.'"

Moses' level of knowledge surprised Rome. She knew the breadth of his experience and knowledge was vast, but even so, his knowledge of ciphers, and the Vigenère cipher in particular, astounded her. "Moses, how do you know this?"

"Ahh, Rome. There are many things about me that you and the rest of the world do not know, and some of those are things no one should know. We all have our secrets. It is part of our human experience. Suffice it to say that in my youth, I spent time with one government alphabet agency or another encrypting and decrypting messages. I do not believe I am able to say much more than that, but my time with the agencies certainly exposed me to the current and some of the more historical cryptographic systems."

Rome never thought of Moses as a man of secrets, and simply said, "I see," as she wondered what else Moses wouldn't or couldn't tell her about himself. "Assuming this is the correct cryptographic system, how can we access the key, Moses?"

"Yes, how indeed? The only thing we can do is continue to consume what you are finding out about Mr. Clarke. As we learn things, I can play with the words that describe what we have learned to see if one of those is the key. Keys can be much like computer and website passwords. And as you know, people tend to use passwords over and over again, and the passwords tend to be words and phrases with which people are familiar and comfortable. It is human nature."

"Moses, while you were talking, I found several websites that can decrypt a Vigenère cipher automatically with the key. We can use such a site to play with possible keys that might reveal a message that makes sense. I've sent you the URL of one of the decrypting websites. Perhaps I can aggregate the posts made by Clarke and develop an app that can submit all those words to one of the decrypting websites and see if any of the decryptions the site generates using the Vigenère cipher make sense."

"Can you do that, my friend?"

"I can give it a try, Moses. Others have done similar work in analogous situations. For example, when a vulnerability in software comes to light, a hacker can find a website whose login fields don't have a limited login attempt feature and use a tool like *THC-Hydra*, *John the Ripper*, or *DaveGrohl* to execute a brute force attack on the login fields by flooding the login with common passwords like '1-2-3-4-5-6' or 'admin.' We call these password-cracking tools an exploit. I may be able to do something similar, and instead of flooding a login with common passwords, I could use Clarke's common post words as the key to see if any of them lead to a decrypted message that makes sense."

"Excellent, Rome. If anyone can do this, it is you. Let's get to work."

Over the course of the next two days, Rome modified a version of a brute force app and fed it the words from the last two months of Clarke's posts. Then Moses and Rome reviewed the many decrypted messages. After two days, she still had a number of words to run, but so far, the decrypted messages she and Moses reviewed were as much gibberish as the encrypted code. During this time, she drank coffee chased with energy drinks, paced around her small flat, racked her brain for anything that might be a breakthrough, and barely slept.

She knew she would have to set this part of the project aside by Saturday evening to play Clarke. At first, she thought of canceling the gaming challenge since she had all the information she needed from the hack into his computer. Then she thought better of cancelling and decided to play the game with Clarke to avoid arousing suspicion that she had set him up.

Saturday evening, she and Clarke logged on, opened a chat, and began. Clarke had selected the Battle of Westport for the environment and had selected a Confederate Army general for his character. Rome whispered to herself, "Battle of Westport it is, and the Union Army general will work fine for me."

They competed into early Sunday morning, and Clarke proved to be a formidable foe. In the end, she conceded victory to him, and in the land of RPG multiplayer make-believe, Clarke's Graycoats won. It was a far cry from the real Westport battle where thirty thousand men fought, thousands died, and the Union forces decisively defeated the Confederates.

When they finished, Rome downloaded the game chat to her laptop so she could review in more detail what Clarke had written. Several posts were curious. One referenced the battle itself and Clarke wrote, "This game is resolving the way the battle should have gone in 1864. Major General Sterling Price should never have lost to Major General Samuel R. Curtis. Righting that wrong tonight."

In another post, Clarke, whose army had just ambushed Rome's Union forces, killing dozens of Union soldiers, wrote, "And that's for all the coloreds we never should have set free! No Fourteenth Amendment citizens. No more Juneteeth."

The two posts repulsed her. In a third post, Clarke wrote, "Don't need me no posse comitatus for this one. My soldiers have things well under control."

Rome decided to go back to Clarke's private chatroom posts, into which she'd hacked, to see if there was any discussion of posse comitatus. She found two discussions, both in chats that her app had not yet grabbed to run through the decryption website.

Before she ran them, she phoned Moses.

After explaining the results of the game with Clarke, she shared Clarke's game chats with Moses.

"Posse comitatus? Interesting," Moses said. "I believe our previous research showed that the phrase is a darling of some of the right-wing groups in America."

"I think we should see if that phrase is the key," she replied.

"Agreed." He paused for several seconds, and then said, "Rome, please go back to the decryption site and run 'POSSECOMITATUS' as the key. No space between the words. Let's see what it reveals."

Rome ran the decryption key. "Moses, the decrypted message is this: 'OBBARJOFRIATEPM.' Seems like more gibberish. Is it the answer or is it another encrypted message?" She stared at the words and asked, "Can this be a message Clarke transmitted in his private chat?"

Moses wrote down the letters and studied them. "I am afraid this might be as big a mystery as the encrypted letters." He continued to look at the letters but saw no pattern. *O-B-B-A-R-J-O-F-R-I-A-T-E-P-M.* "Are you the answer or another cipher?" he wondered aloud. "If you are the answer, what do you mean?"

Then he asked, "Rome, what was your specific agreement with Mr. Pascale about my involvement?"

"He said the project should be between him and me."

"We need to report to him that we have broken that promise and now need his help."

Rome noted that Moses said "we have broken," not "she had broken." The Moses team, she figured, was indeed a team. She sighed. "But I gave my word."

"And events have overtaken that word, my dear Rome. The mission must prevail. We must protect Ms. Jones, Mr. Steinert, and the Melanshins."

"He might fire us."

"Always the client's prerogative. But you know what we do. We shine light on things that lurk in the darkness. He might fire us, but he would do it by the light of day and with all the knowledge we have."

"Rome, please set up a call as soon as he can talk. Do not tell him I'll be on the call. When we connect with him, let me do the initial talking."

"Very well."

"One other thing, Rome. We do not hide things from clients. When we finish this engagement, we can discuss whether we hide things from each other."

Rome sighed again.

"Rome, in Norway, they have a word we don't have in English: *dugnad*. Loosley translated, it means that if something bad happens, everybody turns up to help and work together to solve the problem. That is where we are right now. In a dugnad. The greater good of protecting 3J and the others demands it. We will show up on the call and stay with the problem until we solve it. Both of us. And you will see. Mr. Pascale will show up as well."

The two said nothing for a long moment, and then Rome said, "I still have more information coming in from the enhanced plug-in on Mr. Clarke's computer."

"I do not think we have the luxury of waiting for more information before we make a full report to Mr. Pascale. We need his help to understand the decrypted message, and that help should commence immediately, even as we have more work to do to protect Mr. Steinert and the Melanshins."

Rome quickly set up a meeting with Pascale once she and Moses ended their call, and in short order, she had Pascale on the phone with her and Moses. Moses greeted Pascale quickly to make his presence on the call known and then took charge.

He explained that Rome had shared the project with him and that as a member of his organization, she should not have agreed to take on a project without sharing it with him in the first place. He then explained how and why she had pulled him in. "Rome has accessed Mr. Clarke's technology as you had hoped. She discovered what we believe is an encrypted message that Mr. Clarke posted, and she needed my assistance with the decryption process. Hence the need to violate her word to you and involve me.

"We feel close to breaking the cipher but need your help. With that, we may get lucky and offer some insight into what, if anything, Mr. Clarke has planned."

Moses then briefly explained the encryption and decryption process, using the Vigenère cipher and their reasons for choosing that particular cipher. "Mr. Pascale, while I have been talking, Rome has emailed you the decrypted word. It is fifteen letters: O-B-B-A-R-J-O-F-R-I-A-T-E-P-M. We need your assistance. Does this string of letters make any sense to you?"

Pascale made no comment about Rome's violation of her promise and reported that the email had come in. He paused for a moment before answering Moses' question. "I see several things in the letters. The word 'of,' the word 'bar,' read backwards, the word 'Peta.' I guess I also see a partial word, 'Jo.' As I'm looking at these letters, I also see 'Obbar.' You know, there was a time when a bar in Westport was affectionately called the O B Bar, short for O'Brien's Bar. Jo could be short for Josephina. I think her father used to call her Jo, but no one else would know that. But if one is trying to be efficient in the use of letters, Jo would be better than Josephina."

"It's a who, when, and where message," Rome said. "Something is going to happen to 3J on Friday at eight p.m. at O'Brien's. What else could it be?"

"You are correct, Rome," Moses said. "Mr. Pascale, what is the relevance of O'Brien's and Friday?"

"Bloody hell, folks. Since shortly after 3J started here at the firm, she and I have been meeting at O'Brien's on Fridays for our own version of the week in review—for us, the firm, the cases, and the practice of law in review. We sit at the same table in the back of the bar. We drink the same drinks, wheat beer for me and Irish whiskey for her. We stay an hour and a half or so, and then we leave. Sometimes we leave together. Sometimes we leave separately."

"Mr. Pascale. Rome. My gut is telling me that Mr. Clarke will attempt to cause some physical harm to Ms. Jones on Friday evening after she leaves the bar. With all my soul, I would like to be wrong, but while I can be wrong from my chin up from time to time, I'm rarely wrong from my chest down."

"I have that same gut feeling, Moses," Pascale said.

Rome chimed in. "Me too."

The three were silent for a while. They all knew that several issues had to be quickly resolved, including whether to let 3J know what they had just concluded, how to protect her, and whether to pull in the authorities.

"Rome and Moses, have you found a similar message about the Melanshins and Jacob Steinert?" Pascale asked.

"Not yet," Rome replied. "But now I am totally expecting to. I still have lots of private chat posts to go through."

"Folks, I very much need to figure out what to do here," Pascale said. "I'm going to need some quiet time to do so. Thanks for all your hard work. Stand by."

When the call ended, Pascale sat at the foot of his bed with his Martin resting in his lap. This time, he didn't strum it. He just held it with his left hand stationary around its neck, like a child holds a blanket for comfort. It was not helping him focus. He needed help. He decided to call his friend, Ronnie Steele, and explain everything. And together, he hoped they could figure out a viable plan.

20

Sunday, May 19 through Monday, May 20, 2024

AN HOUR AFTER Pascale called Ronnie Steele, he heard a knock at his front door, and when he opened it, there was Steele. Pascale led him to the kitchen and a cup of freshly brewed coffee.

"You didn't say what it was about when you called, Bill. And now you hand me a cup of joe. I take it that whatever's on your mind isn't going away in short order."

"'Fraid not, Ronnie. Did I take you away from something important?"

"Not tonight. If you'd called last night, you would have had a bit of a problem coercing me to come over since I was at 3J's. But we aren't getting together tonight."

"I'm grateful you could get here so quickly. And funny you mentioned 3J. My problem is about her."

"You got a problem with her? Has she done something?"

"Not at all. Not *with* her. *About* her. Here's the story. All true."

Pascale then recounted the Melanshin bankruptcy cases, Woody Clarke, The Thirty-Six Thirties, and the current state of affairs. He explained how the Melanshins had stung Clarke in a premeditated plan and how he now stood to lose significant sums of money. He relayed Clarke's views of Blacks, other people of color, immigrants, and Jews, to name but a few of the groups that were the subject of his online chatroom rants. He told Steele what Rome and Moses had discovered and how, and he read Steele the decrypted cipher.

"The three of us had the same gut reaction. This guy Clarke is coming for 3J this Friday night as she leaves O'Brien's. I bet he's likely coming with minions."

Steele shook his head slowly, frowning but saying nothing. Pascale didn't expect him to say anything right away. He needed to digest what he'd just been told. Eventually he said, "Well, the part of me that is ex-vice squad thinks two things. First, always best to bring these kinds of matters to the police. But second, I don't see enough here that's hard and fast for the police to do anything with. The decrypted cipher probably means what you three've concluded. But maybe not. You acquired this information through a hack, and an impressive one at that. So if you tell the police, you'll be setting yourself and your hired hands up for lots of questions."

"Then what, Ronnie?" Pascale asked, not trying to hide his anxiety.

"First things first. You've gotta tell 3J. And tell her everything. That would include why you went behind her back to commission the hack."

"I know," Pascale replied in a voice barely above a whisper.

"Then we need a plan. I'm thinking the thing to do here is to intercept Clarke and his group outside O'Brien's. You know, run our own little sting operation. Give 'em some bait that they mistake for 3J. Then right there in the street, we'll flatten them and deliver them to the police. Y'know, tell the officers we saw an assault developing and thwarted it. The police can get Clarke to admit he was after 3J. Attempted assault and battery on 3J. Actual assault and battery on a 3J stand-in."

"Could work. That'd sure keep the hack out of the story line."

"Yeah. The police wouldn't need to know anything about the chatrooms, the cipher, or the hack. They could piece together that Clarke hates folks and couldn't take the bankruptcy pressure of not getting paid, so he tried to take it out on the committee's Black female lawyer. But the damn fool can't tell one Black person from another. And just his luck, he took after the one woman he should never have tangled with."

There was silence for a moment, and then Steele nodded. "Everything you and 3J have told me about this Clarke guy would fit the bill for the story I'm spinning here."

"Except it isn't a story. It's real. Clarke and one or two of his goons would be there to hurt 3J, and we would have to count on hurting them first."

"Exactly. We can do it. I can put together how this should go down," Steele said.

Another brief silence followed Steele's assertion.

"Ronnie, who would play 3J in this sting?" Pascale asked, breaking the silence.

Steele smiled. "I'm thinking that's my former partner on the force, Monica Sterling. Moe to her friends. She's a Black woman who's now in private security. She'd relish the chance to take down a hater. You heard that song 'Bad, Bad Leroy Brown'? Monica is bad, bad Moe."

"Y'know, Ronnie, in the song, things don't end up so good for Leroy. He ends up with some pieces missing, as I recall."

"Well, bad, bad Moe won't have that problem. Clarke and his cohorts will be the ones with pieces missing."

"Does she look like 3J?"

"Doesn't have to for this to work. You're forgetting, Bill. Guys like Clarke think we all look alike. To him, one Black woman looks just like another. And the area on the Pennsylvania side of O'Brien's isn't well lit. One of the streetlights is out too. Our visitors from down south won't get a good look at Moe."

"As soon as they make their move on her, Moe, me, and another guy I have in mind will make our move."

"Who do you have in mind for the other guy?"

"Another former law enforcement guy. His preference is a blackjack slapper, as I recall."

"What'll I be doing in your plan?"

"You'll call the police. You'll be the 911 guy."

Pascale sighed and ran his hand through his thinning hair. "What a fuckin' day, Ronnie. What a fuckin' day." Smiling weakly, he added, "A total clusterfuck."

"Amen to that, brother. The force gave me good training for these kinds of days. For weeks on end sometimes, every day seemed like a clusterfuck." After a few moments of silence, he added, "It'll work, Pascale. We'll make it work."

Pascale knew Steele was trying to reassure him, but nothing was going to make him feel reassured.

INTERLUDE

Friday, May 19, 1995

A THIRTEEN-YEAR-OLD GIRL and her father sat on the front porch of his small, one-story, clapboard house he rented in the Tremé neighborhood of New Orleans. Originally from the Lower Ninth Ward, her father had moved to Tremé when her parents divorced. Since the divorce, the girl and her sister split time between the Lower Ninth and Tremé. The house was blocks from the Louis Armstrong Park and sat on land originally part of a plantation serviced by New Orleans slaves and later developed into the oldest Black neighborhood in New Orleans and perhaps in America.

After the divorce, her mother and father took divergent paths as they tried to carve out new lives as single adults splitting the tasks of raising two kids. Her mother turned to the church for guidance and comfort. Her father turned away. Life lessons the girl received from her parents often conflicted because of their differing points of view.

The girl was lanky, although she was not uncomfortable in her own skin like other teenagers. She was attractive but quickly moving from attractive to striking: hazel eyes, clear skin, high cheekbones. She had an athletic build that she put to good use running track and playing soccer as a high school freshman. She was also intelligent and willing to study. She stayed out of trouble, as much as a teenager could in New Orleans, and she was quiet and thoughtful when she spoke.

Her father looked tired. Very tired. He started his shift at the factory at four in the morning and volunteered for extra hours when workers called in sick. He'd worked twelve hours that day in the heat and humidity of the New Orleans late spring. Later in the afternoon, a series of thunderstorms rolled through the city. But rather than cooling it down, the rain just provided more moisture—fuel for the humidity that was the Deep South's calling card. If the girl and her father didn't move too fast or too much, they could feel the heat leaving the city as the day moved to night.

Her father was proud of her and hoped she might ride the education and athletics train out of New Orleans. "Don't get mad, get smart," he'd said on many occasions, encouraging her to go to college somewhere other than in New Orleans.

Next door, someone played a saxophone, and the sound of a trumpet drifted toward them from across the street and down the block. Kids practicing, most likely, learning New Orleans style jazz born from military marches, voodoo rhythm, and drums. It was rhythm and delta blues married up with gospel hymns, offering the listener its distinctive improvisation, syncopation, altered scale notes, interaction between the musicians, and that *feeling*—the musical version of a traditional dish of New Orleans gumbo.

Kids were learning an instrument to honor their rich history, and for the truly gifted, it might be a chance to chase the music dream. Another way out. Neither the girl nor her father played, but they listened and appreciated. He made sure the girl got a healthy dose of jazz. He wanted to make sure she took that feeling with her no matter how far she traveled from the Crescent City—and from him.

Sitting on the left side of the top step, he sipped slowly from a Dixie Beer longneck while she sat opposite him drinking a sweet tea. Sweat ran down both his bottle and her glass.

She looked over to her father and smiled. "Hard day, Papa?"

"Aren't they all?" He paused for a moment. "Well, not too

hard. You're here, and I'm here with you. That's all that matters to me right now."

There was a comfortable silence between them for a time.

"What's your sister up to?" he finally asked.

"Stayed late to practice her part in the school play."

"Have you heard her practice her lines?"

"Yep."

"She good?"

"Yep."

"And Momma? How's Momma doing these days?"

"She's good. She works, she prays, she helps out at the church, she cooks, she cleans, she loves us. And then she does it all over again." She paused and then asked, "You like it here, Papa?"

"Well, Sha, it ain't no Faubourg, but it'll do."

After a few moments, he turned the conversation away from himself and asked, "How was school today?"

"Not real great." It had been a hard day at school for the girl because of taunting and bullying. Teenagers could be cruel, and that behavior existed long before the internet and social media.

"So what made today such a not real great day at school?"

"I guess it wasn't that bad. But I was on the track after school running for the coach, and some of the boys came by to watch the girls' track team . . . and I guess mostly me. They were hooting and hollering, and it was embarrassing. I expected the coach to do something or say something. Y'know. shoo 'em away. But all he did was blow the whistle around his neck and yell at me to get my head back in the game. He must've thought I was flirting. But I wasn't, Papa. I wanted the boys to go away, not stay and ogle."

"I see," her father said softly nodding his head in understanding of the problem. He knew why a group of teenage boys would hoot and holler when they saw his daughter in athletic shorts. "So you wanted the coach to take care of the problem for you, eh?"

"Well . . . yes. He's the coach."

He smiled. "Jo, let me tell you a little story, just between you and me. Your momma wouldn't approve of this at all, but she's heard me tell it before, and now I'm gonna tell you."

Jo was what her father called her, short for Josephina. Josephina Jillian Jones. Quite a mouthful of a name. She once asked her momma how her parents ever came up with the name, and her momma told her that they liked the name Jillian. Josephina was the name of a favorite aunt on her father's side of the family. Jones was her Papa's name. "And voilà, as they say in France and here in New Orleans, your name appeared like magic," her momma explained.

Only her papa called her Jo. A few years earlier, she had told her sister that she was looking for a nickname. Her sister came up with 3J. She liked that nickname almost as much as Jo.

Out there, she was 3J. On her papa's Tremé porch, she was Jo.

As her father began to explain his story, Jo listened carefully. She liked her father's parables. They usually gave her something to think about and remember. Something to carry with her through life. She hoped she'd never forget what he told her.

"You know the Bible story in the book of Genesis where God created heaven and earth in six days and then rested on the seventh?"

"Yes, Papa."

"God created heaven and earth, and light, and then near the end of that week of work, you remember that God created man in his image?"

"Yes, Papa."

"Well, Jo, that ain't how it went down at all."

Jo raised her eyebrows but said nothing.

"Least, that's not how I think it went down. I can't speak to the science of the creation of heaven and earth and light and the universe, but I can tell you that the Genesis story is missing something."

"What's that, Papa?"

"Well, where God came from."

"Momma says that God didn't come from anywhere. God is just God."

"Yeah, the minister says that in Bible class. I've certainly heard Momma say it too. I respect that view. I truly do. But it's not my view."

"And what do you think, Papa?"

"I think that man created God in man's image. It helped people cope with the things that people should never have to cope with. It helped people explain the things they can never explain. It gave them comfort when they couldn't find comfort."

He paused while Jo absorbed what he said.

"Me? I think we're all on our own. We need to take care of ourselves and our families. We need to solve our own problems. We need to forge our own path."

Jo listened quietly as her father finished and took another sip of his Dixie Beer.

"I think the folks who created God in their own image figured out real quick that they may have overstepped. So they came up with the slogan 'God helps those who help themselves.' But I don't think that worked. It was too little, too late. People still leaned on God too much to solve all their problems. Only God didn't."

"So you think I need to take care of those boys myself and not expect the coach to do anything?"

"I'm just saying, Jo, if it's a problem—if it's your problem—then it's yours to own and solve. Whether that's fair or not. Whether you caused the problem or not. It's yours. If you need help to solve it, you get guidance from your family. God ain't gonna help and Coach shouldn't have to help."

Jo thought about the lesson silently. Silence was a good thing. With Jo, it meant she was thinking and processing. One of the things her father loved about Jo was her willingness to listen and absorb the lessons life had to offer. He smiled to himself.

"Okay, Papa. F'true. I understand."

"Great," her father said as he patted Jo on the knee and stood up. "Now, come on in and let's eat some dinner. I made some groceries today. Got us some of my famous red beans and rice on the stove, about ready to plate. Grandma's old recipe. The best."

"And French bread?"

"Leidenheimer's, Jo."

Jo smiled broadly. "I'll set the table for us, Papa."

"Thanks, Sha. Throw Harry Connick, Jr.'s and Dr. John's *20* disc on the CD player, will ya'? We can hear a little of the boys singing some standards while we eat and talk if that's okay."

It was always okay.

21

Monday, May 20 through Tuesday, May 21, 2024

Right before midnight, after Steele and Pascale decided they couldn't wait until the morning to talk with 3J, they called her on the speakerphone and woke her up.

"Look, 3J," Pascale said, "things have developed, and it looks like our concern that Clarke is a threat is panning out. Ronnie is here with me, and we need to come over and talk with you."

"Jesus, Bill. What time is it?" 3J replied.

"11:50 p.m."

"Ronnie's there with you?"

"I'm here with Bill, 3J," Steele said.

"Fine, fine. Come over. I'll buzz you up. We can talk. I'll have my wits about me in fifteen minutes. Why the hell did I take on these cases?"

Shortly after midnight, the three were sitting around 3J's coffee table. Pascale explained the hack and how Moses, Rome, and he had cracked the cipher. Then he told her that Clarke and maybe others would arrive at O'Brien's in three days and try to rough her up. Steele explained his plan.

3J listened and wondered if any other bankruptcy lawyer

outside of Kansas City was dealing with a physical threat at that moment or if it was only her.

"What about the Melanshins and Jacob Steinert?" she asked when they finished.

"Rome is still working on the Melanshins and Steinert piece. If she can find a cipher out there she thinks addresses them, we believe we have the key to crack it. I'll call Steinert first thing in the morning and let him know what we know. If he asks how we know, I'll defer getting into that," Pascale replied.

"And Judge Robertson?" 3J asked.

"Yeah, not sure how to handle that. I can leave him out of this, or I can call and read him in if he'll take the call. Or we can ask for a chambers conference and see if he'll gather us up to talk. I haven't decided if and when he needs to know."

The three were silent for a while.

"My papa brought me up to solve my own problems," 3J finally said. "To own them and solve them. Doesn't sound like that's what I'm doing here, friends."

"You've told me about some of your father's teachings," Pascale replied. "I seem to recall one: Families help solve problems. It's fair to say we're family, right?"

"Yes," 3J said softly. "But he didn't mean that families shield each other from problems."

"Well, if we've been trying to shield you, we've certainly done a real shitty job of it," Steele offered.

"If I had been shielding you, I would have been much more forceful in trying to talk you out of taking this case," Pascale said. "It's yours to own, but you need help, and that's what family does—24/7 if need be."

3J sat on her couch, feet tucked under her, and thought, occasionally shaking her head in disgust. "Are there any other options besides direct confrontation on the Westport streets?"

"Not that I'm seeing, 3J," Steele replied. "I don't see a way of ending this Clarke guy's craziness other than intercepting him and having him carted off."

"Something could go wrong," 3J observed.

Steele immediately replied. "Well, if we don't do something to head this off, something will definitely go wrong, and we won't be in control."

3J took a deep breath and exhaled slowly. "Look, I know why you did this," she said, looking at Pascale. "And I am grateful. But what you've already done makes me uncomfortable. And what you're proposing to do? Even more uncomfortable. Nothing like this has ever happened to me before, not even tangentially."

"The thing is, 3J, you haven't done anything," Pascale explained. "You had nothing to do with the hack. In Ronnie's plan, you'll have nothing to do with the solution."

"I get that, Pascale. I do. But it doesn't feel that way to me. I'm the reason everything has happened."

No one said anything for several minutes. Then 3J sighed again. "Okay."

She rose, turned, and headed off to her bedroom. "I've got to get some sleep before Judge Robertson's Section 105 hearing this morning, folks."

Pascale and Steele let themselves out. Despite the need, none of the three would find sleep the rest of the night.

22

Tuesday, May 21, 2024

JUDGE ROBERTSON'S PRACTICE was for the parties to appear before him early in the bankruptcy cases, explain the background, and agree to soft deadlines so cases could progress toward completion.

"All rise," the courtroom deputy clerk announced. "The Honorable Daniel Robertson presiding." The judge and his law clerk, Jennifer Cuello, entered the courtroom, and as the judge arrived at his chair on the bench several steps above the rest of the courtroom, the clerk said, "You may be seated."

"All right, everyone. I see we have Mr. Steinert here representing the debtors and Ms. Jones on behalf of the unsecured creditors committee. Are there any other parties here today in the Melanshin cases?" Judge Robertson asked as he quickly surveyed the courtroom. None of the observers rose to speak.

Sitting next to Jacob Steinert at counsel's table were Donnie and Lil Melanshin. 3J was alone at her counsel's table. Despite receiving notice of the conference, neither Woody Clarke nor any of the other committee members were attending. Also in the courtroom was Marshal Sal Viglione, as Judge Robertson had requested.

"Mr. Steinert, let's start with an overview of these Chapter 11 cases please," the judge said as Steinert approached the podium to speak.

"Of course, Your Honor. Mr. Melanshin is in the rural and agricultural real estate business. He buys and sells real estate in Eastern Kansas, and he also leases significant acreage to crop and hog farmers. Currently, he leases over twenty-five hundred acres to one Bill Pearson, who grows wheat on the land. The land business has been good, but the Melanshins got overextended and filed these Chapter 11 cases to assess what land to keep and what to sell. A significant portion of their debts relate to the acquisition and rehabilitation of a historical register, pre-Civil War house they own and occupy in Meadowfield, Kansas."

"Thank you for that synopsis, Mr. Steinert. Any unique issues we can expect in these cases?"

"Well, one in particular, Judge." Steinert explained the contract for deed with Woody Clarke, that Clarke didn't have counsel in the transaction, and that he hadn't recorded the contract in the mortgage records.

"Hmm. I see. Most folks record that type of contract. Mr. Clarke should now appreciate that Mr. Melanshin owns the land, not him. And because Mr. Clarke failed to record the contract, Mr. Melanshin owns it free and clear."

"That is certainly the debtors' position, Your Honor. I'll defer to Ms. Jones to state the committee's position on the matter. It is the debtors' preliminary view that they will sell this unencumbered land, generate north of four and a half million dollars, and use that money to pay down or off a significant portion of their debts. The Melanshins believe that with such a significant pay down, they can service the balance of the debts over a reasonable period under a bankruptcy plan."

"Very well. And what of Mr. Clarke's unsecured debt, which I assume is sizable?" Judge Robertson probed.

"The debtors and the committee have begun to talk about how

to treat Mr. Clarke under a plan. To lay our cards on the table, Your Honor, we are exploring the possibility of treating Mr. Clarke's claim differently than the other creditors. We do not believe that different treatment will run afoul of the unfair discrimination rule."

"I see," Judge Robertson said as he rubbed his chin. "I expect we will have some disputes to resolve between parties on that issue." Judge Robertson paused and then said, "And you say Mr. Clarke has no lawyer?"

"Correct, Your Honor. Not yet."

"Okay. Thank you, Mr. Steinert. Ms. Jones? Comments?"

3J approached the podium. "Thank you, Your Honor." She and Steinert had agreed that she would address all matters pertaining to Woody Clarke. "The committee has seven members, one of whom is Mr. Woody Clarke. Mr. Clarke has participated in committee calls. He and two other members of the committee are members of a group that calls themselves The Thirty-Six Thirties. The name of the group refers to the geographic latitude set out in the 1820 Missouri Compromise that allowed White residents of Southern states, as well as residents of Missouri, to have slaves.

"During this case, Mr. Clarke has made some very threatening comments about the debtors, as well as about most minorities, including people of color and people of the Jewish faith. Someone threw two bricks through the Melanshins' front window with the phrase 'Pay up or pay the price' inscribed on the bricks.

"Mr. Clarke somehow recorded a private conversation between Mr. and Ms. Melanshin and forwarded the recording to me on a thumb drive. I had some concerns that the conversation would be inadmissible in court due to the way it was obtained and because of marital privilege. But last Friday, Mr. Melanshin willingly testified about the conversation stating that he had nothing to hide.

"Your Honor may recall that you ordered Mr. Clarke to appear for an examination. Last Friday, Mr. Clarke testified, at least for a brief period, and then he left the examination room before I completed his exam."

The judge nodded almost imperceptibly with his right index finger rubbing his bottom lip as 3J explained what had happened. 3J and Pascale had decided not to tell the judge about the cipher and the impending conflict that might play out near O'Brien's that Friday. Both concluded neither pieces of information were needed to begin to lay the foundation for a different treatment of Clarke under the plan.

"So far, a majority of the committee members support the debtors' idea to sell the land leased to Mr. Pearson and fully support the notion that Mr. Melanshin owns the land free and clear. On this point, Your Honor, Mr. Clarke and the committee are significantly at odds. The committee is concerned that Mr. Clarke must recuse himself from any committee discussions on this matter."

"Does the Court have any questions?" 3J asked in conclusion.

"Thank you, Ms. Jones. No. I get the emerging picture here. Recusal from deliberations on the land issue may not be enough since it is such a significant matter in these cases. Has the committee given any thought to asking the United States Trustee to remove Mr. Clarke from the committee?"

"Yes, Your Honor. We may make that request shortly."

"Good enough. Thank you, Ms. Jones. Mr. Steinert, so the record is clear, you gave Mr. Clarke notice of this conference?"

Steinert stood at counsel's table and replied, "I did, Your Honor."

The judge nodded. "Anything else to share with the Court this morning, counsel?"

In unison, Steinert and 3J replied, "Nothing further."

"Very well, counsel. Thank you both for your presentations. I will issue an order containing deadlines for claims objections, plan filing, and other routine matters. If things come up, please feel free to contact Ms. Cuello and seek a chambers conference. When you do so, please make a special effort to apprise Mr. Clarke of the request and any conference scheduling. Ms. Jones, if you can get me a motion seeking an order to direct Mr. Clarke to reappear to finish the examination, along with the transcript of his testimony before he departed, I will consider appropriate relief. Thank you, counsel."

Back in his office, as the judge removed his robe, Jennifer headed for the large club chair facing his desk to debrief. Before the judge got to his desk chair, he said sarcastically, "Fun times ahead in these cases. Jesus. The Thirty-Six Thirties. See if you can find out anything on the internet about that group."

"Will do, Judge."

"As I think about this, Jennifer, if Ms. Jones gets me that motion, it looks like I'm going to have to issue an order for Clarke to show cause why I should not find him in contempt of court for violating my prior order. I ordered him to appear, testify, and act appropriately, and he didn't comply. At least not fully." The judge paused for a moment and then shook his head. "I can see already that if there is an easy way and a hard way, Mr. Clarke may be someone compelled to select the hard way."

"And if he doesn't come to the hearing to consider the show cause?" Jennifer asked.

"Well, that would be a huge mistake. Then I'll have to issue a bench warrant and direct the marshals to go get him, handcuff him, and bring him in for violating that show cause order. Another example of the hard way, I'm afraid."

"So we're looking at the potential for multiple confrontations with Mr. Clarke?"

"Quite possibly, Jennifer. Quite possibly."

Both sighed and Jennifer left the judge's office.

3J, Jacob Steinert, and the Melanshins went down the elevator together in silence. In the courthouse lobby, they said good-bye to the Melanshins, and as they left the courthouse, 3J walked Steinert to his car.

"Bill called me first thing this morning and explained some of what seems to be going on behind the scenes," Steinert said. "He told me not to ask how he knows. Second time in a matter of days he's prefaced his comments with a request to avoid asking him something. The 'remain silent' protocol goes against my nature."

3J nodded.

"Bill told me that so far, your folks, whoever they are, had found nothing suggesting a confrontation between Clarke and the Melanshins or Clarke and me. But I gotta believe it's out there, don't you?"

"I don't know, Jacob. But we all need to take steps to guard against the very real possibility."

"I hear you," Steinert said shaking his head. "I'm not in the muscle business, 3J. I'm in the debt business. Repayment and collection are my things."

"Me too, Jacob."

Nodding he said, "Y'know, I'm just a simple bankruptcy lawyer. A solo practitioner at that. I know my way around the Bankruptcy Code and the courtroom. I don't profess to know my way around the protection business at all. The number of times in my career that I've had to use a private investigator, I can count on one hand and not use all the fingers. The number of times I've had to use a security firm in my career is exactly zero."

"Me neither, Jacob," 3J admitted as they reached Steinert's car. "Whatever Bill and I can do to help you, please say the word. But, please. We both need to be vigilant."

When 3J arrived back at her office, she hung her suit coat on a hook behind her door, slumped in her chair, and rubbed her eyes. She was pretty sure that if they weren't bloodshot yet, they would be soon. While she wasn't a coffee drinker, she decided she needed more caffeine than her typical cup of Earl Grey tea could provide. She rose from her chair, made her way to the coffee station near her office, and poured a cup of black coffee into a mug bearing the firm's logo.

Pascale met her there, and she updated him on the Section 105 conference and her discussion with Jacob Steinert.

"Anything yet from Rome on a planned attack on Steinert or the Melanshins?" 3J asked, speaking quietly.

"Still nothing, 3J. It's out there. I can feel it. She just has to find it."

3J nodded but said nothing.

"When you get your second wind," he continued, "Ronnie, you, and I need to meet to firm up what we're doing on Friday. And what we're not. He wants to bring his former colleague, Moe, along, as well as the other former law enforcement person he has in mind."

3J took a deep breath. "I understand. I'd like to meet these folks. Let's set it up for later today if that works for everyone."

About the time 3J returned to her office, Woody Clarke was at his desk, having just finished calling the five Thirties he selected to help with his mission. He had invited them to his barn for a meeting at the end of the day, and they all accepted. His raiders. They would plan the three attacks in detail and then go over the plan again and again to make sure there would be no slipups. He likened himself to a modern-day Confederate general. He was looking forward to this next phase of his plan to get repaid, one way or another.

Pascale had received a call from Moses Aaronson to discuss contingency plans if Rome was unable to locate any express threats against Jacob Steinert and the Melanshins. They agreed it would be a good idea to make an educated guess about when and where an attack might take place against them should one be planned. And to do that, Moses had suggested they discover if either Steinert or the Melanshins had patterns or routines.

That afternoon, Pascale gave Jacob Steinert a call. He began by filling him in on the belief that Clarke and his minions were going to attack 3J on Friday evening, most likely as she left O'Brien's, representing it as a credible threat. Steinert had not been happy about once again being told something important without being told how Pascale knew what he was passing along. He insisted on being told where and how the information had come to Pascale, but Pascale had declined, quickly moving on to the belief that Steinert and his clients were likely in danger too.

Pascale admitted he had no actual evidence that they were in danger, representing it as a credible, reasonable deduction. "We think that if they attempt a strike on you and the Melanshins, it will follow the same pattern they used to plan an attack on 3J as she leaves O'Brien's: identify something you and the Melanshins do habitually on Fridays."

Steinert admitted he did not know the Melanshins' habits and promised to call them pronto. "As for my own habits, my practice is to leave the office at three on Fridays if my caseload and client obligations permit and visit my mom, who's in a memory care facility in the burbs. I usually spend an hour or so with her and then find my wife and get a glass of wine somewhere. We don't have a customary watering hole. But Bill, for God's sake, how the hell would Woody fuckin' Clarke know any of that? It's not like I publish my personal comings and goings for the world to see. I'm a private person, and I'm mostly inactive on social media."

When Pascale contemplated the question for a moment, he realized that Clarke probably already knew the Melanshins' habits and didn't really need to know Jacob Steinert's habits. "He doesn't need to know for sure. He knows where you work. He could follow you and wait for the right place and moment to pounce."

Steinert sighed audibly. "I appreciate the sentiment, Bill. I'm forewarned. And I will be careful. But I need to see my mom and then I need to be with my wife. I'm not adjusting my life for Woody fuckin' Clarke. I will warn the Melanshins. Since they live in the same town as Clarke, my guess is that it will come as no surprise to them that Clarke has said threatening things. My impression from talking to the Melanshins is that Woody Clarke often spouts off, so I expect the Melanshins will thank me for the call and tell me that they've heard it all before from Clarke and The Thirties."

"I understand, Jacob. Please be safe."

"And you as well, Bill."

When the call ended, Pascale tried to return to the never-ending paper sorting project in progress on his office floor, but he was too unsettled to focus on each piece of paper and deposit it in its proper pile. He left his office to check on 3J. As tough as she is, Pascale thought nothing could prepare her adequately for Woody Clarke and The Thirty-Six Thirties.

Pascale, Ronnie Steele, Monica Sterling, and 3J were in the small twenty-seventh floor conference room at 4:00 p.m. awaiting the arrival of the last person attending the meeting, who had called and said he was five minutes out. There were no conscripts in the group. Each came voluntarily with one common mission: No one would hurt 3J.

When 3J's administrative assistant escorted the last volunteer to the room, he extended his hand to shake 3J's, and she was momentarily surprised. It was Anthony Rosini. She had never before met him face-to-face. "Anthony? You're in on this as well?"

"Pascale *asked* me to help. Ronnie kinda *told* me I would help. Moe told me she *hoped* I'd help. Same message; different styles." He paused just long enough to smile. "But yes, I'm in. Wouldn't miss it. No way I'd skip taking down a terrorist."

"You know all these folks?" 3J asked, still surprised.

"I sure do. When I was a sheriff, I worked closely with Ronnie and Moe. They were with vice at the time. Now they're clients, just like Mr. Pascale and you. Happy to help. Wouldn't be here if I didn't mean that, 3J. And so it doesn't get lost in all of this other stuff, it's really good to meet you in person."

Steele took the lead in explaining the situation to make sure everyone was operating with the same facts. He expected Clarke and perhaps others to arrive at O'Brien's with bad intent at some point before 8:00 p.m. that Friday. Steele's plan was to take Clarke and his cohorts down on the Pennsylvania side of O'Brien's. As the group disabled The Thirties, Pascale would alert the police in a 911 call.

Ronnie, Moe, and Anthony had an internet picture of Clarke so they'd have a general idea of what he looked like and would identify him as he approached Moe, masquerading as 3J and standing alone under one of the burned-out streetlights on Pennsylvania Street. When Clarke made his move on her, Ronnie, Moe, and Anthony would intervene quickly, disable Clarke and any others, zip tie them, and await the arrival of the police. The means: Brute force and inflicting pain or breaking a bone or two in the process would be acceptable. The irony: Clarke would go down in Westport like the Confederates he so dearly idolized did during the Battle of Westport, and to add insult to injury, it would be at the hands of immigrants and Blacks.

"All well and good if it works according to plan," 3J said when he'd finished. "What can go wrong?"

Steele smiled. "You really want to know?"

"I don't tend to ask questions the answers to which I don't want to know. I get paid to ask questions, and when I do, people answer." She paused for emphasis and then forcefully said, "So again, what can go wrong?"

Rosini fielded the question. "3J, as long as they don't have guns, we don't see very much going wrong here. Clarke is not much of a physical specimen. He's middle-aged, pudgy, and short. And he doesn't look to be much a boxing ring fighter type. We figure he's relying on the element of surprise and counting on an easy go of it because you're a woman. Moe can disable Clarke all by herself if need be. That leaves three of us to take care of any cohorts Clarke may bring. There's also a huge bouncer at O'Brien's who Ronnie can enlist."

"Indeed, as I think about it, the bouncer is in," Steele added. "All six-foot-eight and at least three hundred pounds of him."

"And what if they have guns?" 3J asked.

"We're ready," Steele said. "We'll be wearing Kevlar, and other than Bill, we're all trained to disable quickly and efficiently in such an eventuality."

3J frowned. "I don't know what's more alarming: That there was a computer hacker who got us to this point, that Clarke is after me, that this is all happening in the twenty-first century, or that someone—like one of you folks—could get seriously hurt trying to protect me."

They all nodded slowly in acknowledgment of her concerns.

She continued. "Suppose I just leave town for a while and work remotely?"

"Is that what you want to do?" Pascale asked softly.

"Of course not. But have you considered that option?"

"Considered and rejected, 3J," Steele replied. "First, it solves nothing unless you're proposing to leave Kansas City altogether and open a Greene Madison office in Anchorage, Alaska. Second, unless we meet this head-on, it doesn't go away, and eventually, you get hurt or worse. We think this is the best option. They think they have the element of surprise on their side, but they don't. We will."

3J shook her head as she slumped in her chair slightly. She felt backed into a corner. There were no good options, and that the others were right didn't make it sit any better with her. She hated the plan, but she also hated doing nothing. And she wasn't going to get run out of town by a domestic terrorist dressed up like a bankruptcy creditor. She wondered again why the hell she'd taken the Melanshin committee case.

Finally, she sat up straight, squared herself, nodded, and said, "All right. I sanction the plan and it's a go. But if any of you get hurt, I'm going to come after you and kick your ass when you heal up. Do you hear me?"

"Loud and clear," Moe said. She turned to Steele. "I like her. Feisty. Could've used her on vice."

Early that evening, Clarke sat in his barn with the five Thirties he'd selected for the mission. His raiders, like Quantrill's.

"Let's start with the Melanshins. Each Friday around 6:30 p.m., they take a before-dinner walk at Meadowfield Memorial Park, holding hands as they walk and talk. They like to walk by the Civil War Memorial plaques, and from there, they follow the path into the cottonwood tree grove.

"This should be easy. Ron, Frank, you boys'll wait for them where the grove begins. As soon as they head into the grove, you'll come up behind them and rough 'em up. Knock them on their heads. If you knock 'em out, that's fine. If you break something, that's fine. But we don't want to kill them. Not this time. We'll scare the hell out of 'em for now. Questions?"

No one had questions.

"Joe and Harry, you draw the Jew-boy city lawyer. Got a friend in KC who tailed this guy and learned that on Friday afternoons, he visits his mother in a nursing home or something like that somewhere in the burbs. Leaves work around 3:00 p.m. Sometimes at 4:00. No real good way to get in his face once he arrives at the nursing home. But my buddy tells me he works in an older office building outside of downtown—so he can penny-pinch, I'm sure. That'd be his way.

"I'll get you the address. My intel says his building has an older attached parking garage. You'll take up a position near his car before 3:00, and when he heads for it, you'll be ready. Jump him. Same program as the Melanshins. Rough him up. Knock him out if you can. Blood's good. A broken bone or two is fine. But no weapons. Don't kill him. Y'hear? Putting the fear of God into him is all we're after."

The others nodded their understanding, but no one other than Clarke spoke.

"You boys all have your cipher and the key?"

They all nodded.

"Good. Like in the past, I'll post a cipher in the usual places if I've got something to communicate, so check before you leave in case I have any last-minute instructions. Use the key to decrypt. I'll also post a cipher to let the other posses know what's up."

Clarke paused and smiled before adding, "Them Confederate generals would be proud of us, boys. Planning this out and using ciphers. Time for The Thirties to start taking some action."

Everyone nodded again. "Last, me and Brian got that colored gal. My same buddy followed her and asked around a bit. Seems she shows up at the same bar at the end of the work day every Friday. Drives a dark blue Prius. Convenient for us. We'll get her when she comes out of the bar and heads for her car. Knock a little sense into her is what I have in mind."

Clarke paused to survey the team. "One more thing. Everyone needs to wear a neckerchief to pull over your face before you rough up your target. Don't want anyone seeing your faces. Right?"

They all mumbled, "Right."

As they stood to leave the barn, Clarke was smiling broadly. He was feeling good about what he had set in motion. "No one fucks with me and gets away with it. No one!" he said loudly in parting.

23

Wednesday, May 22, 2024

"SO WHAT DO we know about this Clarke guy?" Ronnie Steele asked Rosini at a table in the back of Steele's favorite coffee shop not far from Kansas City's Hyde Park neighborhood. When the meeting the day before with 3J and Pascale ended, he, Rosini, and Moe had decided to meet the next morning to talk about the operation in more detail. They agreed it would be better to exclude both Pascale and 3J.

The group had assigned Rosini the task of doing research. As he started to respond, a six-foot-eight Black man weighing north of three hundred pounds entered the coffee shop and made his way slowly to the table: Eugene Martin. Bitty to his friends and acquaintances, as in itty-bitty. He looked imposing but not threatening. Imposing was the nature of his business.

Steele had hired Bitty as the O'Brien's bouncer several years earlier and thought Bitty's presence had measurably reduced the number of incidents at the bar. Bitty's size and his penetrating stare had a way of disarming any developing disputes. His stare silently invited unruly patrons to consider if they wished to tangle with him. Most wisely opted not to. If they dispensed with common sense and decided to take him on, his size and strength permitted him to remove any rowdy patrons swiftly.

Steele introduced Bitty to the others, and he sat and ordered a large coffee and a croissant.

Rosini then began his report. "I spent the morning tracking down the local county sheriff, who I've known for years, and some of the surrounding county sheriffs. The picture is more sinister than I expected. I thought Clarke was an uneducated right-winger who felt he needed to do something to save face after losing his land to a sharper businessperson.

"To be sure, he is some of that. But here are snippets of what else I've learned. He attended Mizzou for a while but never graduated. A few years ago, some bank got a judgment against him, and as is customary, the bank sent the then sitting sheriff out to repossess the bank's equipment collateral. When the sheriff arrived at Clarke's farm with the repossession papers, Clarke met him on the porch with a shotgun, Wild West style. That sheriff turned, got back in his car, and drove away. He resigned the next morning. Told the county officials that when he signed up to be sheriff, he hadn't signed up for farmers pulling shotguns on him."

Steele, Moe, and Bitty listened silently.

"The story continues. Clarke was apparently so mad that he drove to the county seat and burst into the courthouse, past the guards, and into the judge's office. To do what, no one knows. The judge wasn't there that morning.

"When that same bank hired a lawyer and asked that judge for new repossession papers to serve on Clarke, the judge told the lawyer he wouldn't recommend serving the papers on Clarke. He described Clarke as 'capable of violence.'"

The others remained silent for a few more moments. Then Moe narrowed her eyes as she questioned Rosini. "Anthony, how often does this kind of thing happen with Clarke?"

"Couldn't get a good bead on that, Moe. Most folks go their

whole life without pulling a shotgun on a sheriff or bursting into a judge's office, so even if he's only done it once, that's once more than most."

Steele and Moe nodded. Bitty listened but offered no hint of what he was thinking.

"What else?" Steele asked.

"Now we get to the bizarre kind of stuff. Ever hear of a group called The Common Law Citizens? Some call them the CLCs, but most call them the 'Cits' for short."

"Not really," Steele replied, and Moe shook her head.

"Right-wingers. Anti-Black, anti-Jew, anti-working woman, anti-Asian, anti-Latino, anti-gay. You name a group and they hate 'em. They couple their hate with some bizarre views. They believe that Jews have a satanic plot to take over the planet. They believe all forms of government are illegitimate and enslave all Americans, although it's a good bet they mean the White Christian kind—the ones they say are the *real* Americans. They believe all people of color should leave the country.

"The Cits have some other significant—and I should add looney, in my book—conspiracy theories. They believe that after the Founding Fathers set up our government, an evil secret government stepped in and replaced it. They believe that because the United States abandoned the gold standard of backing currency, there are duplicate identities of Americans the government maintains. They believe that each duplicate identity has a Treasury Department account that is funded with huge amounts of money. They believe there's a code that will grant them access to the accounts, so they write and file papers in court peppered with what they believe are random secret codes and symbols. They believe that if they guess and include the correct secret code or symbol on the filing, it will automatically give them access to tens of millions of dollars in these hidden accounts.

"They sign their court pleadings in red and sometimes with

a red thumbprint. Not blue ink or black ink for these folks. Red is the color of choice. The Cits believe that red is the color of the people and black and blue are the colors of corporate America and the illegitimate government. Blood is the best and most convenient red they seem to have. So sometimes they use that as their signature ink."

As Rosini explained the Cits, Moe closed her eyes as if to try to make the conspiracy theories of the Cits, QAnon, and other fringe groups like them go away. With her eyes still squeezed shut she said, "There were always kooks running around. But with social media, texts, emails, chatrooms, the dark web, and the like, we've made it way too easy for these folks to communicate and continue to conduct business. Too damn easy. We now enable these assholes."

Moe slowly opened her eyes and looked at Rosini. "Are you saying that Clarke is a Cit?"

"Don't know for sure. His Thirty-Six Thirties hold many of the Cits' conspiracy views. The Thirties seem to hold other views as well. More than once, one of The Thirties tried to pay his real estate taxes with money he printed up. Didn't work, but some of The Thirties are tax protestor types. Clarke supposedly signs his pro se court papers with a red thumbprint. Presumably, red from his blood. Does that make him a Cit or someone who merely uses filings in a threatening manner? Don't know."

Bitty said nothing but shook his head slowly.

"I'm a little afraid to ask, but . . . anything else?" Steele asked.

"The last tidbit. The sheriff down there dropped his voice to a whisper when he told me this. He said the local rumor is that Clarke ordered his minions to kill several Black farmers along the Kansas/Missouri border. Cold cases. Open, but cold."

"I wonder how vigorously a rural sheriff down that way would try to solve the murder of a Black farmer," Steele replied. "Probably not vigorously, especially if he thought the investigation path might lead to Clarke's front door and the business end of a shotgun."

Bitty spoke for the first time, in a deep baritone voice, but softly. "Many of these rural law enforcement folks have two cold case file cabinets, one containing the files of crimes against Black folks and one containing the rest. That Black folks cabinet doesn't get a lot of use, I hear."

Everyone nodded.

"So are these Cits dangerous and does that make Clarke a killer?" Rosini asked.

Steele, Moe, and Bitty did not respond. Instead, Rosini said, "The FBI considers the Cits dangerous. It's understandable. You need look no further than Terry Nichols, Timothy McVeigh's partner in the Oklahoma City bombing. Nichols professed to be a Cit."

The three sat in silence as they considered Rosini's report.

"I'm gonna go out on a limb here and observe that the four of us need to completely prepare for Friday's festivities with Mr. Clarke," Rosini said, breaking the silence. "We need to go over every possible way this could play out and make sure we have a response."

Steele and Moe nodded. Bitty said and did nothing, but everyone knew it was his business to always have an effective response. The four agreed they would meet at Moe's house in the Waldo neighborhood near Wornall and 75th and plan the "mission" that evening.

3J walked around the hall to Pascale's office. Instead of sitting cross-legged on his floor, he was at his desk, feet on the desktop, highlighter in hand, reading glasses on his nose, as he read a brief filed in one of his cases.

"Wanna accompany me on a short lunchtime excursion in lieu of lunch?"

"Happy to. Where to?"

"I thought I'd go to the Negro Leagues Baseball Museum over

the lunch hour and commune on the museum's ball field." The ball field was the museum's indoor replica of a baseball diamond and outfield, called the Field of Legends. On and around the field stood more than a dozen bronze statues of famous Negro Leagues players.

"Oh? Which player will you hang with?"

"Cool Papa Bell standing behind second base in center field."

"Why him?"

"His speed. Y'know, like the Satchel Paige story. Bell was so fast, he could flip off the light switch and be in bed under the covers before the lights went out. We're gonna need that kind of fast on Friday."

"Whoa there, 3J. There's no 'we' involving you on Friday. Is that going to be a problem?"

She smiled. "No problem, Pascale. That's part of what I can talk to Papa Bell about."

They arrived at the museum on Eighteenth Street next to the American Jazz Museum in less than ten minutes. They entered the common lobby that the two museums shared, 3J bought two tickets, and she and Pascale walked quickly through the exhibits, past cases displaying game-worn uniforms, cleats, and gloves. They made their way to the field separated by chicken wire at the entrance and accessible only at the end of the tour. The statue of Papa Bell stood in center field.

3J walked over to the Bell statue and stared up into his face. It appeared to look back at her in an understanding and all-knowing way. She called to Pascale, "These are the shoulders we stand on today."

He nodded silently.

She sat down on the field, hands clasping her knees to her body, looking up at Bell.

"Some of the greatest ballplayers ever, and only a few got to play in the majors for no reason other than the color of their skin," Pascale said. "The Hall of Fame belatedly admitted some of them. Bell got inducted in '74, and more than a dozen in 2017. More in 2022, including our own Buck O'Neill finally. But those admissions were too little, too late, and didn't change the fact that in their heyday, they couldn't play in the majors."

3J said, "For a while, Cool played in Kansas City for the Monarchs at the old Kansas City Municipal Stadium across from Arthur Bryant's Barbecue joint by the corner of Seventeenth and Brooklyn," 3J said. "The stadium is gone now. Glad the museum carries on the stories and the legacy. This field makes the players seem alive."

She paused and then said, "Jazz and Black baseball. Whites came to listen and watch. But the musicians and ballplayers couldn't get served the next day at the Whites-only restaurants. Part of being Black in Kansas City in the 1930s, '40s, and into the '50s. We could make White people happy in our world, but we couldn't share in theirs."

After a few more silent moments, she rose and said, "Okay," as she exhaled slowly. "We can head back to the shop."

On the car ride back, Pascale broke a period of silence. "Did you reach any state of calm and acceptance on the field, 3J?"

"Actually, I did. As far as I can tell, Bell would've told me, had he been here to do so, '3J, sometimes you just gotta do what you gotta do.'" After another short period of silence, she added, "I'm sure my papa would have told me the same."

As they pulled into the Greene Madison parking garage, 3J said, "I guess that's what's happening on Friday. Doing what's got to be done."

Pascale turned to 3J and nodded.

Back at her desk, 3J tried to write a motion and related pleadings requiring Clarke to show cause why the Court shouldn't hold him in contempt for walking out of the court-ordered examination. It was difficult for her to write the papers. Her ability to focus and block out the world abandoned her, so she left her desk and gazed out of her window at the Power and Light quad. Pascale had taken to staring out his window as he reflected on his career, she thought. Maybe it would help her. But it didn't. Maybe it only worked for Pascale or maybe it only worked to reflect on the past, rather than worry about the future. She moved away from her window and returned to her desk.

With no focus, she set the motion aside with a plan to return to it after Friday. She had already decided not to file it before the Clarke attack played itself out anyway. She saw no reason to poke the beast any more than necessary. And she figured that if it all played out the way Steele planned it, there might be no reason to file it because Clarke might be behind bars somewhere.

She could only hope.

Early that evening, Steele called 3J and told her to remain in her condo until he came and not leave for any reason. She agreed, but she felt certain that was overkill. So she decided to ignore Steele's directive and walked the few blocks from her condo to The Belfrey so Chef Tio could cook her dinner.

On the walk over, she felt hyperalert, and even though it was still light outside, she closely surveyed the people on the street like she would on a dark street after the sun had set. It was no way to live, and she realized she was walking more briskly than usual. When she arrived, she sat down at the bar and then thought better of her location with her back to the entrance. She moved to one of the tables and sat facing the front door. With her rationality hat on, she found it hard to believe that Clarke and his cohorts would burst through the entrance and into a bar that would fill up shortly and somehow navigate their way to 3J. With her paranoia hat on, she thought she couldn't be too careful. She hung her rationality hat on a faraway hat rack and wore the paranoia hat.

Celina Tio came over to the table and sat down with 3J, her

back to the door. 3J decided not to share what was going on and what might be about to happen in forty-eight hours. They exchanged brief pleasantries, and 3J said, "I could really use some of that private stock bourbon tonight, Celina."

Tio rose, went behind the bar, and returned in an instant with a bottle of brown liquor and two glasses. She poured, they raised their glasses to each other, and they drank. Both were from the no ice, no water stable of whiskey drinkers, especially if the liquor was the good stuff. And this bourbon was.

3J hoped the drink would take the edge off. While it smoothed the rough edges a little, for the most part, they remained. But Tio's company was what 3J needed, and the bourbon certainly didn't hurt.

By the time dinner arrived, the bar had filled with patrons stopping off for a drink and a bite to eat before heading home. Tio had to tend to the customers, so 3J ate alone with her thoughts and concerns. And yes, she admitted to herself, a certain amount of fear she could feel growing. After dinner, she paid and walked back to her condo in her secure, high-rise building. Once there, she collapsed on her couch, tucked her feet under her legs, and waited for Steele's arrival. No wine. No jazz. Alone with her thoughts. She needed him. Very much.

Steele, Rosini, Moe, and Bitty sat around Moe's coffee table that evening and discussed every eventuality they could identify, and how they would individually handle the situation. The plan was simple. Simple was best, they all agreed. They would jump Clarke and any cohorts as the attackers reached Moe. When they had restrained the attackers, Bitty would zip tie them and leave them laying on the sidewalk facedown to await the police.

In a physical confrontation, they felt confident they would easily have the upper hand, especially with Bitty on the team. But they needed contingency plans if Clarke and his cohorts brought guns or knives. Guns and knives would be game changers. Steele had a plan if Clarke brought weapons. The team concurred and thought it would work, and they all agreed it *had* to work.

Clarke sat at his kitchen table that evening, alone with his computer, unaware that Rome's malware had compromised it. He was worried about the Friday operation he had set in gear, and he knew any good general would be worried. He had come up with a campaign that was more than workable. He dubbed it admirable. It was going to be his first concrete step in fulfilling the mission to return the country to a path of freedom from people who didn't belong there, systems designed to oppress folks like him, and anyone who tried to fuck with him and thought they could get away with it.

Thinking about his lack of freedom made him angry.

As he thought through his role in the campaign, he decided to arm himself. Not with a gun but with a twelve-inch bowie knife his father had left him. With its cross guard and clip point, it was a fighting knife. A classic. He knew he told the boys that the goal wasn't to kill anyone, but he wanted to be ready if he needed to defend himself. After all, he was the one going to the big city, where he believed everyone carried a weapon. He thought about something he once read from a time when the fighting before the Civil War had started in Kansas. It had appeared on June 10, 1856, in *Squatter Sovereign*, a pro-slavery newspaper in the Atchison, Kansas Territory: "Let not the knives of pro-slavery men be sheathed while there is one abolitionist in the Territory."

Clarke said aloud, "Me and my knife'll be ready. It won't be in the damn sheath. Not at all." He knew the Confederates had taken a beating at the Battle of Westport, and he aimed to not have history repeat itself on Friday. Not under his watch. Not in his campaign.

His only regret was that he couldn't be in three places at once. He'd picked the right part of the campaign for him to lead the charge—the 3J operation. But he wished he could be there as his raiders took down the Melanshins and Steinert. He'd want a full report from everyone when they returned to Meadowfield. Any general would. And he'd share the spoils of a successful campaign with the raiders. Every general should.

He thought that Friday couldn't come soon enough.

Just before midnight, 3J rested her head on Ronnie Steele's shoulder as they sat quietly on her couch. The lights of the downtown buildings twinkled outside her windows. But that night, she had no appreciation for the Kansas City skyline. And she had no words. No Sonos music. Just the silence of the night that roared in her ears as one more day passed into the next.

She wanted to lay her head somewhere and have someone take care of her. She was glad she had Ronnie, and she was grateful he didn't feel like talking. In her silence, she finally let her mind wander freely without thinking about Clarke, right-wingers, Friday, and a fight outside O'Brien's.

Eventually, they both fell asleep on the couch in each other's arms.

INTERLUDE

A FIVE-YEAR-OLD GIRL stood in the back alleyway in New Orleans' Lower Ninth Ward behind the small house where she, her father, her mother, and her newborn sister lived.

"But, Papa, do I have to? I don't want to do this." She was holding back tears as she spoke. It all seemed scary to her.

"Yeah, Jo. We need to. Don't resist it. You need to learn this stuff."

'This stuff' was how to defend herself. She had been playing in the alleyway during the week, and two older boys confronted her, pushed her to the ground, and taunted her before dispersing when a neighbor came to Jo's aid.

The neighbor came by later that night when her father was home from work and explained what he saw and who the perpetrators were. The father made a mental note to have a fireside chat with the boys. If they felt threatened by the discussion, mission accomplished.

In the meantime, the parents talked and decided that it wasn't too early for Jo to start learning the basics of self-defense. The Lower Ninth was a tough neighborhood. She needed to develop a self-preservation tool kit.

As her father talked, Jo listened carefully. "Your fingers, their eyes," he explained. "Your arms, their necks. Your foot and knee, their groins. We don't look for trouble. And when we see it, what do we do?"

"We don't go toward it, Papa."

"Right, Jo. But if there's no exit, what do we do?"

"If we have no other choice, we defend ourselves, Papa."

"Exactly, Jo."

"But I don't want to hurt anyone, Papa."

Her father smiled at her. "Of course not, sweetheart. Of course not. But if they're trying to hurt you, you can't let them. Understood?"

"I do, Papa."

Her father would keep returning to defense lessons as Jo grew up, and by the time she was a teen, he was pretty sure anyone who took her on would be sorry they did. That was the point. He had done his job. He had laid down a marker that no one would hurt his Jo without a fight.

24

Thursday, May 23, 2024

3J CHANGED OUT of her heels and into her walking sneakers. Pascale walked by 3J's office as she stood to put on a cardigan.

"Where're you going, 3J?"

"Down for a walk."

"Mind if I join you?"

Like Steele, 3J knew that Pascale was reluctant for her to be outside alone. 3J sighed audibly. She was getting used to the loss of her precious independence in the days leading up to Friday. She didn't like it, but she understood it, and now she acquiesced without debate. Anyway, she knew that it wouldn't matter if she said she minded. He had that look on his face. He was coming with her and there was nothing she could do about it.

They headed out of the building and onto the streets of lunch hour Kansas City. It was common for the two to spend the lunch hour together. But unlike most of her lunchtimes with Pascale, this walk was in complete silence as they meandered west up the hill on 13th Street to Baltimore and past the President Hotel.

3J knew its history. Opened in 1926, its fabled Drum Room hosted performances by many a jazz artist including Frank Sinatra, Benny Goodman, Tommy Dorsey, Glenn Miller, and Sammy

Davis, Jr. Eventually, the hotel closed and remained vacant for twenty-five years, surviving numerous pushes to raze the building before its renovation and reopening in 2006. Another jazz icon saved. As they walked past it, 3J wondered what the Drum Room's Black jazz artists, who could play but did not drink in the Drum Room of old, would have thought about the 2024 need for her to have an aging White male escort her as she walked by the storied old building.

They turned South on Baltimore, past Sporting Kansas City's headquarters with its mural "For Glory For City," then to the Kaufman Center for the Performing Arts, whose award-winning, complex geometric architecture began with a sketch on the back of a napkin. There they turned north and headed back to the Greene Madison office along Main Street's streetcar route. They walked past Anton's Taproom, housed in an 1898 factory building. Across the way, they passed Tom's Town Distilling, a modern local pur-veyor of alcohol, invoking Kansas City's checkered past of heavy drinking even during Prohibition and offering a reverent nod to the city's boss politician, Tom Pendergast, who made sure booze and vice ruled the nights so every Kansas Citian and visitor could liquor up and cavort, even as the rest of the country went dry and boring.

Normally, a quick walk around downtown Kansas City offered 3J a restorative hour of conjuring up the city's history, and for her, jazz history in particular. "A tune on every corner," she would say.

Pascale would respond, "A story under every streetlight."

But not this time. Appreciating the city's rich history was on hold. It would be there on Monday, assuming she would be as well. The situation was a mess, and she was going to blame herself if anything happened to anyone on the team.

And with that last thought, 3J completed her emotional jour-ney brought on by Woody Clarke, which started with repulsion and moved to disbelief, defiance, concern, fear, and finally guilt. Six emotions she rarely felt in normal times. Normal times were safe but fragile and always one unexpected twist away from the dangerous. Her twist happened when she took on the committee representation. Now, nothing about the Melanshin cases, Woody Clarke, and The Thirties were at all normal. *And here comes Friday. Point A to Point B like a Kansas City streetcar. But for me, there are no stops in between. No place to get off the goddamn Clarke Express before the end of the line.*

That night after dinner, Steele, Rosini, Moe, and Bitty again sat around Moe's coffee table to run through each possible attack scenario and plan out their response.

"Let's go over the weapons scenario one more time," Steele said.

Rosini offered, "Our working premise is that they'll have some form of hand weapon. A gun or maybe knives. They won't approach Moe with their weapons visible because of the risk that someone in the Westport crowds will see them, so we'll have to be ready if they draw the weapons as they begin the attack."

"Let's challenge that working premise," Moe said. "If they're smart, they'll conceal any weapons as they approach. But are they smart?"

"If Clarke is dumb enough to approach with weapons drawn, he may not get close enough to pull off the attack," Steele replied. "He'd be risking someone seeing the gun or knife and bringing the cops into the picture before he can attack. Pascale says he's street smart."

"All right. No weapons drawn," Moe conceded.

Steele nodded and continued. "Bitty's an expert in quickly scanning folks like he does for every patron who enters O'Brien's. If Clarke et al. have weapons drawn, Bitty'll spot it, and we'll go on the offensive rather than wait for them to engage with Moe."

"So if Bitty spots weapons drawn, he'll place himself between Clarke and me?" Moe asked to clarify what would happen.

"Correct," Steele confirmed. "And if Bitty spots no weapons, he'll let them pass toward you. Then he'll come up from behind them as we all converge on Clarke and his boys and take them down."

"Look, either way, this is destined to be a scrum," Rosini said. "The scrum shouldn't last long, but until Clarke and any cohorts are facedown kissing the concrete, there's gonna be risk."

Moe and Steele nodded their understanding. Bitty said nothing and didn't move.

"Any word on whether there's gonna be Steinert and Melanshin attacks?" Rosini asked.

"Still nothing solid, Pascale tells me," Steele answered.

"Let's go over everything one more time, Ronnie," Rosini said. "Where will 3J be throughout this confrontation?"

"If she follows my orders, she'll drive over with Pascale and arrive at the bar as usual. She'll park her Prius on Pennsylvania a little north of the bar entrance. I'll have an orange cone in place to reserve the spot for her. She'll come into the bar and then go back to my storeroom and office, where Moe'll be waiting. Meanwhile, Pascale will enter and take a seat at his usual booth in the back of the bar. In a few minutes, Moe will come out of the storeroom, proceed to the booth, and take a seat opposite Pascale, like 3J would normally. 3J is supposed to lock the storeroom door after Moe leaves and stay in the room awaiting further instruction. At a little before eight, Moe will stand to leave and walk out O'Brien's front door. She'll pass Bitty and make a quick left toward Pennsylvania and the Prius."

They all listened as Steele went through the plan one more time. Then Bitty spoke with his arms folded across his huge chest. "I'll be sitting on my usual stool at the front door. I normally shuttle between the stool and outside the front door to survey any crowd loitering by the entrance and any disorderlies I need to hustle along. As Moe walks by me on the stool, I'll stand and follow her out. That's where I'll assess if I need to be in front of her or behind her. My gut tells me behind her, but we'll have to see how it goes in real time."

Everyone nodded.

Rosini then chimed in. "Meanwhile, Steele and I will be behind the bar. As Moe stands to leave, we'll exit the bar from the side entrance and enter the little alleyway that leads out to Pennsylvania, right under the broken streetlight."

Moe continued. "I'll be walking briskly and pause before getting to the Prius and pretend to look in my shoulder bag for my keys, which I'll then fumble with. If they're going to pounce, it'll be at that moment. I'll let Clarke grab me, and then the scrum will begin."

"The scrum shouldn't last but a second," Bitty said. "If all goes as planned, Clarke and company will be on the ground in a blink, facedown."

There was silence for a few seconds. Then Rosini opened a small box. "I have these in-ear pieces and transceivers for each of us to use so we can stay in communication with each other as this all plays out. I use these little buggers in some of my surveillance work. They're incredibly handy. Got them on the internet. With these, we can talk to each other as needed."

He scanned the group members as he handed each of them their small ear bud and continued. "Bitty, you can use this to tell us what you're seeing outside the front door as Moe's time to leave the bar approaches."

Bitty nodded.

"Has anyone read 3J and Pascale into our details?" Moe asked.

"Not yet," Steele replied. "I'll tell Pascale tonight when we finish up here. Not sure what to do with 3J. The more I tell her, the more information she'll want. And then the more she'll want to do something that's not part of the plan. I want her out of the limelight on this one, but if you know her, you'll know that what I want and what she might do may not be in sync."

Bitty shook his head, expressing his dissatisfaction with the prospect that 3J might try to do something outside the plan. Then he said softly, "I like her. But I don't like that. Not a bit. She needs to stay in the damn storeroom."

"She knows. She says she will," Steele explained.

"Why don't we have her come into the bar as usual but leave after she and Moe trade places?" Rosini asked.

"I offered that option first," Steele said shaking his head in frustration. "3J gave me a hard no in response. In light of that, I don't see any better options than parking her in the storeroom and holding her to her word. Do you?"

No one spoke. There was no other 3J option.

"If that's the case, Ronnie," Moe said, "you'll need to tell her the whole plan. She'll need to know what's planned on Pennsylvania so she doesn't wander out into the middle of the scrum."

"Agreed," Bitty said.

"Anthony?" Steele asked.

"Agreed as well."

"All right then," Ronnie said smiling slightly and raising his eyebrows. "Tonight I'll read in both Pascale and 3J. Pascale will listen and say fine. No questions. He'll leave the plan to the experts. 3J will have lots of questions." He smiled. "You heard her the other day. She asks questions for a living and expects people to answer them. Guess it'll be a long evening for me under her hot light."

The group all nodded and then headed out into the Kansas City late spring evening. It had cooled off and the air was still, as if mother nature had given everyone a lull before Friday's face-off.

Steele's prediction of Pascale's and 3J's reactions to the plan was accurate. Pascale listened in silence and when Steele finished, simply said, "Thanks, man." 3J, however, was an active participant, interrupting Steele's explanations with questions and then follow-ups to his answers. With Pascale, it took thirty minutes to run through the plan. It took two hours with 3J. But in the end, she acknowledged that the group had planned as much as was humanly possible.

And she liked that Bitty was on the team. She figured Clarke had never seen anyone quite like Bitty. Most hadn't. She wondered out loud if the presence of a Black giant would, in and of itself, scare Clarke away. Steele pointed out that at this point, scaring Clarke away was not a goal. "We want engagement with this guy, 3J," he said. "Engagement is the only way to take him down and end this."

She nodded.

Please, counselor. Just stay in the storeroom tomorrow! Steele thought.

25

Friday, May 24, 2024

ROME SAT ON her bed, befuddled and frustrated. She had searched online for more ciphers and had found none. She had searched the Clarke computer files and found nothing. She wondered what she was missing. Clarke had a MacBook Air. Nothing out of the ordinary. On a whim, she decided to scan through the applications installed on the computer, but she saw nothing unusual there.

While it was possible there was nothing to find—no "there" there—in her heart, she didn't believe that was the case. She worried that she was missing something, both in her searches and in her thinking. The less she found, the more she bore in on the problem, to no avail.

She decided to take a walk and see if that would cure the blockage, resolving not to think about the problem or the lack of a solution during the walk. A quick jaunt to the Chelsea Market and a late afternoon cup of fresh roasted Ethiopian beans brewed before her eyes was what she wanted. At the market, she made her way to the Ethiopian coffee vendor, a family-run operation, and greeted the matriarch of the family, Mrs. Baraki, who smiled broadly.

"Welcome back, my friend." After studying Rome's face, Mrs. Baraki said, "You look troubled."

"Nothing a cup of your world's best coffee cannot fix, Mrs. Baraki," Rome said, smiling back at her.

As the beans for Rome's cup roasted in a copper pan over an open flame, Mrs. Baraki said, "Let me put on some music from my homeland. Very soothing. Uplifting. Inspirational."

Rome smiled and nodded as the owner opened her laptop, clicked on iTunes, turned on her bluetooth speaker, and selected a beautiful a capella piece with a gospel tinge. As promised, it was uplifting and soothing. And in an instant, it inspired her, but perhaps not in the way that Mrs. Baraki intended. As the song progressed, Rome ran back through her mind how the owner selected the song: laptop, iTunes, click on song, portable bluetooth speaker.

"iTunes!" Rome said aloud. It was the easiest way to back up an iPhone. Rome had been searching Clarke's computer for breadcrumbs. But she had ignored iTunes and as a result, any backups Clarke made of his iPhone as well. A serious omission on her part. It struck her that Clarke had likely used his phone to post. If she could get the most recent iPhone backup, she hoped she could find the posts.

The owner came around the table between her and Rome and offered the cup of brewed coffee to Rome. Rome accepted the paper cup and then hugged the owner, turned, and raced back to her flat. She knew time was not her ally.

Back on her bed, she perused Clarke's hard drive and found that Clarke used iTunes. Clarke had a choice of backing up his iPhone to his iCloud or his hard drive. He had selected hard drive. To her relief, she found a backup from twelve hours earlier.

She copied the backup to her hard drive. She knew that iTunes did not encrypt iPhone backups by default, and she hoped Clarke had not checked the "encrypt local backup" box in his Finder or iTunes windows. She knew that many did not encrypt for fear of losing the password to unlock the encrypted backup, assuming that the backup was otherwise safe and secure on their laptop.

She opened her iPhone backup viewer app, one of many such apps readily available all over the internet. The moment of truth: no encryption. She exhaled audibly. She was in.

On the iPhone backup, she looked for a *Slack* app but found none. *Slack* was a messaging program that allowed people to use a private, persistent chatroom called a channel. Instead of *Slack*, Rome found an app named *Alert* with which she wasn't familiar. She needed to go online and learn about the app before she attempted to use it or any of the related data on the backup. She learned that *Alert* was a company in almost all respects similar to *Slack* but seemed to cater to right-wing communications. That had to be it.

She returned to the backup, employed the backup viewer, and quickly discovered that Clarke avidly used *Alert*. She found numerous recent posts by him, many containing encrypted ciphers, and began the task of decrypting and reviewing. After an hour, she found two posts that appeared to address attacks on the Melanshins and Jacob Steinert. But these decrypted ciphers lacked the detail of when and where the attacks would occur. She also found a post calling a meeting in Clarke's barn several days earlier "to take action."

She wrote an email to Pascale and copied 3J and Moses, explaining what she found and pointing out that the level of detail from the newly found attack ciphers was insufficient for her to state with certainty where or when Clarke would strike Steinert and the Melanshins. She looked at her watch and made a quick conversion of time zones in her head. It was already after the noon hour in Kansas City, and she hoped there was still enough time to get a message to Steinert and the Melanshins.

As 3J was finishing a sandwich from Pickleman's Deli at her desk, her computer dinged the arrival of a message from Rome. She opened it, saw that she had been copied on a message to Pascale, and read it quickly. Then she hustled around the corner and into Pascale's office.

Pascale spoke before she could open her mouth. "We've got to find Steinert, and fast. It's already 1:30. Let's dial him up right now."

Pascale called Steinert's direct line, but it went right to voice mail. He quickly left a message urging Steinert to call him or 3J because they had credible evidence that Clarke was coming after both him and the Melanshins and that he suspected it would be sometime that day. Then he tried Steinert's mobile phone. When it also went right to voice mail, he left the same message. Then he called the Steinert Law Firm's main office number, and when Steinert's assistant answered, he learned that not only was Jacob not in but that she had no way to get a message to him other than leaving a voice mail on his office and mobile phones.

"3J, unless we talk to Jacob, we have no way of getting a message to the Melanshins. Since they have counsel, we can only communicate with their lawyer."

"You mean *ethically* we can only communicate with Steinert?"

"Correct."

They sat in silence until 3J spoke. "You've left a detailed message for Jacob. You've talked with him many times. He'll get your message and then get one to the Melanshins. He has to and will. I know it in my heart."

"Well, your heart and your gut are almost always right. Almost always," Pascale said.

Jacob Steinert had stepped away from his office and the brief he was trying to finish at 1:00 p.m. and headed to a meeting with a doctor caring for his mother. The doctor had left a cryptic voice mail asking Steinert to meet with him that afternoon without hinting at the topic, and Steinert powered off his mobile phone to be undisturbed in his thoughts on the drive there. He arrived at the doctor's office for what turned out to be a two-hour discussion of Steinert's mother's degenerating cognitive abilities.

After the meeting, he returned to his office, troubled by what he learned at the meeting. He couldn't focus on the brief, so he decided to quit for the day and head to his mother's memory care facility. Moments before 4:00, he made his way to the parking garage. Reaching into his jacket pocket for his keys was the last thing he would remember. The two Thirties came around from behind a concrete support, grabbed a handful of Steinert's hair on the back of his head, and in two quick motions, pulled Steinert's head back and then violently forward into the hood of the car, knocking Steinert out cold.

He came to almost ten minutes later slumped on the ground, his head drooped and his back leaning against his car's front left tire. Blood soaked his white shirt and light gray suit. The source of the blood was his nose, now broken in two places. He tried to stand but could not. Instead of moving, he reached for his mobile phone, turned it on, and called 9-1-1. He felt for his wallet in his suit jacket and it was still there. He still had both his phone and his wallet, so he realized the attack hadn't been a robbery attempt.

Paramedics came and told Steinert he needed to go to the hospital with them for observation and to attend to his nose. Once at the hospital, Steinert settled into his bed and drifted off to sleep. The chart hanging at the end of the bed said he had a moderate concussion. The attending doctor described the beating as vicious and told him he was lucky he only suffered a concussion and a broken nose.

He would not speak to Pascale until Saturday afternoon.

Shortly after 6:30 p.m., Lil and Donnie Melanshin walked down the porch steps of their antebellum home and strolled hand in hand to Meadowfield Memorial Park, a few blocks away. As they walked, they smiled and talked softly about the week that was now ending.

They entered the park, with its many plaques memorializing the Civil War border battles between Kansas Free-Staters and Missouri proslavery soldiers. They made their way to the path that circled the park and weaved its way through their favorite grove of cottonwood trees. After a mere handful of steps into the grove, the two Thirties sprung at them from behind a group of large trees. One grabbed Lil and threw her to the ground. Her head struck a tree root, dazing her. She got up on all fours, moaned in pain, and tried to gather herself.

Meanwhile, the other Thirty grabbed Donnie's shoulders from behind and tried to pull him backward to the ground. Seeing his wife on the ground, Donnie fought back against his attacker. Donnie was easily five inches taller than his attacker, and rather than ending up on the ground, he wheeled around to face the Thirty whose neckerchief had fallen off his face.

"What the hell are you doing to my wife?" he yelled, grabbing his attacker's left arm with his left hand and punching him in the face with his right fist from point-blank range. The attacker instantly fell to the ground next to a dazed Lil and momentarily lost conciousness.

Lil's attacker came up behind Donnie and clubbed him in the head with his fists. Donnie crumpled to the ground, losing consciousness for a minute as he collapsed. That attacker ran from the scene leaving the two Melanshins on the ground beside the unconscious attacker.

Another couple came by on their evening walk within moments and called 9-1-1. As they dialed, the Thirty Donnie had punched gathered himself and stumbled off. A police officer arrived shortly, took statements from the Melanshins and the couple, and summoned an ambulance to take the Melanshins to the hospital.

Donnie Melanshin tried to reach Jacob Steinert to report what had happened. He had to leave a voice mail on Steinert's phone sitting in silent mode on the table next to Steinert's hospital bed.

Each attacker phoned Clarke to report the results of their mission. While not perfectly executed, his team completed the first and second installments of his campaign. They had roughed up Donnie and Lil Melanshin, as well as Jacob Steinert, and had drawn blood. Clarke commended them on jobs well done and asked each if they said anything to the victims during the attacks. They all reported that there were no words spoken during their attacks. Still, Clarke had confidence that he sent his message: No one fucks with Woody Clarke and gets away with it!

All that remained was the third installment of Clarke's campaign. Clarke and his raider, Brian Saber, would be center stage for the final attack. Clarke had his bowie knife. In his view, that colored lawyer had fucked with him, and he was ready to take her down.

Before heading out to O'Brien's, 3J sat in her office in her favorite navy blue pantsuit, replacing her navy heels with a pair of running shoes she kept in her closet. She wasn't sure why she had decided to change shoes, but something in her gut told her it was the prudent thing to do.

She met Pascale at the elevator bank, and they headed out together. They rode the elevator in silence. They drove in silence. There was nothing either could say . . . or should.

3J played no music in the car. There was no jazz playlist she could think of appropriate for the mood. They were driving off to Westport to do battle. Jazz was not the musical language of war. She decided that she would allow none of her cherished music to be associated with Woody Clarke or the attack.

The only sounds were the Prius engine and road noise. They drove past the World War I Memorial but she allowed herself no thoughts about its virtues: Honor, Courage, Patriotism, and Sacrifice. None seemed at all applicable to Woody Clarke, his views and beliefs, and what was about to happen. She hoped she would be around that winter to walk the memorial grounds.

She looked briefly in her rearview mirror and saw her face: a combination of a grim look and exhaustion. It could as easily be a look of fury because fury was how she felt as she drove.

Upon arriving in the Westport District, 3J drove by three sides of the block where O'Brien's sat, ending up on Pennsylvania. Pascale hopped out to move Steele's orange cone and free up the parking space, and 3J parked the car. Each inserted a transceiver in their ear. As the plan called for, 3J entered the bar first, walked past Bitty, and then headed straight back to the storeroom. Pascale entered a few minutes later, walked past Bitty, and made his way through the crowd to his usual booth.

As 3J entered the storeroom, Moe stood up from Steele's desk chair, looked at 3J, and said, "Wish me luck."

"Luck, Moe." They were the first two words she'd uttered since she entered the elevator almost forty-five minutes earlier.

Moe walked from the storeroom into the O'Brien's Friday crowd. It was the beginning of the three-day Memorial Day weekend and the gathering crowd was festive. She had dressed in lawyer-appropriate attire: navy blue pantsuit, heels, and a large shoulder bag in which she carried her sneakers. She blended well into the crowd of off-work, weekend-hungry, party-ready, office patrons. As she approached Pascale's booth, they both surveyed the bar crowd quickly but saw nothing out of the ordinary. Moe sat facing Pascale.

Steele spoke to the team. "Anybody see anything yet?"

Pascale, Moe, Bitty, and Rosini each replied, "Negative."

"Okay," Steele said. "Keep your eyes peeled."

Moe traded her heels for sneakers, and she and Pascale sat in the booth in silence. While Moe looked calm, Pascale was having trouble hiding his growing concerns as the confrontation moment drew nearer.

Steele and Rosini were behind the bar, wearing white aprons. Steele worked the bar crowd as he did every night. Rosini repeatedly scanned the crowd. Bitty scanned from his stool at the front entrance.

Steele, Rosini, and Moe had on lightweight Kevlar vests. Bitty chose not to wear a vest. Rosini wasn't sure he could have found one big enough anyway.

And they waited for the implementation of the just-before-8:00 p.m. plan.

26

Woody Clarke recalls Friday, May 24, 2024

WE LEFT MEADOWFIELD and arrived in Westport at a little past 7:15 p.m. We was looking for a good parking place, one that would give us the chance to exit easily after we finished with that colored gal. We found a spot on Mill Street a few blocks from the bar and parked. Front of some church named the St. James Baptist Church. Old building. Colored folks milling around. We sat in the truck cab for thirty minutes making small talk. Saber seemed nervous. He was talking fast, and he sounded like he was trying hard not to think about what came next.

Me, on the other hand—I wanted to visualize the attack. At one point, I closed my eyes while Saber talked, and in my mind's eye, I saw us grabbing that gal and giving her a good beating. Couldn't string her up on a tree, but with my eyes closed, I wondered how that would've gone down if we could've had that as a part of the plan. Not practical, I concluded. Not in these times. Not in Westport.

At around 7:45 p.m., I interrupted Brian and said, "Time to move." I opened my door, and Brian didn't move. So like the general I was, I gave him the order, "Move out, son!"

Brian nodded, opened his door, and came around to my side of the truck. And off we went on foot. I had my knife sheathed on my hip, hidden from view by my windbreaker.

We headed east on Westport Road past a surface parking lot, toward the bar. There was a crowd outside the bar when we arrived. I had intended to peek into the bar and survey the scene first, but there were way more people there than I expected. There was lots more drinking going on in the big city than I expected. And there was a huge colored guy sitting on a stool by the entryway. Him and me made eye contact for a moment. He smiled at me and nodded slightly. I figured he was the bouncer. Big guy for a big bar. We didn't have no business with him. I looked at my watch. 7:52. I figured she would be coming out any second. We moved on past the bar entrance and settled on standing by the corner under the Westport Road and Pennsylvania Street signs.

Heard they auctioned slaves in this here building before the Civil War. The days of old. Would've been good if I hadda been born back then.

I saw a blue Prius parked a few cars away on Pennsylvania, like my boy told me it would be. Her car. I was ready. Time to start taking this country back, I figured.

27

AFTER CLARKE WALKED past the entrance, Bitty stood and said for the others to hear on their earbuds, "They're here, folks. Looks like two of them. Didn't see any weapons, but Clarke's wearing a jacket, so there may be something underneath it. Clarke's got one of those bad intentions looks on his face. He and his buddy are on the move, so me too. Moe, you're up."

Moe stood, made her way to the front door, and left the bar. Outside, she took a left, head down as she walked briskly. She walked past the corner where Clarke stood and turned toward Pennsylvania and the Prius.

Meanwhile, Rosini and Steele took off their aprons and quickly made their way to the back of the bar and out the side door to the alleyway. Then they turned right onto Pennsylvania. They moved toward the Prius and the place on the sidewalk where Moe would end up.

As Moe walked past Clarke, he and Saber pulled their neckerchiefs over their mouths and noses, turned, and started to follow her, closing the distance between them. Saber had his hands buried deep in his blue jeans pockets. Clarke's arms moved back and forth as he walked quickly.

As Moe neared the car, Clarke accelerated, came up from

behind her, and pushed her hard. She lurched forward grunting and fell to the ground, her knees breaking her fall, tearing her pants. Saber lost his nerve and took off running away from the bar down Pennsylvania, past Rosini and Steele.

Clarke muttered, "Shit!" under his breath.

Rosini and Steele ignored Saber and focused on Clarke, who was reaching under his jacket with his right hand. Rosini saw the bowie on Clarke's hip and yelled out, "Knife!"

As Clarke put his hand on the sheath to pull out the knife, he felt a vice-like grip close around his hand. It was Bitty, who had come up rapidly behind him. For a moment, Clarke tried to pull his hand free but couldn't. He tried to turn his body to face Bitty, but before he could, Bitty twisted Clarke's wrist beyond the point that any wrist could flex. Before Clarke could say or do anything more, there was a loud, gruesome popping noise, followed by another, and Clarke's wrist snapped like it was a dry twig. There are eight carpal bones in the human wrist. Bitty's twist snapped three of them.

"Fuck!" Clarke screamed out in pain, cradling his disabled right hand in his left palm.

As Clarke screamed, Steele grabbed Clarke's shoulders and pulled them forward, driving Clarke's body down to the ground, face-planting Clarke on the sidewalk and breaking his nose. Blood spurted on the sidewalk, as well as down Clarke's mouth to his chin and onto the collar of his shirt. Steele forced Clarke's hands behind his back. With his face on the ground, Clarke spit warm blood out of his mouth.

As Steele grabbed Clarke's right hand to move it into position, Clarke let out another bloodcurdling yell, this time with no words. Then Steele placed his knee in the small of Clarke's back and transferred all his weight to his knee.

Clarke continued to scream, "Get the hell off me!"

Steele ignored him.

Two seconds later, Clarke screamed, "I said get the fuck off of me!"

Steele grabbed Clarke's right hand and twisted it as Clarke tried to wriggle his body from side to side to escape Steele. Clarke screamed again. Bitty handed Steele a zip tie, and as he put it around Clarke's wrists, he twisted Clarke's shattered wrist one more time, breaking a fourth carpal tunnel bone.

Clarke again screamed out in agony.

Steele leaned close to Clarke's left ear and whispered hoarsely, "Listen to me. Shut the fuck up, asshole."

Once the zip tie was in place, Steele stood and Bitty leaned down, flipped Clarke over, and sat him upright. Once on his butt looking up, Clarke saw Moe's face for the first time, blinked, and yelled out, "You ain't that colored skirt lawyer."

Moe leaned down inches from Clarke's broken nose and yelled back, "The man here told you to shut the fuck up! And fuck you! Y'hear me? You tore my best pants."

Clarke spit blood at Moe but missed his target. She leaned close and hissed, "You piece of shit!" Then she made a fist and pulled it back, preparing to punch Clarke's face. Clarke squeezed his eyes shut as he readied himself for the blow.

But Rosini interceded, grabbed Moe's coiled fist, and said softly, "You don't need to do that, Moe."

"Yeah, you're right. But I want to," Moe replied, breathing hard through clenched teeth, still looking at Clarke for a moment longer before she moved away.

While the events unfolded under the malfunctioning streetlight, 3J left the storeroom, exited O'Brien's back door, and peered out from the alleyway to observe what she could. She knew she should stay in the storeroom behind locked doors. She had agreed to do so, and she remembered she had promised her father all those years ago not to run toward trouble. And she knew the others were trained in law enforcement and personal protection while she was just a lawyer. She knew her way around a courtroom, not around a right-wing attacker.

She knew all that. But this was all about her, and she could not, *would not*, hide out. So she peered around O'Brien's brick wall and saw Moe getting up off the street, Steele, Rosini and Bitty surrounding Clarke, and Saber running past her down Pennsylvania. Saber didn't see 3J. Without taking a moment to think, she took off running after Saber.

As she headed down the block, closing the distance between Saber and herself, Rosini saw her take off and yelled, "3J! No!"

She ignored Rosini or might not have heard him in the moment. Either way, the chase was on. Saber was surprisingly fast but 3J was faster, and in less than a minute, she caught up to him and jumped on his back, draped her arms around his neck, locked her legs around his waist, and hung on.

No one ever accused Rosini of being fast, and he had at least a full city block to go before he could catch up to where 3J and Saber were scuffling.

Saber tried to twist his body to flick her off, but she had a solid grip on him and wasn't letting go. She reached for his eyes and managed to rake her fingernails across his right eyebrow and part of his eyelid, and when he screamed out in pain, 3J pulled hard. Saber lost his balance and fell over backwards, landing on top of 3J. As the two fell to the pavement, her head hit the concrete and her body cushioned his fall, knocking the wind out of her. From beneath Saber, she kept her arms wrapped around his neck and her legs around his waist. She tried to gouge his eyes again, but he pulled his head up and away. As he avoided her attempted rake, he hissed, "You slut!"

She pulled as hard as she could trying to cut off his airway.

Slowly, the larger Saber managed to flip himself over to face 3J, and they struggled as 3J thrashed from side to side. He managed to pin her arms flat to the street and placed his knees over her arms to free up his hands. He screamed, "You colored bitch," reared back, and punched her in the face. She turned away from the punch as he struck her face, and the blow glanced off her cheek, making only partial contact with her cheekbone.

She freed her knee and quickly forced it up into his groin as hard and fast as she could, making solid contact as her father had taught her all those years ago. It was a fierce kick, and Saber recoiled, screaming in pain and rage as a feeling of nausea came over him. He leaned closer to her face and yelled, "That's gonna cost you, bitch!"

3J could feel the steam from Saber's mouth as he screamed and could smell his sour breath. She tried to force him off her but couldn't.

Rosini arrived as Saber was about to punch again and just as 3J freed her leg and kicked him with her foot once more, even more forcefully. Saber inhaled a lungful of air and opened his mouth wide to scream again in pain. But before he could, Rosini struck him with a blackjack across the back of his head, instantly knocking out Saber, who collapsed from the blow as 3J pushed him to the sidewalk.

Rosini's first order of business was to secure Saber before he woke up. With 3J still lying on the ground, Rosini pointed to her and said emphatically, "Don't move," and then began to drag Saber's limp body to a small tree nearby. Ignoring Rosini's directive, 3J sat up but didn't try to stand up. Rosini saw her moving out of the corner of his eye and said sternly over his shoulder, "Please, 3J, just wait for me to tie this guy up." 3J slowly nodded.

Rosini put Saber's arms around the narrow tree trunk as if the attacker were hugging it and attached a zip tie to his hands so he couldn't move away from the tree once he came to. "This scum is going nowhere," Rosini announced as he made his way back to 3J. "Are you okay?" He kneeled down next to her to examine her injuries and looked into her hazel eyes to see if she was clear-eyed and focusing.

"I'm fine," she replied, trying to convince herself of the correctness of her reply and wondering if she was. She spoke slowly and closed and opened her eyes almost as slowly. She felt foggy-brained, and she hoped blinking would lift the fog.

"Let's wait a few minutes here before we move you," Rosini said softly.

3J nodded. The small head movement left her woozy. After a few minutes, she said, "Okay. Ready."

"Take this slow," Rosini said as he grabbed her under her left arm and helped her up.

When she got to her feet, she was wobbly, and he held onto her arm. Her cheek and the back of her head hurt. Her ribs were sore from the weight of Saber's body falling on her. After a few more moments, she gathered herself and the two walked the several blocks back with deliberate steps to where the rest of the team waited with Clarke.

As the team disabled Clarke and 3J took off after Saber, Pascale called 9-1-1. The crowds always filled the Westport streets on Friday nights, and the police department deployed beat cops to walk the bar district and keep the peace. Two foot patrol cops were nearby and arrived in minutes. They surveyed the scene before them. A small crowd had gathered and encircled the place on the sidewalk where Clarke now sat.

One of the Westport beat cops, Officer James Lin, was of Asian-American descent. He knew Bitty well and respected him. Though Lin was a tall man, he still had to look up five more inches at Bitty. "What the hell do we have here, m'friend?" Lin was in the classic law enforcement pose with his thumbs wrapped around his belt and his left forearm resting on his holstered weapon.

"Saw these two guys as I made my usual rounds on the O'Brien's perimeter," Bitty replied. "Saw that the little guy and his buddy were waiting on the corner." He pointed at Moe. "And as the lady turned the corner, this dude accosted her. Pushed her to the ground from behind." Shaking his head in disbelief, he added, "A real man's man."

Bitty looked down at Clarke with disdain. "The other one took off running. Must've lost his nerve. I approached to come to her aid. This little guy here reached for a knife. I was behind him and needed to act. Didn't leave me options. 'Fraid I had to break his wrist. He screamed and struggled, and Steele came to assist me and it looks like someone may have broken his nose as well. By that time, Ronnie and Anthony came out of the bar. We zip-tied him for you. Pretty mouthy. He wouldn't shut up. Kept yelling about a colored lawyer."

"Colored lawyer?" Lin asked, surprised.

"Yeah. I didn't much like to hear that." Bitty smiled at Lin and said, "Don't know what color he might have been referring to. Purple? Green, maybe?"

Lin nodded.

The second cop, whose name tag read Officer Ralph Finkle, looked at 3J, standing three feet from where Clarke sat on the ground, rubbing the back of her neck. "And what's your story, ma'am?" he asked 3J.

Pointing north, Rosini replied for 3J. "If you folks go a few blocks on Pennsylvania, you'll find a man I believe is the accomplice. The one who ran away." Rosini stared at Clarke, who looked away.

Finkle raised his eyebrows, surprised by the revelation.

Rosini continued, "Yeah. Bump on the head and zip-tied to a tree trunk."

"A tree trunk? Ah. Quite the eventful evening for you folks," Lin said, shaking his head.

"He was out cold and hadn't come to when we left him back there," 3J explained.

"Knocked out? We?" Lin asked. "What's your involvement in this, ma'am?"

"I ran him down when he fled the area."

"You did, now did you?" Lin said, again surprised.

"Yeah. I got to him, we scuffled, and then Anthony here came to my aid and knocked him cold. My guess is that he'll have a little trouble walking when he wakes up."

"Why's that, ma'am?" Finkle asked.

"My knee and foot. His groin." 3J paused before continuing with a hint of smile on her face. "More than once. I played some college soccer. A striker. I made pretty good contact with him below the belt."

"I see," Lin said with a knowing look on his face and a tone of approval.

As Finkle listened, he made notes in his pad and then scanned the six members of the team. "Look, this all makes sense and we should thank you, but instead, and sorry to do this to you, we're gonna need to take formal statements from each of you folks down at the station. I'm thinking tonight, not in the morning."

The six team members all nodded.

"And you, sir," Lin said to Clarke, who was still sitting on the ground, facing up to the team and the cops. "It is my great pleasure to inform you that you are under arrest for assault and battery, for starters." Clarke looked away from Lin, who read Clarke his Miranda rights and asked, "Do you understand these rights?"

Clarke turned his head back to face up to Lin and hissed in response, "Fuck you, you fuckin' immigrant!"

Lin glared at Clarke. Never breaking eye contact, he said, "Immigrant, huh? We've lost our good mood tonight, have we? That can happen when plans go so terribly awry. And what might you be? One of those good old, brave American citizens who assaults women from behind?" Lin scowled at Clarke, who remained silent.

Lin paused, and then exhaled. "All right. Enough banter. On

your feet. It's your lucky evening. You get a free backseat ride to the KCPD station, courtesy of my partner and me and this fair City of the Fountains. Let's go."

As Lin finished, Finkle reached down to assist Clarke up off the ground, but instead of grabbing him under his left arm, he grabbed his right wrist and tugged. Clarke screamed in pain. "Oh. I'm so sorry," Finkle said. "Is that the bad hand, sir?"

Clarke writhed in agony but said nothing, and Finkle placed him in the back of the first of the two squad cars that had arrived.

Bitty smirked as he turned away and faced the small crowd. "Okay, people. Thanks for coming. Show's over. The night's young. Go back to your festivities or go home to your families."

Steele popped back into the bar and made some quick reassignments, telling the staff that he was unexpectedly called away. A new bouncer for the evening sat at the front door—one of the dishwashers. And one of the waiters was now serving as bartender. Steele told them both he'd check in and said with encouragement, "You got this."

Finkle walked the several blocks along Pennsylvania and found Saber restrained, beginning to come to, and moaning softly. Finkle cut the zip ties off, placed Saber's hands behind his back, handcuffed him, and walked Saber back to the second squad car. As 3J had predicted, Saber walked hunched over, gingerly, apparently trying to manage the serious pain in his groin, courtesy of 3J's kicks. With each step, he groaned. One block into the walk, Saber stopped, bent down, and threw up from the pain.

Finkle and Lin transported Saber and Clarke to the downtown police station, booked them, and placed them in separate holding cells. A doctor examined Clarke's wrist and determined that he would need surgery to pin the broken bones. For the moment, the doctor wrapped it and placed it in a sling, awaiting the availability of a surgeon in the morning. He offered Clarke no pain killers. The same doctor cleaned the cuts on Saber's face. No one offered to attend to Saber's groin.

The team started to make their way to the station to give their statements. 3J handed Pascale the car keys and said, "You've got the reins, Bill. Be gentle on the bumps. My ribs really ache." Pascale's eyes got wide, but he said nothing. He knew this wasn't the time to chastise 3J for her heroics. There would be time for a meaningful discussion about failing to follow the plan and unnecessary risk-taking.

At the station, the team gave consistent statements and excluded the fact they knew the real target of the attack was 3J. Also excluded was any information about the Clarke computer hack. Their collective story was simple: They happened to be patrons at O'Brien's or they worked at O'Brien's. Steele, Rosini, and Bitty were glad they were in the right place at the right time to help avert a more serious incident. They were glad that Moe wasn't seriously injured.

As she gave her statement, one of the police officers told 3J that Officer Finkle found a small gun on Saber's person when he handcuffed the attacker and said she was lucky that all she got were bruises and a bump on the head. 3J thanked him for the information and added to her to-do list the decision of whether she should share that nugget with the rest of the team, and if so, when.

28

FTER THEY GAVE their statements, the six met on the steps of the police station and breathed in the cool spring air being moved by a gentle breeze. They wanted to be together, so they agreed to meet back at Moe's house for debriefing.

On the drive to Moe's house, 3J had Pascale stop at Mike's Liquors in Brookside on Sixty-third Street. She went in and bought the largest bottle of Irish whiskey on the shelf and three six-packs of beer for the beer drinkers in the group. 3J thought the others would need the booze to smooth out the edges of what turned out to be a rough evening. And she would also need ice—for the back of her head, not for the whiskey. She wondered if Saber had an ice bag clamped between his legs. She hoped so and smiled at the thought.

When she brought the liquor to the checkout counter, the cashier stole a quick look at her face while ringing up the purchases. 3J figured she must look quite the sight. The cashier said nothing and didn't let on if 3J's appearance was alarming. 3J hoped it was nothing that a Kansas City liquor store clerk hadn't seen before on a Friday evening.

As 3J paid with her credit card, she again thought of her father's training sessions and realized that he had taught her well, even if she ignored all the good reasons her father had told her to be cautious about running toward danger. She knew Pascale and Steele would remind her that she hadn't followed the plan and she could've been seriously hurt or killed. She knew it was coming, but she also knew they would be right. She was lucky to be alive.

Her ribs reminded her of that fact as Pascale arrived at Moe's house, turned into a parking spot, and hit one of Kansas City's famous side street potholes lingering from the winter. The car shook, and as it did, 3J groaned.

"Ribs?" Pascale asked.

"They're fine," 3J replied, grimacing.

"If you say so," Pascale said.

Moe answered the door dressed in jeans and led them to the living room, where the rest of the team was sitting. Moe held up her ripped dress pants. "Goddamn Clarke ruined my pantsuit. Gonna send that son of a bitch hater a goddamn bill."

Everyone smiled.

"Got another call from Lin," Rosini reported. "Seems that Clarke's not talking and declined to have a lawyer. Strange strategy to decline a lawyer. Unless something changes, it means he'll represent himself at the arraignment."

"Do you know which judge has drawn Monday's arraignment docket?" Steele asked.

"Lin says it's likely gonna be Judge Roundtree," Rosini replied.

Judge Sanford Roundtree was one of several Black Jackson County District Court judges who handled the criminal docket.

Steele smiled. "Not Clarke's lucky couple of days, I guess. Can't imagine how Clarke's gonna react to a Black judge setting his bail . . . or denying him bail."

"Clarke was bleeding pretty good. He'll look a mess in front of Roundtree," Moe said.

"Well, remember what John Brown said just before the Confederates hung him in Virginia," 3J offered. "'I, John Brown, am now quite certain that the crimes of this guilty land will never be purged away but with blood.' I don't think a little Clarke blood will change how Judge Roundtree handles him."

Everyone nodded.

"I still haven't heard from Jacob Steinert," Pascale said. "I'm worried."

"I wonder if we should divide up the hospitals in the Country Club Plaza area where he works and call them to see if they've admitted a patient named Steinert?" 3J said.

Everyone thought it was a good idea, so they began calling hospitals. 3J called St. Luke's, located in Kansas City's core between the Country Club Plaza and Westport. After waiting on hold for several minutes, she talked with one of the admitting nurses. It was after 11:00 p.m. The nurse was uncomfortable sharing information with 3J but finally, with some cajoling, told 3J that an ambulance had brought Jacob Steinert to the emergency room that afternoon, and the hospital had admitted him shortly after 5:15 p.m. 3J hung up the phone and reported to the team what she'd learned.

Pascale shook his head. "Shit. Just what I feared. Did they say anything about his condition?"

"The nurse wouldn't share any more information with me."

"Look, we need to call the hospital in Meadowfield and find out about the Melanshins," Rosini said.

"Agreed," Pascale replied.

3J was ahead of them and had already found the phone number of the sole regional hospital servicing Meadowfield and the surrounding area. She called, and this time, the nurse who answered was more willing to speak. "Yes, we admitted the Melanshins to the hospital at around 7:15 p.m. today for observation."

The nurse explained that they weren't seriously hurt and said that it appeared someone had knocked them out while they were in the park. They had moderate concussions, as well as cuts and bruises, and they had been discharged at about 9:30 p.m.

3J thanked the nurse for the information and reported what she learned to the team.

"My Lord," Pascale said. "Three attacks. Multiple assailants. This is awful."

"Obviously a coordinated effort carried out by Clarke and his folks," Steele added.

"Absolutely," Moe agreed. "No other explanation."

Pascale nodded. "Like the decrypted ciphers said."

"I wonder if we're gonna have to break cover and reveal how we knew what we knew," Steele pondered aloud.

"Not necessarily, and not just yet in any case. Let me see if I can extract any more information from Lin before we make any decisions," Rosini said.

Bitty broke his silence and said, "Anthony, let me give Lin a call in the morning. I know him pretty well. He may be willing to share information with me. I can tell him that I'm following up as a concerned citizen and a Westport employee."

"Works for me," Rosini said, ceding the task to Bitty.

Before they started drinking in earnest, the group agreed that in the morning, Pascale and 3J would visit Jacob Steinert at the hospital as soon as visiting hours began, which they thought was 8:00 a.m. Bitty would call Lin to see how much more he'd be willing to share. By now, it was 11:30 p.m., and Moe turned on the television to see if the local streaming news had reported anything. The third story was about the confrontation in Westport, but it was a cursory piece with no video footage. The next story was about Steinert. It included a video showing Steinert's car in the garage and a stain on the ground near the tire, presumably blood.

The group watched in silence and began to drink. They collectively opted not to revisit the day's events. No debriefing. Just drinking.

3J was happy for the silence. Silence was a sound in its own right. And at that moment, it was the single best sound for 3J's state of mind and body.

29

Saturday, May 25, 2024

DRESSED IN JEANS, 3J was standing outside her condominium building with a travel mug in her hand at 7:45 the next morning when Pascale pulled up. Her ribs hurt less than they had the previous night and she felt better than she expected to.

She got in the car and they headed for St. Luke's. Once there, they checked in, learned where Steinert's room was, and headed for the elevator.

At his door, cracked open two inches, 3J knocked softly. "Hello? Jacob? 3J and Bill Pascale. You up?"

"Come in," Steinert said weakly.

The pair entered his room and found him propped up on two pillows, toying with his hospital breakfast, most of which remained on the plate. He had a black eye that was swollen and partially closed and cotton packing in his nostrils.

Pascale surveyed Steinert's face. "Jesus, Jacob. I am so sorry."

Steinert attempted a smile. "Hey, could be worse. I mean, I'm here and I'm talking to you, right?"

3J shook her head slowly in disbelief.

Steinert continued. "Just a knock on the head. Moderate concussion." He paused and then acknowledged as he sighed, "But a concussion nonetheless."

As Steinert spoke, his wife, Nancy, entered the room. 3J and Pascale introduced themselves and she shook their hands. They exchanged pleasantries and listened as Steinert recounted the little he could remember.

"Two attackers, I think. Slammed my head into something. I assume the car. I folded up and hit the ground." He made eye contact with Pascale. "I guess you were right, Bill. I should've been more on alert, although I'm not sure what I could've done. They were ready for me and had done some homework. The attack was quick and efficient."

"I understand, Jacob," Pascale replied.

"The police came by earlier this morning and took a brief statement," Steinert explained. "But I don't remember much."

"Understood," Pascale said. "Look, I don't want to sound like an alarmist, but whoever attacked you is still out there—not in police custody. I want to get you a security guard for here, home, and frankly, wherever you go. For a while."

Steinert's eyes were closed and he said nothing.

His wife said softly, "Listen to him. You need to do this, Jacob."

Steinert opened his eyes, tried to smile, and said, "You heard the woman, Bill."

"Okay, Jacob. I'll take care of it."

When they had finished their visit and were back in the car, 3J asked, "Who?"

"Come again?"

"I assume you're going to give me the same treatment as Jacob. So who are you going to get to watch me?"

"I'm going to say a team will watch you. We have Ronnie and me. And we have Moe."

3J sighed deeply. "Fine. Who for Jacob?"

"Anthony will do it."

They rode in silence for a time, and then Pascale asked if 3J was hungry.

"Sure," was all she said in reply. When he suggested they stop at Ibis Bakery she again said, "Sure." She was not feeling very talkative.

Bitty called Officer Lin and left a voice mail. Ten minutes later, Lin returned the call.

"Recovered from last night?" Lin asked.

"I'm fine, James. In my line of work, you learn to recuperate quickly." He paused and then added, "The rest are still recovering. They'll be fine."

"What's up?"

"I keep going over last night in my mind. Occupational hazard, I suppose. Most folks I need to deal with have had too much to drink. Didn't seem like our friends were drinkers, and they certainly didn't come out of O'Brien's and into the limelight. So I'm trying to understand what went down. Help me make a little sense of it."

"Happy to share," Lin replied, "but I doubt it'll make sense. Some of it is scary stuff. Clarke continues to say nothing. He's stone-faced. The only words he's muttered so far were 'raiders' and 'Quantrill.' We haven't had time to figure out what either means yet. Oh, and he again mistakenly thinks I'm an immigrant. I should have shared with him that my grandparents ended up in a World War II internment camp in California, but that might have started a Clarke-style history lesson I don't need to hear."

Lin paused and collected his thoughts. "Clarke'll need surgery on his wrist, apparently later today. He'll be out in time for his arraignment on Monday. We'll have a cop outside his hospital door in case he decides to try to check out early."

Bitty listened in silence.

"Now that other guy, Saber? The one Ms. Jones ran down and whose reproductive organs she roughed up? That guy is talking in between complaining about his black-and-blue balls. Now that he's started talking, he can't keep his mouth shut. Says Clarke heads up a group called The Thirty-Six Thirties. Strange name. Has something to do with the latitude of the state of Missouri and slaves. In any case, they're a right-wing group. One of the detectives did some research. The ADL considers them dangerous.

"According to Saber, this guy Clarke planned three attacks to occur almost simultaneously. One, a lawyer here in town named Jacob Steinert. Apparently a bankruptcy guy. Saber referred to him as 'that Jew-boy lawyer.'"

Bitty exhaled audibly.

Lin continued. "Two, Steinert's clients down in Meadowfield, where Clarke and Saber come from. A couple named Melanshin. Country of origin unknown. And now here's the unusual part. Saber says the third was not supposed to be Moe. They wanted to attack your friend, Ms. Jones. Ms. Jones must be the 'colored-law-yer' Clarke was ranting about. I take it she's a Kansas City lawyer."

"Yeah, that's strange. Jones is a Friday regular at the bar. Nice lady. The staff likes her. I wonder how these guys crossed up their signals between Moe and Jones."

"You're not going to like the answer to that question. Saber said he and Clarke couldn't tell the difference between the two women because they're both Black."

Bitty grunted and said angrily, "I'm betting that's not exactly how Saber phrased it, now did he?"

"He did not. I'm cleaning it up for you. He was much more, let's say, George Wallace and Confederate in the words he used."

"Yup. I imagine so. What a goddamn world."

"I gotta say, this guy Saber is downright indignant in how he describes folks. Like he has the right to talk that way. He's either tone deaf or he gives not one shit what people think about him. Or he thinks everyone agrees with him."

"I wonder how they knew where Ms. Jones drank."

"Saber said he didn't exactly know. Said that Clarke had a guy in KC who tailed Jones and Steinert."

"So one of The Thirty-Six Thirties is here in Kansas City?"

"Apparently. Maybe more than one."

"Guess I'm not surprised," Bitty replied. "Did he happen to say why they planned the attacks in the first place?"

"Said he couldn't exactly explain it but it had something to do with the Melanshins screwing Clarke out of lots of land and money and then filing bankruptcy."

"So this whole attack was over money and to get back at the Melanshins and their lawyer, Steinert?"

"Apparently. At least that's the story so far."

"Then why Jones, other than she's Black?"

"Saber didn't understand that fully either. Just said she pissed Clarke off when she wouldn't help him. Said she took sides against Clarke. Said she fucked with Clarke and no one does that."

Bitty sighed. "Clarke wanted help from a 'colored' lawyer? That also makes no sense. You'd think he'd want nothing to do with Ms. Jones."

"Y'know, Saber had a gun on him when Finkle cuffed him in Westport."

"Yeah, I heard that," Bitty said.

"That Jones lady is real lucky that Saber didn't use it when they scuffled. Real lucky."

"Yes she was. Damn fool. Okay, James. Thanks for filling in some of the blanks. I appreciate it. You guys going to turn this over to the Feds to pursue a hate crime?"

"My understanding? We haven't done that yet, but I'm sure that'll be the plan, Bitty."

"And since both of these folks were carrying weapons, I assume that kicks up the charges a notch?"

"Or two notches," Lin replied.

Bitty paused. When Lin said nothing, Bitty said, "Okay. Thanks for all the info, James."

"My pleasure, Bitty. I owed you."

"How so?"

"With you around at O'Brien's, my partner and me have got to deal with far fewer Westport drunk and disorderlies."

"All I mostly do is sit and watch the crowd. If they start to get out of line, I give them the Bitty look. They usually calm down rather than screwing with me."

"Sometimes, that's all that's needed to keep the peace, m'friend. And your look makes our job a little easier."

"Well, happy to help the city's finest out."

Bitty arranged for another meeting of the team to go over what he had learned when the call ended. "Need to stick with our story," he muttered to himself. "Anything else would be bad for the mission and bad for the team. We're dancing on the head of a pin here."

30

Woody Clarke recalls Sunday, May 26, 2024

I SAT THERE in the cell with my wrist throbbing, waiting for some guards to take me to the hospital, where a doc would fix me up. I'd heard from a guard that Brian Saber could barely stand up straight. I guess that colored gal, Jones, kicked him good and hard where the sun don't shine. And then did it again. Tough luck for Brian. He wasn't finished having kids. Or at least, he wasn't until Friday evening.

I kept wondering how the plan failed. I mean, we took down the Melanshins. We took down that Jew-boy lawyer. How come my part of the operation failed? It was as if that enormous colored guy and the others knew we was coming. It was as if they'd seen and cracked the cipher.

It's okay in life to have a healthy dose of paranoia. Comes in handy. Keeps a guy on his toes. And I was on my toes waiting to go to the hospital. No fuckin' way they all just happened to be exactly where me and Brian waited for that Jones skirt. No fuckin' way that bitch I pushed just happened to be dressed like that Jones gal.

It was as if them Union generals from the Civil War rose out of their graves in the nearby Union Hill Cemetary and read my mind . . . or my cipher. And Saber went absent without leave, big time. What the hell was that about? No commitment to the cause. He weren't no Graycoat of mine. No wonder the South lost.

I heard them guards coming for me and my hospital rendezvous. The wrist hurt like a bastard. Glad they were at least willin' to patch me up before I had to go before a judge for my bail.

I figured I'd be out by Tuesday morning. Then that bitch lawyer, Jones, needed to watch out. I wasn't done with her. I had no intention of surrendering on this one. Not at all.

INTERLUDE

Sunday, October 6, 2002

"HI YA, JO. WHERE y'at?" 3J's father asked, invoking the traditional New Orleans greeting. She and Papa talked every Sunday morning. "How's my college girl's college life?"

"It's all good, Papa. We have a game right after lunch against our league rivals, Lewis and Clark."

3J was a sophomore at Whitman College in Walla Walla, Washington. There on a full scholarship. She was a striker on the soccer team and ran track in the spring. The league named her to its Northwest Conference All-Academic team.

"How's those feet of yours, Jo?"

"Working good, Papa. Working good. Lot's of scoring chances. Some go in."

"And . . . campus life?"

3J sighed. "Not too many Black folks here, Papa. Even fewer from down our way. I don't always feel like I belong at social events. Still a wallflower, I suppose. Seems safe."

3J's papa worried about her social life, or lack thereof. College was a time for both academic and social education. Whitman, the alma mater of Supreme Court Justice William O. Douglas, lacked nothing on the academic side. He was sure it would open doors for her after graduation. That's what he hoped for his oldest. Maybe she'd continue with her interest in psychology. Maybe she'd go on and get an MBA and run a big company. Or maybe she'd veer in another direction, like law school. He was sure that whatever she did, she would be great at it. That was his Jo.

"You might oughta push yourself to get off that wall, Jo. Meet people. If they're not worried that you're Black, don't worry so much that they're not. Enjoy their company. They'll surely enjoy yours."

"Easier said than done, Papa. But you're right. You're always right."

Neither said anything for a moment, and then 3J asked, "Will you be able to come up here for Parents' Weekend, Papa?"

"I wish, Jo. Don't see how I can get time away from the plant this year. We're real busy."

"Busy's your middle name, Papa."

He chuckled. "I suppose that's so, Jo. I suppose that's so."

3J needed to run to a pre-game lunch with the team. "Love you, Papa."

"Love ya', Jo."

When the call ended, 3J's father had a big smile on his face. He always had one after they talked. He thought to himself, *Her ticket out of the Big Easy. Big things for her on the horizon.*

He hoped he would still be around to revel in her success. He had a doctor's appointment in a week. Something didn't feel right every morning. He hadn't shared the appointment news with 3J. No reason to alarm her. *It's probably nothing*, he thought, hoping he was right.

31

Sunday, May 26, 2024

THE SIX SAT around Moe's living room coffee table one more time, and Bitty reported his discussion with James Lin.

"So here's how I'm seeing this. Some of us commissioned an illegal computer hack. I assume our operative has eliminated the hacking trail. We should confirm that. Our operative cracked the private ciphers. Nothing illegal there. We developed a plan to protect Ms. Jones, and we set up a decoy that worked. We took down a couple of bad actors. Cops now know that Saber and Clarke were after Ms. Jones, not Moe. Lin didn't seem particularly concerned about that. Clarke's not talking. I wonder how long that'll go on. From what Lin says, Saber doesn't know everything. But he knows enough. We haven't lied to the cops because they haven't asked us the right questions. And this all gets turned over to the Feds at some point soon."

"That's about the sum and substance of it," Rosini said. "To me, as long as the operative has withdrawn the malware and left no trail, it'd be real hard for anyone to figure out it was the hack that led to the plan that led to our takedown."

"Look, I commissioned the hack," Pascale replied. "None of the rest of you. I'm not asking anyone to lie on my account. I need to circle back with the investigators and see if they've covered the malware trail. I'm sure they have, but I'll get confirmation. Then I don't see how or why the authorities would challenge what we've told them. Hell, if we had never met but all of us found ourselves at O'Brien's last Friday, the same series of events could have gone down. Right? The only real vulnerability here is that we knew what would happen beforehand, and we took steps to protect 3J."

"It's good to keep talking these things out," Steele said. "Can't be too careful and can't plan too much. But for my money, people, we stay the course. I don't think we'll have to lie. 3J and Pascale were going to be at O'Brien's anyway. Like always. Bitty and I work there. Bitty patrols the perimeter regularly. I use the alleyway regularly. Rosini and Moe go there after work from time to time. If Clarke starts talking, my feeling is he'll say he failed in his mission like his Southern generals did back in the Battle of Westport. He presents as someone more interested in advancing his racist narrative than examining how he failed."

3J sat silently listening, feeling it was all her fault. "Look, I'm not going to have anyone lying on my account," she said softly. "If things take a turn here and there's something we've missed, or Clarke figures it out, or the Feds figure it out, and the choice is between lying to the authorities or coming clean, I'm gonna vote for coming clean." She looked around the room for a reaction.

"Given the choice between jailing a right-wing hater who's on the ADL's list, who hacked the Melanshins, and whose son sells heroin to teenagers versus prosecuting lawyers for a hack that led to the demise of the hater, the Feds will punish the hater every time," Rosini observed. "They might even thank us. That's my take for whatever it's worth."

Everyone nodded again. "I agree completely," 3J said emphatically.

"So, bankruptcy gurus, what happens next to Clarke and the Melanshins in the bankruptcy cases?" Moe asked.

3J smiled. "That's one I can answer. Once Jacob has the use of both of his eyes again, we'll collaborate on a plan, file it, get Judge Robertson involved, and get it approved. The only open question is how Clarke will fare under the plan, since, attack or no attack, he's still owed millions."

Jacob Steinert's wife led the lawyer to the car, and he gingerly folded himself into the passenger seat when the hospital discharged him mid-afternoon on Sunday. The discharging doctor told him to try to take things slow for a few days. But slow wasn't his usual gear, and he decided to do nothing productive on Sunday and be back at his desk Monday.

Once home, he wrote and filed a short motion for an extension of time to file the brief he had hoped to finish over the weekend. His wife frowned, and he gave her the only explanation he could—one she had heard too many times. "Honey, you know one of the main drawbacks to being a solo practitioner is that there's no one to lean on in an emergency. I'm not the chief cook and bottle washer in my firm. I'm the *only* cook and bottle-washer. Concussion or no concussion."

His wife turned and left him alone.

"Two cops—a Black driver and a Latino passenger—transported Clarke to the North Kansas City Hospital for his wrist surgery. They stationed themselves outside the operating room, and when the hand surgeon finished, the orderlies moved Clarke to a room, followed by the cops. When the anesthesia wore off, the surgeon examined him and discharged him back into the officers' custody.

On the drive back to the jail, the Black cop asked Clarke if he wanted to talk now. Clarke said nothing and turned to look out the patrol car window.

The Latino said to the driver, "I wonder what old Judge Roundtree will make of this one."

"No idea," replied the driver, smiling. "But I was wondering what this one will make of old Judge Roundtree."

"Good point. This one doesn't seem to like folks like you and me and is happy to share that with about anyone. When he sees Roundtree is Black, who knows what this one will do. Should be an interesting morning with old Judge Roundtree."

The driver chuckled.

Clarke listened and thought, *My God. Is everyone here who's in a position of authority colored? Or an immigrant? What a fucking world!*

32

Monday, May 26, 2024

WOODY CLARKE SAT in the traditional orange Jackson County jumpsuit that said "Inmate" across the back. The police had used a zip tie to connect his right arm cast to his left wrist, and both hands and arms were across the front of his body, resting for the moment in his lap.

In due course, the bailiff announced, "Case No. 24-70731, State of Missouri vs. Woody Clarke. Defendant shall rise and come forward with his counsel."

Clarke stood and walked alone to one of the lawyers' tables facing the judge. He had no lawyer. The prosecutor, Barnaby Steward, stood at the other table.

The nameplate on the bench said "Judge Sanford Roundtree." The judge looked down at Clarke and read the charges. "Mr. Clarke, the State has charged you with aggravated assault and battery and conspiracy to commit assault and battery, as well as attempted murder. Where's your lawyer today, sir?"

Clarke said nothing.

"Sir, did you hear me?"

Clarke said nothing.

"Look m'friend. It's a simple process we have here. Nothin' fancy. I ask questions. You answer them. Do you understand me?"

"Oh, I heard you all right. I ain't your friend. That's for damn sure. I got nothing to say. Leastwise not to you."

"So it's me, eh? That's your problem? What is there about me has you all bothered?"

"You're colored."

"I am?" The judge feigned surprise. "I see."

Some of the people in the pews watching the proceedings chuckled audibly at the judge's comment.

"Did the officers read you your rights?"

"Yep. Many times."

"Did you understand those rights?"

"Not that hard to follow."

"Good. Good. So the police officers told you that you had the right to an attorney?"

"Yep."

"And you declined to have one."

"Yep. Also told me I had the right to remain silent. But apparently not in here."

There was more chuckling, and Judge Roundtree looked out to the pews where mostly lawyers sat waiting for their turn to appear in front of him and shook his head, silently commanding them not to laugh. Then he looked back at Clarke. "All right. Your choice. No lawyer. We're making some progress here. Now you have to tell me whether you plead guilty or not guilty. Do you understand that?"

"Yep."

"How do you plead?"

"Well, I ain't guilty. And you ain't got no authority over me."

"I see. We'll enter a plea of not guilty for you."

"Mr. Steward," the judge said, turning his attention to the prosecutor and the issue of bail. "What is the state's position on bail?"

"Your Honor, we request that the Court deny bail. Mr. Clarke is a flight risk and, we believe, a danger to the general public. He's the leader of a right-wing organization named The Thirty-Six Thirties and, as you can tell, he denies that the government has any level of authority. He signs his court pleadings pro se in his own blood, we believe."

As Steward finished the explanation about Clarke's blood, many of the lawyers in the pews leaned forward to listen more closely.

Steward continued. "His group is on several terrorist lists, including the Justice Department's, the ADL's, and the Southern Poverty Law Center's. He plotted to attack two attorneys, officers of the court under Missouri and federal law. Two of his group members carried out his wishes and put one victim in the hospital with serious injuries—Jacob Steinert, who Mr. Clarke refers to as 'the Jew-boy lawyer.'

"Two others in his group carrying out his wishes attacked two bankruptcy debtors who owe him money. Put them in the hospital as well. He plotted to attack attorney Josephina Jones, a Black bankruptcy attorney here in Jackson County. Mr. Clarke refers to her as 'that colored gal.' But he didn't succeed in attacking Ms. Jones because he mistakenly attacked another Black woman in Westport instead. If you let him out on bail, we submit he'll continue to try to attack Ms. Jones, Mr. Steinert, and the debtors. Judge, this is not someone who should be out on the street awaiting trial."

Turning his gaze to Clarke, the judge asked, "Mr. Clarke, if I set bail and let you out pending your trial, will you agree not to flee?"

"I ain't agreeing to nothing."

"Are you going to try to hurt anyone if I let you out?"

"Still got the mission. No one fucks with me."

"The mission? I see. Mr. Clarke, do you believe that you have the financial capacity to make bail?"

"Well, I mighta before that son of a bitch Donnie Melanshin swindled me out of millions."

"I don't know Mr. Donnie Melanshin, sir, but it sounds to me that if I set bail at a million dollars or higher, you couldn't or wouldn't post bail, and if I let you out pending trial, you're reserving the right to complete your mission, as you call it, as well as flee. Do I have that about right?"

"You ain't far off."

"And you still want to attack Ms. Jones?"

"I ain't answering that question."

"I see. Probably wise. All right. I agree with the prosecutor. You're a flight risk and a clear and present danger to society. I will not afford you the chance to be free pending trial. Rather, you will be a guest of Jackson County for a while, and I'm returning you to the custody of these fine officers, who will escort you back to your jail cell. Bail is hereby denied."

The judge paused and glared at Clarke. "Mr. Clarke, any further business before this court?"

"I don't got no *further* business 'cause I never had *no* business with you in the first place and still don't. Like I said, you ain't got no authority."

"Well, Mr. Clarke, you and I don't need to debate that point here today. Let's have these good officers take you back to the jail, where you can sit alone and contemplate your fate for a good while and even heal up a little, authority or not." The judge turned away from Clarke, turned to his courtroom staff, and said, "Bailiff, call the next case."

Later in the day, Pascale called Moses Aaronson, who conferenced in Rome, and explained everything that had happened. Rome admitted she felt her heart in her stomach as she learned that despite her efforts, she had been unable to prevent the attacks on the Melanshins and Steinert. "I feel awful. I should have thought to check for an iPhone backup on Clarke's hard drive sooner."

Pascale responded quickly in a reassuring tone, "Rome, please don't beat yourself up. You did everything you could, and we're grateful for the assistance. Truly. By your good work, we suspected enough to warn Steinert. Jacob made a decision not to adjust his life. That decision is what led to the beating, not the timing of your review of the iPhone backup."

Rome said nothing, and neither did Moses, so Pascale continued. "The reason for my call is to discuss what happened to your malware after you completed the operation."

"Recall that the plug-in he downloaded and used to game with me was where the malware resided," Rome replied. "I pushed an updated plug-in to his computer early on the Saturday morning after the attacks, and the plug-in that now resides in his browser is free of any malware."

"So all gone?"

"All gone, Mr. Pascale," Rome concurred.

"If the FBI took Clarke's computer, their forensics team couldn't detect that there had been malware on Clarke's computer?"

"In my opinion, the FBI would not detect it."

"*Would* not or *could* not?" Pascale asked.

"Would not." She paused, and then added, "They would have to be looking for traces of the malware, and it would be hard to find. They would have no reason to look for malware, would they?"

"Am I hearing that if the FBI set out to look for malware on Clarke's hard drive and their forensics folks were good, which they are, they might find evidence of the malware?"

"In my opinion, they might. Rarely is something ever completely wiped from a hard drive. But in my estimation, they would have to be looking for evidence of malware to find that Mr. Clarke had downloaded an infected plug-in that I've now updated to be malware-free."

"Hmm, I see," Pascale said slowly. It was not the answer he had been hoping for.

"Recall, also, Mr. Pascale, that Mr. Clarke had a penchant for online gaming. He was active on the internet, to include shady websites on both the dark web and clearnet. He is obviously willing to download things from the internet. In other words, a forensics analysis of Mr. Clarke's hard drive could easily conclude that given Mr. Clarke's surfing habits, any traces of malware could have come from any number of sites rather than from my plug-in."

"Yes, I suppose so," Pascale replied as he rubbed his chin, unconvinced.

When the call ended, Pascale stood, put his hands deep in his suit pockets, and turned to stare out his office window.

3J knocked softly on his doorjamb. "More contemplation?"

"Not this time, 3J. Not contemplation. Complications. Looking outside for inspiration, I'm afraid. Rome says that if the FBI is looking for malware on Clarke's computer, they might find evidence of her plug-in. It's gone now, she tells me, but evidence that it was present may not be."

"Bill, it'll be fine."

"Yeah. I hope so. But I wish there was more I could do than just hope."

3J grinned. "Well, look at it this way. I'm here. I'm smiling. Clarke is in jail. The perfect trifecta."

Pascale did not smile back and ignored her grin. He was not prepared to have his spirits lifted. "Let's hope that Clarke's incarceration has put an end to all of this." He pursed his lips and added softly, "Let's just hope."

33

Tuesday, June 4, through Friday, June 7, 2024

CHET LANDRY ARRIVED at the Jackson County jail as visiting hours began. After emptying his pockets and passing through a metal detector, an officer led him to a communication room. He took a seat in a narrow area in front of a thick pane of plexiglass with a phone hanging on the dividing wall. An identical chair, phone, and wall were on the other side of the plexiglass. Prison guards on both sides of the glass kept a watchful eye.

A guard led Clarke to his chair opposite Landry. Clarke's phone was on his right side, and because of his wrist cast, he had to reach across his body with his left hand to grab the phone and put it to his ear. The black-and-blue bruising from Clarke's broken nose had begun to fade into an ugly blend of yellow, green, and brown colors.

Clarke spoke first. "Good to see you, Chet. You're my first. What's the word from the outside?"

"How you doing in here, Woody?"

"I'm fine so far. Colored judge sent me back in here rather than letting me out. Seems like everyone in these parts is either colored or an immigrant or both. A big steaming pile of shit is what it is, Chet. This is our America, and that sound you hear every night is the big flush of us going down the toilet and into the sewers. I smell a lot of that sewage here in the big city."

"I know, I know," Landry agreed. "Look, Woody. Word is that the Melanshins traveled up here to meet with the Feds about the attack. We heard that them Feds might talk to the Jew-boy lawyer and that colored gal as well. Hate crime is what they're talking about. That's some serious stuff."

"Yeah, well . . . we always knew we was on them lists. So not too surprising."

"What're we gonna do, Woody?"

"I'll come up with a plan. Won't be able to get it to you by cipher from inside here, but this whole thing ain't gonna be my Appomattox Court House either. That's for damn sure."

Landry nodded slowly. "Woody, gotta tell you something else. You ain't gonna like it."

"Ain't a whole lot I've been liking lately. Go on."

"Have you seen Saber in here?"

"Nah. They keep us separated. Ain't seen him since we got arrested and booked."

"Well, Saber is in here singing like a bird. Telling 'em everything. Telling them about the heroin. Telling about us Thirties. I seen Saber here yesterday morning. Surprised he was even willing to see me. Didn't have much to say. But he told me that the Fed in charge of the hate crime investigation is a prosecutor named Robert Hickman."

"Never heard of him."

"Well, I'm thinking you gonna hear a lot about him and from him. And soon."

"Maybe so. We'll see."

"Something else you ain't gonna like. Hickman's colored."

"Well . . . sheeeeit!" Clarke shook his head slowly and said, "Like I said. It's like there ain't no White Christians at all left in these parts."

3J received a call from Robert Hickman on Wednesday. The two had never met but she guessed he had done his homework on her.

Hickman asked if they could meet and talk in person, and 3J agreed to come to his office on Friday. Pascale and 3J agreed that she should go without him or another Greene Madison lawyer accompanying her. They both felt the presence of other lawyers would set off an alarm that 3J was concerned, and they agreed that 3J should present herself as she was—the lucky-to-be-alive intended victim.

Then they did what all good lawyers do: They spent hours preparing 3J for the interview and practiced and refined her answers to the likely questions Hickman might ask.

That Friday morning she arrived at the courthouse, made her way upstairs, and was led by a receptionist to a spartan conference room in the office occupied by the attorneys of the Western District of Missouri Office of the United States Attorneys, part of the United States Justice Department. Hickman, an Assistant U.S. Attorney, an AUSA, was one of the Justice Department's many litigators stationed throughout the country and charged with enforcing federal laws, including investigating and prosecuting criminal cases.

Hickman came in shortly after 3J arrived with a tall FBI agent named James Diaz. The three shook hands. Diaz sported a gray-and-white handlebar mustache and a full head of pure white hair combed straight back. He introduced himself as Jamie and spoke with a slight Texas accent. Hickman was a career prosecutor in the U.S. Attorney's office with a reputation as a hardworking, no-nonsense criminal litigator. He sported a constant overworked and understaffed look on his face.

Hickman thanked 3J for coming and got down to business immediately. He asked for her spin on what had happened. She explained her interactions with, and impressions of, Clarke. Then she said, "You know. I have some lingering concerns that this is not necessarily over, whatever *this* is."

"As do we, Ms. Jones," Diaz replied. "The investigation is in its infancy, but I feel you're entitled to know that we're quickly heading down a path to present to Mr. Hickman here sufficient information for him to decide if federal hate crime charges are appropriate. And not just against Woody Clarke and Brian Saber. We have a bead on the two who attacked Jacob Steinert and the ones who attacked Donnie and Lil Melanshin. It's fair to say that we're rapidly zeroing in on the rest of these Thirty-Six Thirties group members."

"What exactly do you mean by 'a bead on'?" 3J asked.

Hickman replied for Diaz. "Can't answer that, Ms. Jones. But rest assured that we share your concerns."

3J nodded.

"Tell me something, Ms. Jones," Hickman said slowly. "Something I've been wondering about as I'm gathering facts. How exactly did it come to pass that there were six of you at that bar at the same exact time and on the same exact day Woody Clarke was planning to assault you?"

3J had practiced how she would answer this question and answered without hesitation. "Can't speak for each of the six, Mr. Hickman. William Pascale is my law partner at Greene Madison. He and I often meet at O'Brien's on Fridays to grab a drink and review the week. Ronnie Steele works behind the bar at O'Brien's and manages the operation for the owners. Eugene Martin—people call him Bitty—also works there. I'd describe his role as private security to keep the peace. If you meet him, you'll quickly see why he's good at that job." It was clear to 3J that Diaz was not just looking at her but studying her as she spoke.

When she paused, Diaz said, "Here's the thing, Ms. Jones. Witnesses have told us that, indeed, you're a regular at O'Brien's and that, indeed, you and Mr. Pascale usually sit at the same booth. But even though you were there, you weren't sitting in the booth that night. Someone was sitting with Mr. Pascale. Just not you. No one was able to tell us where you were." Diaz paused and smiled. "So where were you?"

3J answered confidently, "I went back to the storeroom behind the bar."

"And why would you be in the bar's storeroom?" Diaz asked.

"I needed to talk to Ronnie Steele. His office is back there." 3J paused, smiled, and said casually, "He and I are seeing each other. I didn't want to talk to him in front of Bill. Y'know, personal boy-girl stuff."

"I see," Diaz replied. "Ms. Jones, witnesses also told us a former Jackson County Sheriff, one Anthony Rosini, was also behind the bar that night wearing a white apron, as if he worked at the bar. He does not. Know anything about that?"

"I really don't, Mr. Diaz. I know Anthony. My firm uses him to serve papers for us. Ronnie and Anthony know each other pretty well. Ronnie worked vice for KCPD for many years before transitioning to bartender. They probably bumped into each other professionally from time to time back in the day."

Hickman jumped in. "Well, it's not just them who go way back. Right? We understand Mr. Steele and Monica Sterling, the woman Clarke attacked, were partners working vice together for many years."

3J kept her composure and didn't react.

Hickman continued. "Here's what we're wondering, Ms. Jones. And mind you, my personal opinion is that Clarke is bad with a capital B, and he's gonna go away for a very long time if I have anything to say about it. And this'll be a better city, county, state, and country as a result. He and his Thirties colleagues."

Hickman paused, looked down at the table, and continued without looking up. "But I'm looking at Friday evening's events, and in all candor, here's what I'm seeing. I've got two lawyers from Greene Madison—you and Mr. Pascale. But it just happens you're not sitting with Mr. Pascale in the usual booth. I've got two former law enforcement folks with a history wearing aprons behind the bar, but it just happens only one of them belongs there. I got a bouncer who just happens to be making the perimeter rounds when the bad guys arrive and station themselves to wait for you."

Hickman paused again and then looked up at 3J. "I've got another former law enforcement officer who just happens to be Mr. Steele's decades-long vice squad partner and who just happens to be wearing a dark-colored pantsuit not unlike the kind folks say you wear from time to time, including that evening. And then I got Clarke who mistakenly attacks the wrong woman, thinking it's you.

"I've got you in the alleyway, not in the booth and not in the storeroom, and you just happen to be there when the bad guys strike and when one of them runs for it. And you just happen to be a former college track runner. A sprinter, I believe. Probably lucky for you that you played soccer, I would guess, given how you rearranged Saber's family jewels."

Hickman paused and looked intently at 3J. She continued to have no reaction to his analysis.

"You see, Ms. Jones, I do well in this office because I work hard—harder than most—and I got a little voice in my head I always listen to. Always. The little voice gets all agitated when I'm explaining things and have to say, over and over again, 'who just happens to.' Lots of coincidences here, Ms. Jones. Too many. The little voice inside my head? It doesn't much like coincidences." Hickman narrowed his eyes at 3J and added, "Me neither." Hickman paused and folded his arms across his chest. "I'm sure you see my point."

As she had practiced with Pascale, 3J locked eyes with Hickman and replied, "No, I don't, Mr. Hickman. Hundreds of people drink at O'Brien's on any given Friday. Even more on Memorial Day weekend. As I understand it, Clarke had me followed to learn my habits." Quietly but sternly she added, "Hear me. This racist had me followed."

She paused to gather herself and then continued. "Creepy

beyond description. He hates Black folks intensely. I'm sure you've figured that out and are as troubled by it as am I. He illegally listened in on the debtors' private conversations in their kitchen. He's on multiple domestic terrorist lists, including your employer's list. As you say, he's a bad man. And it was just by the grace of God, and the fact he can't tell the difference between one Black woman and another, that he failed to come after me. If he had, he might've killed me. First time I can remember the 'we all look alike' racist stereotype helped me out. And it's a good goddamn thing he didn't seriously hurt the woman he attacked."

3J paused to see if there was any reaction from either Hickman or Diaz. There was not.

Hickman and 3J continued to lock eyes after 3J finished as if neither wanted to break the eye contact. Finally, Hickman broke the silence, smiled, looked toward Diaz, and said, "Well, like I said. Clarke is bad with a capital B. The Thirties as well. It will give me great satisfaction to move him and his crew from the watch to the incarcerated list."

Then he shifted his gaze to 3J. "Watch your news feed for the next couple of days, and do me a favor. Try to lie a little low. Don't get into any fights for a while."

3J nodded. The three shook hands and Hickman rose to walk 3J out. When he returned to the conference room, Diaz was pouring a glass of water. He held the glass in his left hand while he aimlessly twirled the end of his mustache with his right. "She's impressive, Robert. Very composed."

Hickman said nothing.

"Very prepared, as well," Diaz added. "Someone very experienced spent some serious time prepping her. That's my opinion."

"That they did, my friend," Hickman replied. "That they did. In my book, a little too damn prepared."

"So whataya think, Robert?" Diaz asked after a few seconds, smiling.

"Like I told her, that little voice in my head is a bit agitated right now. Something doesn't seem to add up for the voice and me. Six people all at the bar at the same time Clarke arrives, admittedly with terror on his mind. Three of the six have worked in law enforcement. One is a mountain of a man who could snap a person in half with his bare hands. Two were once vice partners. One dresses like Ms. Jones. And all six find themselves outside near enough to Clarke that as he strikes, they swiftly and efficiently take him and Saber down. And I mean, really take them down. They were ready, like a professional hit team. Like they had a plan. And if they did, it worked. Clarke may not write for a while, and Saber may not be having any more babies."

Hickman slowly shook his head. "So what do I think? It feels to me like they were all there that night to take down Clarke and Saber, not to drink."

"Humor me for a moment, Robert," Diaz said. "And what if they were? Anything wrong with that? Maybe we need more people like these six to stand up to the Clarkes and The Thirties of the world." Diaz clasped his hands behind his head and looked up at the ceiling. Then he looked back to Hickman. "Seems like if they were there for that purpose, we ought to be giving them a heroes' ceremony, medals, and the key to the city."

"No argument there. But if they were there for that purpose, I'm wondering how they knew the attack was going down right there and then."

Diaz continued to play with his mustache as he looked down at the floor and then back up to Hickman. "Same question, Mr. Prosecutor. Why does it matter?"

"Maybe it doesn't," Hickman admitted. "And in this case, maybe it shouldn't. These may be loose ends that won't matter when the sun sets on this case, but then again, tying up loose ends is what I get paid to do."

After a few moments, Diaz replied, "Yeah, well. Unless you

direct me otherwise, I'm not gonna lose much sleep over the possibility these six folks somehow had information at their disposal and used it to come up with a plan—a successful one, I might add—to take down Clarke and that Saber guy. If they knew ahead of time about the planned hit on Ms. Jones, more power to them and maybe I don't think I need to know how they found out. My team can attend to the business of Clarke and his right-wing Thirties without tying up this particular loose end." He paused, smiled, twirled the end of his mustache and added with a more pronounced Texas drawl, "At least that's my esteemed opinion, counselor, for what it's worth."

Hickman offered an understanding head nod. "I hear you."

3J left the courthouse and walked back to her office along Grand Boulevard. Once a downtown street aptly reflecting its name, the stretch from River Market south to Fourteenth Street had fallen on hard times. Other than the Ambassador Hotel with its Reno Club and live jazz within, its streets were now lined with empty storefronts, commercial tenants who seemed to lease their space for a month and then disappear, high-rise office buildings in disrepair, low-rise buildings that gave new meaning to deferred maintenance, and empty lots that served as small garbage dumps with mice and rats scurrying around. A now-shuttered Federal Reserve Bank high-rise, opened in 1921 and once described as a magnificent tower of strength, was dark as it appeared to gaze down on the boulevard. The business of money had moved away from downtown Kansas City and left behind a moneyless urban blight in its wake.

Normally, she would try to think of some Kansas City jazz history facts relating to the street on which she walked to make the journey more interesting. But not on this walk. No stories came to mind about Kansas City's Ben Webster and Lester Young blowing their tenor saxes in smokey, 1940s, Grand Boulevard establishments like the Vendome Cabaret.

Instead, her thoughts about the Hickman meeting consumed her. She revisited the questions and her answers over and over as she approached the Sprint Center, near where Civil War Union soldiers had housed female prisoners, then walked west on Twelfth Street one block to Walnut Street and her office building. She stuck to the script, and Pascale's prep had been invaluable, but she still wondered if she gave anything away?

Then her thoughts turned to Hickman's dislike for coincidences, a trait she shared. But this time, she was the reason for many of those coincidences, and she wondered if they knew something. At Moe's house, she had emphatically agreed that the Feds would never come after the team for a hack, but now she suddenly felt concern seeping into her thought process. She told herself to get a grip because she didn't want to let Pascale see her concerned. He was already concerned enough.

Once on Greene Madison's twenty-seventh floor, her first stop was Pascale's office, where she made a detailed report to him. He shook his head and frowned, obviously concerned, and mustered only, "Sounds like you did well. But we still gotta hope no one in the Justice Department cares how we knew what we knew."

"Bill, it went well. The prep was great," she replied confidently, but he still looked ill at ease, and she could see the concern on his face. She added softly with conviction, "Bill, it really will all be okay." But they both knew there was insufficient evidence to back up her statement.

34

Wednesday, June 12, 2024

ROBERT HICKMAN HEADED down for his car and the short drive to the FBI's new Kansas City regional headquarters at I-29 and NW 112th Street. Once there, he showed his credentials and headed to the small conference room steps from Jamie Diaz's desk.

Hickman asked where they were on the Meadowfield case and Diaz advised him that he expected to have search warrants within a couple of hours. Saber had told the KCPD that The Thirties were scheduled to have a barn meeting that evening to discuss the Clarke and Saber arrests, and Diaz planned to have each of them nabbed at their homes as they left for the meeting. That way, they could avoid the potential for mob behavior they might encounter if they nabbed them at the barn.

The search warrants would cover electronics, homes, offices, barns, and vehicles. They would also be arresting the two Thirties who attacked Jacob Steinert and the two who attacked Donnie and Lil Melanshin. They had both Kansas and Missouri jurisdictions involved: Kansas, where the Melanshins were attacked, and Missouri, where Steinert had been taken down. All four would be processed in the Western District and all four would then be moved to the same place to be held pending arraignment.

Diaz didn't need anything from Hickman at that point, but he was willing to accommodate Hickman's request to ride along with Diaz, who was going to be on the team to arrest one of Jacob Steinert's attackers.

Promptly at 6:00 p.m., the agents fanned out in Meadowfield and FBI teams stationed themselves near the homes of The Thirties who lived in Meadowfield proper. For The Thirties who lived on a farm, a team stationed itself at the end of the private farm road connecting the farmhouse to the public road. The FBI intercepted each of The Thirties as they headed out for the barn meeting, served the search warrants, and began to collect documents and property. The Thirties who had attacked Steinert and the Melanshins were arrested and handcuffed.

The only hitch was that one of Steinert's attackers had a small handgun he reached for when Diaz yelled, "FBI! Don't move!" But before he could grab his gun, two large agents pinned him flat to the ground and sat on his back while they read him his rights and handcuffed him.

While the FBI encountered grousing, other than Steinert's attacker, The Thirties did nothing to interfere or resist. As Diaz and Hickman would later learn, unlike other right-wing groups, The Thirties had neither trained nor planned for a confrontation with authorities of the magnitude of the FBI raid.

Diaz and Hickman rode back to Kansas City together in their unmarked government vehicle. At first, they said little. Then after twenty minutes, Hickman said, "I've got access to Clarke's electronics seized by KCPD with the help of Meadowfield's finest. Between that and what your teams seized, I'm going to need some FBI computer forensic help pretty quickly here to start to get to the bottom of what makes this guy Clarke tick."

"Not a problem. I'll assign some help for you when we get back."

"Y'know, we're pretty lucky here. I've already got my grand jury convened. I can present the case against Clarke to the jurors quickly, and so far, it's straightforward. I've got at least six people who will testify about what happened out on the street that night. Even if I have my suspicions about how they knew the where and when, they're credible witnesses for what happened. If need be, I bet I can get Saber to testify.

"With all that, I expect I'll get my indictment against Clarke and the four attackers, file my charges, and we'll be off and running. Meanwhile, you'll have processed the evidence we seized and done some forensics, which will give us a start on some insight into Mr. Clarke. And then I'll have to go through arraignments for these folks. For Clarke, it'll be a repeat experience. That reminds me. I gotta get a transcript of the state court arraignment hearing. From what I heard, it was a doozy and might be sufficient to convince my federal judge to deny bail."

Diaz nodded.

After a few moments, Hickman mused, "I wonder if Clarke learned from his Jackson County arraignment experience how to conduct himself before a judge."

Diaz smiled. "I doubt it."

35

Friday, June 14 through Monday, July 1, 2024

STEINERT HAD EMAILED a draft plan to 3J. The email it accompanied had explained that his clients hoped the committee would join with the debtors in jointly filing the plan. Of interest to 3J, the plan had two classes set up for unsecured creditors, designated Classes 4 and 5. Class 4 contained all the unsecured creditors except one, Woody Clarke. He was the sole creditor in Class 5.

As Steinert had signaled in court, the plan proposed to sell the land formerly owned by Clarke and use the sale proceeds to make a lump sum payment to all creditors except the one Class 5 creditor. The debtors would pay the balances owing on claims, after the initial payment, quarterly over eight years at six percent interest. In their plan, the Melanshins also promised they would make adjustments to their lifestyle to assure sufficient cash flow to make the plan payments.

The plan treated Class 5 totally differently. It proposed to pay Clarke only five percent of whatever Judge Robertson said the Melanshins owed him over fifteen years with annual payments at four percent interest. 3J knew such a provision was in the works, but seeing it on paper was jarring, even to her. She couldn't even imagine how Clarke would react. She wondered if the prison guards allowed inmates to scream in their cells.

In the email, Steinert wrote he would need her help in coming up with a strategy to make the separate treatment of Clarke's claim fly and survive the "unfair discrimination" test. She was looking forward to her meeting with Steinert that day to brainstorm ways to get Judge Robertson's approval of the treatment of Clarke's claim.

3J arrived at Steinert's office just after lunchtime. Steinert's assistant brought her into the small conference room adjacent to his office at which Steinert was already seated, surrounded by neatly organized Melanshin case papers. It had been three weeks since the attacks. His face had begun to heal, although a careful inspection revealed remaining bruising faded but still noticeable. He stood, and they shook hands.

"Jacob, so good to see you. How are you doing?"

"Healing up. The brain fog seems to have mostly lifted. I've never boxed, but I suppose I feel like how a boxer must feel a few weeks after getting knocked out. Except I have more body fat, fewer muscles, and lower stamina, speed, and coordination."

3J smiled.

"And how about you, 3J?"

"I didn't get it nearly as bad as you. But my ribs still ache when I take a deep breath. Having Saber land on top of me as we fell backwards was not part of my plan." 3J didn't tell Steinert she had no real plan. "So I'm not jogging for at least another week, and then I'll hope to get back to the exercise routine."

"When I graduated from law school, never in my wildest dreams did I think that someday I'd get beaten up because I represented debtors someone didn't like," Steinert admitted. "It's not something they teach you to watch out for in law school."

"You got that right."

They sat silently for a few moments.

Steinert pulled one pile of papers closer to him. "Well, why don't we dive into it, if that's okay with you."

"Sure thing. I read the plan. I like it. The committee will like it, or should I say, the reconstituted committee now that the U.S. Trustee removed Clarke and The Thirties from it."

"How could they not like it? They'll all get paid in full, including an immediate significant pay down."

"You and I need to figure out how to get this to fly in Robertson's court," 3J said. "In our circuit, the ability to separately classify unsecured creditors, while not prohibited, is pretty limited. We'll need a credible reason. Have you come up with any ideas?"

"Still working on it. We need to identify what makes Clarke different from the other creditors and see if that leads to a permissible reason for separate classification."

"Well, of course, there are the obvious ones: He's a felon. He's a racist. He's a misogynist. He's violent. He threatened the debtors. He tried to kill us. And he illegally eavesdropped."

"Yeah, but what has me concerned is that if we set all that aside and look at him with only his creditor hat on, he's not much different from the other creditors."

"Pascale had an idea he wanted me to pass along. What if the Melanshins didn't owe Mr. Clarke over four million dollars?"

"The Melanshins confirmed the math. The sale deal was worth a little over four million to Clarke."

"No, that's not what Pascale meant."

"Explain," Steinert said, looking intrigued.

"Suppose the Melanshins had a claim against Clarke that offset the four million dollars."

"Like what kind of claim?"

"Well, the man *did* direct his goons to try to kill them, and the attack put them in the hospital. And I'm certain he directed his squad to throw bricks through their front window."

"Suing Clarke for damages will take time. Not that we couldn't, but the outcome of the litigation could delay the plan process, and I know the Melanshins want to move forward as quickly as possible. Also, since part of the offset would be a personal injury claim, I'm not sure the Bankruptcy Code permits a bankruptcy judge to try that case, so we'd have to find a district court judge. More time, I'm afraid."

They both sat there, silently pondering. "Jacob, suppose you said in the plan that his conduct damaged the Melanshins and it was so outrageous that in a lawsuit by the Melanshins against Clarke, a jury would award them actual and punitive damages of a total of, let's say, four million dollars, or whatever amount an expert would say."

3J could tell from Steinert's expression that he was warming to 3J's developing theory.

"Yes, I like this," he said. "We could object to Clarke's claim, give as the grounds for objection exactly what you're saying, and then provide as part of the plan process that Judge Robertson will have to establish the amount of the Clarke claim. Estimate the claim for payment under the plan. The Bankruptcy Code lets the bankruptcy judges do that."

"Exactly. It could work," 3J agreed.

"Yeah, but while it would reduce the claim, it wouldn't address whether the Melanshins could still keep Clarke in a different class."

"True," 3J said slowly as she thought through the remaining issue.

"The Melanshins are pretty adamant they don't want Clarke to get a dime from the sale of the land. Not a dime. To pull that off, he'll need to be in a different class. My clients might be able to pay him less in that separate class."

"Not sure if that will work," 3J said.

"Well, remember, the Melanshins carried out the contract for deed scheme to get back at Clarke for the death of their son Toby. That's a pretty powerful motivator to keep Clarke far away from the land proceeds." Steinert paused. "It won't bring Toby back, but it will bring meaning to the phrase 'make Clarke pay.'"

"Indeed," 3J said. "It's certainly in the interest of other unsecured creditors for Clarke to get paid less. That would free up more money to pay the rest of the creditor body faster."

"Exactly."

Once again, they sat in silence. Finally, 3J said, "There must be some way to make this work. I just need to do a little research. I'm sure there's something here, but I'm not seeing it. In the meantime, why not edit the plan along the lines we've discussed to reduce Clarke's claim and put some meat on the bones to support the extent of the Melanshins' damages."

"Agreed."

3J stood to leave. Then, turning toward him, she bent over at the waist, placed her hands on the conference room table, and said slowly, "Listen, Jacob—."

Before she could finish the thought, Steinert said softly, "No need, 3J. We're both here. We're both back at it. We're both lucky. And with time, we'll both be fine. Below the neck and above."

3J nodded. "It's a messed up world, Jacob."

"My Jewish Russian Grandma used to say to me, 'Jacob, it's a messed up world sometimes. But still, there's a lot of good around. The good and the bad speak to us, although admittedly, the bad tends to yell more loudly and drown out the rest. But the good gets us through the day.'" He paused, smiled, and added, "You and me, 3J, let's both try to remember that."

She smiled back at him. "Jacob Steinert, your grandma was a wise woman. She sounds more and more like my father."

"He must have been a very wise man."

"The wisest," she said in agreement.

Over the weekend and into the next week, 3J read dozens of cases permitting a plan to separately classify an unsecured creditor saying it didn't unfairly discriminate. She felt strongly that Judge Robertson would want to, and would in fact, permit it, *if* the lawyers could give him the ammunition to support the plan treatment. But finding the hook to support the treatment had proven to be illusive.

She sat at her desk staring at her computer screen and the Westlaw legal research database trying to fashion yet another search to unlock the key to permitted plan discrimination. Just before she was ready to pack it in for the night, a search returned a hit on an article written by a well-known Stanford Law School professor discussing unfair discrimination. Professor Amanda Lee was a regular on the bankruptcy seminar circuit, and 3J had heard her speak on several panels at conferences. She was impressive.

3J decided to delay leaving the office while she read the article. The author noted Chapter 11 creditors vote on plan approval, like a mini-election. The lawyers counted the plan votes class by class like electors counted political votes state by state. The author pointed out that a bankruptcy court had the power to deny a creditor the right to vote if the creditor had done something egregious and the court found that the creditor had acted in bad faith. Often, the article noted, the courts equated bad faith with the creditor having an ulterior motive. One example offered by Professor Lee was a competitor buying a claim from a legitimate creditor and then voting "No" to try to put the debtor out of business.

In a footnote, the author argued, "Of course, if a creditor cannot vote because it acted in bad faith, a court should not normally consider putting that creditor in its own class as unfair discrimination." It was the nugget of gold 3J had been searching for. Those were the exact words she hoped Judge Robertson would utter as he approved the Melanshins' plan. But the footnote contained the statement and no supporting citations to cases or other articles to support the professor's conclusion.

3J frowned and leaned back in her chair. She was so close. On the one hand, an article from a well-known Stanford bankruptcy professor was good. But on the other hand, she wished the respected professor had offered support for the footnote. In light of the lack of support offered by Professor Lee, 3J didn't know how Judge Robertson would react.

She attached the article to an email to Jacob Steinert and copied Pascale. Her message said, "Jacob, take a look at this article, and in particular, footnote 157. What do you think?" She hit the send button, disconnected her laptop from its docking station, put it in her backpack, and headed out of the offices and down to Walnut Street.

On Tuesday morning, 3J received a subpoena from Robert Hickman's office to testify before a grand jury Thursday morning. Hickman also subpoenaed Bitty, Moe, Rosini, and Steele. Pascale spent time preparing and practicing with each of them to hone their expected testimony. Each would appear alone because a witness's attorney could not be present when a witness testified before a grand jury.

The five arrived outside the Grand Jury courtroom at the Western District Courthouse at 9:15 Thursday morning. The subpoenas scheduled them all at the same time, but as Pascale reported, Hickman would summon them in one by one to testify in whatever order he deemed best.

3J was first up and took forty-five minutes to answer Hickman's questions and explain what happened. The other four followed her, and Hickman completed the testimony by lunchtime. By 2:30, the grand jury completed its deliberations and found probable cause to return an indictment against Clarke and Saber on multiple counts: aggravated assault and battery, conspiracy to commit aggravated assault and battery, and attempted assault and battery. The jury further indicted them for attempted premeditated murder. Finally, the jury found that the defendants had perpetrated the crimes based on race. Therefore, the jury also indicted the defendants for federal hate crimes.

Friday morning, the scene was repeated, but this time, only two witnesses received subpoenas to testify: Jacob Steinert and Brian Saber. Steinert explained what he remembered. Saber provided the damning testimony that Clarke planned everything and that two of his goons had carried out the plan. Saber quoted Clarke in describing Steinert repeatedly as that "Jew-boy lawyer."

The grand jury indicted Clarke for conspiracy to commit assault and battery, and because the squad carried out the crimes at Clarke's behest in part based on Steinert's religion, the jury indicted Clarke for a federal hate crime. The jury also indicted the two assailants for assault and battery, conspiracy, and a federal hate crime.

Friday afternoon, the scene repeated one more time, this time with Saber and Donnie Melanshin testifying about the attack on the Melanshins. The result was the same: assault and battery indictments against the goons and a conspiracy indictment against Clarke and the goons.

The pressure on Clarke was mounting.

Neither 3J nor Pascale were ready for their traditional Friday trip to O'Brien's to drink, talk, and unwind after work that Friday. The attacks were too fresh, and 3J said she wasn't ready yet to resume a "business as usual" routine.

So instead, they sat in Pascale's cluttered office and talked as the sun set over the confluence of the Kansas and Missouri Rivers. No booze, no booth, and no bar noise. No jukebox, no twang, and no Dwight Yoakam or George Strait singing about exes. Just the week in review custom they both enjoyed. 3J had learned that the arraignment hearings would be at the courthouse Monday at 4:00 p.m. "I'd love to go over and see those proceedings," she confided in Pascale.

He smiled but shook his head no.

"Just an aspiration. But I *am* involved," she said as she shrugged her shoulders. "I'm not a bystander reading about this in *The Kansas City Star*."

"Well, for my two cents, it'll be a potential shitstorm. A repeat of Clarke's performance in state court. The better move is to stay away."

"For sure," 3J admitted. "I saw that Judge Sandy Wilson will preside. I've never appeared in front of her. But I hear she runs a tight ship courtroom. No mistaking who's in charge when she's on the bench. You think Clarke'll be happier and on his best behavior because the judge is White?"

"Oh, I kinda doubt it. First, Clarke doesn't come across as a happy sort and second, she's still a woman, or a 'skirt' as he likes to call you."

3J smiled. "Well, I'm more of a pantsuit gal, but I have to admit, that derogatory comment resonates in my head, over and over." After a few moments she asked, "Bill, did you have a chance to look at Professor Lee's article? I copied you on it in an email?"

"I did. She's the real deal. Deep thinker, congressional bankruptcy law influencer, and well-known. She spoke most recently at the National Conference of Bankruptcy Judges' annual event in Chicago. Robertson attended. He'll know her name and reputation. I'm thinking her opinion might be enough to sway him. It's not another bankruptcy judge's opinion, but it's a close second."

"Maybe. I don't know, but I sure hope so. Jacob likes the idea and is going with it as the basis for plan confirmation. The plan will drastically reduce Clarke's claim, assert that Clarke can't vote because of his bad faith, and then justify separate treatment of his claim because he can't vote anyway."

Pascale nodded. "It's a little cutting edge, but not so much so that it'll be a bridge too far for the judge. At least, that's my reaction." He paused and added, "Great catch, 3J—finding Lee's article and that footnote buried within it. Not an easy research task."

"I had days of failed search attempts, so I'm feeling kinda lucky, I suppose."

"When it comes to research, good analysis and work make their own luck."

3J surveyed the office, still as cluttered as ever. "Bill, every time I come in here, I'm expecting to see more of the carpeting. But I don't. Just more piles of papers. Where does all this stuff come from? Are you making any progress at all?"

"I feel a little like the kid whose mother serves him fried liver, lima beans, and cooked spinach for dinner. The kid hates all of it, so he moves the food around on the plate, hoping it looks like he ate when he didn't. All he did was rearrange to create the illusion there was less on the plate. I'm worried that all I'm doing here is rearranging." He paused momentarily and added, "Rearranging and reacquainting."

3J smiled knowingly.

Pascale then added softly, "Rearranging, reacquainting, and . . . maybe even reconsidering."

"Reconsidering?" 3J asked, surprised. "Reconsidering what?"

"Perhaps my departure date."

The last comment took 3J completely off guard. Her serious look and raised eyebrows were a request for him to elaborate.

"Bob Swanson came by. Even though he said he wouldn't, he sat down with the firm's board of directors, and a couple of days ago, they gave me an offer to stay on part-time for twelve months. My new title would be 'consultant.'"

3J cupped her left hand around her chin. "Thoughts?"

"None yet. It's a generous offer. Too generous, to be honest. There are a couple of bad reasons to consider taking the offer. Like not wanting to finish cleaning out my office and needing more time to clean out. Cleaning aside, there are other more legitimate pros and cons. I just need to sort it all out."

3J nodded.

"Who knew it would be so complicated to address my goal of getting on with my life?" Pascale said after a few moments passed. "I just don't trust that the practice of law allows us to get on with our life, even in a consulting capacity."

3J understood. She knew well that the practice of law could be a formidable and sometimes relentless competitor to the goal of having a life.

U.S. Marshals led the six Thirties defendants in orange jumpsuits into Judge Wilson's courtroom on Monday afternoon, right before 4:00 p.m. Except for Woody Clarke, each had a lawyer present. Judge Wilson had read the state court arraignment transcript. She left Clarke for last. One by one, the judge read the charges against the other five accused. She asked each for their plea and all said, "Not guilty." She quickly denied bail after hearing argument.

The guards led the five from the courtroom, leaving only Clarke. Sal Viglione sat in the pew near where Clarke stood. Clarke and Viglione made eye contact, and Viglione smiled and tipped the brim of an imaginary hat in greeting. Clarke looked away. Shackled and alone, he stood at the defense counsel's table facing Judge Wilson.

"Mr. Clarke, before we get started with your arraignment hearing this afternoon, I had the pleasure of reading the transcript of your state court arraignment hearing before Judge Roundtree," Judge Wilson said. "Someone should give Judge Roundtree a medal for maintaining his composure. His patience with you during that hearing was extraordinary—above and beyond the call of duty. I want to warn you that I'm not as composed and not nearly as patient as Judge Roundtree. I won't hesitate to remove you from the courtroom if you don't behave yourself. Am I clear?"

Clarke shrugged his shoulders as if to say "Whatever."

"I see you are alone. Have you rejected the notion of having counsel represent you?"

"Don't need no lawyer. Don't trust them neither."

"I want to advise you that failing to have counsel represent you is a terrible mistake. These are serious charges against you: attempted murder and hate crimes. Criminal proceedings are not for the uninitiated. It is a mistake for you to appear before me on these charges pro se."

"Got nothing to add."

The judge looked down at her papers. "Very well," she replied as she looked back up. She read the charges aloud and asked Clarke how he pleaded.

"Not guilty," Clarke said emphatically.

The judge moved on to the bail portion of the hearing. When she asked Hickman for his views, he mostly followed the script offered by the Jackson County prosecutor. He added, pointing at Clarke without looking at him, "In light of the serious nature of the hate crime charges, Clarke should not be out wandering the streets conspiring to do bodily harm to people of color, debtors, people of the Jewish faith, and who knows who else."

As he spoke, the judge showed no emotion, and when Hickman finished, she asked Clarke what he had to say in response.

"Same things I said before that Roundtree colored judge. Got nothing to add."

"So you are adopting your prior statements in the state court arraignment proceeding?"

"Yep."

"All of your statements?"

"Yep."

"That is your right. And then this is my ruling. You are a flight risk and a danger to society, including protected classes under our Constitution. And you are a danger to lawyers who are officers of this court. I order the marshals to hold you without bail. I remand you to the custody of the U.S. Marshals Service, and you shall remain incarcerated pending trial of the charges against you. Do you have any questions, Mr. Clarke?"

"Donnie Melanshin still owes me a fortune. I'm gonna need to get out of jail to go to them bankruptcy proceedings. I got a right to appear in court and collect my money."

"Mr. Viglione," the judge said.

Viglione stood. "Yes, Your Honor?"

"Please ensure that there is a protocol set up for Mr. Clarke to get notices in those bankruptcy proceedings, to file pleadings, and to appear in court, either in person or virtually. When Mr. Clarke appears, please ensure that you or other marshals are present." She paused and stared at Clarke before adding authoritatively, "To keep the peace." She paused again before adding, "I will alert Judge Robertson of these matters."

Viglione nodded. Clarke stared off into space.

The judge looked around the courtroom and asked if there was anything further.

"Nothing further, Your Honor," Hickman replied.

Clarke looked like he was about to say something, but before he could, the judge rose, turned, and exited her courtroom.

Once back in chambers, she phoned Judge Robertson and gave him an update. When the call ended, Judge Robertson walked to his window, stared out across the early summer scene to the Missouri River beyond, and thought that the Melanshin hearings were going to be unorthodox, to say the least.

36

Wednesday, July 3 through Friday, July 19, 2024

THE DAY BEFORE the Fourth of July holiday, the committee signed off on the plan. Steinert amended it to say the debtors and the committee jointly proposed it, and midafternoon, he filed it as he packed up to leave the office. Judge Robertson read it before he headed out for the extended holiday, noted the treatment of Woody Clarke's claim, and asked Jennifer to schedule a conference for late afternoon, Wednesday, July 17 to discuss the plan and set hearing dates. The marshals set up a video conference at the jail so Clarke could participate.

Late afternoon two weeks later, 3J, Steinert, the judge, Jennifer, the court clerk, and an IT tech sat in the courtroom. Clarke appeared in his orange jumpsuit on a large flat screen from a room at the prison. Guards stood on either side of him. A guard attached his zip tie to a steel ring imbedded in the spartan table where he sat.

"Okay, everyone. Thank you for making yourselves available this afternoon to discuss the Melanshin plan and schedule some deadlines and a court hearing," Judge Robertson said.

But before he could continue, Clarke said gruffly, "I want you to appoint a lawyer for me, Judge."

Judge Robertson looked up from his notes to the screen,

smiled, and said, "Mr. Clarke, we don't interrupt each other in my courtroom."

"I thought you was done."

"I was not. But since you raised it, let's turn to your request. We don't appoint lawyers for parties in bankruptcy court."

"When they read me my rights, they said I had a right to a lawyer and if I couldn't afford one, they'd appoint one. That Judge Wilson said the same. You're one of them 'they' folks. I want you to appoint a lawyer for me."

"Mr. Clarke. The marshals read you your rights when they arrested you. I'm sure the KCPD officers did the same in Westport during that arrest as well. Those rights are called Miranda rights. You have Miranda rights in criminal matters but not in bankruptcy cases. So this court cannot appoint a lawyer for you, but you are free to hire your own attorney. You can hire one from the prison."

"How'm I gonna do that? I got no access to things like lawyers."

As 3J listened to Clarke's contentious tone, she wondered what bankruptcy lawyer in their right mind would take Clarke's call and agree to represent him, knowing, as the media had reported, that he might get mad and try to kill the lawyer.

"The marshals can help you with access to a phone so you can find a lawyer to hire."

Clarke scowled.

"Okay. Let's continue, please," the judge said. "I've read the plan, Mr. Steinert. I see you have two classes of unsecured creditors. Your clients will pay the creditors in Class 4 in full. Class 4 contains all the unsecured creditors except Mr. Clarke, who is alone in Class 5, and the plan treats him substantially differently. Correct?"

"Yes, Your Honor," Steinert replied.

"Mr. Clarke, have you had a chance to read the plan?"

Clarke nodded but said nothing, and while the judge might have admonished him for not answering audibly, he did not.

"I see that you assert an offset against Mr. Clarke for damages caused by the attack on the Melanshins."

"Correct," Steinert replied. "For clarity, both attacks, Your Honor. The bricks and the assault in the park."

The Judge nodded. "Okay. Here's what I want to do. We'll have an expedited hearing to determine the claims issues. That is, I'll estimate how much the Melanshins owe Mr. Clarke, if anything, for purposes of determining if I can confirm the plan. Whatever number I determine will govern payments, if any, under the plan to Mr. Clarke."

"There ain't no 'if any' about it," Clarke interjected loudly. "Oh, they owe me lots of money all right. They stole my land out from under me."

Once again, Judge Robertson looked up at the screen and smiled. "Well, Mr. Clarke, that's what we will determine at the hearing: how much money they owe you, as I said, *if any*. The hearing will be evidentiary, so you will be able to call witnesses and testify if you wish."

Clarke nodded once.

The judge continued. "What witnesses do you envision on the claims issue, Mr. Steinert, so we can gauge how much time to set aside?"

"We expect our witnesses will be the Melanshins, Mr. Steele, Mr. Saber, and a damages expert. Perhaps Mr. Clarke as well."

"Okay. Thank you."

"Ms. Jones, I note that the committee is a co-proponent of the plan, correct?"

"Yes, Your Honor."

"News to me," Clarke interrupted. "I'm on the committee and I never voted for no plan like this one and never would."

Once again, the judge looked up at the screen, this time without smiling. "Mr. Clarke, please don't do that again or we will mute the audio and all you will be able to do is watch and listen. Understood?"

Clarke glared. The judge ignored him.

"The United States Trustee's office removed Mr. Clarke and his Thirty-Six Thirties colleagues from the committee for more than enough good cause," 3J replied. "It goes without saying, but in case there is any doubt, when a committee member tries to kill committee and debtors' counsel, committee participation is no longer appropriate. Mr. Clarke did not vote on cosponsorship of the plan because he's not on the committee."

"Thank you, Ms. Jones, for the explanation," the judge said. "Does the committee have witnesses it plans to call in the Clarke claim hearing?"

"We will reserve the right to examine Mr. Steinert's witnesses," 3J replied. "In addition, we will probably call Mr. Steinert to the stand to explain what happened to him."

Judge Robertson nodded. "All right, I'll set this down for a two-day evidentiary hearing beginning first thing in the morning on Thursday, August 8 and continuing through the end of the day on Friday, August 9. After that hearing, I'll rule on the claim issues and we'll set a time for plan voting, followed by a confirmation hearing where we can handle the separate classification legal matters and determine whether I should confirm the plan.

"To be clear, at the confirmation hearing, I expect we will take up whether I should count Mr. Clarke's vote, whether his claims may be in a different class, and if it is appropriate to treat his claim differently by paying him less over a longer time period. In other words, whether the proposed plan treatment amounts to unfair discrimination against him or not."

The judge paused and looked at both Steinert and 3J but avoided looking at Clarke on the screen. "Questions?"

No one had any, including Clarke, and the conference ended. The judge asked the clerk to terminate the video feed and thanked the lawyers. He and his law clerk, Jennifer, headed back to chambers and his office.

As the lawyers packed up their materials, Jennifer came back into the courtroom. "Judge Robertson would like to see both of you in his office for a moment."

3J and Steinert left their materials on the courtroom tables and followed Jennifer back to the judge's office, where he was standing behind his desk. "Please, come in and sit down. This will only take a second."

He gestured for them to take the two chairs facing his desk, hung his robe, and sat down at his desk. Clutching a yellow pad, Jennifer leaned against a wall behind the two chairs and watched.

"A few things, folks," Judge Robertson said. "First, I want to extend my deepest sympathy about Clarke's minions attacking you, Jacob, and Clarke hunting you, Ms. Jones. All of this happened as a result of a bankruptcy case pending in my court, and I feel the system, my system, failed you. I am without words. I am glad you appear to be on the mend, Jacob. I am sorry that both of you have to deal with the aftermath of the whole sordid affair."

Both nodded their heads in appreciation.

"Second, I also want you to know that at any hearings in which Mr. Clarke appears in person, security will be top of mind. There will be marshals everywhere. Anyone trying to come through security on the main floor will pass through the metal detector, of course. But the marshals will also wand and frisk them. That's everyone. No exceptions. No frisk, no entry. You will be safe in this courthouse and in this courtroom. That is my pledge to you."

"I appreciate that, Your Honor," Steinert said. "After what happened, I'm all in with erring on the side of protection."

3J nodded.

"Last, it seems that often, when one of these fringe group members appears in bankruptcy court, there is a hometown contingent of supporters who show up as well. So please, let me assure you that I am considering additional security measures to manage that potential risk, and I will report to you on my efforts before the next hearing. All the judges in this courthouse have met to discuss this, and we are all in agreement."

"Thank you, Judge," 3J said.

The day was drawing to a close when 3J returned to her office and found Pascale waiting for her. She explained the court hearing settings and the post-conference meeting with the judge to discuss security.

"How do you feel about venturing out to The Belfrey for a drink before we call it a day?" Pascale asked.

3J nodded, and the two headed down to Walnut Street and over to Grand. It was less than a ten-minute walk to The Belfrey. Once there, they each ordered a glass of private label Bourbon, neat.

"Bourbon? You? What's that all about?" 3J asked.

"I'm stepping out and stepping up," he said with a huge smile.

"Is everything okay, Bill?"

"All good. I'm worried about you. The strain must be enormous."

"Thanks. Mostly, I'm managing it. Ronnie's around a lot. You're around as well. When you and Ronnie aren't around, Moe is nearby. That all helps. But I'd be lying if I said this stuff wasn't on my mind."

"How could it not be? Will shop talk help?"

"Like what?"

"What's your gut tell you about Clarke's claim and the plan treatment."

"I expect Steinert will successfully offset a good chunk of the Clarke claim. Not sure if it goes down all the way to five hundred thousand, but it'll go down a lot. But on the plan treatment and voting, I don't have any feel from the judge's comments how he might be leaning. That worries me as well."

Pascale nodded. He knew she had lots on her mind. He decided to wait to tell her he took Swanson's offer to hang around and "consult" for twelve more months. He had also vowed to himself to use the time to better plan out what would come next in his life.

After the meeting in Judge Robertson's office ended, Jennifer lingered. Both were silent for a few moments before the judge spoke. "Well, this is why they pay me the medium bucks, I suppose." He exhaled slowly. "Momma said there'd be days like this. But when she said it, I don't think Momma had these Woody Clarke days in mind. I need to set up a meeting with Viglione and make sure he has the security plan and the bodies to staff it. I'm not going to let a group of right-wing fanatics change how this court operates. I want to make sure they think many times over before doing anything crazy."

Jennifer nodded. "What do you need from me on this one, Judge?"

"First things first. I would like you to be present for the meetings with courthouse personnel, the other judges, and the marshals to plan security for these hearings. Clarke will be coming to the courthouse. He's not going to remote in like today. The marshals will shackle him, but we can expect that some portion of his crew will be present in the pews. I want you as conversant in the security protocols and the plan as me. Understood?"

"Of course, Judge."

"Okay. Then, to the bankruptcy business at hand. We both need to dive into the separate classification and unfair discrimination issues. A broad search: all jurisdictions; all districts; all articles and treatises, published and unpublished. I don't care if it's not a local case and I don't care if I've never heard of the commentator. I want to know if something like the Clarke situation has provided cover for another judge to separately classify an unsecured creditor."

"On it, Judge," Jennifer replied.

"I know you are, Jennifer."

When Jennifer left, the judge finished reading the Lee article, and footnote 157 in particular, attached to Steinert's filed Memorandum in Support of Plan Confirmation. He decided to set up a call with Professor Lee to ask about the footnote and any leads she might have to offer. He had met her at the bankruptcy judge's conference cocktail hour the year before, enjoyed talking with her, and was sure she would take his call.

He wasted no time in making that call, and he was surprised when she answered her phone the next morning because it was only 6:30 in California. Instead of leaving a voice message, he got her live on the second ring. After introductory pleasantries, he told her he'd read her article, briefly explained the Melanshin case situation, and asked if she had any insight she could share about footnote 157.

"A creditor on the committee tried to take out both committee and debtors' counsel? My Lord!" she exclaimed.

After a moment, she exhaled audibly and continued. "Well, let's talk about my now infamous footnote 157. The courts are all over the map on this question, Judge. But for what it may be worth, this is how I look at it. Some courts seem to look at the type of claim at issue, that is, whether it is an unsecured claim or not. These courts end the inquiry quickly. If both claims are unsecured, the bar is pretty high to treat the claims differently. Your circuit leans this way. But even in your circuit, I still believe there are permissible ways to separately classify them and provide disparate treatment, especially in your unusual situation.

"Others look at the relationship between the debtor and the creditor. Is the debtor's relationship with the creditor somehow different from the relationship it has with other creditors? So for example, those courts might say, 'Well, the debtor needs to continue to do business with Class 4 creditors. But the debtor no longer does business with Class 5 creditors.' These courts ask if there is a valid business reason to treat the claim differently. In my example, many courts permit separate treatment. There is some of that in your circuit.

"It seems to me that the claim in your case could qualify for separate treatment. Not sure if there's a business reason for different treatment, but maybe there is. Maybe they don't do business anymore. Maybe Clarke is the only one who lost his land. Maybe he's the only one who failed to record a mortgage. Maybe it's good business and policy to discourage trying to kill the debtor. I say that without any smile on my face, Judge.

"There are some other things to consider. If the debtor disputes a creditor's claims and it's substantially reduced because of offset, it seems to me that creditor holds a claim that is different from the claim of the usual run of the mill unsecured creditor. Creditors who can't vote are also different creatures. If Clarke has done something so egregious—such as try to kill counsel—that you don't let him vote, setting up a class of nonvoting bad actors might make sense. If you reduce his claim and he can't vote, his claim would be a different animal than regular unsecured claims. His claim would lack the usual rights of an unsecured creditor: to have their claim allowed in the full amount owed rather than offset for personal injury and punitive damages; to sit on a committee; to vote. Ultimately, you'll have to decide if it seems different enough."

"So I have discretion, and my decision is subjective."

"I might call it subjective objectivity, Judge."

"Clear as mud," the Judge replied.

The professor chuckled.

The professor was as impressive on the impromptu phone call as she had been presenting her thesis at the judge's conference. Judge Robertson had his pad and pen out and took copious notes. While Lee didn't offer a case to support her thinking, she certainly provided a road map to support her thesis.

When the call ended, he walked to his window and stood in

silence as he watched the river flow. Predictable. Inevitable. Consequential. The longest river in North America, carrying water, mud, fish, boats, stories, and the secrets of everything upstream east across Missouri to the Mississippi River and then south to the gulf. Was that how the Clarke hearings would be?

As he thought, he doubted Clarke's hearings would be predictable. How could they be? He hoped nothing that Clarke would do would be consequential. But he wondered. And he worried that trouble would be inevitable in this case.

37

Woody Clarke recalls Thursday, July 25, 2024

ALL I WAS doing all day was sitting and thinking and waiting. Not much else to do in prison. They was keeping me separate from the rest of the prisoners. Not sure if that was to protect them or me. I ain't seen Saber since we was arrested. Good thing for him. Not sure what I would do if we was together.

So far, my hearings were remote. Virtual from a prison room. I thought I needed to start going on road trips to the courthouse.

I had a contingency plan to cover me if I got arrested. Any leader of a posse would, and I did. Once they locked me up, the plan was that my son, Junior, would post a cipher. It would explain when the court hearing would be and what court it'd be in. That message would say something like, "eighteightwdmo." August 8 in the Western District of Missouri. The cipher key would be "quantrill." Encoded, it would read "ucgumvqrsjqdzh."

The boys would see it posted and decode it. They'd know what it meant and they'd know what they needed to do. They'd know it would be a call to action like we talked about when we set up the plan.

They'd get the message: Come to the courthouse. Intimidate and disrupt, plain and simple. They wouldn't let me down.

38

Monday, July 29 through Thursday, August 1, 2024

JUNIOR CLARKE POSTED the cipher message for his father on *Alert* late that Sunday, and the boys saw it the next morning. But so did the U.S. Marshals Service.

Different agencies in the federal government regularly monitored the right-wing message boards. Weeks before, they had figured out that The Thirty-Six Thirties used *Alert* to post encoded messages. An agency passed that information along to the U.S. Marshals Service, which had developed an app to decode the messages, thanks to one of their tech gurus. As soon as the tech saw the ciphered message, he quickly figured it out. He briefed Sal Viglione, who set out to develop a plan to deal with any Thirties who came to the courthouse.

Viglione informed Judge Robertson and his law clerk of the findings and the marshals' plan in person. The judge listened somberly and thanked Viglione for the good work. Once Viglione had left, he and his law clerk sat in silence for a time.

"I need to let Ms. Jones and Mr. Steinert know," the judge finally said after taking a deep breath and letting it out. "I'm wondering if that means I should also let Mr. Clarke know that we are aware of his call to action. Sal should make a recommendation."

"The date and place message is a little vague, Judge. It doesn't say what will happen."

"Precisely. This was an activation message. My guess is that they've already baked the 'what' into the plan. Meaning The Thirties already know what they're supposed to do if they see this kind of message."

"And what do you think that is, Judge?"

"No idea, Jennifer. No earthly idea."

The judge frowned. "Let's go for a walk, clear our brains, and then grab a sandwich, Jennifer."

"Sure. Let me get my sneaks on."

The two headed out of the courthouse and turned north over the highway to River Market, formerly known as the River Quay. They walked in silence as they made their way to the northernmost part of the River Market district and a wrought iron balcony overlooking the Missouri River. The river was high and moving fast after torrential rains upstream in Nebraska. They watched the river race by without speaking.

"You know, people have described this river as ornery," Jennifer finally said. "They say that drinking from it gives the state animal, the Missouri mule, its attitude."

The judge smiled. "Didn't know that tidbit. Are you saying we need more attitude?"

She smiled but didn't respond. Then he turned away from the river and said, "Let's get a bite. How about the Farmhouse?"

Jennifer nodded.

As they walked back through River Market to the restaurant, the judge said, "It's so quiet here. A far cry from the bygone days when the mob ran the River Quay. No more red-light district down here. No more strip clubs owned by the likes of Willy 'the Rat' Cammisano. No more Dirty McNasty's Boiler Room. Or Madame Lovejoy's. Or Annie Chambers' place. Or Yesterday's Girls. They were colorful days, but all's quiet now. I guess that's what happens after mobsters blow up three establishments and each other in a turf war."

"Yes, Kansas City is certainly tamer than the days of the mob wars. Let's hope it remains tame as the Melanshin hearing approaches," Jennifer replied.

When the judge and Jennifer returned from lunch, on their desks was a pleading written and filed by Woody Clarke. Clarke signed it in red, and given the width and imprecision of the signature's letters, it appeared that Clarke had signed his name using his bloody index finger. Next to the signature was a red thumbprint. The pleading demanded that the judge and the Marshals Service recuse themselves from the bankruptcy case. Clarke asserted that both had shown bias against him and that he couldn't get a fair shake from them. Clarke filed a similar pleading against Judge Wilson.

It was well-written, and Judge Robertson figured a lawyer ghostwrote it for Clarke. Judge Wilson acted first and summarily denied the relief requested in a three-line ruling. Judge Robertson and Jennifer talked and he decided to write more than Judge Wilson had to explain his ruling. By the end of the day, the judge had written and filed an order in which he set out his ruling denying the request. He pointed out that the Marshals Service could not recuse itself from performing its duties and stated he would preside over the case because he had no personal bias or prejudice concerning Clarke, no personal knowledge of disputed evidentiary facts concerning the proceeding, and no financial interest in the outcome of the case.

It was the first time a party had asked Judge Robertson to abstain from hearing a matter since he'd taken the bench, and it confirmed to him that nothing about the upcoming Clarke hearing would be typical. He wondered what else Clarke had up his sleeve.

39

THE COURTS HAD incarcerated six of The Thirties without bail, awaiting trial. Of the remaining five, two begged off the idea that they would go into a federal courthouse and attempt to disrupt proceedings. They had families and farms to run, they said, and while they wished the rest the best of luck, they wouldn't participate. Early on Thursday morning, the remaining three of The Thirties and Junior Clarke piled into an old van and headed north for Kansas City and the courthouse.

Junior and two of the three carried 3D-printed plastic knives they had bought on the internet that had been built with rugged filament. The knives were sheathed in their pockets. They figured the plastic would make it through the metal detectors undetected.

Woody Clarke woke early, dressed, and awaited his armed escort from prison to the federal courthouse and his bankruptcy court hearing.

At 7:30 a.m., Sal Viglione awaited the arrival of Woody Clarke and his prison transport guards at the courthouse loading area where prisoners arrived. Once Viglione secured Clarke in a holding cell at the U.S. Marshals Service office, he would head down to the security station and await the arrival of The Thirties.

As Viglione waited, the judge, Jennifer Cuello, 3J, Pascale, Steinert, Steele, Rosini, Bitty, and Moe all got ready and headed to the courthouse.

In all, sixteen people converged at the courthouse just as the spokes on a Wild West wagon wheel converged at the wheel's brass hub.

Viglione had considered arresting the remaining Thirties on conspiracy charges before they even traveled to the courthouse, but he had two problems. First, he didn't know which of The Thirties were coming to the courthouse, so he didn't know who to arrest. And second, he didn't know what they intended to do once they arrived. The intercepted cipher did no more than communicate an encrypted date and place. It gave no instructions.

Whatever was up was understood by The Thirties, but because of what he didn't know, he saw no legitimate charges he could bring to support arrests. So he determined he had no choice but to let the morning play out and provide the best security the Marshals Service could muster.

To that end, he beefed up the number of marshals who would normally be on duty at the courthouse. He stationed twelve marshals with firearms in the courthouse lobby, plus two more outside the revolving entryway door for The Thirties to see as they arrived. He also stationed four other marshals on the sixth floor near Judge Robertson's courtroom. The main floor looked more like a war zone safe house protected by an armed security team than the normally quiet, federal courthouse public lobby.

He had advised the other judges and court personnel that August 8 should be a work-from-home day. If people insisted on coming to work at the courthouse, he strongly recommended that they make sure they closed and locked the doors to their chambers and offices. No visitors and no exceptions. He wanted August 8 to be a remote working day and hoped that as many people as possible complied. With only rare exceptions, everyone who normally worked at the courthouse followed Viglione's near edict and stayed home. As a result, the courthouse was eerily quiet and empty, like the deserted dusty main street of Marshal Dillon's 1870s Dodge City just before a scheduled shootout.

Viglione didn't mind the quiet. He didn't mind the emptiness. He didn't mind that he would be the modern-day Marshal Dillon as the day's events played out. But he wasn't looking forward to the possibility of a confrontation, let alone a violent one, at a federal courthouse.

Junior pulled the van onto a side street several blocks from the courthouse and parked in front of a ten-hour meter that took quarters. He had no money, so he ignored the meter.

The Thirties and he gathered in front of the van and walked to the courthouse and up the entryway steps. They hadn't discussed what they might encounter at the courthouse, and when they got to the steps, they saw the armed marshals outside. One of The Thirties decided to abandon the mission upon making eye contact with the marshals.

One of the outdoor marshals signaled ahead to the team inside. "Four total. One turned around and walked away. Three remaining and coming in. I don't see any weapons, but they're not here for a party. That much is clear."

The remaining Thirties and Junior walked up the steps menacingly, made no eye contact with the marshals, and entered the revolving door, one by one. They were now only steps away from the security station. As they walked toward it, the marshals in the lobby fell into step and encircled them on three sides. They ignored the marshals and slowed their pace, staring only at the security station in front of them.

At about the same time that Junior parked the van, Sal Viglione met the prison transport vehicle. The guards had shackled Clarke's hands and feet, and he could only shuffle when he exited the car. A guard stayed with him.

Viglione approached, took Clarke by the elbow, and said, "This way, sir."

Clarke beamed a Cheshire cat grin from ear to ear. "Why, Marshal Viglione, we meet again."

Viglione ignored him.

"Lovely day for a field trip, ain't it? Like my momma used to say, always good to get a little natural light each day."

Viglione continued to ignore him.

"I hear we're gonna decide today how much I'm owed. Fun day in court, I expect."

He got no response from the marshal.

"Cat got your tongue there, Marshal?"

Marshal Viglione remained mum. By then, the threesome had arrived at the Marshals Service offices. Viglione led Clarke inside, placed him in a holding cell, and locked the door behind him.

"Can a guy get a cup of coffee, Marshal?" Clarke asked. "Got up real early. Black with some sugar would be right fine. Black's my color of choice, y'know?"

Without replying to Clarke, Viglione turned away, leaving the guard in front of the holding cell area for extra protection. "Dirt bag," he muttered under his breath as he looked back at Clarke and then hustled down the staircase.

Based on the communication he'd just heard in his earbud, he feared confrontation was moments away. On the main floor, he opened the staircase door and saw The Thirties and Junior approaching the security station.

Junior was first to the station. Viglione stepped quickly to the metal detector area. "Empty everything you're carrying in your pockets into the basket, and then await my further instructions," Viglione commanded.

Junior smiled at him and placed a wallet, comb, and mobile phone in the basket.

"Anything else?" Viglione asked brusquely.

Junior continued to smile and shrugged his shoulders as if to say, "I guess not, old man."

Viglione motioned Junior to walk through the metal detector. Junior walked slowly through the portal and triggered no alarm. Once on the other side, he began to walk toward the X-ray machine conveyor belt where his basket now sat. But before he got to the basket, Viglione said, "Not yet. Arms out. Marshal Beltman here will frisk you by hand."

Junior stopped smiling. "You mean lay hands on me?" He shook his head and continued, "Not necessary, Marshal. We're all just law-abiding United States citizens exercising our right to observe a federal bankruptcy court hearing. Harmless students of the system in action."

Viglione ignored him. "No frisk, no passage. Your choice. You have three seconds to decide or I'll deem that you declined and we'll send you on your way out the courthouse door you came in."

Junior shook his head in disbelief, quickly reached down into his pants pocket, retrieved the 3D printed knife, and charged Viglione, yelling, "You fuckin' Fed! You took my father! You ain't gonna take me!"

Junior's charge momentarily caught Viglione by surprise, but he recovered in time to sidestep his attacker just enough to avoid a serious knife wound. Still, Junior made contact with Viglione's left forearm, which immediately began seeping blood onto his crisp white shirt and led Viglione to exclaim, "Sheeit!"

Junior smiled, and as he lunged at Viglione again, slashing the air with his knife, one of the marshals yelled, "Knife!" and the marshals who had encircled The Thirties immediately engaged them, forced them to the ground, and zip-tied them.

Initially, it appeared that Viglione had Junior under control, so the marshals' attention turned to restraining The Thirties, and they left Viglione alone with Junior. But Junior was persistent. He and Viglione locked arms in a wrestling match, crashing to the floor and rolling around with Junior on top of Viglione and then Viglione on top of Junior. Junior continued to wave the knife at Viglione and made several failed attempts to stab him. But one caught Viglione on his ear, and it began to bleed as well.

Finally, Junior was on top and Viglione was trying to force his hand to open so he would drop the knife. A moment later, a six-foot-six marshal came running to Viglione's aid and grabbed Junior, his fingers wrapping completely around Junior's forearm. He squeezed and Junior lost control of the knife and dropped it to the courthouse floor. The marshal pulled Junior up and off Viglione, and less than a second later, Junior's face joined the knife on the courthouse floor.

With the remaining Thirties and Junior all on the floor face-down, the marshals quickly determined two others in the group also had knives, relieved them of them, and read them their rights before arresting them. As the marshals collected them for processing, Viglione held his bleeding forearm with his now bloody hand and said to them collectively, "I guess you fellas won't be observing a bankruptcy court hearing today. I'll let Mr. Clarke know you boys won't be attending and that you send your regrets and wish him the best of luck on his day in court."

Steele, Rosini, Moe, and Bitty had left the courthouse coffee shop as the confrontation between the marshals, Junior, and The Thirties began. Seeing Viglione in trouble, they were about to come to his aid before the tall marshal intervened. Bitty smiled his approval when the marshal disabled Junior Clarke in an instant. He looked over to Steele, nodded approvingly, and said, "That's what I'm saying. That marshal is muh man."

40

"ALL RISE," THE courtroom deputy commanded. "The Honorable Daniel Robertson presiding. You may be seated."

3J, Steinert, and Pascale sat at one of the counsel tables. Clarke sat at the other, shackled and under the constant watch of the prison guard and a marshal assigned to him. The marshal sat next to Clarke, and the guard sat right behind him. As the judge and Jennifer entered the courtroom, Clarke turned to survey the pews. He saw no Thirties. He saw no Junior. All he saw were Steele, Rosini, Bitty, and Moe. They stared at him. Bitty smiled and nodded. Clarke looked away.

Judge Robertson saw Clarke looking out over the pews as he sat down. "Mr. Clarke, they're not coming today."

Clarke turned to face the judge, stood, and said, "Come again?"

"They're not coming today, Mr. Clarke," the judge repeated. "Your son's little cipher to them? Intercepted. The marshals arrested them in the lobby moments ago because they carried weapons. I'm sure you must understand it is a serious federal crime to carry weapons into a U.S. courthouse. Your boy even tried to stab a marshal. He's in custody now."

Clarke sat and stared at the judge but said nothing.

The judge continued. "Today we will take up the matter of

how much the debtors owe Mr. Clarke . . . if anything." Looking at 3J and Steinert, he said, "Counsel, this is your joint plan and your request to estimate and adjust Mr. Clarke's claim. Are you ready to proceed?"

"We are," Steinert and 3J said.

"Very well. Mr. Clarke, are you ready to proceed?"

"No, I ain't ready," Clarke said petulantly. "And you know damn well I'm not. I asked that you give me a lawyer, and you said no."

"Mr. Clarke, you asked that I appoint a lawyer for you pursuant to your Miranda rights, and I explained that we don't do that in bankruptcy cases. Indigent parties get appointed lawyers only in criminal matters. I advised you that you could hire a lawyer if you wished. Did you attempt to do so?"

"Did not."

"Hmm. Well, that was a personal choice. We are here today, witnesses are here, and the hearing will proceed, notwithstanding what took place in the courthouse lobby and notwithstanding your lack of an attorney." The judge looked at Steinert. "Counsel, proceed."

Jacob Steinert went to the podium and in efficient, elegant prose explained to the court that his clients had been brutally attacked. He also stated that Clarke's Thirties attacked him and tried to attack 3J. The judge listened attentively, and Clarke fiddled with his handcuffs. Steinert explained that if his clients sued Clarke for their injuries, pain and suffering, emotional distress, mental anguish, and punitive damages, a court or jury would award them at least three and a half million dollars in actual and punitive damages.

"Judge, here in bankruptcy court, those damages serve as an offset against the amount Mr. Clarke says the Melanshins owe him. We submit that when you hear the evidence, you should estimate Mr. Clarke's unsecured claim and rule that after offset of the Melanshin damages, they owe him no more than five hundred thousand dollars."

When Steinert said the phrase "unsecured claim," Clarke stood, and as Steinert was completing his sentence, he interrupted and bellowed, "It ain't unsecured. I own that land! Melanshin stole it from me! Him and his wife are thieves, plain and simple!"

In an even toned voice, Judge Robertson said, "Marshal, please restrain Mr. Clarke and return him to his seat."

The marshal grabbed Clarke by his damaged arm and pulled him back down into his chair, eliciting a cry of pain from him. Once seated, Clarke stared up at Judge Robertson with a threatening look on his face.

"Mr. Clarke, one more outburst and we will employ some other measures," the judge admonished. "Please, sir. Do not make me show you what those will be. I am certain you will not be happy if we have to use them."

Based on Jennifer's research, the judge had learned what his options were if a pro se litigant like Clarke was unruly in his courtroom. The litigant could remain in the courtroom, bound and gagged. Clarke was already bound, so that left the option of gagging. The Judge asked Viglione what type of gag the U.S. Marshals would use and learned that duct tape was the preferred method. Jennifer also discovered the judge could have the marshals remove the litigant from the courtroom under a 1970 Supreme Court ruling. The judge decided removal would be the better option and had arranged a room in the U.S. Marshals' office, where they could take Clarke, if necessary, to watch the proceedings on an office screen and where everyone in the courtroom could see him on the courtroom screens. To speak, he would have to raise his hand, and the clerk would control when he was on mute and when those in the courtroom could hear him talk.

Steinert called the Melanshins to the stand, and they explained the brick-through-the-front-window incident and the Meadowfield

Memorial Park attack. They stated the damage to their property and the cost of repairs. They testified that the attacks had put them in the hospital and described their physical injuries and lingering emotional struggles.

Clarke asked no questions. He stared down at the table and shook his head in disgust.

Steinert next called Ronnie Steele to explain the attempted attack on 3J. When finished, Clarke again declined to ask any questions, saying only, "Them colored folks. We all know they stick together."

As Steinert finished up with Steele, a marshal opened the courtroom door and led a shackled Brian Saber into the courtroom and to a seat in the pews. Clarke saw Saber enter and narrowed his eyes angrily.

3J called Jacob Steinert to the stand. He testified about the brutal beating he took and said he never got a good look at his assailants because they had come up behind him and knocked him out.

"Mr. Clarke? Questions?" the judge asked when Steinert finished testifying.

Clarke paused while he thought and then said, "Got nothing to ask this Jew-boy."

With her back to Clarke, 3J looked at Judge Robertson, raised her eyebrows, and rolled her eyes in disgust. "The committee calls Brian Saber to the stand," she then announced.

As Saber passed Clarke on his walk to the front of the courtroom, Clarke hissed at him under his breath, "You gonna pay for this, Brian, and for all that damn yacking you been doing. You ain't no Thirty. You and that family of yours, you be careful, y'hear?" The microphone at the counsel's table was on and amplified Clarke's voice for everyone in the courtroom to hear.

Judge Robertson said, "Okay. That's more than enough. I've been patient and tried to be accommodating. But threatening a witness is where I draw the line. Mr. Clarke, I don't know your plan, or maybe you have none now that the folks with the knives in the lobby are in custody. You have no lawyer and you ask no questions. But you have made racist pronouncements and disruptive comments. And now you have threatened a witness in a federal courtroom. Mr. Clarke, I hereby rule that by your conduct, you have waived any right you may have to participate in person in this hearing today. Marshal, please remove Mr. Clarke from the courtroom and take him to where we have arranged for him to sit so he can observe and speak—when it is appropriate and only then—so we can hear him."

As the marshal nodded and grabbed Clarke by the elbow to lead him out, Clarke yelled as he thrust his index finger at the judge with each phrase, "You ain't no judge! And you ain't no sheriff. You ain't got no authority. Not over me. Not over the posse. Not over no one! This whole goddamn fuckin' system! You're lucky I'm shackled!"

The judge, who had looked down at his pad after ordering the marshal to remove Clarke, looked up, locked eyes with Clarke, and said, "And now, sir, we add to your growing list of serious problems threatening a federal judge. Marshal, gag him and remove him."

The marshal smiled, nodded, and placed duct tape across Clarke's mouth. Then he slapped his hand across Clarke's now gagged mouth with force to ensure the tape would stick, and Clarke's head recoiled. Clarke continued to yell, but his words were muffled by the tape. The marshal led him out of the courtroom, followed by the prison guard.

3J had a look of disbelief on her face. "Would Your Honor like to take a short break now?"

"Let's take a ten-minute break to allow Mr. Clarke to get settled into his new environment," Judge Robertson replied.

Ten minutes later, the proceeding continued. Saber took the stand, and under questioning by 3J, he explained that Clarke had planned and was behind the attacks. Saber testified Clarke directed The Thirties to attack both Steinert and the Melanshins. Clarke watched and listened from his small room where two marshals and the prison guard stood.

When 3J finished examining Saber, the judge gave Clarke the chance to cross-examine. Clarke's duct tape had been removed, but he was on mute. The clerk took Clarke off mute, and the judge said, "Mr. Clarke, you may proceed."

Instead of questioning Saber, Clarke screamed, "Brian, I'm gonna get—"

But before he could complete the sentence, the judge looked at the clerk and gestured a slash across his throat. She pressed the mute button, silencing the screaming Clarke.

The judge said, "Mr. Clarke, I gave you the chance to examine Mr. Saber, not threaten him . . . yet again. We will assume you have no questions to ask." Turning to Saber he said, "You may step down." Saber stepped from the witness stand and back into custody of a marshal, who led him out of the courtroom.

Viglione—patched up with ten stitches in his arm and three in his ear, clean hands, and a new white shirt—was back in the courtroom to observe and protect. He sat next to Robert Hickman, who had quietly entered the courtroom and sat in the last pew to watch the events unfold. When the clerk muted Clarke, Viglione looked down to his lap and smiled.

"Any further witnesses, Mr. Steinert?"

"One more, Your Honor. The plan proponents call Hannah Ling to the stand. She is our damages expert."

Steinert established her qualifications and then elicited expert opinion testimony from her as she assigned dollar amounts to the out-of-pocket medical expenses, pain and suffering, emotional distress, and mental anguish suffered by the Melanshins. In her expert opinion, she testified, the shock of the attack would stay with the Melanshins for years. She foresaw they would not feel safe walking together and might find themselves always looking over their shoulders. Only through extended therapy, she said, would they have any chance to return to some semblance of normality. She identified three significant real estate deals that Donnie Melanshin could not close as a result of the assault. In all, the expert said that the Melanshins' actual damages were in the amount of one and a half million dollars.

The expert also testified that Clarke had significant land holdings in Eastern Kansas. She valued those holdings at over eight million dollars. Punitive damages had to be substantial enough to punish Clarke and send a message that his conduct was unacceptable.

"Ms. Ling, based on your analysis of Mr. Clarke's assets, what amount of punitive damages would you suggest would send such a message and appropriately punish him?" Steinert asked.

"Mr. Steinert, I would suggest twenty-five percent of his net worth, or a total of two million dollars."

"I see. So the total damages, actual and punitive, in your expert opinion are how much?"

"Three and a half million dollars."

"And if the Court agrees with you, what is Mr. Clarke's resulting claim?"

"Five hundred thousand dollars."

"Any questions, Mr. Clarke," the judge asked when Steinert finished his expert witness examination.

"It's all a bunch of BS, Judge," Clarke said disdainfully. "It's all rigged. Fake facts. I ain't gonna validate this immigrant's opinion by asking her a damn thing."

"That is your prerogative, Mr. Clarke," Judge Robertson replied. "And I'll take that as a no." He turned to the witness and said, "Thank you, ma'am. You may step down." Then he turned to counsel. "Any further evidence from the plan proponents?"

"None, Your Honor," 3J and Steinert said in unison.

"Okay. We'll take a fifteen-minute break. When we return, Mr. Clarke can put on whatever testimony or evidence he may have."

The judge and Jennifer left the courtroom and entered his office. With eyes wide, he shook his head slowly but said nothing. She raised her eyebrows and said nothing as well. Unlike almost every break they took while a trial was in process, this time, they said nothing. There was nothing to say. No teaching moment for Jennifer. No need for the judge to solicit her views about a witness or answer any of her questions. No conflicting testimony for the judge to sort through. Just silence. It was the only appropriate thing they could do.

After ten minutes, the judge turned to look out his window, and with his back to Jennifer, he sighed and said, "All right. Let's get them back in the courtroom and ready to go. We need to get this over with, Jennifer."

Back in the courtroom, the judge asked Clarke what evidence he had to present.

"Just me. Unless you're gonna cut me off like you been doing," Clarke replied.

"You can testify, but at the first inkling I have of threats, I will shut you down, and we will complete our hearing with you watching and listening. The first inkling. Do you understand me?"

Clarke ignored the judge. The clerk stood and told Clarke to raise his right hand. "Do you swear to tell the truth, the whole truth, and nothing but the truth."

Clarke sneered into the camera and said, "Damn right. Unlike these other folks. Here's my testimony. My whole damn country has gone to shit. My country! Them Melanshins stole over twenty-five hundred acres from me. Right out from under my nose. They planned it and they executed it. Damn real estate moguls. Not even real farmers. Now they gonna sell my land and pay everyone exceptin' me. What the hell kinda country let's that happen? What kinda supposed judge let's that happen?

"Now they say they got damages against me and they ain't even gonna pay me what they owe me. Damages? Shit. They ain't damaged in the least. They got pushed to the ground and from that, they come in here and say they got harm of . . . how much? One and a half million? That's some kinda crazy bullshit. They ain't been hurt. They're lying.

"That oriental bitch expert was paid to testify against me. Pay her and she'll say anything. Brian Saber ain't one of us no more. Far as I'm concerned, never was." Clarke pointed at the screen "And them two lawyers—the Jew and the colored bitch—what kinda damn country lets them types run the show and decide not to pay me? I'll tell you. It's my country, not theirs. But they're trying to take away my rights, my land, my freedoms, my country. A White, Christian, man's country, and all you people're flushing it down the toilet. That's all I got to say. Exceptin' this. No matter what you rule, Judge, it ain't gonna matter none. 'Cause you ain't no real judge. You as much a part of the problem as them two lawyers, the Melanshins, and that Far East, expert bitch. That's all I got to say."

When Clarke finished, Hickman slowly stood to leave the courtroom and Viglione nodded to him. As he left, he decided that he wouldn't look into how six folks knew Clarke would be at O'Brien's. He concluded it wouldn't advance justice. Not in the least. He smiled as he went through the courtroom doors. The little voice and he had reached a consensus.

"Anything further, Mr. Clarke?" Judge Robertson asked.

"Not in this fake court," Clarke replied sullenly.

"Very well. Ms. Jones? Mr. Steinert? Anything else?"

"Brief closing comments, please, Your Honor?" 3J said as she rose.

"Certainly," the judge replied.

3J placed her hands on either side of the podium, looked at Jennifer Cuello and then the Judge, and said, "Judge, the evidence speaks for itself. There is no dispute here. Woody Clarke tried to assault, and perhaps kill or have killed, four people. Two were the debtors. One was Mr. Steinert. One was me. And I won't even get into what happened in the courthouse lobby this very morning. Ms. Ling credibly quantified the damages the debtors suffered. Uncontroverted evidence. We submit that based on today's proceeding, Your Honor must rule the Melanshins' damages against Mr. Clarke would total three and a half million dollars in any lawsuit they might bring, and as a result, you should reduce his bankruptcy claim to five hundred thousand dollars. Unless the Court has questions for me, I have nothing further."

The judge nodded but said nothing to 3J. "Anything to add, Mr. Steinert?"

"Nothing more, Your Honor."

The judge didn't ask Clarke for his summation. "Very well. I'll take a thirty-minute break and then come back in and announce my ruling."

In his office, the judge admitted to his law clerk that he wasn't sure he would need all thirty minutes and asked if she had any input.

"Frankly, Judge, I'm speechless. So much hate from one person. So much denial. So much anger."

"It is indeed an angry, denying, hating, divided, and fearful country we live in these days. I would like to think that Clarke is an anomaly, but sadly, I know he is not. He is one of many. They have always been there, but now, they're no longer playing possum. Empowered, on social media, and now vocal."

They sat quietly. The judge took a deep breath and exhaled slowly. "I'm sure you know how I will rule. Claim reduced as requested. Let's get back in there and end this."

They returned to the courtroom, and Judge Robertson thanked counsel for their presentations.

"Here is my ruling. In short, I agree with Ms. Jones. The only evidence presented to me is that Mr. Clarke is responsible for the assault on the debtors and the damage to their house. As well, he is responsible for the assault and attempted assault on counsel. The only evidence is that the actual damages total one and half million dollars. I agree with the expert witness, Ms. Ling. The punitive damages must be sufficient to punish Mr. Clarke. I will accept her analysis completely. Indeed, it is the only analysis presented to me today. In a lawsuit brought by the Melanshins, the total damages would be three and a half million dollars. Therefore, I estimate those to be the damages and hereby reduce Mr. Clarke's allowed bankruptcy claim to five hundred thousand dollars."

The judge paused before continuing. "You know, when I came back out here, I was not sure if I would end my comments with my ruling. But today's events started with violence in my courthouse's lobby and injury to a brave U.S. Marshal who has admirably protected the judiciary for decades and protected it again today. Now we have endured Mr. Clarke's relentless verbal assaults during this hearing. All of this has been on the heels of Mr. Clarke's abominable attacks on debtors who sought protection in my court and two officers of this court who regularly practice before me.

"I could stop with my ruling. But today I will exercise my prerogative to press on and have some last words. In law, there is a Latin word, 'dicta.' That word means a judge's expression of opinion on a point other than the precise issue involved in deciding a case. Some might view what I am about to say as dicta. I don't view it that way. It is not dicta in my life and no one should consider my following comment as dicta. My comments are necessary."

The judge again paused and looked at the courtroom screen to see Clarke with his back to the courtroom.

"Marshal, turn Mr. Clarke around to face me."

The marshal complied.

"My comment is this. Mr. Clarke, this is not your country. It is ours."

The judge paused for emphasis, gathered himself, and continued. "It belongs to all of us. Every single one of us. While the word 'us' has wrongfully excluded some in our history and continues to do so today, the aspiration—my aspiration—is that someday, it will exclude no one. And when that happens, when 'us' is every one of us, I hope I am around to find you, Mr. Clarke, and repeat to your face that this country is not yours. It is ours. All of ours.

"I know I can't convince you. But if you've listened today, perhaps, my words will give you something to ruminate on, and if my comments cause you to lose sleep, then lose sleep. If my words make you angry, be angry. If my words make you and others like you even more violent, we—and I do mean we—are ready for you. You cannot and will not win whatever it is you are trying to win."

As the judge spoke, those in the courtroom could see an animated Woody Clarke yelling, head back, eyes closed, to no avail. A muted tantrum. No one in the courtroom knew what he said. No one wanted or needed to.

"Court is adjourned," the judge said softly as he looked around the courtroom somberly and rose.

When the judge and Jennifer left, 3J remained at counsel's table, elbows on the tabletop, watching Clarke on the courtroom screen continue to bellow, chin up and face tilted to the ceiling. Still on mute, he bellowed in silence. No audience was forced to listen to him. Just Clarke in his little room screaming toward the heavens in silence.

Heavens? she thought. And she said softly, "No one in heaven's listening. No one there's gonna help him out."

Donnie and Lil Melanshin drove back to Meadowfield. For the first sixty minutes they were silent. When they were fifteen minutes from home, Lil said to Donnie, as he navigated a curve, "Woody seemed a little out of sorts today, didn't ya think?"

"Well, that happens sometimes when things don't go as planned."

"Yes, indeed. Didn't expect that Junior would try to come to his pop's rescue, did you?"

"I kinda figured that Woody would try something, and if he did, it might involve Junior. Now that boy's gonna be in a world of hurt." Donnie paused, and then, allowing a small smile on his face, continued. "Bringing a knife to a federal courthouse. Whatever was that boy thinking?"

Lil nodded. After a few minutes she said, "Figured we'd have a chance of pulling this all off against Woody. Didn't expect that we'd also get the prize of gettin' rid of Junior for a while. Won't bring Toby back, but I gotta believe that he's watching this from up above with a good-sized smile on his face."

"Yes, indeed," Donnie agreed. "I wonder if old Woody was yelling up to the heavens to try to talk with Toby?"

"Kinda doubt it, Donnie. Don't think Woody has given Toby one second of thought. Not one." Lil shook her head in disgust. "That's a big part of Woody's problem. He's not a real thoughtful sort. Says he's a Christian, but he's not my kind of Christian."

"Well, now he'll have plenty of time to think about a lot of things, Toby included." Donnie looked over to Lil. "I'm thinking we should take a walk in the park tonight after dinner, Lil."

"It's not Friday, Donnie."

"A new tradition. No need to wait 'till Friday."

Lil nodded and reached out for Donnie's hand.

41

Friday, August 9, 2024

3J ACCOMPLISHED LITTLE at her desk the day after the Clarke hearing. Burned into her memory was the image of a muted Clarke screaming for no one to hear. It reminded her of Norwegian surrealist Edvard Munch's 1893 painting, *The Scream*, a work of art she liked, even as it gave voice to dread, anxiety, and loneliness. She and Pascale had decided August 9 would be the day they resumed their Friday post-work O'Brien's ritual. Ronnie would be working behind the bar with Bitty manning the door. Pascale said he would like to invite Moe and Rosini, and 3J offered to invite Steinert.

By 6:45, O'Brien's was hopping with its usual crowd. The Bastard Sons of Johnny Cash were belting out "Hard Times" on the jukebox. 3J entered the bar and walked past Bitty sitting on his high stool at the entrance. She smiled at the bouncer as he raised his eyebrows, waved to Ronnie Steele behind the bar, and made her way to a booth in the back.

Pascale was already seated at the booth. It was different than their usual booth—one that could hold more people. New tradition. Already seated were Pascale, Steinert, Moe, and Rosini. 3J grabbed a chair and pulled it to the side of the table. Moe slid 3J a shot glass of a double barrel Irish whiskey, neat, that someone had ordered for her. She picked up the glass, held it up, and silently toasted everyone at the table before closing her eyes and taking a swig.

As she put the glass down, she smiled and said, "I'm late. Sorry. I had a hard time focusing today, and then next thing I knew, I was still at my desk and realizing that I was going to be late. You can coax only so much speed out of a Prius driving up Main Street, I'm afraid."

"No worries. You're here now," Moe said.

Steele arrived at the table to greet everyone.

Rosini smiled. "We're gonna have to stop meeting or that Hickman guy may get ideas."

"Did you guys catch him in the back of the courtroom yesterday?" Steinert asked. "Sat next to the injured marshal."

"I saw him there a few moments before he left," Moe said.

"He left before the hearing ended," Pascale said. "After Clarke offered his manifesto. Guess he'd heard enough."

"This is the same AUSA who went after Quincy Witherman a few years ago," 3J offered. "Tenacious. That won't bode well for Clarke."

Everyone nodded.

"I don't see him pursuing us after Clarke's performance," Steele said. "My gut tells me the government will use its resources to put away Clarke, the other five attackers, and the lobby insurrection crew. Followed by a news conference on the courthouse steps and a morning *Kansas City Star* headline that reads "Bad Guys Go Down for the Count." Then they'll close their books on this one. Hickman won't have time or interest to figure us out. Not after he got a gander of Clarke in action."

"So, then, it's all's well, as Shakespeare wrote," Rosini added.

"3J and Jacob haven't quite finished up yet, folks. They still have some heavy lifting ahead to get the plan approved," Pascale pointed out.

Steinert raised his beer mug and said in agreement, "To plan confirmation."

3J lifted her glass and added, "Hear! Hear!"

INTERLUDE

Tuesday, May 17, 2005

"JOSEPHINA JILLIAN JONES," the Whitman College president announced at the commencement ceremony for the 2005 graduates. The audience clapped as 3J walked across the outdoor stage, accepted her degree in her left hand, and shook hands with the president and other dignitaries before exiting the stage. Pomp and circumstance at one of the country's elite colleges. It was her moment in the Walla Walla sun.

Celebrated alone. Three months earlier, her father had died of acute renal cancer, stage four and incurable. He passed quickly. That was the only good thing 3J could say about the process. Her mother had died two years earlier, so the death of her father left 3J and her sister to fend for themselves.

At a post-graduation party, one of 3J's college acquaintances asked her if she planned on returning to the Big Easy. "No," 3J replied with a wistful smile. "My Papa wanted me to ride the education train out and not the graduation train back. No, I'm off to law school in Topeka, Kansas."

"Wonderful, 3J. I'm happy for you," the acquaintance said and quickly added, "I meant for you starting law school."

"Not to worry. I know what you meant."

"I see great things for you, 3J."

"We'll see. But thanks. That's what my Papa would have said."

One hundred and four days later, Hurricane Katrina made

landfall in New Orleans, washing away her mother's empty Lower Ninth Ward home.

3J was two weeks into her freshman year at law school. She had heard that law life was all-consuming. She now knew the notion was all too true. In her few moments of spare time, she wondered if she had rushed into the decision to start law school so soon after college graduation and Papa's death. Maybe she needed time off from school, she thought. But then she decided Papa would not want her to use his death as the reason to delay the rest of her life.

Before Katrina, she thought about a brief trip back to New Orleans to get the remaining post-death affairs in order. Her father had shipped her his music, his only valuable possessions, shortly before he died. So, before Katrina, all that was left was her mother's house. There was now no reason for that trip. The house was gone, just like her parents. It was as if Mother Nature had washed all of 3J's past out to the gulf to clear the path for her law career and the rest of her life. A life without weekly calls with her papa and the strength of her mother's deep faith.

She wondered if she was tough enough to weather all the recent events and remembered her father's favorite quip: Don't get mad, get educated. As she opened a torts case book and sighed, she also wondered what the future would hold for her with so much of her past disappearing so quickly. Her father would also say, "Look forward. That's where all the good is hiding."

42

Thursday, September 12, 2024

IT WAS PLAN confirmation day. Three weeks earlier, Steinert and 3J tallied the votes. All creditors voted to accept the plan except Woody Clarke. His preprinted ballot offered him the option of checking either the "accept" or "reject" box. Instead, he circled reject twice in red and wrote "Hell No" below the boxes. He didn't sign his name. He affixed a red thumbprint to his ballot, and 3J presumed it again might be blood, not ink. "Guess he hasn't run out of blood yet," 3J mused.

The only remaining issues for Judge Robertson to decide were whether he would count Clarke's vote and whether 3J and Steinert could separately classify Clarke and pay him less. Jennifer had completed a lengthy research memo for the judge analyzing the classification and voting issues. Prominent in the research was Amanda Lee's article and several unpublished conference presentations by other law school professors who came to the same conclusion as Professor Lee: If the creditor can't vote, the debtor can separately classify the creditor and treat it differently. In other words, egregious conduct permits different payment treatment and does not amount to unfair discrimination.

Seated at counsel's table were 3J and Pascale for the committee and Steinert for the debtors, along with his clients. Once on the bench, the judge asked both sides for opening comments. Clarke watched from the same room he had watched the claim hearing in after being ejected from the courtroom. The clerk had his audio on mute.

3J and Steinert spoke persuasively. Woody Clarke's conduct was egregious. That was a given. He had tried to kill four people, including the bankruptcy debtors. They each suggested that if it was egregious for a debtor's competitor to buy a creditor's bankruptcy claim and then vote "no" to try to put the debtor out of business, then it was even more egregious for a creditor to try to kill the debtors and counsel to coerce a quick repayment.

The judge listened dispassionately. 3J and Steinert could tell that the judge had already decided what he would do, but they weren't sure what that decision was.

The lawyers asked the judge to accept the testimony from the claim hearing as evidence in the plan confirmation process, and he agreed. Clarke said nothing.

When the lawyers completed their presentations, the judge looked at the courtroom screen and said, "Mr. Clarke, your turn. You're up."

The clerk disabled the mute, and Clarke stood at the table in his room and began to speak. Without raising his voice, he said, "They stole my land. That's a crime. I just want my money back. That ain't a crime. You cain't let these Melanshins get away with this plan thing. You just cain't. It ain't fair."

Clarke sat. That was all he had to say. 3J wondered if incarceration had begun to smooth Clarke's many rough edges. Prison could do that to some. But she had her doubts. Clarke surprised the courtroom clerk with the brevity of his comments, but she recovered and quickly pushed the mute button. Clarke would have no further time to speak.

"Very well. Here is my ruling," the judge said. "Mr. Clarke

has identified one of the issues: Is his treatment in the plan unfair? But before I turn to that, I have before me a request to disallow Mr. Clarke's vote. The Bankruptcy Code permits me to designate a claim as nonvoting if the creditor has acted in bad faith. To Mr. Clarke, the law is a sham. To Mr. Clarke, the bankruptcy law in particular is of no consequence. The Constitution is of no consequence. Our monetary system is of no consequence. His need to play within the rules of society is of no consequence. And as he has so eloquently stated, *I* am of no consequence.

"It is my ruling that Mr. Clarke's attempt to take matters into his own hands, repeatedly, and his wanton attempt to kill parties and lawyers who appear before me in this case is the highest form of bad faith I can imagine. Every creditor in bankruptcy has the right to vote. Some earn their way out of that right. Mr. Clarke has earned his way into nonvoting status. I hereby purge his vote from the record."

The judge paused to look at the courtroom screen. Clarke hung his head over the table and made no eye contact.

"The plan proposes to pay Class 4 unsecured creditors an initial significant pay down and the balance in full with interest at six percent over eight years. By contrast, the debtors propose to pay Mr. Clarke's Class 5 claim five percent of five hundred thousand dollars over fifteen years at four percent interest. So Mr. Clarke can count on receiving only 1,667 dollars each year with interest over many years. Quite different treatment indeed.

"Now, turning to this different treatment. One common definition of the word 'unfair' is 'contrary to justice.' One definition of 'unfair discrimination' is 'conduct that undermines fundamental dignity.' Neither of those are the bankruptcy definitions, of course. But if they were, it would be easy to rule that nothing proposed in the plan is contrary to justice, and it promotes, not undermines, dignity.

"But there is no bankruptcy definition for the phrase 'unfair discrimination.' And as many have pointed out, the Bankruptcy Code does not ban all discriminatory treatment of unsecured creditors, only treatment that *unfairly* discriminates. So as others have observed, I can deduce as well that in bankruptcy, some discrimination is acceptable. Perhaps it is the only place in society where some discrimination *is* acceptable.

"There is a certain irony I must not fail to recognize. How ironic that the bankruptcy law sanctions some level of discrimination of Mr. Clarke's claims at the same time he promotes so much discrimination in his day-to-day life. I can sum up his position this way: Discrimination *by* him is good, but discrimination *against* him is not. But I do not wish to conflate Mr. Clarke's enormous social shortcomings with his substantial legal shortcomings.

"In deciding whether to approve plan discrimination, courts and commentators seem to focus on whether the separately treated creditor's claim is different in some way than the other unsecured claims. Others look at the creditor's conduct to see if they have done anything egregious in the bankruptcy case.

"I don't take lightly the need for me to police the fair and equal treatment of most unsecured creditors. But here, I find nothing unfair in Mr. Clarke's treatment. He is different from the other unsecured creditors. Egregious does not begin adequately to describe his conduct in the few months I have gotten to know him. His claim is different as well. All other unsecured creditors retained all their rights in bankruptcy—the full amount of their claims and their right to cast their vote for or against the plan. Mr. Clarke has lost most of his claim amount and now his right to vote because of his conduct. And as Mr. Clarke himself has so eloquently testified in his examination, neither he nor the Melanshins need each other going forward to conduct their businesses.

"I do not have to find that Mr. Clarke's treatment is fair, although, under the circumstances, I would be well within my rights to do so. No. All I have to find is that the treatment is not unfair. And I so find and rule.

"In the absence of Mr. Clarke's vote, the plan is hereby confirmed. He should keep in mind that in order to assure he receives his annual payments in a timely manner, he should make sure the parties have an updated mailing address." The judge smiled at the courtroom screen. "When one becomes available." Looking to 3J, Pascale, and Steinert, he added, "Please submit an order memorializing my rulings here today. Court is adjourned."

43

Woody Clarke recalls Thursday, October 17, 2024

I SAT IN jail waiting for my trial. My world: the four corners of my cell. I thought about how I had gotten there. I realized that no matter what you do, what you try to build to protect yourself, the world comes in. Into your head. Into your house. Into the hand you've been dealt. And that world . . . it's just no damn good anymore. Lincoln said a house divided can't stand. Bullshit. We need to burn this house down and build it again. This time in my image. Only real Americans.

In my new world, I had lots more time to think. I thought, *So there you have it, Woody. Lost my land. Lost my money. Lost my side business with Junior. Lost my freedom. Lost my country. That one's been coming for a long time. Lost it to a group of coloreds, and Jews, and immigrants, and a no authority federal judge. A judge who thinks this country ain't mine. Yeah, well, what does he know and who the hell asked him, anyway?"*

Gotta figure out a way to get a message to the boys. Time for another raid on the border. Them prior ones were just practice runs. Still a few of them Black farmers left we need to deal with. Y'know. Just culling the herd.

Open your eyes, people! Do something, goddammit, before it's too late!

I ain't got no more to say to you.

44

WOODY CLARKE AWAITED trial. He decided to exercise his Miranda rights and have counsel appointed for him. Judge Wilson, however, found he was not indigent and required him to pay for counsel, even if it meant mortgaging his land holdings. He hadn't talked since the plan confirmation. And even if he wanted to, there was no one to hear him.

Junior Clarke hired counsel and pled guilty to carrying a concealed weapon into a federal courthouse. He remained in jail, awaiting sentencing.

Pascale headed to O'Brien's. Two days earlier, he had told 3J that he'd accepted the firm's offer to consult for a year. He told her he was glad that no one on the board had said he had an "amazing ride" or a "good run" in his career. He hated both phrases.

He grimaced when he told her, expecting her to call him a damn fool for not getting on with his life. Instead, she smiled and said, "I'm happy for you, Bill. Now I have time to roll up my sleeves and help you clean up this freakin' mess. When I'm done, your office can look like mine: everything in its place."

"But everything *is* in its place," he'd replied. "As it should be. As it's always been."

He didn't know what "consult" exactly meant. He was the first in the firm's history to assume the role. But he was sure it was the first step in the process of an amicable divorce from the practice of law. He hoped it meant the band he was gigging with could book some sets at a local bar or two. Maybe debut his new song, "Don't Ever Change." He thought he was ready.

Rome booked a flight to New York City. She had processed her concerns about her investigatory performance and was looking forward to seeing Moses and Emily for the first time in way too long.

Pascale had called Moses to let him know the outcome of the Melanshin case. He asked Moses to thank Rome for him. As Pascale talked, Moses stood and stretched at his desk, under the watchful eye of his best friend, Emily. When the call ended, Moses asked Emily if it was time for a walk.

His loyal companion answered by walking to the door and awaiting her harness. Once it was on, they made their way down to the bustling city Moses loved. This day, instead of walking directly to Madison Square Park, they diverted, heading a few blocks north on Fifth Avenue, now limited to pedestrians and vendors. They walked past street vendors and merchants. Some knew Moses and waved as he and Emily passed by. Two bent over to give Emily a treat and a pet. *My people*, Moses thought.

After meeting up with Pascale at O'Brien's, 3J started back downtown to her condo to await Ronnie Steele's arrival. As she drove, she listened to an old recording of Lester Young from the late 1930s, *The Kansas City Sessions*. She adored the eccentric, porkpie hat-loving, and larger than life tenor saxophonist who arrived in

Kansas City in 1933 and bridged the gap between swing music and bebop. He and his Kansas City Six band played "I Want a Little Girl," and it made her smile. Papa had played that song for her. She thought it was heaven.

As she got to the World War I Memorial, rather than continue north, she made a left and headed into the park. There was no snow on the ground yet. She certainly hadn't dressed for a hike, but she decided to park and walk anyway. She took off her heels and carried them as she made her way to the wall on the northernmost part of the memorial, where she sat, her back to the shaft. It was by far the best view of Union Station and the Kansas City skyline beyond.

She thought of Kansas City's place in Black American history. There had been so much poverty and pain through the decades. Out of that pain came jazz. Jazz was good, she thought. The genre, like her papa, was always finding a way to see some good in a sea of bad.

Was that the lesson of Woody Clarke? Was there even a lesson?

Clarke had exhausted her, and here she was on her own time, still thinking about him. She headed back to her car and mumbled, "Girl, you've got to get that damn guy out of your head."

Ronnie arrived at the condo at 12:30. 3J had fallen asleep on the couch. When he arrived, she opened her eyes sleepily and they kissed. She was wearing only a white, wrinkled, men's dress shirt. She hadn't buttoned it up all the way, and it wasn't hiding much. On the Sonos, she cued up Ben Webster's "Our Love Is Here to Stay" from his album, *Stormy Weather.* It was another classic by Ben "The Brute And The Beautiful" Webster, his nickname referring to his seamless use of growl and altissimo notes.

They put their arms around each other and swayed slowly in half-time to the tune with the twinkling skyline lights of downtown Kansas City as the backdrop. No words, just music by one of Kansas City's greats. And resting in the arms of someone she now realized she loved.

Papa was right, she thought. She was officially no longer leaning on the wall. If he was still around, she knew Papa would like Ronnie. Then, because her father would have approved, she stopped thinking of him, opened her eyes, looked deep into Ronnie's eyes, smiled, and motioned to the bedroom.

Acknowledgments

My sincerest thanks to the following people, who helped me create *Unfair Discrimination*.

Zac Shaiken, who is always willing to talk with me and give me leads about tech. It's a full-time job to keep a baby boomer technologically true, isn't it?

Celina Tio, chef extraordinaire at the real *Belfrey* in Kansas City, for letting me keep it real by including you in *Unfair Discrimination*.

Avant Jones, wherever you may be, for teaching me so much and for being my friend.

Loren Shaiken, for being there and accepting me for what I am, whatever that might be.

Emily Shaiken, the sweet miss. The best miss. And the inspiration for Emily Aaronson.

Melanie Mulhall and *Dragonheart Writing and Editing* for all the great editing work and guidance. You really turned my dread of the editing process into one of fun and education.

Damon and Robynne of *Damonza.com* for the great book design and formatting work.

Xpressvideos for the great book trailer.

John Wilcockson for all his editing and proofreading.

Marla Keown for the book cover shot of me and for making the photoshoot work even when I was the subject matter. You are the best! *https://www.marlakeownphotography.com*

For my research, thanks to *All Music* for all its content rich history of jazz. I also relied on the following books for background, history, and inspiration: *Storied & Scandalous Kansas City: A History of Corruption, Mischief and a Whole Lot of Booze* by Karla Deel; *Kansas City Jazz: From Ragtime to Bebop: a History* by Frank Driggs and Chuck Haddix; *Racism in Kansas City* by G.S. Griffin; *Black America Series: Kansas City* by Delia C. Gillis; *Forgotten Tales of Kansas City* by Paul Kirkman; *Tom's Town: Kansas City and the Pendergast Legend* by William M. Reddig; *Take Up the Black Man's Burden: Kansas City's African American Communities 1865-1939* by Charles E. Coulter; *Bleeding Kansas, Bleeding Missouri: The Long Civil War on the Border* edited by Jonathan Earl and Diane Mutti Burke; and *Wide-Open Town: Kansas City in the Pendergast Era* edited by Diane Mutti Burke, Jason Roe, and John Herron.

About the Author

Mark lives with his wife, Loren, and their dog, Emily, in Denver, Colorado. He schooled at Haverford College and Washburn University and practiced commercial bankruptcy law for several decades before moving on in 2019 to write, volunteer, travel, and play music.

In addition to his award-winning legal thriller, *Automatic Stay*, he is the author of *And . . . Just Like That: Essays on a Life Before, During, and After the Law*, and *Fresh Start*, the first legal thriller in his 3J series. He will soon begin work on the next book in the series, *Cram Down*.

Connect with Mark at *http://markshaikenauthor.com*.

Amazon Review

You would make an author happy if you would please leave a short review of *Unfair Discrimination* on Amazon.

CRAM DOWN
A 3J BANKRUPTCY THRILLER

Watch for the release of my next thriller, *Cram Down*, starring Josephina Jillian Jones, with her supporting cast, and a host of others.

Enjoy my other books:

And . . . Just Like That:
Essays on a Life Before, During and After the Law
http://aws.org/HNT9GF

Fresh Start
https://tinyurl.com/49dkfs7w

Automatic Stay
https://tinyurl.com/4pmvt44y

Automatic Stay Litigation in Bankruptcy
(co-authored with Cindi Woolery)
https://tinyurl.com/9hh9bdz3

Connect with me and join my mailing list to stay up to date at *http://markshaikenauthor.com*.

12034451R10204